CU00370340

Rob pumps his dick harder with each rise and fall of his his knees higher and higher. entrench the boot's sole mo.. ... . nuts. Finally, Rob's left ankle, still crossed by his right ankle, almost touches Rob's ass, and the boot between his legs really mashes his testicles which are prominently kept elevated by the way the front of his jocksock is still latched beneath his cum-bulged testsicles.

"Oh, yes," Rob congratulates. No way does he stop the onslaught of orgasm this time. Doing so would require more know-how than he's mastered during all of his admittedly extensive sexual experimentation.

He pumps his dick harder, and each downward pass of his hand over his cock jams the heel of his fist against his balls and additionally squashes his gonads between Rob's fist and the strategically placed jocksock-hammock accordianed more and more by the pressure of boot leather.

Rob turns his cheek into closer contact with the boot sleeve laid up along his neck. His taut nipples are made more tender by the continual chafing provided by the slight rocking motion of the boot-sole edge atop them.

Rob licks that portion of the boot sleeve available to him. He takes a bite of the leather, holds fast, and sucks his mouthful.

"Ugh! Ugh! Ugh!" he grunts as his nuts, chock full of sexual cream, blast their carload of cum.

Rob's cum exits his pulsing cockmouth in syrupy, tail-trailing comets that, because of their wet-weight, are airborne mere fractions of a second before they lose all altitude and splatter down.

The first couple of gooey wads leapfrog the boot atop Rob's chest and splatter: one to Rob's left cheek, one in a drool of his chin. The next three slugs plop onto the boot on his chest. The last of his projected mess lattices Rob's muscled stomach and pools within his bellybutton.

Other books in the PROWLER BOOKS collection:

Fiction:
Diary of a Hustler
• ISBN 0-9524647-64
Slaves
• ISBN 0-9524647-99
Young Cruisers
• ISBN 0-9524647-72
Corporal in Charge
• ISBN 0-95246478-0
Hard
• ISBN 1-90264401-8
Virgin Sailors
• ISBN 1-90264403-4

Photographic:
Planet Boys
• ISBN 0-9524647-13
Kama Sutra of Gay Sex
• ISBN 0-9524647-05

Travel:
New York Scene Guide
• ISBN 1-90264400-X

▶ **CALIFORNIA CREAMIN'** & OTHER STORIES | by **WILLIAM MALTESE**

PROWLER BOOKS

California Creamin' and other stories by William Maltese

Copyright © 1998   William Lambert
3 Broadbent Close London N6 5GG. All rights reserved.

First printing October 1998
Cover photography © 1998 Prowler Press

web-site: prowler.co.uk
• ISBN 1-902644-04-2

Printed in Finland by Werner Soderstrom Oy.

British Library Cataloguing in Publication Data.
A catalogue record for this book is available from the British Library.

▶ CONTENTS

WHAT IF?

I'm wearing a white shirt, grey shorts, sneakers. Six other guys wear the same, although the colors differ. It's the costume geared to make us all look younger, and it basically does the trick. When I see my reflection, I looked about twelve. It's hard to believe I, and the other six, are legal and then some. One of the guys, Brent, looks so young even I have trouble believing his balls have dropped or his cock is capable of achieving boner-status.

The way I have it figured, Rodrigo Maurez liking his one special boy-toy to look young, Brent is the one of us about to collect $200, do not pass Go.

The party we're attending isn't being thrown by Rodrigo but by a Mr. Sanchez who Rodrigo knows from their early days in Cuba. Mr. Sanchez, from what I can tell, just by following the way he works his own party, prefers his tricks a little older-looking than Rodrigo does, although he's well aware of how we young-looking stuff liven up things, if just by providing something seemingly-chicken to look at.

"Mingle, my lovelies," is what Mr. Sanchez said when Rodrigo made introductions. "Make everyone envious of Rodrigo who has undoubtedly bought you all just for that very purpose."

It's admittedly all kind of exciting. A lot of money and pretty people, all around, including some genuinely studly numbers who aren't wearing much of anything but designer swimming trunks. It's a different kind of ambiance than on the West Coast where most of the big-dollars are movie-generated. This crowds attractiveness is more diversified than the West Coast's movie-star ideal.

There's this dark-complected guy, name of Andrew deSilva, with whom I exchange glances most of the evening. He's one of these exuberant types who always seems the center of attention, although his encircling coterie of admirers varies, like a twirling astronomical something (sun? black hole? galaxy? double-star?), that keeps peeling off matter from the surrounding area but occasionally letting some go.

Eavesdropping from a distance having already given me his name, the same now affords me the insinuation that he's well-known by, and knows of a lot of, the people present. He's recently been away. Minnesota I hear from more than one direction. But, what in the hell is in Minnesota? Maybe home to see mother? Even more fascinating is the twice-heard reference to his being "The Black Widower": sotto voce, once even with accompanying girlish titter.

Left to myself, the evening will end as uneventful as it has begun, nothing lost or gained by my harmless bit of long-distance flirtation. I'm well aware that Rodrigo has given all seven of us boy-toy candidates carte blanche, by way of sexual fun and games for this particular evening. I haven't a clue if it's some kind of test or not. Maybe he's measuring our capacity for faithfulness even before he's prepared to make a commitment. Maybe he's out to judge our potential for inflating his ego, if and when, he should commit; after all, if his potential boy-toy attracts a whole gamut of men, like a magnet brings on the iron filings, the fact that Rodrigo can end up with the magnet, might well count for something.

Granted, I find exciting the idea that, my evening already paid for by Rodrigo, I'm free -- for the rare occasion -- to solicit and/or be solicited for free sex. Money for fucking and sucking can be ego-bolstering, but some of the most handsome guys, who aren't on the giving or receiving end of payments, stay clear of sex that requires any monetary remuneration.

Also, I admit that Andrew DeSilva fits within my parameters of what I consider sexually attractive. Even though, it looks as if he might have been an even better match for my want-list when he was a few years younger. Not that youth matters all that much to me. It's just that he looks as if he may have once had an exceptionally well put-together physique that's been allowed to deteriorate just a bit. There's a slight puffiness to his face, to his neck, even to the vee of hairless chest seen beyond his open shirt collar. There's a slightly disconcerting roundness to his muscled arms, although they still fit well through his short shirt sleeves. There's merely an over-all straight edge sharpness that's missing from the way his still-nice ass fills his white trousers.

I like his dark hair, his dark eyes, his dark-complexion, all of which offer nice contrast to my blond hair, blue eyes, and tanned peaches-

and-cream complexion.

He takes the initiative, crossing the distance to me, actually leaving three good-looking guys who have been playing orbiting planets to his sun, their circling continuing within the space he's left vacant behind him.

"Hi," he says, coming to a stop very near-touching. "I've been noticing you noticing me noticing you noticing me, all evening."

He smells of some indefinable but probably very expensive cologne.

"I've been thinking how your tan is more Caribbean or Mediterranean that Minnesotan," I say, and he gets this strange look on his face. "Rumor being that you just got in from Minnesota," I clarify for him.

"Oh!" He laughs. He has a laugh that sounds like a nice laugh should sound, while being a little off key.

"Gossip," I say. "Innuendo. You seem to be a popular subject for this evening's conversations."

"Don't much care what the hell they say, just as long as they're saying something."

"Why do they call you The Black Widower?"

"My, but the tongues have been wagging."

So what that his accompanying laugh, this time, too, is a little less than genuine. He's handsome. He's studly, if on the verge of going to seed. He's interested. He's interesting. And I'm bored with being of legal age and masquerading as a prepubescent juvenile. I remain all the more disconcerted by my natural young looks, and by my attending unnatural teenybopper game-playing, because I continue to suspect I don't have the chance of a snowball in hell of making the final cut as far as Rodrigo Manuez's next permanent boy-toy is concerned.

"I have a tendency to get male sugar-daddies who end up thinking a few bucks buys me, hook, line, and sinker," he says. "Can't help it. Some flaw in me draws them to me, like bees drawn to honey, or like flies to raw meat. Except, I can only take so much of their possessiveness shit and usually pull out and leave them hanging. They're so upset, they turn straight." He laughs, this time genuinely light-hearted.

People turn to look. I feel how envious they are that the two of us have shared something privately amusing -- a joke from which they've been excluded.

"Straight as good as dead," he says. "Ergo: The Black Widower."

I smile. I can't help myself. It's so fucking absurd, it can't be anything but true. Or, maybe, I'm just dumb.

"Enough about me," he says. "Rumor has it that you're about to become the next permanent boy-toy in Rodrigo Manuez's stable."

"Not likely. Way I see it, I'm merely here enjoying a free few days of fun in the sun."

"Come on, kid," he says. "I find you sexy as hell, your competition pure shit. You think Rodrigo hasn't figured out the same?"

True or not, it's exactly what I want to hear.

"I've been getting horny just thinking about you sitting on my face, my rolling my tongue and fucking it up your hairless ass," he says. "I'm assuming Rodrigo, as usual, still insists all his boy-toy candidates keep themselves hairless as a baby's ass."

"God, please tell me you're not into all of that, too!" I have visions of being hairless and passing for fourteen when I'm a hundred and fourteen.

"I like you, kid, hairless as a balloon, or hairy as an baboon. However, since I figure my window of opportunity is very limited, before Rodrigo latches onto you like a vampire onto a virgin vein of blood, for you and me it's either now or never."

"Trouble is, I can't figure out if Rodrigo means it when he says the night is mine to do with as I like."

"He means sow the last of your wild oats now, because, come tomorrow, your ass, and every other part of your body that's for sale, is his."

Don't I wish.

"So, why don't you and I go somewhere, and do something, while the getting is good?" he says. "I'd suggest my place, but I've just dumped my latest sugar-daddy, and I wouldn't want him showing up and spoiling things with a scene. So, how about we go to your place?"

Rodrigo has me and the other candidates booked in a nearby hotel. The accommodations aren't exactly five-star, but we each have a room to ourself. All within easy walking distance of the party-in-progress.

"Okay," I say. "Why not?"

Eyes watch us leave. Rodrigo Manuez's eyes? I can't tell. I know pretty much where Rodrigo is in the house, but I don't make it a point to search him out for eye contact. If he doesn't want me going with

Andrew, he shouldn't have made the rules of the game the way he's made them.

We're at my hotel in no time.

Once in my bedroom, I shift my black backpack from the bedspread to a nearby chair.

Andrew unbuttons his shirt and peels it off.

As I suspect, he has a nice body that was once better. His chest is pretty much naked of hair, except for a halo of single strands at each nipple and a line of pubic hair from his navel to the waistband of his trousers.

He drops his pants and undershorts in one swift let's-get-to-it movement and reveals a cock that's ready-made for whatever fun and games either of us has in mind.

"I'm going to have trouble eating your asshole as long as you keep wearing those sexy shorts," he says.

I realize I'm staring. Quite frankly, I can't believe he's really here. Of course, I'd fantasized returning from the party with an I'll-show-you-Rodrigo trick to fuck my brains out, but I'd never really thought I, or any interested stud, like Andrew, would be gutsy enough to make it happen. Maybe because I'd had myself convinced that Rodrigo's insistence that the night was mine "to do with as you please" was more a test of my faithfulness than it was an exhibit of his genuine magnanimity.

No turning back now, though, so I come out of my clothes faster than any butterfly ever shed its chrysalis.

My nakedness, in comparison to his slightly over-the-hill appearance, is that of someone not having yet reached full maturity. Perfection, to my way of thinking, lies somewhere between. But since perfection of that sort is hard to come by ...

"Hairless wonder, indeed!" Andrew says, referencing my now naked and pretty much completely shaved body. "You really do have me imagining I'm some old pervert, just having successfully prowled some school yard."

He means it as a compliment: I can tell by the way he says it. It should make me flattered that the desired effect has been achieved by the regular shedding of every hair on my body, except the hair on my head. Nonetheless, it's always a bit disconcerting to realize that every guy I meet enters into our sex with the image of me so young and innocent that I've not yet sprouted pubic hair.

"Sit on the edge of the bed, kid," he says.

Whether Andrew sees me as six or sixty, it's only straight ahead from here, though. I've found him sexy from the beginning, and he only gets me more so as the minutes progress.

So, I sit as instructed, and he kneels before me. His hands touch my thighs and send tingles all of the way to my balls that hang suspended from the base of my not quite eight-inch circumcised erection.

"Now, lean back, kid," he says.

I lean back, and he opens my thighs and hoists my legs to hook his shoulders with the bends behind my knees. He rises, all the while pushing with his shoulders to put my legs up and over my head. He anchors my legs in place by putting his hands to the backs of my thighs while his face travels down my chest and belly, his tongue licking all the way.

"Skin smooth as silk," he says, down at my navel and savoring as a stag enjoys a salt lick.

My cock isn't all that far away from all his licking, and it begs for a lick of its own by giving a noticeable jerk and an oozing of clear preseminal juice.

"God, our baby, here, has a leaker," he says in evidence that he sees the results of his labors even before he's touched my cock.

For the moment, though, he's not interested in my cock, or in the flavorful elixir that leaks from it. He bypasses my dick, en route to my ass, but detours at my balls. He kisses my scrotum, then exerts the sucking pressure to siphon first one of my nuts, then the other, into his spit-wet mouth. My testicles collide with each other and ricochet against the interior of an oral chamber seemingly way too small to contain them.

When he's through mouthing my nuts, he doesn't just open up and let them drop out. He pulls his face away from my crotch and pulls my nuts right along with it. My scrotum stretches as far as it can from its continued anchorage beneath my cock, my two balls suddenly grouped and pressed tightly to the inside of his pursed lips.

When my balls do come free, it's a quick and pleasurably painful pop-pop exit. Their spitty veneer turns them cool as soon as they're exposed to the air. My rubber-band scrotum draws them back to my crotch but hangs them in not nearly as flaccid a sac as when we first began. Before, sacked, my gonads looked like dual pendulums. Now, they appear exotic fruit grown sexily to the base of their tree.

Andrew burrows beneath my nuts, like a pig burrowing for truffles. The pressure of his hands against the backs of my legs, cements my body into a tighter coil. Suddenly, I've a very good view of my cock, its head poked into the arch of my belly and drooling wetness to my furrowed hairless skin.

He licks from the base of my balls, right into the crease of my ass. He finds my asshole but licks right on by it after, first, making sure to lash it twice with the full length of his roughly taste-budded tongue. He reaches the base of my spine before he begins licking right on back.

Something tells me Andrew has eaten ass before. There's nothing tentative or half-assed about his enthusiasm. He's like a conscientious janitor who knows exactly how to completely clean and buff a floor with minimum effort and to maximum effect.

His rolled tongue becomes a miniature dick, slick as any dog's prick. It probes my sphincter and beyond, clearing away whatever residue tastes and accompanying smells linger at the gateway of my asshole.

His pursed lips anchor around the opening of my butt, like a spaceship docked with its pod. He sucks, even as he tongue-fucks, with such vacuum force that he has me figuring he's out to turn my whole asshole inside-out.

Helplessly, I wiggle my ass in all the tighter to his feasting face, pugging his sexy nose against the depth of my asscrack.

Strange how something so obviously insignificant as tongue, compared to hard cock, leaves me feeling so empty when it finally pulls out. I do a bit of butt humping to try and get my rectum re-speared, but his tongue is already unrolled and back to licking its way to my balls.

He doesn't swallow my nuts, like last time, but pretends they're lollipops, and he's a kid crazy for their sweetness. Then, he again licks from my asscrack, all of the way up and over my nuts. Not once, not twice, but several times. At each completed lap, his curled tongue forces my balls into a very small corner of my almost fully compacted scrotum. The result is more pleasure/pain that has my cock leaking even more goo.

He's waited so long to give my dick any attention that it's almost too pleasurable a shock to endure when a final full licking of my nuts spills over onto and up the belly of my dick.

"Oh, stud ... stud," I say as his tongue reaches the flare of my cockhead and keeps right on going to the leaking goo oozing from the pouted mouth of my erection. There, without any pause, his mouth converts to a small culvert for my cock to fuck. His wet-warm tunnel swallows my stiff dick as swiftly and as completely as any train tunnel ever gulps streamline locomotive.

I put my hands into the dark hair on his head, and I comb strands, exerting pressure to keep him over my dick even as he attempts to come up for air. Finally, I give him leave of passage, and his head swings up from my crotch, and his mouth spills inch after inch of my spit-drenched boner.

While his continued upswing momentum would allow him easy exit from my erection, like the sheath of a straw having achieved escape velocity, he stops with only the flared head of my cock encased within closed doors. His rolled tongue plays my cockmouth much as it has played my asshole before it. My dick leaks another gushing of goo, and the tip of his tongue claims it all.

He's down, up, down, up, down my dick in quick, successive bounces. The resulting wet friction is a sensuous source of heat that sets the total length of my dick all aglow. The warmth travels inward to steam-heat my whole hairless crotch. My hairless testicles use the conjured heat as an incubator to coax new cum to life within my balls.

I'm aware all of this is pretty one-sided, except for whatever pleasure he gets from sucking my dick. Were he to hop up on the bed with me and maneuver into convenient sixty-nine position, I'd suck up his cock, even his balls in the package, and suck him silly, too. Except, he stays right where he is. My reflexive sucking mouth movements go to waste, as does the spit suddenly overflowing and drooling the side of my chin.

"Easy, stud," I say. "Easy, or you'll have your full before you've had a chance to serve me up a meal of your own."

He doesn't go easier, though. He clamps down all the harder for another sliding to my balls and another ride back up again.

My dick suddenly leaks within the sensuously compressing tube of what more and more seems a python's digesting belly. I swear to God, the intensity of his suctioning over my dick gives my cock the eight-plus inches I've always wanted it to have.

As much experience as I've attained in my days of hustling, and I have to admit that I've not been in the body-selling business all that long, there's no way I'm in control of this situation. Andrew plays my hard dick and my taut body like a masterful musician plays whatever his chosen instrument. He's conductor as well, self-deciding when to bounce his head fast or slow over my cock, whether to blow hard or soft, whether to work my cock straight up and down or with a slight torquing of his head in ascent and/or descent.

"I want your cock, stud-bastard!" I say, my words all juicy and wet-sounding with saliva. I figure since my mouth and throat are going through all the reflexive motions, mimicking his slobberings over my dick, I might as well have his cock inserted to take advantage.

He, though, doesn't go anywhere, except right where he is. He provides heartier and heartier efforts to suck for my cum through the straw of my dick, and there's nothing I can humanly do to stop my balls from going helplessly artesian beneath his skillful ministrations.

"Build your ark, stud," I say. "The deluge is about to ..."

"Come" is hardly the word to describe it. Pulse, riptide, explode, gush, spew, jettison: all seem more apropos of the way my sperm suddenly wrenches from my gonads, during the final full drop of his head over my dick.

His cheeks puff with my cum shot to fill them. His cheeks collapse as he swallows each and every drop of my teenage cream. His cheeks balloon again.

I'm sucked bone (boner?) dry. Anyway, that's how it feels. Only a history of fast recoveries and re-found boners, after but one orgasm, leaves me to believe I just might not be as completely done in by Andrew's admittedly vigorous sucking as I might at first imagine.

He releases my spent dick and comes up for air. I see him licking my cock clean, his handsome face parenthesized by my still-uplifted legs.

"My prick would like to fuck your hairless baby-ass, pretty please" he says; the least I can do, to my way of thinking, for his having so generously given of his head.

"There's a rubber in the end-table dresser."

"Think we really need one of those?"

I laugh nervously. He has to be kidding, right? He knows I'm a hustler, right? Albeit a hustler with a free night for fun and games, but how's he to know how many rubberless dicks I've had up my butt; even if, by careful count, there haven't been any? I certainly haven't a clue as to how many assholes his cock, free of protection, has screwed, in his past.

"There's a rubber in the end-table dresser," I repeat.

I'm relieved when, without additional argument, he finds the lubricated rubber and rolls it down his dick.

I'm disappointed he's even partially diluted my pleasure by having provided me even the slightest notion that he's sexually careless. His cockhead at my butt, I'm suddenly devoting concentration on telling the difference between rubberized dick and naked dork, confirming the former, when I prefer concentrating on the pure pleasure of the moment.

However, once assured his cock is protected as it begins its slow and easy shove up my rear, I'm better able to disregard whatever my previous fears and better concentrate on what new pleasures Andrew's obvious expertise holds in store for me.

"Tight, baby-boy asshole," he says, his chest coming to rest against the support offered by the backs of my legs. His dark hair seductively bangs his dark eyes. He licks his lips. His hips shoot his cock to his dark-haired balls.

My body curls more completely, and my cockhead leaks goo as it rides up the center of my chest.

"Feels virgin asshole, kid," he says. "Feels as if my cock is in for the very, very first plug. Feels ... oh ... so ... good."

It's my tight-tight asshole, as well as my young-boy good looks, which I've been assured by my johns and by my manager, will make me an even bigger success in the body-selling business than I already am. Helped along by the fact that while my seven-and-a-quarter inches of cock aren't liable to hold the interest of a size queen, they're more than adequate in an arena where the illusion of youth is often more important than cock size.

"Virgin ass, just for you, stud," I say. "Feel free to take my cherry with all the vigor your studly phallic muscle can muster."

"Lucky ... lucky ... Rodrigo Manuez," Andrew says, pulling his dork out to its cockhead and putting it right back in. "Money like his does buy the very ... very ... best, doesn't it?"

I suspect Andrew was the very best in his time. If he's a little over the hill for the crowd I presently run with, there are undoubtedly still men out there willing to pay for the kind of good times he can offer. If he can just keep from being bored with them. Just milk them of whatever cash they're willing to spend before he drops them by the wayside and moves on. For a guy who looks the part of a hustler, who can perform with the expertise of one, who has the additional advantage of considerable charm, his attitude, all along, hasn't struck me as conducive to milking the profession for all he can get from it. Of course, buyers are going to think they own you for the dollars they spend on you and for your services. The secret isn't to drop them because of their illusion but, rather, to make it damned expensive for them. Hustling a business, for Christ's sake!

"Yes ... oh, yes ... yes," he says. His hips have put his cock into a smooth and regularly cadenced push and pull up my rectum. Despite the industrial-strength lubricant on the rubber, there's plenty of friction generated by his cock against my inner ass to make for heat hot enough to kindle sticks.

Having once figured I might be totally drained of cum by his suck-off, I realize my cock has never really gone soft. I take hold of it and beat it off in time to the rhythmic pumping of Andrew's cock up my butt.

"Whip your teenage dick, kid," he says, having a good view of me manhandling my meat. My balls are again contained within a thick-skinned scrotum that has very little elasticity remaining to it.

As usual, that I beat a dick sprouted from a completely hairless belly gives me a weird feeling, quite aside from the pleasure, because I remember the hair that once grew there, as well as the hair that will sprout again if given half the chance. Always a mystery is how my skin remains so stubble-free.

"Sexy ... sexy ... sexy," says Andrew. "So nice ... fucking ... young ass ... instead of fucking the sagging butt of some old fart who thinks it's all about control and money."

His lower belly slaps my ass, my fingers providing slippery wet sounds in their drag of my preseminal goo up and down the shank of my erection.

"Oh, we do right well together ... ohhhhh ... don't we?" he says.

I can only agree. It's always strange when such seemingly perfect fits occur because, more often than not, they have nothing to do with cock- or ass-size. Probably because cock up ass is only the half of it. Other parts of the participating bodies have to mold just right, as well, to make it a really good-fit fuck, like this one.

"Feels good," I say.   Actually, it feels more than good.   It feels fucking great!

There's something to be said for two guys getting sexually linked up when they know enough about what's going on so that they're not under the complete control of primitive centers, whether in the brain or elsewhere, that can seek -- always sooner than wanted -- to take complete control.

My asshole needs a certain degree of pounding, beneath the onslaught of any hard cock, for me to achieve maximum benefit from it, in the end (figuratively and literally).   Sometimes the length of time needed for such a good fuck, from my standpoint, isn't achieved, because my paying customer is too quick on the draw, or could go on but doesn't want to.   After all, it's never the hustler's pleasure that's most important in any paid-for relationship.   This sex not being paid-for sex, however ...

"Make it last longer, stud," I say, feeling I have every right to telegraph just where my pleasure quotient exists within the scheme of things.   Of course, considering he's already been considerate enough to give me one orgasm to his upcoming one, I can't bitch too much if he plunges right ahead to erupt his overdue load up my butt.

"You tell me when, kid," he says.

Do I believe he actually has the kind of control needed to keep his first eruption in abeyance until I'm primed for climax number two? There are guys who can do just that, but I've run across damned few. It's a degree of mind over pleasure that I'm not sure I'll ever master, putting me in complete awe of anyone who has.

I beat my cock harder, faster.   I strangle my prick as if I'm mad as hell at it and am anxious to twist all of its life out of it.   All my manhandling only makes my dick harder and hotter.

"Oh, sweet, sweet, boy-ass," says Andrew.

"Oh, sweet, sweet, man-cock," says I.

I shut my eyes.   I arch my head back into the pillow.   I open my mouth and grunt.   I salivate, then swallow my spit.   My tongue lolls from the corner of my mouth.

The guy is a virtual fuck machine, apparently prepared to screw me forever, if that's what it takes.   His finger may be poised on whatever the trigger that will set him into orgasmic oblivion, but he refuses to pull that trigger until I've given him the go-ahead.

"Amazing, truly amazing," I define his expertise and the newest rush of pleasure that threatens to swallow me as completely as my greedily eating asshole swallows his dick.

"You about ready ... kid?" he says. It's the first indication he's given that he may not be as much in control as I've come to imagine.

Is he close to blasting his wad? Is he so far along that he's prepared to let go his cum, whether I tell him to or not?

Frankly, I'm infinitely pleased that he may not be so much the cool cucumber to the very last. After all, if I'm supposedly so sexy to him, as he's made me out to be, can he so easily proceed along his merry way, at his designated speed, no matter how slow, completely immune to my substantial charms?

Possibly out to cut off my nose to spite my face, I'm suddenly prepared to sacrifice my building toward a second climax to see if I can't entice him out on the edge and over without my toppling off with him. I decide to hang on for the limits of his ride, and I release the pressure of my handhold on my dick, so that I'm fucking a far looser hole.

"Come on, kid ... come on ... come on!"

He's really working to keep control. I can tell by the full dilation of his eyes, by the line of sweat along his upper lip, by the muscular ridges that appear in bas-relief along the column of his sexy neck. His nipples are hard. His tanned flesh visibly shows the underlining pinkish tinge of sexual blush.

"Go ahead and blast-off, stud," I say. "Feed your spunk up my hairless backside. Baste my asshole with stud cream. Poke me so far and so deep that I can taste your spewing spunk from the inside-out."

ESP tells me that he knows I've decided to outlast him.

"Clever ... playful ... masochistic ... sadistic ... little ... sexy shit!" he confirms.

By now, though, there's not much he can do about it. His hips are fucking right out of control, his cock a piston gone wild inside me.

I grab a handful of my nuts and squeeze, confident the resulting flood of dull ache, arisen from my hand-molested gonads, will provide whatever further breather I'll need while he proceeds to ride me into his blast-off.

"You're good!" he bellows and slams his cock home one more time.

His contracted scrotum and two nuts mash tightly against my butt. "You're so ... very ... very ... very ... good."

His cock goes so additionally large, all over, it's as if a cannon, its muzzle blocked, prepares to split asunder, in every which direction.

"Agghhhhmmthhhh!" he says with the very first spit of his fiery cream up my asshole.

"Yes!" I'm triumphant.

So intensely do I experience my success, Andrew's cock continuing to fire-hose his cream up my butt, my dick remaining poised on the brink, my gamut of felt sensations are almost as enjoyable as orgasm itself.

I'm still basking in the joy of his splashing cum, and my skill in having outlasted him to orgasm, when the phone rings.

"Jesus!" Andrew protests the interruption, except he and I know the peak of his climax is over and done. All that remains is for him to remove his cock and his rubber-contained deluge. "Don't answer it."

I'm tempted to let it ring except, after the seventh ring, I'm convinced whomever is on the other end isn't going to hang up.

"Okay, okay, answer," says Andrew, apparently as convinced as I am of the intended long-lasting insistence of the interruption.

His dick slides free and leaves my asshole in a state of deprivation-collapse.

I roll for the phone.

"Joey, here?" I say, as if any caller who has the number wouldn't know who's on this side of the line.

I'm on the phone for less than fifteen seconds.

"Rodrigo?" intuits Andrew, as soon as I hang up.

"Rodrigo's go-fer, Sean Cortez," I say. "Know him?"

"Vaguely."

"Rodrigo's car will be downstairs for me in five minutes."

"He calling you in to give you the good news that you're to be his new permanent boy-toy?"

"More likely to break the bad news that I'm out on my ass." I can't help feeling I've violated some unwritten rule by having taken Rodrigo at his word that I should feel free to take any advantage of whatever the party had to offer. Oh, well, easy come, easy go. And what a delightful easy come it's been!

"Why not stay here?" Andrew says. "We can spend the rest of the evening fucking and sucking each other's brains out."

"Since Rodrigo makes the effort to break the bad news to me face-to-face, I feel kind of obligated to be as good a sport about it," I say. "Quite aside from how I might want to spend some time, now or later, in this fun city, without the baggage of coming off a bad loser."

"So, I confess I'm only thinking of myself," he says. "Not only because we're off to such a good start, but because I was kind of looking for a home away from home, at least for the evening. I especially hate to ruin how good I feel now by any confrontation with an ex-sugar daddy who figures the cum I just fed you should have been his."

"Stay here," I say, already out of bed. I bypass my discarded clothes and grab fresh ones from the closet. I stuff my still-hard cock into a real pair pants, not kiddie shorts. If I'm off to get the ax for not looking prepubescent enough, I prefer the butcher-but-not-much look of me in jeans and a T-shirt. "I'll wake you when I get back, and we can take up right where we left off."

"Sure?"

"Sure!" It's not as if there's much he can make off with, if he turns out to be a thief. Not expecting to stay too long in this city, I haven't brought all that much with me, having correctly assumed all extras would be provided by Rodrigo, along the way. I need only my wallet, fished from my jettisoned shorts, to give me all, by way of a survival pack.

"I can't think of a nicer way to come awake," he says and stretches seductively to put all of his body parts in its best possible light. His cock, still pretty much hard, even after its climax up my ass, is a poker he hooks with one thumb and pushes to an aimed-for-the-ceiling position. I'm tempted to tell Rodrigo Manuez and his unscheduled summons to both go to hell, but ...

The intercom buzzes.

"Bastard must have been parked on your doorstep when he phoned," Andrew says.

I answer the buzzer and say I'll be right down.

"Keep your cock at the ready," I say as I head out the door and close it behind me.

I keep my each and every thought on Andrew, and on my acute desire to get back to him, to his cock, and to his ass, until Rodrigo tells me he wants me to move in to his South Beach mansion that very evening.

Even before Rodrigo gets into the how of my having lucked out by winning his look-like-chicken lottery, I've pretty much forgotten Andrew at my hotel. If I do think of him, it's only to remind myself that all he had probably been looking for, anyway, was a place to spend the night, and that I'd provided, as well as a good cock fuck of my rear, and meal of my sperm in the bargain.

Come morning, courtesy of a night with Rodrigo, I'm nursing a thoroughly cock-fucked asshole, a friction-burned dick, and the decided residue (but not distasteful) of Rodrigo's cum on my taste buds. Rodrigo is in the other room, taking a conference call, and I'm in bed about to enjoy an on-tray breakfast of bacon, eggs, hash browns, orange juice, and milk. I click on the television.

First thing I hear is the Special News Broadcast as to how Andrew Cunanan, alias Andrew deSilva (wearing what I would only later learn is my grey shorts, white shirt, and black backpack), is suspected of having shot and killed, earlier that morning, Gianni Versace on the steps of the fashion designer's Mediterranean-style South Beach palazzo.

POETIC DEFENSE OF ONE-HAND READERS

Okay, I admit,
Of those certain hours, of those certain days,
When I'm more than content to learn of the ways
To build a small house or a boat.

I, also, confess,
Of those other times, when mood is just right,
I'll summon a book to give me a good fright
With hauntings of gossamer ghosts.

Or, maybe, I want,
With drink close at hand, perhaps by the pool,
To be confused and beguiled, even quite fooled,
By mysteries hot off the press.

Or, read of some man,
Whose life, out of control, nearly goes mad,
And strives against odds, to make good out of bad,
And actually solves all the mess.

But, oft come the times,
When all that I want, by way of a book,
Is nothing requiring too detailed ⌐ look,
But still can provide what I need.

A book for one hand.
My other hand free to fish from my jock
The sensuous writhings of my horny cock.
My hairy balls, likewise, set free.

William Maltese

So that, as I read,
Of deep-spearing cock, up teenager's ass,
My fist can commence spanking, equally fast,
The boner upthrust from my lap.

As teenager squeals,
With each hearty thrust of cock up his butt,
And mewls to announce faster probes of his guts,
I milk for my own creamy sap.

Fuck-grunts come loudly.
Hip movements faster, with each pumping thrust.
Teenager screams wildly his spiralling lust.
I hard-beat my cock to the brink.

The unselfish guy
Who rides young man's rear, and offers a fist
To wrap teenager's dick, fulfils our each wish
For pleasure from which deep to drink.

"Oh, God!" fucker says,
"I'm cock-sticking vise that can't be mere ass.
I'm fighting brave battle to make this screw last!"
While I, likewise, pray for more fun.

Timing so crucial,
For those who don't know, is often hard won
To well-time my tiring with character's gun.
But so good, when masterfully done.

When characters come,
Shoot youthful asshole, shoot boy-fucker's hand,
I match each of their squirts, as well as I can.
Which leaves me no trace of a frown.

Far less the bother --
Though flesh-and-blood partner might be more nice --
Reading and beating, will quite often suffice,

In place of a night on the town.

So, critics out there,
Who complain of gay books needing more plot,
I say this to you: "What a fucking pure crock!
Stop whining, and don't make me scoff!"

For hear this from us,
Who read with one hand, and don't need complex:
"If we want more detail, besides steamy sex,
We'll read Moby Dick and jack-off!"

COWBOY BOOTS

Rob Pitt knows right where young Jim Templar's scruffy cowboy boots are. He visits them regularly when Jim's dressy Tony Lamas boots are out on the town with the kid. Like tonight, Jim's dressy boots with the teenager, line-dancing at the O.K. Bar and Grill. Or, the Cuban heels of Jim's dressy boots hooked over some other bar rail. Or, Jim's dressy boots underneath some lucky girl's bed. Or, the side of one dressy boot rested on Jim's left knee, the way Jim crosses his legs in that young-manly ankle-to-knee way, as opposed to knee-over-knee, to provide amply bulged teenager's jean crotch for sexy viewing.

These left-behind-in-the-bunkhouse boots are Jim's work boots. These aren't cut from exotic leather. Not from ostrich skin, like Jim's Tony Lamas dressy boots. Not from lizard. Not from antelope. From plain old-fashioned cow leather. Not dyed any fancy color, either. Not red. Not blue. Not even black or grey. Natural brown. So scuffed as to appear suede, although they aren't suede. No brand name, although there once was one, now worn away along with any original indication of boot-size.

Each boot heel worn down at its back rear edge. Each toe slightly upturned. Notched boot sleeves drooped as thoroughly as any hound-dog's ears. Once-fancy stitching, but not too-fancy, up each boot front, back, and sides, now broken in places, threads feathered. Dark stains, here, there, everywhere, making brown leather browner.

These boots are on the floor, toes forward, just under the foot of Jim's bunk, although Rob needs lift the drape of a wool blanket to see them.

Rob is down close. On his hands and knees. He goes to his elbows, and his face lowers even closer.

He sniffs. Smells. Not new leather, here. New leather may turn others on, but not Rob. Rob likes just this aroma. A combination of old, worn leather, dust, dirt, cow shit, horse piss, sweaty teenage feet, sweat-wet wool socks ...

He tastes the leather with the tip of his tongue. Rough leather against rough taste buds.

One of his hands to each side of one boot, he pulls the boot forward. His nose and his tongue travel the leather toe. A dusty taste. The leather dries his tongue; his tongue doesn't wet the leather.

He pauses, his lips atop the boot's instep. His head, as well as his face and eyelashes, against the leather. His lush black hair feathers the boot's brown-leather sleeve.

He closes his eyes and concentrates on smell, taste, touch ...

Both hands up the back of the boot, he straightens the drooped boot-sleeve and cups it open, as if making it ready to accept its owner's foot. He puts his face into the opening, as if the boot is an oxygen mask designed specifically for his face. He holds his breath and waits with avid anticipation.

When he finally inhales, it's a deep and lengthy siphon. His reward: an aroma funky, rich, warm, and complex.

His cock throbs in his pants. His dick has been hard since long before Jim and the others left for the evening. Hard with anticipation. Waiting for this. Waiting for what's to come. How wondrous, Rob's face wearing Jim's boot, Rob's hard cock strangled in jockstrap. Rob's nose savoring the smell of boot; of absent sock and teenage foot; of stale teenage sweat, long-evaporated.

Rob's hand adjusts the lie of his cock within his jeans and within the cupping elastic of his jockstrap codpiece. His large balls are cramped within the crease at the small end of the jockstrap's vertically veed hammock. The swell of his stiff meat embosses the sensuously stretched cocksock, as well as the crotch of his jeans. Rob knows, though he can't see it, that the bulbous tip of his prick extends so far upward that it peeks above his jockstrap's elastic waistband.

His cock leaks sticky goo. Clear. Preseminal. It wets the jockstrap's waistband as well as the black pubic hair that haloes his navel. Black hair fans his entire lower belly but grows thickest at the delta punctuated by the anchorage of his stiff cock.

He massages his concealed dick. He rubs the ridge of his prick from his hairy balls to his fist-like cockhead.

All the while, he breathes. Long, deep intakes. Slow exhalations. The smells are aphrodisiacal. His cock all the harder. His petting fingers detect each new bit of stiffness added to his already impressively swollen erection.

Jim's boot-smells are suddenly too intense for Rob to bear. If he's not careful, he'll cream without milking the moment for all its worth. He doesn't want that. He wants all he can get. Not too fast, either. Weekends, the only time these boots are available, seem an eternity apart. His pleasure, one small dose at a time, requires all Rob's patience and control.

His face comes up for air. He pushes himself to a kneeling position. His firm asscheeks sit on the backs of his ankles. He scoots closer to both boots, his thighs open at his knees.

He turns the nearest upright boot so its toe aims away from him, and he pulls its heel securely into the vee formed by his kneeling legs. Boot leather contacts his trousers' denim crotch. His hard cock, evident beneath the worn-thin crotch of his faded jeans, presses the worn leather of the boot and boot-heel. Rob can't help himself as he lifts his ass slightly to rub the length of his denim-sheathed cock against the back of the brown-leather boot sleeve.

He presses the boot's heel more tightly to his crotch. His tender nuts are smashed. The resulting pain is pure pleasure. An even tighter pressure conjures an even more intensely pleasurable ache.

"Ahhhh, yes," he says. He can't help himself. It's good. It's so very good. It always is with this pair of teenager Jim's cowboy boots. Maybe it has something to do with Jim, maybe not.

No doubt Jim is handsome. Young. Blond. Studly. A real cowboy and not the urban variety. God would his young good-looks turn city-slicker heads in some city-slicker bar! Jim's slight drawl is as if his Montana origins are really somewhere south of the Mason-Dixon. His black eyes have flecks of iridescent green. His lips are pouty, his jawline square, his dimples deep. His physique is teenage wiry, not from any lengthy exposure to gym equipment, but because of his long hours spent on a horse. So many hours in the saddle that Jim is slightly bowlegged. Not enough to notice, unless you really look. Rob has really looked. Rob liked what he saw from the very beginning, including Jim's work boots which had convinced him to give the teenager the go-ahead as a ranch hand.

Mr. Jefferson takes seriously all Rob's recommendations for hiring and firing the help. Rob is ranch foreman, as his father was ranch foreman for Mr. Jefferson's father. Rob is as much a cowboy as Jim, more if counting years spent on a ranch, years spent in the saddle, years spent herding cattle.

Then again, as much as there's no denying how much Rob likes Jim's young blond cowboy looks, Rob has gotten boners over scruffy boots worn by some real dogs. Jeffrey Petrie, for instance, who is two-hundred pounds of overweight acne. Which doesn't stop Rob's cock from going rock hard at the mere sight of that pair of Jeffrey's boots that are literally deteriorating under all that weight. Then there's Warren Tork, a real jerk of a human being. One eye a mere pucker, the result of a knife fight with a gay who wasn't, as it turned out, the sissy Warren accused him of being. Warren's grotesqueness not enough to keep Rob's cock from going stiff as a board every time Warren wears that one pair of boots so old that their leather comes across as almost see-through.

Rob's hands coax Jim's boot sleeve into an erection, his fingers around the leather, as if the leather is Rob's cock. The boot sleeve stays stiff until Rob's hands drop, at which time the leather sleeve droops. An upswing of Rob's hands re-props the leather as erect as if the boot were new.

Rob's thighs close tighter against the upright boot, parenthesizing it from its heel to its toe. Rob looks down into the opening of the leather sleeve, his hands again keeping the boot sides from flopping. The darkness of the hole is as exciting an invitation as some men find the tightness of another man's funky asshole.

The upright boot still held tightly between Rob's thighs, Rob unfastens his belt and unbuttons the crotch of his pants. His denim fly peels open and reveals his manly cock-and-balls-stuffed jocksock. He scoots closer to the boot and his cloth-covered nuts squash more visibly beneath the additional pressure of the boot heel.

Rob hooks the elastic of his jockstrap's waistband with his thumb. He pulls outward to better reveal his cockhead which is heart-shaped and leaks goo. His stiff cock remains tight against his hairy belly, even without the snugness exerted by any containing jocksock. His scrotum is a compact mass of big nuts and furry, prune-like skin.

He releases the elastic waistband. It responds with an audible slap-back that stings his cockhead. He so much enjoys the sting, he repeats the process.

After which, he pulls the waistband out yet another time, drops it down and hooks it, and its accordioned jocksock, under and up beneath his balls. His impressive cock, and most of his equally impressive and now-elevated balls, completely unveiled.

He upends the boot between his thighs and slides its sleeve down over his cock, like an extra-extra large sheathe over his cock's head, neck and torso. No matter that Jim's boot over Rob's cock isn't a tight fit, even for Rob's big cock. Rob's pleasure has nothing to do with the friction or lack thereof. Whatever contact made between the leather inside this boot and his erect cock is enough. When he lets go of the upended boot, it remains entirely supported by the continued stiffness of Rob's erection.

His cock, though, is well aware of the weight hung on it. His prick isn't nearly as upright as it was before Rob hung boot leather on it. The boot has made Rob's cock another Leaning Tower of Pisa. So weighty the boot, it seems to Rob, for a brief moment, as if it'll cause Rob's thick prick to snap off at his impressive cockbase.

Rob relieves some of the pressure by supporting the boot with his hands. He pulls the boot up, its leather sliding the back of Rob's erection. Whatever slug-like trail of slime his dick leaks to the interior of the boot will evaporate by morning. Jim will never know his boot was fucked by Rob's cock by the time Jim's sock-sheathed foot slides in for Monday's workday.

Rob wishes for Jim's teenage foot up the boot, here and now, as Rob's cock fucks the leather. Except, Rob still isn't sure Jim is gay, or even bisexual. Even if Jim were gay, it's not clear the young cowboy would appreciate this thing Rob has for Jim's boots. Even some liberal gays don't understand such needs, and since Rob doesn't really need the men in any of the boots he sexually covets, he won't endanger what pleasure he now feels by whatever the possible risk of bringing Jim physically into the picture.

By crimping more tightly the sleeve of the boot, Rob successfully collapses the leather tube more tightly around his erect dick. The boot is suddenly a roomy leather asshole, a giant leather mouth.

Rob fucks the boot over his dick. Up, down, up. Down, up, down.

"Mmmmm," Rob hums to himself.

Rob's free hand pulls the other of Jim's two work boots from beneath the bed. His fingers caress that leather while the leather inside the other boot caresses Rob's stiff cock.

He picks up the second boot and tips it slightly to straighten its dog-eared leather sleeve. He angles the boot so its opening fits over his mouth and nose. Its inside smells are as excitingly sensual as those Rob has already found within the boot Rob's big dick now fucks.

Rob remembers his very first sexually stimulating boots. His father's boots. In this same bunkhouse. His father in the shower. Rob drawn to the boots like a bee drawn to nectar. Rob's cock made hard by the mere thought of his picking up those scruffy boots and caressing them. His cock exploded within his pants from his having done nothing more than sniffed the interior of but one of his father's foot-funky boots.

How many boots sniffed since then? How many licked? How many caressed? How many coveted? How many fucked? How many enjoyed?

Not that many. It isn't just any boot that does the job. In fact, Rob isn't yet sure why some boots turn him on and others don't. Except, they have to be cowboy boots, and they have to be scruffy. Of that much he's certain. After that, who knows? Not Rob. Except, there's definitely something more, as yet indefinable.

Because, Daniel Grime's cowboy boots, and Paul Waynelot's cowboy boots, and Carl Farenick's cowboy boots are scruffy, old, faded, stained, and they do nothing for Rob.

In the final analysis, Rob's isn't sure he really wants to know the why and the how of it. He's afraid too much delving into its mystery might ruin it. He doesn't want it ruined. It's too good to lose. Better than any more conventional sex he's ever had, and of conventional sex he's had more than his share and variety.

Still sheathing his cock with the one upended boot, he puts the toe of the other boot to his shirted chest. He rubs its leather toe against the material of his shirt and against the swollen center of one of his taut nipples. What he's doing feels good, but it can feel even better if there's nothing between his nipple and the leather.

He puts both boots to one side until he can strip down. He goes whole-hog and takes off everything, except his jockstrap which he likes hooked up and under his balls to provide his scrotum even greater prominence than normal.

He tosses his discarded clothes to his bunk which is nearby. Nightly, he sleeps so close to Jim, and to Jim's sexy boots, that he often goes to sleep only after masturbating, with attending fantasies of Jim's boots. No one pays any mind to Rob's masturbatory grunts and groans. To do so would be to be pots calling the kettle black, in that there isn't a ranch hand who doesn't flog his hog regularly, Jim included. Of course, no one knows, besides Rob, that Rob's one-hand fantasies all revolve around Jim's boots, not around visions of some broad's tight pussy.

Rob's striptease doesn't take long. Not that there's any real need for him to hurry. It's still early Friday night, all ranch hands off for their Friday-night blowout, after five days of working so hard that it sometimes hurts. No one is sick and hanging around the bunkhouse. No one will be back until the wee hours of the morning. No one having found Rob's staying behind all that unusual. He always stays behind, even when there isn't a pair of boots that has caught his sexual fancy. After all, he's ranch foreman, and he has paperwork that has to be done. He has the next week's work roster to complete. If Rob joins his men in town, on any Friday night, and he often does, it's always much later in the evening.

Rob is back on his knees in no time, the one boot again upturned and dancing over his naked cock, the other upright boot's pointy toe pushed against one of Rob's pointy and now-naked nipples. Rob's nipple goes even harder with each new chafing. By turning the upright boot sideways against his chest, Rob manages, besides the side of the boot toe still kept against his nipple, to press the side of the boot heel against his other nipple. The center of each nipple is a miniature hard-on made excruciatingly tender by its ongoing molestation by boot leather.

Again, Rob puts both boots to one side. He stretches for his discarded T-shirt on his nearby bunk. He begins an expert wrapping of his T-shirt around the length of his uplifted dick. When he finishes, he stuffs T-shirt, hard cock, and all, into the sleeve of one boot which, first placed upright on the floor, he then tips to one side.

He leans more forward, and eventually stretches completely out, belly-down, on the floor. His cock is fucked into the on-its-side boot now lodged firmly beneath Rob's pressing belly and the floor. One side of the boot's sole horizontally bisects Rob's belly, at his chest, just below his nipples. The weight of Rob's body flattens the boot sleeve against the T-shirt that flattens against Rob's cock inside. When Rob's hips lift slightly, his cock slides slightly outward from the cocoon of cotton cloth and leather. When Rob lowers his hips, his cock sinks right back into the cocoon, as far as Rob's balls.

It's more a dry fuck than a wet one. Not because Rob's cock isn't, as usual, drooling up a storm, but because all the wet is so thoroughly soaked up by the T-shirt and, therefore, provides no slippery slide for Rob's prick. Nonetheless, the fuck is pleasurable in its own right, as Rob's cock more and more makes its nesting form-fitting with each subsequent slip and slide.

Rob can blast his wad easily enough, the way he is. If his fucking of boot and T-shirt stuffing isn't the same as fucking tight male ass, there's something about his fucking the boot and its stuffing that makes what Rob does thoroughly exciting.

In the end, though, Rob comes back to a kneeling position, simultaneously lifting and upturning the still-fucked boot to keep his straining erection securely fucked inside the scruffy leather.

Rob raises higher on his knees. He drags the other boot into a position on the floor between his legs that aims the boot's open sleeve toward his balls, its back seam against the floor, its toe aims upward. Rob's ass slides forward along that boot's sleeve, lifts, then comes down over that boot's toe.

The boot's toe-tip slides into the hairy cleft of Rob's sweaty ass. By jiggling his butt, Rob positions his pucker snugly against the boot's toe-tip. If he sits hard enough, which he does, his pucker actually opens somewhat beneath the exerted pressure. Rob would like the feel of the whole boot kicked up his tight ass, but that would require lathering the boot with a mess of lubricating grease; something Rob would be hard-pressed to explain to Jim, upon the teenager's return to the bunkhouse.

Rob makes do with merely fantasizing his ass fucked hard and deep by leather boot, even as his cock fucks, and fucks again, the leather boot upturned over his erect prick.

Rob does what he does for the longest time. Pure willpower keeps him from popping his rocks into that T-shirt-packed boot sleeve. That he's able to hold off his orgasm emphasizes just how much Rob genuinely wants his playtime with Jim's boots to last, uninterrupted by any climax which would ebb his passions in the aftermath of any cataclysmic finale of his spurting spermal goo.

He unsheathes his cock from the leather boot but leaves his erection swaddled in the bulky T-shirt. He puts the once-fucked boot, upright, toe away from him, directly in front of him, between his open thighs. When he lifts slightly to pull the other boot forward, breaking its toe's contact with his asshole, that boot's toe bumps under Rob's balls on the way out front. Rob's large nuts remain especially vulnerable, thrust into high relief by Rob's jockstrap still folded down and tucked up beneath them.

Rob aligns the boots, side-by-side, their toes aimed away from him, between his thighs. Rob scoots closer to the results. He puts one hand into the sleeve of each boot, and his hands and forearms, like feet and ankles and calves, fill the boots. He leans farther into his hands, in the boots, and his cock is provided a fuck-space between the side-by-side boot sleeves. Rob fucks his T-shirt wrapped cock through that made-available space. He draws his leathered forearms as close together as possible in order to parenthesize more tightly hispoked-between cock.

With rabbity fuck movements, Rob fucks, and his forearms provide additional squeeze that allows both boot sleeves to convert into a tighter and tighter alley for Rob's cock to screw.

Rob humps this way until he genuinely about reaches his final limits of sexual endurance, perched on the very edge of orgasm. He shuts his eyes tightly and concentrates on keeping his cum inside his balls. When this exercise of willpower succeeds, it takes him a full minute to realize he's not begun squirting cum from his sperm-strained nuts.

He doesn't know whether to congratulate himself on his skills at keeping his orgasm at bay, or whether he's an idiot for having prevented himself needed release from pressure that'll likely soon see his un-emptied balls turn blue.

He pulls his hands from the boot sleeves. He gathers both boots in his arms and lies out on his back against the rough-grain wood of the bunkhouse floor. He stands both boots on his chest, toes toward his feet, while he unwraps his cock and tosses the used and abused T-shirt to his bunk.

He lies one boot on its side, across his chest so that its heel covers one of his nipples and its toe covers the other. By turning his head slightly, he places his cheek against that boot's leather sleeve that extends up along the right side of his neck. He smells the leather and can even physically taste it if he so desires.

He drops the second boot down between his legs, its sole aimed toward his crotch, its toe aimed toward the ceiling. He locks the boot's sole securely against his balls. If he could forget his erection (not likely!), now bare and laid out on his stomach, from his crotch to the indent of his navel, he might imagine the toe of the upjutted boot, positioned between his legs, as a leather erection sprouted from his crotch and aimed skyward.

With his left hand, Rob hooks the pseudo leather erection, up-shot between his legs, and he pulls its boot sole even more securely against his scrotum. He crosses his legs at his ankles, right ankle over left. By squeezing his thighs and, lifting his knees, he exerts more pressure of boot against his nuts.

His right hand fists as much of his naked dick as it can manage. No way do his fingers and thumb completely circumvent his erection. Still, there's enough of a grip so Rob exerts a firm stranglehold of his meat, needed to be viewed over the boot laid out, sole across his chest, boot sleeve along his neck.

A tug on his impressive handful of dick pulls its velvety outer layer of cockskin up Rob's solid cockcore. Although his dick has been so expertly circumcised that there's no webbing, nor any other identifiable scar tissue, there's enough loose skin to provide, albeit temporarily, a pseudo foreskin that completely pouts his impressively heart-shaped cockhead. A clear bead of preseminal juice appears at that snout and is about to drop stickily to Rob's belly when a downward stroke of Rob's fist converts the drop to an oily veneer that soaks Rob's cockhead and the first inch of Rob's burgeoned cockshaft.

There are two large veins noticeable on Rob's dick. One on each side of his cockshaft. Rob's palm feels one of those veins as Rob's fist commences a steady up-and-down motion over his solid penis. Simultaneously, he robs his cock of even more sticky juices and smears those over his cock. His cock, soon grown thoroughly soaked with preseminal deluge, emits wet sounds that resound as Rob's fingers work the sticky wash up, down, and around his prick.

Rob pumps his dick harder and faster. His pleasure swells with each rise and fall of his fist over his stiff meat. He raises his knees higher and higher. His knees, thighs and feet tightly entrench the boot's sole more and more firmly against Rob's nuts. Finally, Rob's left ankle, still crossed by his right ankle, almost touches Rob's ass, and the boot between his legs really mashes his testicles which are prominently kept elevated by the way the front of his jocksock is still latched beneath his cum-bulged testsicles.

"Oh, yes," Rob congratulates. No way does he stop the onslaught of orgasm this time. Doing so would require more know-how than he's mastered during all of his admittedly extensive sexual experimentation.

He pumps his dick harder, and each downward pass of his hand over his cock jams the heel of his fist against his balls and additionally squashes his gonads between Rob's fist and the strategically placed jocksock-hammock accordianed more and more by the pressure of boot leather.

Rob turns his cheek into closer contact with the boot sleeve laid up along his neck. His taut nipples are made more tender by the continual chafing provided by the slight rocking motion of the boot-sole edge atop them.

Rob licks that portion of the boot sleeve available to him. He takes a bite of the leather, holds fast, and sucks his mouthful.

"Ugh! Ugh! Ugh!" he grunts as his nuts, chock full of sexual cream, blast their carload of cum.

Rob's cum exits his pulsing cockmouth in syrupy, tail-trailing comets that, because of their wet-weight, are airborne mere fractions of a second before they lose all altitude and splatter down.

The first couple of gooey wads leapfrog the boot atop Rob's chest and splatter: one to Rob's left cheek, one in a drool of his chin. The next three slugs plop onto the boot on his chest. The last of his projected mess lattices Rob's muscled stomach and pools within his bellybutton.

His cum that isn't forcefully blasted is milked free of Rob's dick by another upswing of Rob's fist along the total length of his exploded cock. The resulting drool is a pearly, magmatic, mess that soaks his fingers and webs the black hair of his groin.

"Sweet Jesus!" Rob says around the boot leather his teeth still grip. His body gives a great and final shudder that shakes him from head to feet.

"Sweet Jesus!" he repeats and releases the hold his teeth have on the boot. He's left teeth marks that he knows from experience will vanish by morning.

It's now merely a case of mop-up. He has the routine down pat.

He uses his shirt to wipe down Jim's boots and clear the boot leather of any cum; although, the boots are already so stained a few new blotches aren't likely to be noticed by their teenage owner. Nonetheless, Rob takes particular care to rough up the area around his teeth marks to make sure the indents will more quickly rebound to nonexistence before morning.

He replaces the boots under Jim's bunk, and even makes sure that the drape of the bunk's wool blanket, over the bunk, is as he'd originally found it.

He uses those parts of his T-shirt and shirt not already cum-soaked to wipe up the mess his spunk makes on his belly, chest, neck, cheek, and chin.

He rolls his T-shirt, his shirt, and his pants into a tidy ball, ready for the wash, and deposits that ball on the bottom of his bunk.

He peels off his jockstrap and adds it to the pile.

He heads, bare-ass naked, into the bathroom that immediately adjoins the room he's in. He starts one of the row of showers and steps under its nozzle's noisely cleansing spray.

Jim Templar waits outside, as he always does, until the sounds of water, running through old pipes, tells him Rob is in the shower. Better the plumping clue him in than he try to spy through bunkhouse windows, someone wondering why Jim plays Peeping Tom.

Jim has devised a workable excuse for being back early: the same one he has ready every time, in case Rob, for whatever reason, isn't in the shower, despite what all the running water says. Jim needs only lie he has a headache and has returned with the hopes that turning in early will see the pain gone by morning.

Stepping into the bunkhouse, though, the studly teenager knows he's lucked out again. Rob is in the shower, and Rob's clothes are in their usual compact and discarded pile, jockstrap on top, atop Rob's bunk.

Jim hardly controls his ongoing excitement.

Thoughts of what he's once again come upon stiffen his young cock into an even more painful erection than it's already in.

Jim walks hurriedly to Rob's bunk and reaches for Rob's discarded jockstrap.

Even as Jim brings the sweaty jock, smelling excitingly strong of male musk, to his face, his free hand undoes the buttons of his pants crotch.

His circumcised cock, as always, proves too largely swollen to be conveniently pulled to freedom through the fly of his undershorts and through the open fly of his pants. Jim unfastens his belt and unbuttons the waistband of his jeans. His pants fly conveniently gaped, he pulls his shorts down around his hard cock and bares all of his youthfully stiff prick and most of his naked-except-for-blond-hair balls.

Quickly, he takes a condom packet from his pocket and removes its rubber. Pinching latex nipple, he caps the top of his steely dick with the prophylactic and expertly rolls the excess rubber down the length of his erection.

Then, he again sniffs Jim's jockstrap, long and hard. Simultaneously, he begins a hearty beating of his teenage meat, his fist having taken a firm hold of his dick in order to pump a velvety smooth layer of outer skin around a stiff cockcore that gets even stiffer by the second.

Sooner than later, Jim's huge prick sprays hot and heavy teenage cum, along with his accompanying grunts and groans. The room is made soundproof by the continuing flush of shower water through archaic plumbing.

Quickly, Jim puts Rob's jockstrap back to the pile on Rob's bunk. With consummate skill, and a minimum pulling of blond pubic hair, Jim slips the cum-filled rubber off his slightly softened penis. He ties off the open end of the rubber and slips the total into his right front pocket for disposal elsewhere.

He stuffs his cock and his cum-depleted balls into his underpants and jeans, then fastens and buttons up.

He sneaks out of the bunk house, Rob, whom Jim feels would never understand, hopefully none the wiser.

PUMPING GAS

True story.

I'm seventeen and a runaway.

Actually, I've just turned eighteen by the time I realize I must have taken a wrong turn. Probably got disoriented the night before when, dropped off by my last ride, just outside of Elkhorn, Nevada, I'd walked casually off the side of the road to unroll my sleeping bag and had almost bedded a rattler. No matter that I only remember there being one road of choice, at the time, because I'd already been distracted, since Elkhorn, due to it having been from there that I'd called my parents collect to let them know I was okay. My being eighteen and all, there was no longer any official way for them to track me down and haul my ass back home. My call made my mother cry. She'd figured me for dead, or worse. It made my Dad cry, too, which still makes me feel shitty.

It's not like I'm on the road because my parents are mean, or nasty, or horrible. If they're God-fearing and church-going, that doesn't mean either is the kind of religious fanatic you read about who can make a living hell on earth for any of their naturally rebellious children, or are automatically bigoted, anti-cosmetics, anti-liquor, anti-movies, anti-dancing. They're none of the above. They're just your average, everyday sort of parents, not bad, probably better than most. Trouble is they, and I, for most of my life, lived in a very everyday kind of town, where everybody knew everybody else and everybody else's business; everyday as comfortably everyday predictable and everyday average as the next. I'd had recurring nightmares that I'd never get out of the place. So, one Sunday, promising to meet my parents at church, I'd packed up and headed in the opposite direction.

My having discovered, in time spent since then, that it is, indeed, as I'd always suspected, a big wide world out here (although I've really yet to get beyond a very few U.S. states). Someplaces are a helluva lot better than where I'm from, and a helluva lot more exciting.

Someplaces are a helluva lot worse.

I now walk a highway that stretches forward and back, from seeming horizon to another horizon, seemingly as straight as any stick. Not a car or a building or a tree in sight, not a car or a building or a tree having been in sight since I woke up that morning. Last night, after my experiences with bawling parents and the rattler, I'd tried to keep on walking but had finally become just too damned brain-dead to keep on. I'd literally fallen to the wayside, saying as I did so, "Any venomous rattlers or heart-broken parents can come get me, because I'm just too damned dead on my feet to give a rat's ass!"

Of course, I have a road map. I'm not a complete scatterbrain and usually have a fine sense of direction. I figure to pull the damned map out as soon as I spot a road sign, or any other sign, that'll give me some sort of clue. Signs, though, seem to be in as short supply as cars, buildings, and trees.

Therefore, without even one, "Last Chance for Gas!" or "Eats!" or "See the Live Gila Monsters!", I'm damned surprised when the rickety and bleached-to-monkey-grey building suddenly appears, like magic. Of course, the thing has been there all along. The seemingly straight road I've been walking has, unknown to me, been on a slight upgrade for God only knows how many miles, the gas station having become visible only as I'd crested one edge of the slight depression in the landscape in which the building sits.

I know it's a gas station, because there are two pumps out front. Although, there's no identifying Texaco, EXXON, or Shell logo. It's one of those middle-of-nowhere kind of gas stations that lurks as if having been sitting right where it is since before cars or trucks were ever invented In fact, the premises look so God-awful and ghost-townie, my excitement would have been considerably less if it wasn't for the very red and very expensive-looking sports car pulled off the road and parked beside, albeit toward the back of, the building. Maybe a Corvette like the one the guy was driving who picked me up outside Topeka, Kansas, and drove me through cornfields at one-hundred-plus miles an hour, with the top down. Top-down, where I am now, as soon as the sun manages to climb a bit higher, will be fried-brains time.

I adjust the straps of my backpack and head on down. Hopefully, there's a bit of water to be had to refill my water bottle for a trip back to somewhere that'll allow me to reconnect with civilization.

Nearer the car and the building, the road becomes less expansive, foreshortened to include only the shallow curve-up of road behind me, and another curve-up of road ahead. My whole world becomes this bit of depressed scenery, couched within its shallow dip of roadway.

When I give the old water pump, located just a few feet from the gas-station door, several hearty pumps, I never actually expect water to result. Let's face it, I'm talking vintage piece of equipment here, seen only in old movies or certain kinds of museums. Pre-inside-toilet stuff. Rusty as hell. Squeaking like sixty, under obvious protest, but eventually spilling a surprisingly forceful gush of crystal-clear water into an accepting dry-as-a-bone trough.

I figure the water is poison. That's my mind-set at this point of the game. So, I don't fill my water bottle directly. I dip a finger into the small pool left on the rusty snout, and I sniff at it, as if I suspect it may be dog shit if only I can detect the telltale aroma. It smells of nothing. So, I tentatively lick the tip of my finger and taste nothing but wet. I figure poisoned water can be tasteless, but I've always figured it tastes of alkaline. Rather, that it tastes bitter, since I haven't a clue as to how alkaline really tastes.

Only then, pretty much convinced of temporary salvation, as if I were some desert traveller having stumbled upon an unmapped oasis, in an ocean of sand, I do a lot of exuberant face-splashing, water-gulping, and wetting-down the nape of my neck. Then, I fill my water bottle and access the gas station through a screen door that squeaks so spookily it completely alleviates whatever goodwill I've been cajoled into experiencing from having discovered potable water.

"Hello!" That's what I say. Exactly like one of those silly-ass teenagers, in all those dumb horror flicks, who somehow thinks the ghosts are going to answer back, or the deranged madman with his ax is going to reveal his presence with any kind of friendly how-are-you? aplomb.

The place seems as deserted on the inside as out, except, of course, for a cash register that looks as if it's old enough to have arrived in the same shipment as the water pump, and display cases and shelves with more than their dusty share of cigarettes, snacks, chewing gum, motor oil, canned goods, and various sundries.

I'm spooked by a sudden noise that I eventually identify, my heart finally down out of my throat, as a refrigerator unit going into chill mode, somewhere on the other side of the shelves.

I listen for the buzz of flies. Fly buzzing always what leads to all those dead bodies. Victims -- of aliens from outer space, or of a military experiment gone awry, or of a modern-day Bonnie and Clyde, or of a disgruntled kid who, sick to death of having reached puberty in the middle of nowhere, offs mom and Dad and Brother Bill and Sister Sue and the Dog Mo and the Cat Rusty, and heads out into the big wide world. All of these would-be killers, at least the human ones, mentally deranged in having left behind so expensive a means of get-away as the car parked outside.

I tell myself to cool it. Actually say the words aloud which leaves me feeling a complete ass. I hear no buzzing of flies, so how can there be any bodies, unless the driver of the car is, even now, out back, burying the corpses? I check for another door to the outside, and I'm still looking for one when I'm distracted by a peripheral view of the glass-door refrigeration unit whose shelves are lined with cold soda.

I detour for a Coke. Nothing like one to quench the old thirst, although someone once told me Coke's caffeine content makes it a diuretic and something to be avoided when dying of thirst. Hell, what did that someone -- whomever it was -- know? I know that the only thing better than a cold Coke to quench a thirst is a cold beer. And, what do you know, there's beer in the unit, too. Except the last thing I want -- or, rather, need -- is to get shit-faced drunk and go wandering off into the blue, never to be seen again, no need for interfering outer-space aliens, government-induced plague, some gangster and his moll, a deranged teenage psychopath ... et al.

I stand in the draft from the temporarily opened cooler, then retrieve a can of soda and pop its tab. As I know it will, the pop tastes cold and downright refreshing all of the way down.

I can't find any other door but the front one. I head back for it, figuring to check outside. Hopefully, the car is still there, not hoisted, from the beginning, on blocks, only looking as if it has but recently arrived, via some time time-warp, into this seemingly past century.

I pause at the entrance/exit counter to anchor a paper dollar to the dust with my empty pop can. The last thing I want anyone to think is that I'm out to stiff him the price of a Coke, especially if this is the only sale the guy has made in the past few hundred years. If a dollar seems too much, I figure I might luck out and get change once I find the proprietor. If it's not enough money (I once unwittingly had to pay two-fifty for a draft beer), I figure ...

"Jesus, fucking Christ, you scared the holy shit out of me!" I literally scream, having turned from the counter to confront the originally squeaky screen door having miraculously been opened without a sound, posed within the excavated doorway the loomingly large and back-lit shadow of a ...

"Wasn't exactly expecting anyone." Definitely a man. No woman's voice has, or should have, exactly that low-kind of timbre.

While I still can't see that much of him, I do know that only a man could, or should, be his size. Although I'm a bit biased, coming in only at five-nine, which means anyone six-feet or above seems pretty much gigantic as far as I'm concerned.

"Not many people through here, these days, since the expressway went through years ago," he says. "Your car break down?"

"I'm thumbing."

"Along this stretch of hell?" He doesn't elaborate. The way he says it indicates just how thoroughly he pegs me as someone whose mental elevator doesn't stop at all floors.

"Took a wrong turn," I say.

"Obviously," he agrees and finally gets out of the doorway and comes on in. As soon as he releases the screen, it reverts to its old creaky self, complete with a bang, in finale, that dislodges an all-enveloping grey tornado of dust.

He comes on by me and takes a position of authority behind the counter.

He's big all right. Well-muscled, too, in that there's hardly a chance of missing the way his body is so snugly poured into his black T-shirt and his tight faded-to-pale-blue jeans.

His hair is comic-book black, tousled, and banged sexily all of the way over his forehead to where it catches not only in his eyebrows but in the thickest, longest, lushest eyelashes I've ever seen this side of Vince Gill. His eyes are grey, made greyer by his deep and burnished tan which velvety veneers his high cheekbones, his square jawline, his cleft chin, his well-muscled arms. His lips are equally golden, and cupid's-bow to boot. His teeth are even and downright sparkly.

His crotch is ... well, although I'm well aware what his crotch is: obviously stuffed to capacity with a package likely to have King Kong green with envy ... I don't let my thoughts or my eyesight linger overly long in that particular direction. The last thing I need is to give this butch number the wrong -- or, rather, right -- impression; namely, that I'd like to see unwrapped the enticing package sprouted between his legs. Let's face it, whoever this guy is, he's bigger than I am, and he outweighs me by several muscular pounds. Encountering a card-carrying homophobe, under these conditions, isn't to my liking. Whose to know if I disappear into the wilds of Nevada, disposed of by a queer-hating stud who takes offense when he figures my gaze becomes too much an ogle focused on the ridge his obviously uncut and large meat makes in one paper-thin leg of his trousers? In that, I haven't told my parents I'm in Nevada, merely said I was safe -- location horribly vague -- in case they decided to call in the authorities with the info that I'm still underage and carrying false ID.

I finally tear my charmed-like-a-snake-by-a-snake-charmer gaze away from his basket of genital goodies, feeling lucky and relieved to discover he's not looking at me but at the can-anchored dollar I've left on the counter.

"Couldn't find anyone around but didn't want you to think I was out to stiff you the price of a Coke," I say.

I catch an unwanted glimpse of myself as reflected from a particularly dirty, discolored, and hopefully distorting bit of window. I look as if I've crawled in on my hands and knees. My short brown hair is spiky beneath my baseball cap which I've turned backwards, tufts sprouted through the space between cap material and size-adjustment tab band. My brown eyebrows and lashes are grey with screen-door dust, and so are my lips. My eyes are so puffy I'm hard-pressed, even knowing their color, to guess brown. My experimentation with the water pump, out front, has streaked the front of my shirt with dry river-runs dried into a kind of discolored mud-cracked tie-dyed design.

"I like to run across anyone, in this day and age, who's honest," he says and pockets the dollar; I don't have the guts to ask if there might be change. "You say you're thumbing?"

"Trying to get to the ocean." At the beginning, the Atlantic had been closer, but the Pacific -- maybe because of all my fantasizing of fabled studly beachboys -- holds far more attraction.

"You saved up for the trip, or you working your way through?"

"I look independently wealthy, do I?" I say, talking as much to my mirror-image as to him.

"How about you stick around for a few days?" he says. "I'll pay you to pump gas -- or whatever."

"No way you're talking commission basis," I say. "I've counted your potential customers on this stretch of highway this morning and came up with zero, aside from me."

"Fifty bucks a day, merely to keep me company, then. My old man died, and I'm going through his things. Thought I could better manage it by myself, probably still can, but I forgot -- although how I could possibly have managed that, I've not a clue -- that this place is so fucking out-of-the-way dreary."

Do I really want to be stuck out here in the middle of nowhere with a big-basket queer-hating stud-muffin? Not that I know he's queer-hating, only the big-basket and stud-muffin parts undeniable. It's just that I try to come up with the odds in favor of his being where he is, looking the way he looks, inviting me to stick around as he has, all delivered up with the icing on the cake of his being gay as well. I stop thinking of the odds against any such miracle when I reach something like six-hundred-million-to-one.

On the other hand, I've always enjoyed just looking. That's all I did until I hit the road, wasn't it? No way could I have come out of the closet to enjoy an openly gay life in our little town where everyone would have known it before I did. For that matter, who to come out with? Granted, there were more than a couple of good-lookers in the neighborhood, each as straight as the other, all just as straight as the bit of Nevada highway just outside this doorway, except without even a hint of hidden deviance.

I figure I can get a lot of mileage out of ogling this stud on the sly. Hell, as the day gets hotter, he might even take off his T-shirt and give me enough fantasies to keep me contentedly beating my meat for days and days after I've eventually pulled out and left him behind.

"Look, I'll throw in all the shit you can eat and drink." A wave of one powerful arm encompasses the total contents of the room. "Anyway, whatever's still edible. I sampled a bag of the potato chips which weren't too stale, and the beer and soda're still okay."

Can I risk a beer, now or later, this guy in the same vicinity? Having not been out all that long, I'm a little disconcerted, let me tell you, by whatever the animal pheromone this dude exudes, me eagerly ready to suck it up (double-entendre intended). So far, I've been the passive one in every gay game I've played. It's simultaneously exciting and scary the way I may actually contemplate taking on more than I can chew (yes, take that any damned way you please, too!).

"I'll even try and come up with a decent evening meal with the supplies I've ferried in," he says, as if he'd boated across a lake to get here.

Good God, the guy can cook, too?

"Nothing gourmet," he says, "but I can serve up a good steak with the best of them."

Sure as hell no doubt about that, what with all the evidence of good steak he sports in the crotch of his trousers.

"Sure, why shouldn't I stick around?" I say. "That is, if you promise to throw in a ride to the nearest town, job-over, into the bargain."

"Deal!" he says and extends one of his large hands to seal the bargain.

Do I confess to the gooseflesh that shivers me timbers just because of the way his massive paw loses my smaller one inside it? The thrill I experience because of the way his fingers press inward and over those of mine? Sure, why not?! No denying I like the guy. Like the way he looks. Like the way he talks. Like the way he smiles. Like the way he graciously controls all the power his fingers have to squeeze mine to oblivion. Hate the way his hand too soon removes from mine. Fear he'll not only notice the swelling in my pants but rightly suspect he's the cause.

"Name's David, by the way," he says. "David Freon."

Goddamn!: a good-looker, a good cook, with a good and definitely non-homophobic sense of humor. My wide smile and accompanying chuckle compliment him on the latter.

"You know," I say, "that could have gone well over my head, except my uncle works with refrigerators?"

"Does he?"

"Regular Maytag Man. Otherwise ..."

Something about the way he looks brings me up short. Suddenly, I feel pretty much the fool.

"Your name really David Freon?"

"Last time I checked."

"Jesus!" How do I talk my way out of this one? Even knowing it had been too good to be true, I'd let a prime bit of coincidence lead me down the garden path. Hoping against hope, like a goddamned love-sick girl.

He didn't come right on out and ask for an explanation. Nevertheless, he was patiently waiting for one. Everything about him, from the beginnings of his silly-ass grin, to the slight cock of his handsome head to bang his hair into an even more attractive slant, insisted he be let in on the joke.

"Look, I feel like an ass," I say. That's an understatement.

His grin becomes a bit forced.

"I really could use this job," I give it the old college try. "If my tendency to conjure a sick joke out of nothing screws this up for me, I'm really going to feel like shit."

"I've been known to laugh at more than a few sick jokes, in my time," David says and waits.

"I wouldn't want you to get the wrong idea." Actually, I'm more concerned that he might get the right idea. "I mean, having made a tenuous connection that allows me to see any humor at all is likely to make me come off as queer as a three-dollar bill."

Which, to my dismay, is the perfect lead-in for him to ask if I am, indeed, as queer as three-dollar bill. I, not having any idea how I would response to such a direct in-my-face query. I'm out of the closet, for Christ's sake, and should be beyond putting on any kind of hetero-charade. On the other hand, a guy like I, who can get off just looking at a good-looking straight man -- in particular, at this good-looking straight man -- can well bite off his nose to spite his face by slipping into any militantly gay-is-good mode.

Thank God, he doesn't ask. This time around, I'm fully behind the Clinton administration's "Don't Ask, Don't Tell!" policy, as regards gays (in the military or anywhere else).

"Freon, I'm sure you already know, is a refrigerant -- a gas, " I say. "So, what with you having asked me to stick around to ... well, you know?"

He laughs. A genuine belly-laugh. From somewhere deep inside him. A sounding filled with seemingly good humor.

"'Pumping gas', you mean?" he says and laughs again, more a controlled giggle, this time, than his previous full-blown guffaw. He comes across positively youthful. "Jesus ... that ... is ... funny!" He regains most of his composure, flicks his tumbled hair out of his eyes only to have it fall right back again. "Lucky for me that you did see the humor in it. Otherwise, you might have seen it as my making some kind of sexual come-on."

I should have been so lucky!

"Well, come on," he says, "if you'll excuse that blatant play on words. You look as if you could use a bath."

"Thought you'd never ask." I'm relieved that a difficult moment has passed with relative ease.

I'm confused when he doesn't head for the front door but leads me back toward the cooler. I've been back there. There's no second door to the outside.

Except, as it turns out, there is a second door, unnoticed because it's in the floor, needing to be yanked up to reveal its descending stairway.

"Do-do, do-do. Do-do, do-do," David chants the theme from a scary TV series that's become a classic, what with constant reruns. "Underground is more cooling. Nothing even vaguely more nefarious about that."

I suspect Jeffrey Dahlmer, serial killer, was just as charming as he did his welcome-to-my-parlor routines that enticed gay men to drop their guard and be killed and cannibalized.

"You really want to leave the shop up here unlocked and unlooked-after?"

"Anyone who'd take the time and effort to clean the place out would be doing me a favor," he says. "The only money even to come near that cash register in days is your dollar that's now in my pocket."

He disappears down the stairs

In for a penny, in for a pound. I follow after, pleasantly surprised that it isn't the typical basement I expected. This one has one whole wall opened by a bank of windows that overlook a small gully.

"Dad, of course, always insisted on a green lawn," David says. "I'm afraid I've let the place go completely to hell since he died."

"There's enough water for lawn?"

The submerged living quarters are really quite cool, kept from darkness not only by the windows but by cleverly placed lighting. Lots of manly deep sofas and chairs. A smell of old leather and old cigar smoke. Plush brown rug. A small kitchen. A small dining area. What looks like a couple of bedrooms with attending baths."

"Plenty of water for one house, one family, one small gas station," he says and automatically helps me off with my backpack, making no big deal of his assist. "Dad, of course, had visions of there being enough water for another Las Vegas. Turns out only to be slow seepage, though, of million-year old water rained down somewhere, probably miles from here, but just where not even the scientists are able to decide."

He heads for accordion doors off to one side, folds them open to reveal stacked washer and dryer. He opens the latter and fishes out two large white bath towels, one of which he tosses to me.

"Come on," he says and heads not toward one of the two bedrooms, and their attending bathrooms, but for a large glass panel at one end of the glass wall. "More fun bathing in the great out-of-doors. Cleverly concealed reservoir makes for a rather impressive waterfall. I checked the water level when I first got here and figure there's plenty available for however much sybaritic usage we'll demand of it over the next couple of days."

No sign of his swimming suit. I've mine in my backpack, but he's talking baths not swims. Exciting idea: he and I, naked, in a desert waterfall, soaped up, sun glinting off our sex-heated skin. "Here, let me wash your back. Better yet, why not soap up mine? Hell, slick up your ass, and I'll get to work, earning my keep, fucking gas."

I'm getting a rampant hard-on. No way do I strip on down, my stiff dick uplifted before my belly and weaving back and forth like a metronome. If David has graciously passed over any suspicions I've give him that I'm gay, not even he's going to be able to overlook my stiff prick. Hetero men are supposed to be able to strip down in each other's presence without going into obvious heat.

"I should warn you," he says. "Outdoor bathing sometimes gives me an erection. Can't explain the how or why of it. Can't say as I've ever tried. Only know it happened so often, while I was growing up, my old man swore I had the hots for Mother Nature."

Obviously, he's spotted my cock as its presently swelling in my pants. He's being diplomatic to put me at ease. When I end up the only one with a stiff dick, under this waterfall of his, he'll likely be just as diplomatic in his explanations as to why that's happened. But if he can be graciously okay about it, so the hell can I. Besides, I'm hot to see him naked, no matter what the circumstances. Whether I see his unclothed cock completely soft, completely hard, or anywhere in between, I don't care. Seeing it steely hard, of course, would be the preferable, but ...

"Almost forgot," he says and heads back on by me just as I join him at the sliding glass door.

I take advantage of David's back turned toward me to manhandle my bulged crotch and try and to get it into some more comfortable alignment. If the brief glance I've allowed myself of David's basket, during his brief moment of passing, has provided me every indication that his cock is already as stiff as he predicts, I believe I'm doing nothing more than indulging myself in wishful thinking. Or, true to his word, it's simply no more, nor less, than his being turned on by outside bathing; I've known people with far stranger fetishes.

"A gun," he says, working the barrel of an automatic pistol downward beneath the waistband of his jeans. If the gun goes off, his other gun, and accompanying balls, will likely pay an horrible price.

"A gun," I say. Okay, I'm back to thinking I'm in possibly more danger than just embarrassing myself with a look-at-me-I'm-queer boner. I'm deluged with such a wave of renewed paranoia that my cock actually loses a good deal of its starch.

"Snakes," he says. "I can take one out at fifty feet. Any bigger animal can usually be scared away by a one-shot noise."

He's through the door, giving me a chance to run for it. Although, how far do I get if he comes running after, his gun drawn? And I'm talking the metal gun, not the other impressive weapon he so obviously carries in his pants.

I catch up to him, fall into step beside him. With just the flesh-and-blood gun between his legs, he seemed powerful, big, strong. The metal gun only makes him seem even more ... what ... dangerous? Whatever, no denying that I'm tremendously excited, although I remain unsure of all the contributing factors.

"If we should chance upon a scorpion," he says, "you can trust in me to make it one dead arachnid. A tarantula, on the other hand, every man for himself, and I'll be the first whose ass is seen cresting the horizon. Woke up, as a kid, with one of those hairy things in my bed, and ..."

He visibly shudders in emphasis.

Does he similarly shudder during sex? His big balls spewing cum? His hips bouncing within the couching pelvis of some cunt?

My cock pretty much gone soft, pretty much goes hard, and pretty much keeps getting harder.

I like David all the better now that I know he's afraid of tarantulas. Rather, I like him because he's told me he's afraid of tarantulas. It's something personal. A confidence. How many men, gay and straight, have I met since I've left home, none of whom I've really known a damned thing about? With what bit of something personal, about myself, have I ever left even one of those men?

"I'm afraid of roosters," I say.

That brings him up short.

"You're afraid of cocks?"

"Touché, Mr. Freon Gas," I say with a wide smile, "but it's roosters I said, it's roosters I meant."

If he wants to see how afraid of cock I'm not, all he has to do is pull out his and see how fast I'm on it.

"When I was three, I quite unexpectedly came upon my grandfather's rooster heartily pecking out the eyes out of one of grandfather's dogs. I thought for sure the damned bird had killed it and would kill me. Didn't believe them for a minute when they told me the poor old dog had died of old age, the poor old bird having come along after and had merely taken advantage of the situation. Damned bird still gives me nightmares."

We're on the move again. We walk an old streambed and now angle upward through the extended arms of its vee-shaped arroyo. Nothing looks flat, this close-up, although I would have sworn, from the road, that everything was.

The natural passage narrows to a space pretty much filled with a large metal door. We approach via a series of stepping stones that raise us to a level where we won't be bothered by the foot-high grating upon which the door sits. Before opening the door, David first opens the smaller spy hole and takes a look on through.

"Dad took all sorts of technical precautions to keep the wildlife out," he says by way of explanation, "but creatures can be quite inventive when it comes to accessing water in a place this bestial dust-bowl. Once had a bear, or maybe a damned Sasquatch, come through and rip this very door off its hinges."

Which makes me a little less paranoid about his carrying a gun.

He fishes a key from a selection on the ring he retrieves from his right front pocket.

"Know how many of God's little creatures have brains, as well as little hands? Raccoon can probably open this door in a shot if ever I were fool enough to leave it unlocked."

I believe him. It's easier than imagining David some modern-day Bluebeard providing entrance to his before-now don't-even-think-of-opening-this doorway.

"Fucking beautiful!" I'm surprised by what the opened door reveals. It's the colors, as if the space beyond is a shimmering kaleidoscope.

"For a while, Dad was really into stained glass," David says.

The area beyond the door isn't open to the sky but covered by a canopy of multi-colored panels though which sunlight filters to our side in myriad hues.

Church-like comes to mind. Except, no church I've ever attended ever made my dick get as hard as mine is. Usually quite the opposite. Of course, I've not had anyone as sexy as David along for devotions.

"Actually, Dad had a knack for a lot of things," David says and leads the way through the natural narrow hallway via additional steeping stones hard to see because of the distracting colors. "If he'd merely chosen one thing and stuck to it, instead of always looking for the quick get-rich scheme, like seeing this hellhole another Las Vegas, he would probably have made two or three fortunes."

"Truly, truly amazing!" I say and stop dead in my tracks. I genuinely can't believe how the passageway, instead of narrowing farther, opens into a room-size cavern illuminated by sunlight through a virtual dome of colorfully interlaced shards."

"It's not really glass at all, but some kind of translucent but durable plastic," David says. "Dad tried actual glass, but it kept breaking, usually tumbling some little critter who'd been clever enough to get as far as the skylight."

The stepping stones veer in a leftward procession around the room, and I follow David along them to where a small arrangement of low rock formations provide convenient benches and seats.

"Not really natural rock formations at all," David says and drops his towel on a convenient rock bench, balancing his pistol on the cushion of folded material. "Mother Nature not having managed anything, in original, even close to what Dad considered aesthetically outdoorsy. He used molds and some kind of fast-drying cement, then got rid of all the dangerous rough edges by sanding."

Mid-sentence, David disappears, as if by magic, behind a rock slap that I'd assumed was part of the main wall but turns out to be only veneer. Almost immediately, I hear a gurgle, look in the direction from which it's coming, and spot water emerging from somewhere high on an adjoining rock face.

"All achieved by gravity," David says as he reappears. The initial run of water disappears momentarily at a slightly lower level, only to reappear over another lip of stone to tumble a couple more feet to another disappearance. "Never have quite figured out the physics."

I hear the water but, except for the initial two cascades, it doesn't give any clue as to when or where it'll next make its appearance.

"This part takes the most time," David says.

We wait.

Somehow the water, when it finally deigns make its latest appearance, does so in a curtain-like descent, a good eight-feet across, and in such a seemingly unbroken and well-coordinated line that I swear it's not water but filmy green silk. Only its whoosh, and final watery splash, proclaims the truth of the matter.

"Sir, your bath is drawn," David says and flashes a wide smile.

The initial cascades, plus the latest curtain of water, remain in place, fed by additional deluge. The floor of the cave, once bone-dry, floods with run-off. The total effect, in the face of the miles of dryness outside, seems almost too much of an extravagance.

David sits, unties his boot laces, slips off his shoes. He peels off white sweat socks. I've never thought myself with a foot fetish, but I'm amazed by just how sexy I find his feet.

"You know," he says, maneuvering, while still seated, to begin the peel of his T-shirt from his torso, pausing midway so that what I get is a tantalizing view of his washboarded midsection, punctuated by a navel so flush with its surrounding muscle that it might be nonexistent: David seemingly as umbilical-less as Adam in the Garden of Eden. "I don't think you even told me your name."

"Jamie," I say, my mouth dry with the mere prospect of what additional wonders any continuing unveiling of his body is going to provide. "Jamie Grandler."

"Well, Jamie Grandler," he says, and his voice becomes temporarily muffled through black cotton as he tugs his T-shirt up and over his head, his hair emerging sexily tousled in finale, "you might want to remove some of your clothes before bathing. Dirty they may be, but better washed in the washer and dryer than here."

Which very well may be true, except I'm momentarily powerless to do much of anything but gape. At the confirmed magnificence of his scalloped belly. At the exquisite sculpturing of his chest: two chiselled pectorals facing off across a deeply serrated pectoral cleavage. At a thin fan of black chest hair funneling to a heavy straight line as far as his navel, then onward to disappearance beneath the waistband of his denims. At two too perfect nipples, coppery and dime-size.

He stands and unfastens the top of his jeans, smiling as he does so.

"I did mention this thing I have for Mother Nature," he forewarns and proceeds to drop his pants. Not a quick drop of them, mind you. So slow a drop, in fact, that I'd suspect him a professional stripper, paid extra to titillate his audience, except even I can see his pants, too tight even for him to wear underwear, aren't easily maneuvered down and over the mouth-watering twin-mounds of his bare ass, nor down and over the additional stiffening his naked cock has achieved since he'd first donned his clothes that morning.

Truly, I've never seen a more perfect stereotype of the ideal male of the species. To me, he appears without imperfections. From the tips of his sexily tousled black hair, to the toes of his sexily slim feet. A face to die for. A body to kill for. A cock to shrivel all competition.

Except, my cock goes all the harder in my pants and has me suddenly wondering if I'll be able to get my own pants down around the presented obstacle.

"So," David says, having stepped out of his pants, like a butterfly leaving all traces of confining cocoon. From somewhere, among the grouping of rock benches and seats, he produces a still-wrapped bar of soap and gives it a toss in my direction, caught by me by pure reflex.

With an already unwrapped bar of his own, he steps down into the runoff that's now flooded as far as the exit grate beneath the far door, and he dips his head into the waterfall to cause a resulting spray that reaches all the way to me.

The water caresses and covers his body, refracting already colored light into an even wider assortment of color.

"Water's fine," he says, his head out of the spray. The marvellous acoustics of the place (specifically engineered by his father?), allow me to hear him over the audibly low hiss of the water, without his having to shout.

Boner or not, it's obviously time for me to strip down and join him. My staying put and merely gaping will make me seem more queer than if I, as unselfconsciously as he, merely walk my stiffy into the water.

I strip so hurriedly that it's only when I'm stepping down into the flow, my cock so bloody hard I'm truly beginning to think its going to cause me to tumble forward on my face, that I realize David's just standing there, watching.

"I'm too thin," I say, though I have to real intention of saying any such thing. I just figure he's making the inevitable shower-room comparisons, and it's less painful for me to point out my flaws than imagine his doing it.

"Who says you're too thin?"

"Every mirror I glance into."

"Do those same mirrors tell you there's a difference between skinny and streamline? Between skeletal and honed? I don't know how long you've been on the road, kid, but however much walking you've done, and I can't imagine it's been all that much, looking as good as you must to all the perverts out cruising for handsome young men just like you, you've been toned pretty much to perfection. Not an extra ounce of fat on you that I can spot. Tightly muscled ass. Flat stomach. Fantastic legs."

"Maybe if I took to walking on my hands I could do something about developing my upper body." I've always wanted a chest like his chest. His sculptured muscularity says all-man. My willowy thinness, whether whippet-like or just plain scrawny, says kid, says boy, says undeveloped teenager.

"You're still growing, aren't you, Jamie?" As if he's read my mind. As if he's pagan priest, given second sight by his god. "You even eighteen?"

If he were queer, would he want me eighteen? younger? older?

"Come here," he says, not pressing for an answer. "I'll show you something I used to do all the time, in here, starting long before I was your age and continuing right on down to my bath last night."

I walk on over, as he asks, only wishing my dick wasn't quite so obviously aroused by how sexy I find him. I suspect, before this is done, I'll finally get to know the true meaning of blue balls.

"Over this way a bit more," he says and steps back from the sheer curtain of water that pours down before him and splashes at his feet.

I move between him and the water, the coolness of the spray against my back and rear, the heat of his body furnace-like as I realize there's little more separating us than his swollen cock and my own.

"Face the water," he says.

Do I really want to make myself even more vulnerable by turning my defenseless back to this man?

"This isn't going to hurt, promise," he says. Bastard could probably charm the cassock off a priest; although from what I've heard, that might not be all that difficult.

I face the water, hoping against hope that he's a rapist out to sodomize my ass.

"Now," he says, up real close behind me, his lips nearly brushing my ear, "move forward, ever so slowly, your hips thrust slightly forward, so that just your hard cock gets fucked into the falling water."

Straight, or not, would he fuck my ass if I asked him? Because, while he talks of my fucking a curtain of water, it's my getting fucked by him, or my fucking him, that consumes most of my imagination.

His hands, strong, forceful, large, clamp my hips, his fingertips curling forward to lock securely into place over the sharply leading edges of my predominant hipbones.

Jesus, I think, he's going to fuck me! There is, indeed, a God in heaven.

Except, he uses his handholds not to keep my ass contained for the lustful onslaught of his fucking erection but to maneuver my lower body into the slightly forward curve he's requested of it, but which I'd yet to give him.

My standing-tall dick slides into the falling water, my cockhead raised to meet the caressing liquid like a thirsty man with open mouth aimed toward a suddenly opened and rain-filled sky.

Okay, so it's not the exquisite pleasure/pain I'd expect from the lustful thrust of his unlubricated dick up my behind. It's nowhere as exquisite as any passage of my stiff dick up his funky rectum. However, there's no denying that the rush of cool but not-too-cold water, down the uplifted shaft of my submerged dick, is distractingly pleasurable enough.

"Stand there long enough, and the water will jack you off," he says, up so close and personal that I can't believe the hardness of his dick isn't securely pressed against the small of my back.

"Maybe I'd better not," I say but see this as a perfect solution to my dilemma, even acceptable to a straight David who's done the same thing himself and, therefore, can understand my falling equal victim to it. Where he'd not as likely accept my fantasies of him speared on my cock or me speared on his.

"Why not get your rocks off?" he cajoles as skillfully as Eve enticed Adam to sample the apple. "One should be open to new experiences, right?"

Even if such new experiences for David are his cock up my ass, my dick probing his asshole until he screams?

"Move your dick about a bit in the water until you experience just the right caress," he whispers. Marvellous how I hear him so distinctly over the watery sounds, and over the distracting buzz of pleasure the fondling water sets off inside my brain.

As if I might not have gotten the gist of his instructions, his hands shift my hips in varying degrees of forward and back, side to side, pausing briefly after each so that I might better judge which angle of splash best conjures for me the best of all available pleasurable results.

"A man can tell what he likes, can't he?" David says.

For just the briefest bit of a heartbeat, I think I experience the glancing touch of his hard cock along my back. Real or imagined, no denying the thrill. No denying, either, the pleasure caused by the continuing flush of moving water down upon the head of my dick, down around the neck of my cock, down and over my balls.

"Which angle of fuck-the-waterfall is best for you, Jamie?"

Ever so slightly, his hands surrender their guiding pressure. Suddenly, they're only along for the ride as I retrace my hip movements to rediscover that one particular position of my cock in the spray that ...

"Mmmmmm," I hum as I get my prick right where I want it. The slight variations of slippery liquid, caused by water not perfectly aligned for each and every drop from height to finale, offers just the right degree of subtle variation to make it seem as if the waterfall is somehow a living, breathing thing.

"Feels good?" David says.

Feels good, yes, but I risk losing it by leaning back slightly-- I hope innocently enough -- to make some kind of much-desired physical contact with the man behind me. Nonetheless, I'm surprised by just how close he is, immediately assaulting my shoulders with the tack-hard centers of his nipples. Now, if I can just manage to feel the heaviness of his big ...

"Oh, sweet Jesus, yes!" I say, both to the water that does everything David said it will do, and to express my sheer ecstasy in experiencing David's hard cock finally locked against me.

"I want you to let the water make you cream," David says, his lips hot and wet against my ear, his cock hot and hard against my back, his balls cascaded down my rear end, his hands on my hips, his chest all the tighter against me. "Can you do that for me, Jamie? Not too big a favor to ask is it, to have your dick seed the water and the spray?"

"For you," I say and arch my head back so that it rests atop the notch at the base of his neck, his chin suddenly nesting amid my spray-dampened hair.

Sure, I'll allow a water-induced orgasm, but not just because it's what he asks of me. I'll do it, because it's something I want. While no denying he's the primary cause of my being so horribly horny, the sexual release, made possible by the falling water, is suddenly an acceptably sufficient substitute for orgasm caused by my cock up his butt or by my butt anchored over his stiff erection. I now so badly need blast-off, it's orgasm, in and of itself, that's all-important, not how orgasm is or isn't achieved.

"Oh, Jesus," I say, though it's more of a sigh. My hips automatically provide minuscule fucking motions, as if I now actively fuck the water, where moments before I'd been passively content to let it give me good head.

"Getting close, Jamie?"

"Close."

"Really close?"

"Really close."

"And you'll let me know just when? Because, I want to know the when, Jamie? Not too much to ask to hear you tell me when, is it? Your cum boiling from your nuts. Your spunk squirting upward through the impressive tube of your cock. Your creamy bullets like young and healthy salmon swimming up stream and leaping full-blown cascades.

Your balls ..."

"Jesus, now!" I interrupt him, squeeze my eyes shut, and try to keep my dick right where it is so that the falling water can successfully manage the very last of the performance David and I have booked from it. "I'm coming ... I'm coming ... I'm ... Jesus ... fuck ... coming!"

David's hands leave my hips, but his supporting chest and belly keep me firmly in place. His fingers bypass my erection and slide inward and downward along my thighs to curve over my compact scrotum. The tips of his fuckfingers actually poke as far between my legs as the entrance of my ass, his thumbs crossed and locked over the back of my dick, where my cockshaft anchors securely to my lower belly.

I climax like I've never erupted cum in my whole life, and his cupping palms simultaneously compress my scrotum and testicles. The tips of his fuckfingers concave each side of my sphincter, and my pearly streamers of spunk pulse out of me as I unsuccessfully attempt to cram my willing asshole down all of the way over both of his hands, down all of the way over both of his arms.

"Oh, dear God!" One final spasm shakes me, through and through, although I can't imagine there being any remaining cum to be expelled by it.

I'm so weak, in aftermath, it's only David remaining so firmly tucked behind me that keeps my knees from buckling.

That I turn within his arms is only because my legs once again have enough starch to support my weight. My cock, surprisingly still in erection, has grown hypersensitive after blast-off, and its continued fondling by falling water becomes more irritant than pleasure.

David's hands end up locked to my ass, instead of to my balls. His hard cock ends up pressed hard against my belly, instead of to my back. My erect dick gets fucked into the space between his thighs, my cockhead likely to be draped by his balls should his scrotum lose even a fraction of its present compactness.

If I can somehow levitate a few more inches, my cock might well slide up and under his nuts and right on into his asshole.

His head bows into place beside mine, his tongue actually licking a sexily wet line from my forehead, over my ear, along my cheek and jaw.

"Now, how about you fuck you my ass?" he speaks into the crease where my neck joins my shoulder.

"You're gay," I say, my face turned slightly and speaking into his hair.

"Unless there's some other explanation for a grown man having fucked his cock up against a young teen's back and having anchored his hands on the same kid's exploding nuts."

"You're gay!" I say with more finality, not quite able, yet, to accept the sheer wonder of it.

"I thought I made that fairly clear with my Freon -- pumping-gas -- invite. Congratulations, by the way. I was going to say I was David Oxygen or Hydrogen, but I figured that too damned obvious when I like my young men to have brains as well as good looks and bodies."

"Which means if my uncle hadn't worked on refrigerators..."

"I would merely have found some less subtle way of getting my message across. No way I let a handsome catch like you, even if dumb as a stump, slip through my fingers."

"A bit sadistic, yes, not to bother, at the time, to let me know I gotten your message, loud and clear?"

"Oh, I know, there are gays who think the best kind of sex is a quick ëWant to fuck?' and an equally quick 'Sure, why the hell not!?', followed by an even quicker wham-bam, thank-you, man. I prefer, though, a longer lead-in, kind of foreplay, if you will. You think shedding our clothes in the gas station, like two ears of corn in a shucking bee at our local grange, you screwing me silly on the dusty countertop, or vice versa, among stale potato chips and cans of motor oil, would have come even close to how it's going to be when you finally get around to fucking my butt?"

All this while, my hands slide along his back to a final resting on the muscled mounds of his ass. His asscheeks are hard as steel, warm despite their water-wet veneer.

"So, what's your real name?" I give his rear a squeeze, although my fingers, despite concentrated effort, hardly dent the surface.

"David Bristol."

"Well, David Bristol, I suspect I should be more angry than I am for you having led me on this little song and dance, me as often as not wondering if I'd hitched up with a gun-toting serial killer who'd shoot me dead after shooting my ass full of cum, if he ever did get around to his-cock-up-my-butt stuff."

"You're kidding, right?" His hands, on my shoulders, push me to partial arm's-distance.

I've a good close up of his muscled chest, strong neck, handsome-to-die-for face.

"You actually figured I brought the gun along maybe to shoot you?"

"You think some hairy things haven't happened to me, since I've been on the road?"

"All I figured was that it hardly seemed possible a sexual turn-on, young as you, was likely to have gotten this far without having at least unzipped your pants, somewhere along the line, to let some cock-hungry guy go down for a sample. Guess I was too busy planning my moves to realize you might just see me as the next possible creep on the prowl."

"Except, I've a good sixth sense that's gotten me safely this far," I say. "I'd have expected genuine warning bells if I'd really had you pegged for a creep. Besides, while I know it's probably the kind of reasoning that's gotten a lot of kids into big trouble, I just couldn't bring myself to believe someone who came in such attractive packaging as you do was going to turn out providing me anything but one helluva good time."

"Speaking of one helluva good time," he says and takes my hand to lead me away from the waterfall and back to the low stone formations.

The seat he chooses is slightly bowled. When he leans back and lifts his legs, his ass slides slightly forward and up to present his suddenly viewable and sexually exciting asshole right on the lip of the stone chair.

"Pretty much perfect, wouldn't you agree?" he says, his head and back against stone, his hands folded behind his neck.

"Pretty much," I refer to his positioning and to his asshole.

No doubt what I see is literally breath-taking: his offered ass, his balls whose scrotum is conveniently compact enough to have raised the scrotal curtain far enough to provide me full viewing of his puckered sphincter; his big cock poked away from me and toward his chin; his hard-muscled belly barely creased by his lie-back; his well-delineated chest, his neck, his face, his sexy black hair ...

"Would have reason to think my old man made this seat, knowing you'd come along one day, and I'd need something to plop in to in order to put my ass easily on target for your young prick," he says. His hands clamp his asscheeks, pull them open along heir crack, and make his sphincter move slightly, like a pouty mouth. "Actually, daddy had this for growing moss, but tell me it's not more suited for my butt getting fucked by your hard cock. No denying your cock hard, by the way, is there? As I suspected, your fuck of the waterfall only drained enough to allow you, now, to show me a nice long and leisurely screw."

I walk up closer to prove him right on a couple of points. His chosen spot has, indeed, perfectly positioned him for my needing to do nothing more than pull my dick down, parallel to the floor, and walk it until my cockhead meets up with his anal door. No squatting required, thank-you very much. No going up on tiptoes, either. And, if my luck holds out, I'm going to give him the long and leisurely fuck he hopes for.

Can he know this is the first asshole my cock will ever have fucked? The way he's so carefully planned to temper my youthful horniness to a more workable level, arranging for my rocks to first get off in the water, leads me to suspect he does. He's been right on the mark, about so many things, like the number of times I've unzipped for a hungry mouth in order to pay for a ride.

Had a few assholes offered me, in my time, too, but I've turned them all down, each and every one, just as I've never let anyone's hard cock up my ass. Which doesn't mean, I don't continue, even now, to contemplate David Bristol's prick rammed to his bull-like balls up my behind, as much as I presently picture my erection very soon filling his asshole.

"I need a rubber," I say. No need to provide him proof-positive that I'm such a complete novice I don't know when safe sex is called for.

"Check the watch pocket of my jeans."

"You always carry around one and a spare?" I ask, finding what he's predicted, just where he's predicted. "Or, were you so sure you were going to get lucky, this afternoon, with me, in daddy's bathhouse?"

"Can't fault a guy for wishful thinking," he says with a smile. He still holds open his asscheeks, wide and inviting.

I put the head of my well-lubricated and rubberized dick right to the target.

"Who knows when dreams might come true," he says.

Exactly!

"Well, Mr. Freon Gas," I say and put my hands to the rock bench, on either side of his elevated legs and his uplifted rump, my cock kept on target by sheer pressure, "this boy is about to start pumping gas."

I feed him a good half of what I've got for him. That I don't keep on going, giving him the rest, isn't because he's suddenly screaming "Oh, Jesus, kid, you're splitting my bunghole from my balls to the small of my back!" 'Cause he doesn't say any such thing. All he does is provide me an expression about as close as anyone can possibly come to pure, unadulterated contentment, this side of the expression on my face upon blasting my load into falling water. Nor do I stop because his asshole is so fucking tight that I simply can't feed it any more of my cock. Although, frankly, yes, I am surprised by just how fuckingly tight the tunnel of his asshole is.

I stop because it's just too fucking wonderful, half of my cock fucked up his butt, to go any farther without taking more than a few deep and hopefully calming breaths.

"Ahhhhh!" That's what I say. My head arches back, my Adam's apple pops into high relief, my mouth opens and shuts, opens and shuts, like I'm a fish out of water. Or, as if it's my butt, rather than David's, speared by the hearty inches of half a stiff erection.

Quickly enough, thereafter, I'm struck by the admittedly terrible realization that all of David's preplanning for this moment hasn't been preplanning enough. If we'd both figured my nuts once erupted would have me calmed down enough to fuck David's ass with the longevity and skill of a man who knows what he's doing, we were both wrong.

"No! Damn-it, no!" That's what I say, as if the saying makes it so. When, even as I hope for some saving miracle, my guts are all a-rush, my balls are elevated so close to the base of my cock that anyone looking would think I was pure castrato, and my dick (both the half of it up David's butt and the half still out), throbs in response to the bullets of cum already en route to ballooning the rubber my cock has pushed halfway up David's butt.

I'm embarrassed and mortified, followed by wondrously lost within my euphoric spasms of ecstasy, followed by being embarrassed and mortified. Then, I'm so concerned that my obviously cum-sopped dick is so slick that it will automatically shed its skin, up David's rectum, like a snake shedding skin in its hole, I yank out my cock so quickly that I almost leave the cum-filled rubber behind.

"Shit! Shit! Shit!" I'm that bloody frustrated, standing there like a little kid told he can't go to the fair. Only this little kid's fingers are slick with his own cum, the rubber having safely spilled its contents into my hand.

"We're not talking the end of the world here, kid," David says. Though, if I'm not mistaken, he says it more than once before I hear it. "It's not as if my ass is going anywhere. It's not as if your cock is going all soft and good for nothing but pissing. It's not as if we don't have another rubber handy to start all over again. Hell, I've a whole gross of Trojans in the glove compartment of my car."

"I don't want to wait for the rubbers you have in the glove compartment of your car," I say, a precocious kid deprived of pizza for even a few minutes.

"So, we make due with what we have. You want a rubberless fuck of my mouth before we raincoat your young pecker for another go at my asshole?"

The invite is inviting, except I presently want to fuck his ass far more desperately than I want to fuck his mouth. I certainly don't want to find myself suddenly so drained by the former that I'm too soft to perform the latter.

"I've never popped two loads in such quick succession," I say, although that might not quite be true. Vaguely, I do recall having done so, way back when I first discovered the joys of masturbation that ...

"Come ahead, then, sexy," David says. "I want to see if I was as close to orgasm, just half of your cock up my butt, as I thought I was."

"Flattery will get you that other look-see," I say, so quickly having discarded the used rubber and replaced it with the new one that I have to double-check to make sure the cum-drooling sock is the one I've put to one side.

"I sure hope so," he says, his hands back and spreading his asscheeks.

I walk back to him. My right hand reaches out for and grabs hold of his large prick, my fingers barely managing to complete the required circumference. My sudden manhandling of his pecker must take him pleasantly unawares, because his resulting sounds are that of a large cat purring. I marvel at the sparks of pure electricity that tingle my fingers and race the length of my arm, as if I've taken possession of a live wire.

The thumb of my left hand hooks the back of my uplifted dick. The weight of my hand drops my boner to horizontal. Only a slight lean, my feet right where they stand, and the head of my dick pokes his pucker.

I provide the pressure needed to keep my nuzzling cockhead in place, while I add my left hand to my right on his phallic shaft.

"Pump me, stud," he says, his neck slightly arched back, his head pressed tightly against hard stone. His Adam's apple, not nearly as predominant as I've seen on some men, moves up, then down, as he swallows in anticipation of being fed the dick I have every intention of feeding him.

Careful to keep my cock snugly at the opening of his asshole, my handholds on his cock tug upward to slide his velvety outer cockflesh over his solid inner cockcore. Although his cock is perfectly circumcised, its corona cowls with pseudo foreskin. There's an artesian gushing of preseminal lubricant from his pouty cockmouth that pools within the provided snout of flesh.

I pull downward along his dick and release the until-then pretty-well contained flooding of preseminal ooze. It drools the neck of his pecker and smears my gripping fingers. At the same time, my dick, like the camel through the eye of the needle, begins its threading of his asshole.

As I provide his ass with more and more of my big stiff dick, my grip of his cock pulls his buttocks down and over my entering erection. A fourth of my prick disappears inside of him. A half as quickly achieved. Another fourth joins with the buried rest, and I'm farther inside him than I've ever been.

I fight to maintain control of the exquisite pleasure again set loose inside of me. Whether I've gained expertise from my previous quick firing of cum up his butt, and/or from the cum I've drained from fucking the falls, my passion seems tempered sufficiently, this time around, to allow me at least the chance to proceed more slowly toward climax. Suddenly, I'm actually confident, like never before, that I'm actually going to manage some kind of long-run performance.

"Give it to me," he says.

I do. All of it. From the rubber-nippled tip of my cock to that bit of my erection still naked at the very base of my cockneck. My pelvis punches hard against his butt and comes to a grinding halt. His cock leaks a new gush of ooze that's claimed by my cock-massaging hands.

I continue the full-stop, after complete insertion. Maybe just to marvel at my success. Maybe just to realize how quickly we've seemingly become one man, partly hard muscle, partly willowy teen, joined at the crotch and sharing but one massive erection with two sets of balls. His scrotum, pillowy-compact, hugs the base of my submerged meat, up top. My scrotum groups tightly against the underside of my stiff dick, at the base of my erection. It's David's hard cock, though, held to perpendicular by my hands, that rises so impressively from the nesting of our four testicles, like a long-necked bird sitting on a clutch of eggs in a brown-and-black haired nest.

He lifts his legs higher and hooks them to my shoulders, allowing me to lean even more heavily into him, although there's no more of my cock to give. He provides a distinct grind of his lower body that stirs his asshole sensuously around the whole length of my deep-drilled penis.

"Fuck me, stud," he encourages, his voice low-low sexy. He licks his lips, providing his mouth a kissable gloss. His hair, seemingly always tumbled over his forehead, bangs all the more.

Having never before fucked a man's asshole, I nonetheless know there's more to it than stuffing cock completely home and then leaving it put. To comply with his request for me to fuck him, to comply with my want (actually, need) to fuck him, I now have to withdraw what I've stuck. I do just that, and feel his asshole so reluctant to let me do so that it's only the hard inner core of my cock that begrudgingly moves, leaving stuck to his anal walls the softer veneering of my lose skin that encases my dick even in its erection. So much of the loose skin refuses to withdraw with the hard part of my exiting dick that my prick momentarily achieves an elephantine trunk more cowling than were it genuine foreskin. However, like tension produced by attempts of one land plate to move against another, the need for slippage finally becomes too great, and my loose skin follows the hardness of my retreating pecker out of David's hot butt, like rubber having been stretched taut by a sling Suddenly, my cock, actually paused with nothing more than its large head slotted up David's butt, has a turtlenecking of its own loose skin come to join it My cock pushes back through turtleneck and sphincter in a return to the funky depths of David's tight and eagerly awaiting bowel.

"Oh, kid, fuck my ass, beat my meat, screw and flog me 'til I scream!"

Goddamn, he's sexy, once again speared completely by my hard cock. Where the waterfall's spray once glazed him, his sweat now does the same, a trickle of which spills from the jugular notch, at the base of his neck, and begins a slow flow along the deeply etched gully that separates his pectorals.

I lean over his cock and balls and lick that drooling sweat. Its saltiness is aphrodisiacal in that, having tasted the essence of this man, I'm all the more giddy and hungry for even more. My tongue vigorously licks upward along the saline-tainted pathway left by the sweat as it drooled. My tongue laves his neck, his jaw, his chin, finally his lips that have been made so sexily wet by his own licking.

When we kiss, I experience the additional flavors of this man as they exist within his spit. The sampling becomes all the more intense as his lips part slightly, and I claim just a bit of the thicker moisture slicking his tongue.

His hands clamp each side of my head, his palms earmuffing my ears, his fingers in my hair, this thumbs along my jawline. He kisses me all the more deeply, and I respond in kind. Not a swallowing of each other's face, or a kiss that's so wet it sounds as if we're two cows returning to the barn through a mire of thick muck, but a slow and gentle exploration of tongues. My tongue in his mouth, my cock up his butt ...

"Mmmmmm," I moan with the utter magnificence of the moment.

Between us, the arching of my belly overhangs the rippled floodplain of his own, and I fondle his big dick in yet another two-handed masturbatory stroke that milks even more preseminal goo.

I'm hot for the suspected more-concentrated tastes of him inherent within his gooey mess that runs my fingers. I wish for the flexibility to suck up his dick while my cock remains fucked full up his rear. I even attempt that impossibility. Obviously sensing what I'm about, he doesn't insist upon holding his lips to mine but actually provides the pressure necessary to get my face farther down his chest than I ever could have managed on my own.

In the end, however, his leaking cock, and my wet fingers that wrap it, remain an illusive treasure trove seen, marvelled at, desired, but forever out of reach for immediate sucking.

I convert my frustration, at being unable to eat his dick, into a focused determination to do the very best job possible with my cock up his asshole.

I resume a more fully standing position, and he lets me, his hands slipping free of my head and resting gently atop his thighs.

"Screw me silly," he says.

Again, I slip my cock outward from his asshole until only my cockhead is gummed by his pucker. Again, my fingers tug the loose outer layer of his cock high along his cockneck to overflow his cockhead.

As I return the full length of my prick up his butt, I pump my hands down the total length of his stiff meat. The result is my simultaneously fucking a vacuum and ramming another vacuum tightly into place over my lap.

I proceed to a concentrated pumping of David's ass and an accompanying pump-pump-pumping of David's cock. My coordination becoming less and less perfect as my combined efforts flood more and more pleasure throughout my body.

"Fucking tight ass!" It takes me a full second, after I've said it, to realize the triumphant voice is mine. "Beating stiff meat!"

"Yes, yes .. oh, fucking, yes!" David agrees. No way he, no matter how many cocks he may have had up his butt, denies that my prick does some fancy plumbing of his sweet and saucy anal depths.

I assume an even more pronounced standing position, correctly assuming it's best for the increasing rhythm of fuck strokes I desire to provide his ass. My midsection becomes a pile-driver of sorts, swinging forward and back, forward and back, quickly providing staccato sound effects from my hard belly's slapping against his cock-stuffed hard buns.

"Oh, cock ... teenage ... teenage cock," David says and punctuates with a long, low groan. His hands slide from his thighs to a tenting over and along his compact scrotum and cum-filled balls. "Fuck this sweet daddy to sweet Kingdom-coming!"

His eyes shut. His whole body responds, like a tuning fork sent into vibrations. His gyrations and shifts, his bounces and grinds, continuously vary the angle of penetration achieved by my gone-wild fucking. Angles of penetration which would have been kept to a more purely repetitious groove had I been left entirely responsible for them.

"Oh!" I say, as if surprised that having lasted this long I'm not going to be allowed to proceed indefinitely. My surprise should be that I've mastered my fuck of his sexy ass as well as I have, on but my second try. Because, nothing quite so exciting, quite so pleasurable, quite so ball-popping good has ever happened to me before, in my whole life.

Like this tightening of my scrotum around my balls ... this tensing in my neck sinews that makes it difficult to swallow ... this out-of-control rushing of energy inside of me that suddenly converts my rocking hips and cock-whipping fingers into runaway dynamos ... this sudden focusing of my total being inward, from each and every extremity, to a congregation of blinding hot flash at one specific spot deep, deep within my groin.

"I'm going to come, you sexy bastard!" I think it's me, so well do the words relay my feelings of the moment, but it's David. "I'm going to cream sweet jism ... to ... the ... Jesus, oh, Jesus ... ceiling ... fucking ceiling ... fucking ceiling."

So completely in sync is his creamy eruptions, from his pulsing boner which I have squeezed within my hands, with the explosions from my cock into the rubber I have, one final time, stuffed as far as it will go up his butt, that it's as if his parabolas of cum spurt not from his cock but from my own.

"Take it, take it, take it!" I command for my final reflexive hump that pulls then pushes my dick within his butt in that one shudderingly intense ramming of my belly tightly into place against his rear.

All the water that's plunged the falls, since we've first entered this church-like bathhouse and turned on the plumbing, doesn't compare to the seeming gallons of my spunk that spurts up David's ass, let alone compare with David's hearty emptying of thick spermal bullets in all directions.

"Oh, fucking Christ!" I wail as one final and thoroughly unexpected bolt of thick cream ejects from my body, leaving a reservoir completely empty behind it, to join the rest of its kind up David's asshole.

I'm so weak from orgasmic cataclysm that it's a literal momentary buckling of my knees that brings my thoroughly spent cock completely out of David's butt. The rubber on my dick is so cum-filled, at exit, that it slides, under its own weight, along and off the drooping length of my depleting erection. The spent-cum container lands with a splat in the water at my feet and floats lazily away on the current.

"You're a natural, kid," David says breathlessly.

His appreciation expressed even farther by how he's more than ready and willing to spend our every spare moment, over the next few days, fucking and sucking up a storm. He so often leaves off the chores of getting his dead father's estate in order that I'm sure our sexual asides add literal days to his original schedule. Best indication of our excesses may just be the final day, again in the waterfall bathhouse, my butt this time the one experiencing the joys of being filled with hard cock and hot spunk, my balls the ones enjoying simultaneous releasing of cream into David's pumping hands. In that, the large reserve of water that once supplied the cascades suddenly fades to nothing more than a slow trickle. As if the waterfall's sizable nuts, like David's and like mine, refuses to shot any more gallons until given a suitable time to recover.

So, David and I move our fucking to his home in Las Vegas. It's a really nice home, with palm trees and a pool, even a weight room where David, who it turns out owns not one but three local health spas, starts me on a couple of weight routines that he correctly predicts will provide me with some of the upper-body definition I so yearn for.

It's perfect, for a time, until I wake up one morning and realize I've yet to see the ocean. More frightening is the revelation that I've entered another rut. Granted, it's a more luxurious rut than the one I'd had at home with my parents. Granted, it's a rut with a helluva lot more attending pleasures. But, it's a rut nonetheless.

One Saturday, I tell David I'll meet him for lunch downtown, but I pack up my bags, instead, and head for the breaking-blue waves of the Pacific. I catch a ride with a straight trucker who's not in the least interested in my body, only in my keep-him-awake conversation as he takes me as far as Pasedena.

When I get to the ocean, it's all that I expect it will be and more, probably because it comes with a young surfer, Tim Reckly, who likes my cock up his ass just as much as David did. Trouble is, that's about all Tim likes, in the sex department, and my sex with David has programmed me to expect a bit more variety. So, though Tim tells me he loves me, and I believe him, I head off to Hawaii with Jarod who likes to give cock, up mouth and ass, as well as take it up his own.

I end up with Carl in Tahiti. He's been through what he calls "the gay rat-race", and he wants to settle down, just with me. We can sail the world and fuck each other's brains out. Which is just fine with me, until Gregory appears on Bali, there on a photo shoot for a men's fashion magazine.

Gregory persuades me to pose for a few candid shots for him to take to the show's producers. I end up in a photo spread, and both Gregory and I feel I'm going to be an even hotter property on the printed page than I am in bed.

Heading to Los Angeles with Gregory, he arranges for me to meet up with Tina Maclalyne of THE Tina Maclalyne Modeling Agency who signs me to a contract, on the spot, and schedules me for an important shoot in two-days' time. Gregory and I head back to his place and fuck ourselves silly to celebrate. Except he conks out early, because he has a shoot the next morning and doesn't dare get totally wasted. So, a bit more partying still left in me, I head off to the bars, get even more completely smashed than I started, and wake up, albeit barely, three days later, on what turns out to be the beach at Malibu, my cock and my asshole red-raw sore as hell from fucks I can't even remember.

I call Gregory, but he's pissed royally, and Tina Maclalyne is so pissed at my having been a no-show at my first scheduled shoot, that she's guaranteed David, to pass on to me, that I'll never get another shot at the modeling business, and she's just powerful enough, at doing what she does, to know what she promises is Gospel.

Kelly, though, who picks me up from a street corner, doesn't care that I've bummed out as a model, only that I look like one, and he's willing to pay for the pleasure of taking me to bed for just one night. Except, the one night turns into two, then into two years. But Kelly, compared to Lyle, who I find in the baths, is damned boring! Besides which, I've never really forgiven Kelly for having mistaken me for a common hustler, although I was eager enough to capitalize upon his mistake at the time.

Lyle, compared to Peter, who I find in the park, is old and jaded. Peter is sweet and innocent and never been fucked -- at least until I show up. Though I figure it's pure pure puppy love that has him so often insisting "I love you, Jamie. So, when I get the chance to screw around with Peter's best buddy, Porter, supposedly straight as a stick, but who wants, one drunken night, merely to do a bit of man-boy experimentation ...

And, so it goes, my youth, then middle-age, filled with life in the fast lane, me speeding down life's highway at one-hundred-plus an hour, figuring the obliging gas stations will continue to exist over each hill, or around each bend in the road. Figuring it's always better somewhere at bit farther along, with someone other than with whomever I happen to be at the time. Convinced there's always going to be someone or someplace better.

Until the day (and I recognize it just for the day of revelation it is), when I wake up to the fact that I've not only virtually run out of gas, but there isn't a filling station within miles that's willing to give me a hand ... or an ass ... or a cock ....

MENSUR

Night. Whispers. A prevailing aura of secrecy. The Verbindungen. The Mensur. The Schlager.

Peter, eighteen, and I stand face to face, swaddled in padded material, like two exotic insects in their chrysalis stages. Eyes protected by steel glasses.

Deja-vu: the feeling in my guts! There's actually a psychosomatic paining along my left eyebrow, but no blood. The blood, the river of red that made the world seem more than rose-tinted as it washed my left eye at the time, has long since dried and been washed away. The cut made and stitched is now healed, almost lost except to those who were there to see it. Admittedly some of the uninitiated do still notice and ask the cause. I lie and tell them I fell from a chair.

That night of my ritual scarring, when I was but eighteen, was at a large university in Germany. This Verbindungen is at a large university in the United States.

My sense of excitement hasn't paled. I sense excitement, too, in those around me: these handsome young men with their serious faces. In that, they have every right to take this seriously. There's a heritage upheld here: a long tradition followed; the American Verbindungen societies the bastard children arrived on these shores quite without the official sanction of those spawning organizations that exist thousands of miles away. These American colonizers are Promethean in their defiance. For there are, after all, those who prefer keeping such German things strictly in Germany. No denying the Verbindungen, the Mensur, the Schlager, are German. I've run across their likes nowhere else -- until now.

Just how many American "fighting corps" exist is hard for me to say. They are as secret here as they are in Germany. But, I know of three whose ranks grow larger yearly. Breaks-off from these will occur as times progress. As in Germany, the Verbindungen in America seem to center in and around university campuses and, thus, gain new members with each school year.

The Verbindungen is not for everyone. Its exclusiveness can be accounted for by the prerequisites for entrance. Fencing with saber not your average American skill. And, even if you're willing to put in the time and the money to acquire that training, not every American city has its master or the facilities. Then, even if the saber skill is achieved, there's no guarantee you'll be approached for membership. Not because you're not good potential but because you're simply in the wrong place at the wrong time. With American Verbindungen few and far between, potential candidates and club recruiters often fail to meet. And then, of course, the Mensur ritual requires a person to endure a degree of genuine physical pain, with genuine bloodletting, and the resulting scar.

While the Mensur uniform has evolved over the years into padded encasements that protect except for cuts to the head (the eyes covered by special glasses), a duel continues, once begun, until blood is drawn.

I began fencing in college. It's been my experience that's where most Americans begin. In Europe, the sport is more popular, and there's a gamut of clubs available for such training. But in the US, the better masters are at the universities or in the surrounding environs.

My fencing master was a member of the German Olympic team. He was studying two years in the United States on a scholarship. At my first meeting with Dieter, I knew nothing of the Verbindungen, the Mensur, the Schlager. While fencing had an esoteric quality that I found appealing, I'd really received instructions from my family to look Deiter up at the university. His great-grandfather and mine had been officers together in the Prussian army in the days of Frederick William I.

Deiter was blond. Blue-eyed. Five-foot-eleven. Tanned. Muscled. Completely hairless except for the silky strands on his head, the surrounding halo at each nipple, the line up the crease of his ass, and the fuller veed bush at his crotch. He had sensuously full lips. Square jaw. Cleft chin. Ten-inch, uncut cock.

He had a scar that was an inch of slight discoloration on his right cheek.

We became lovers. He taught me foil and saber fencing. He, also, taught me a hell of a lot more. His term of schooling ended, and he asked me to spend some time with him in Germany before I continued with my schooling. I did.

It was in Germany that I found myself initiated in protective cocoon: neck guard, forearm pads, steel glasses. Verbindungen. Mensur. Facing Deiter, quite close to him, my Schlager (a heavy basket-hilted saber), held above my head with my forearm in front of my face. I had a hard-on.

I came away with a cut above my left brow. It bled a good deal. I still vividly remember the sting of its salty fluid washing my eye. It took twelve stitches to suture the wound. My sex with Deiter, shortly thereafter, was the best sex I'd ever had.

Deiter wrote me last year, mentioning a rumored Verbindungen at a particular American university.

I contacted Rolph Gunsen, that university's fencing master. He asked me by to watch an advanced class in official saber dueling.

Official saber fencing differs from the dueling in the Mensur in that target areas include the opponent's body from the waist up, his arms, as well as his head. In the Mensur ritual, the target area is exclusively the head. Official saber fencing gives more leeway in movement, while the Mensur requires a combatant remain immobile from the top of his head to his rear foot. Defensive moves in the Mensur are restricted to blocking an opponent's strokes with forearm and/or with saber hilt.

Rolph asked me about my scar. I told him I got it falling off a chair. I asked about his scar, along his right jawline. He said he got it in a car accident.

He loaned me a fencing jacket, gloves, and a hard leather elbow guard. By that time the practice room had been emptied by Rolph to only him, me, and one other young man.

"I've asked Peter to stay, if that's all right," Rolph said. "I'd like him to see your technique."

Later, as we showered, Rolph and Peter displayed excellent physiques. Fencing, by itself, isn't going to turn anyone into a Mr. Universe overnight, but it has a nice way of firming body contours. It's particularly good for delineating abdominals; both Rolph and Peter had hard and scalloped bellies to prove it.

While I dressed, Rolph watched me closely. I looked up to see him smile. He ran the tip of his left forefinger back and forth through his left eyebrow, leaving no doubt that he was again going to question me about my scar.

"The Mensur," he said. It wasn't a question. And, this time, I didn't deny it. Hadn't I come all of this way in the hopes of discussing the Mensur -- the American Mensur?

Rolph had been a member of a military fencing club when he'd been stationed with US forces in Germany. He'd asked for his discharge overseas and had enrolled in one of the German universities, where he'd gained entrance to that university's elite and secretive fighting corps; thus, his scar.

When he returned to the States, Rolph missed the camaraderie of the Verbindungen. Teaching fencing at this university gave him an excellent opportunity to begin selective recruitment for an American Verbindungen.

I went to several of his club meetings. I fenced with several of its members. There were seven in all. Peter, up for initiation, would hopefully make eight.

I liked Peter from the beginning, although I remained unsure of his sexual orientation. He was a friendly teenager but shy. I was pleasantly surprised when Rolph told me Peter asked specifically for me to play master at his initiation. I was more surprised when Rolph asked if I were completely straight or could swing "the other way". While I'd never come right out and announced my sexual preference, I'd certainly made no big secret about it.

"My swinging 'the other way' makes a difference?" I asked. I'd long suspected, and rightly so, that while Rolph wasn't adverse to one guy fucking another guy's ass, he actually preferred cunt for his own large penis.

"Peter's gay," Rolph said. "I don't know how you were after your first Mensur, but I needed sex. I think Peter has that in mind, too. Not that I can blame him. How many initiates get marked by a master and then fucked by the same master afterwards? Had the option been available to me, I might even have gone for it. But if guy-guy sex isn't your scene, we'd best get everything out in the open, here and now, and save disappointments and misunderstandings, in some quarters, later."

I cut Peter above his right eye. If the cut had been a little lower it would have been the mirror-image to my own

His cut bled a lot. It took ten stitches.

I went with him into the privacy of a back room.

God, he was handsome! Made even more so by the cut on his eyebrow. His cut signifying to me that here was a real, honest-to-goodness, man-boy soon to be stuck on my hard cock. In a world of technological marvels, Peter had had the guts to stand man to man with me on a battlefield. Together, we'd known the exultation of fear, and the pump of adrenaline through our veins: a natural high that beats all to shit any of those had on narcotics or chemicals. It was a thrilling experience in this day and age when man (the need to give battle imprinted on his genes), is more often than not frustrated by his wars fought by inanimate machines, death, although in the millions, supplying few faces in real closeup.

Is the Mensur, then, a reversion to the primitive, a yearning for simpler days? Maybe so. Whatever, it offers satisfaction to a basic need within Peter, within Rolph, within me, and within countless other men in Germany, and a growing number here in the States.

My hard cock and Peter's hard cock, both obvious beneath our fencing breeches, were part of it, too.

His flesh was covered with a glossing of perspiration when his clothes came off.

His lips were salty with sweat and blood when I kissed them. He groaned softly into my mouth. His hands wrapped my body, held tightly, squeezed so hard it took my breath away. Between our naked, muscled bellies, our cocks mated, slid one against the other, became wedged between our rippled abdominals.

I told him to lie on his back on a bench. He did so. I raised his legs, one of his calves rested against each of my shoulders. I straddled the same bench and sat facing his ass. My cock was so stiff I was going to have trouble prying it down to the luscious target offered by his asshole.

I rubberized my dick and pushed its large knob of a cockhead into the tight little pucker centering the crack between Peter's teenage buns. When my cock was held in place by the tightness of Peter's sphincter ring, I cupped one of my hands around each of Peter's thighs. I scooted forward, my drooped balls sliding along the top of the bench and, simultaneously, pulled on Peter's lower body to slip his butt down deeper over my cock.

"Jesus, fuck!" Peter grunted. I'd stabbed him almost as far as I could. My cock had rammed into his guts so that his sphincter was like a rubberband around my cockroots. The whole length of his bowel vibrated along the whole length of my meat, spasming anal muscles and tissue desperately trying to adjust to my sticking.

My cock up to my balls in Peter's butt, I moved Peter's legs down around my waist. He automatically locked his ankles behind my back.

In our present position, he supine on the bench, his arms along his sides, his hands gripped my thighs. I sat with my cock up his ass and my hands holding his hipbones. My fingers glided the curves of his buttocks, anchoring in the firm, sweaty warmth of his asscheeks.

"Oh, fuck, screw me!" Peter said.

My gaze ran up his body. His cock a monster laid out on his belly, its roots anchored in a bush of strikingly blond pubic hair, its head leaking a mess of translucent juices that pooled to overflowing within his indented navel. His blond balls flowed over his asscrack, actually touching my plugging erection.

There was a definite line of sweat that ran upward, halving his torso along his deeply delineated pectoral cleavage. His jugular notch was pooled with more sweat. His nipples were hard, and I leaned forward and pinched both of them.

"Oh, Jessssus!" Peter groaned. His cock thumped loudly against his muscled belly. His asshole gave another series of excruciating shudders. His head rocked from side to side. His mouth was open, his tongue a pink snake wetting the surface of his lips. His eyes, once gone wide with the shock of my initial insertion of cock, were now shut, twitching behind closed lids. His right eye was severely swollen, the saber cut looking downright vicious now, still raw, its meaty redness an interesting contrast to the neat black asterisks made by the row of stitches.

Goddamn, I was excited! My balls had already elevated, pulled upward from their initial resting on the bench to form a grapefruit-like mass at the base of my still-buried erection. Peter's balls had pulled up, also. I watched, fascinated by the way his teenager gonads rolled within the wrinkled flesh of his compact scrotum.

"Fuck meeee!" Peter squealed loudly and sounded like a very young boy. His lower body bounced so that it pulled up along the neck of my cock and then sank down again.

I savagely dug my fingers into his buttcheeks, lifting his ass upwards again. His suctioning asshole pulled my loose outer cockskin around my hard inner cockcore.

"Stab ... the ... shit ... out ... of ... me!" he begged. His hands went claw-like on my legs.

I put his lower body down again, completely over my dick. I added a complementary little bounce of my own butt against the bench. I felt the sweat from my asscheeks making a butterfly stain on the wood.

"Oh, master, yes ... oh, yes," Peter grunted. His voice was low, gravely, gargled somewhere deep in his throat.

I gave him what he wanted. I gave him my hard cock. I fucked his eighteen-year-old butt. I stabbed his young ass. I did so not because I was victor, he vanquished. I did so because the two of us had shared something which brought us closer together than the mere union of our bodies, there and then. We'd dipped back into the past, dredged up collective memories of ancestors who belonged to a simpler day and age: a time when there were less reasons to question one's masculinity, if just because the guidelines that determined identities had been more clearly defined. We'd peeked back into that other time, and we'd seen our worth. We'd judged and been judged in battle. We'd come out more confident of whom we were, and where we were in the mighty scheme of things. And, who is there to deny that we're better off for having achieved that inner revelation?

"Oh ... my ... God ... I'm ... coming!" Peter groaned. And he was! His thick wads of spunk pumped free while his untouched cock went into ejaculatory spasms. Streamers were laid down in lacy designs on Peter's belly, chest, and neck.

"Take my cock, kid!" I commanded. "Jesus ... God ... take it!"

I placed his butt one final time over my full penis. I clutched hard to his buns. I fired my hot and heavy loads into his body.

He was man-boy. I was man. There was no one on God's green earth who could any longer tell us differently.

FUCKING DRUNK

Major hangover. No doubt about it. Eyes gummed shut. Mouth dry with a lingering taste of stale booze and vomit-on-the-way. Splitting headache.

"Oh, Jesus," I moaned.

No way I'd make it through this one without some hair of the dog, except a trip to the refrigerator for a cold beer, presuming there was a cold beer left to be had, seemed way too long a journey at the moment. Especially in conjunction with the trip to the can I was going to have to make, and damned soon, if I hoped to save myself the additional embarrassment of pissing the bed.

Not that the sheets weren't already damp with sweat, with spilled booze, with cooled-to-flaking cum (mine? someone else's? a multi-contributed-to spermal cocktail?).

Where in the hell was I? Hopefully in my own apartment. The refrigerator whine assuredly familiar. As was the should-have-been-fixed-long-ago leak in the kitchen sink.

"Shit, oh, shit, oh, shit."

It hurt, inside and out, to even move, but move I had to do, as my filled to the brim bladder threatened, once again, to give way.

No other way to have managed but to keep it slow and easy. Felt myself on a roller coaster instead of a bed, about to upchuck cotton candy and hot-dogs and sugary elephant ears, all apparently deep-sixed in booze before having gone down. Except, I hadn't been anywhere near an amusement park in six years.

At least there was no job on which I had to be that morning. Although I might have been far better off it there had been. Needing to earn my way in the world might have confined such excesses of the night before, then again ...

I felt it fair to blame my mother and father. Dead in a car crash, for Christ's sake! Whose parents ever died in a car crash, these days, except in hackneyed movie scripts or in trite novel plot-lines?

"Up, up, and away!" I said. Normally, I might have been amused by the tenuous connection between that Superman tag line, Superman's girlfriend, Lois Lane, no relation to me, Myles Lane, who was trying his best to provide suitable accommodation for my insistent need to piss. But all humor escaped me.

I kept my eyes shut, as if my eyelids were what would have prevented any upchuck if it came. I came to a slightly tilted sit-up position, my feet over the edge of my bed, my feet unable to locate any suggestion of a slipper to cushion me from the effects of the clammy cold floor.

"You've survived before, old boy," I said by way of self-encouragement. Although, it was a damned pitiful admission when you came right down to it. I couldn't count the times I'd indulged just such insurance-money-funded binges on booze. "You ... can ... do ... it ... again. You can ... you can ... you can."

As if I were that children's book choo-choo train trying to make it up and over the hill. Although that fucking choo-choo came through with far more hope for eventual success than I felt possible at that particularly painful moment in time.

"You need help?"

My guardian angel? Or, my condo manager fearing one more bed-wetting, from one more deluge-producing drunk, would see my neighbor's below complaining of urine seepage?

"You need a beer or a toilet?"

"I need a beer and a toilet."

Somehow, I managed a forceful assault on the gunk sticking my eyelashes together with the exportioo of superglue, rewarded by a painful influx of morning light to my overwrought brain pan. Although the room should have been dim, my not able to remember when last I'd thrown the drapes.

"Maybe if you looked as bad as you felt."

My father's ghost?

"When in reality, you remain downright handsome, in a genuinely dissolute sort of way."

"And, I thank you very much for that ... I think," I said.

Normally gravely, my voice was downright riverbed without any lubricating river.

"You need one day of waking up and looking run over by a semi."

"I feel run over by a semi," I said. "I feel run over by a semi and a street car. I feel run over by a semi, a street car, a bulldozer, a backhoe, and a steamroller."

"But you need to look that way. The way it is, you figure, 'Hell, I can go on like this forever!' When that's not going to be the case. Take it as Gospel from someone who knows from having had an alcoholic father."

"Who in the hell are you calling an alcoholic?"

Aha, I spotted him!

Oh-oh! Because if this wasn't my guardian angel, the kid looking as angelic as he did, there were only one other god-awful alternative: it highly unlikely that I had died and gone to heaven. Had I just spent an unremembered night of fucking and sucking with an underage kid?

"You and I just spent a whole night of fucking and sucking," he confirmed.

The truth is, I didn't ever recall finding his kind of prepubescence in the least bit sexually exciting.

I tried to open my eyes wider for a better look. Maybe my hangover-blurred vision, like cheesecloth over a camera lens, made the kid only look .

Nope! No placing the blame on fucked-up vision!

He was young all right. Just a kid. Short-cropped blond hair. Blue, maybe grey, eyes. Pouty little mouth. Snub little nose. Juvenile physique tucked away in a too-big T-shirt and too-fucking-baggy Bermudas. He virtually smelled of Colonel Sanders.

"Should have known better," he said, "but, then, I couldn't keep my hands off my father, either. You two having a lot in common."

Jesus ... Jesus ... did he insinuate I was old enough to be his old man? I, at only twenty-four, for Christ's sake! Or, did I just look that old? Booze and dissolution could do that for a guy, couldn't they?

"Just how old are you?" Of course, what I really wanted to know was, "Are you really the shotgun, I think you very well may be, taking dead aim at my poor hangover head?"

"Old enough to have fucked you to screaming," he said. "Used a rubber, in case you wonder. Although, you didn't much seem to care if I did or didn't at the time. Something you might want to pay more attention to in the future. The next guy up your rectum might not be as considerate."

I definitely recalled reading of some teenybopper school kid putting it to his teacher; the teacher, not the kid, all those statutory rape laws later, the one sent up the proverbial river without a paddle.

"I really do have to piss," I said. The child molester's last wish: to piss one last time in the privacy of his own can before being forced to whip his dick out for public display in the restroom of some prison.

Except, naked as a jay, I wasn't offered much privacy, although I was afforded the right to pass. Truth of the matter, I was so unstable on my feet, the kid did everything but take hold of my dick and aim it at the toilet.

"God, you're still pretty much wiped out, aren't you?" he said, once he'd manhandled me back to the bed.

"Now, about that beer," I said as soon as my ass made touchdown. That I was naked didn't phase me. I'd always been proud of my body. It being one of those natural physiques that looked as if I worked out when all I really did was abuse it, I'm not talking masturbation, either.

He gave me the cold beer before I realized he'd even gone after it. He'd even managed, slight of hand, silently to uncap it.

And didn't that cool elixir taste refreshingly good as it poured, half a bottle in one gulp, down my parched throat.

"If you're okay," he said, "I'll head on out."

What? The kid waited around long enough to see if I hadn't died of liquor overdose and, then, obligingly leaves, without calling in the coppers?

Had he really fucked me? Truly, had his underage cock been inside my butt and pumped to pearly teenage climax?

It would have been nice if the one time I'd gone against character and played lecherous chicken hawk to this little chick -- did he even have pubic hair? -- I could at least remember one tiny little bit of what sex had transpired between us.

"What day-care school ground did I pick you up on?"

He giggled. A pleasant enough exhibit of infantile laughter, except that it reminded me of some two-year old having just been told he'd shat his pants.

"I picked you up at Delaney's Brass Rail," he said.

"You had to have had fake ID?"

"You think I'm underage," he said; it wasn't a question. "You do, don't you?"

As if it weren't a logical assumption to spot a kindergartner and correctly identify him as such.

"That why I had so much damned trouble persuading you to bring me home?" he said. "You told me you didn't like blonds."

I love blonds. Blonds are my very favorite. Possibly because I enjoy the contrast of their peaches-and-cream Scandinavian against my olive-oil Mediterranean.

"You thought I was chicken," he said. "You still think it, right?"

If he wasn't chicken, I would have been even more disappointed that I couldn't remember ever having been at Delaney's Brass Rail, let alone remember anything that came after -- until major hangover time. How often does a guy get picked up by a kid who not only looked chicken but who enjoyed fucking his kiddy-cock up man-ass?

Was this little prick's prick little, or large? Fat or thin? Cut or uncut? Veined or smooth? Streamline or cumbersome? Good fuck or bad?

"I'm legal," he said, but he'd have to show me the ID to prove it; although, if he had been in Delaney's Brass Rail, a bar known for its stringent checking of IDs, whatever paperwork he carried around had to at least look valid, even pass a phone check.

Was my asshole sore from its workout? I tried to focus on my rectum, coming up with nothing more than a vague suspicion I might soon have to shit. So, maybe his cock, like everything else about this little-kid studly, was neither too large, nor too small, but just right enough to have left behind no residual soreness.

"I need another beer," I said.

Granted, briefly, I entertained the possibility of taking up, right then and there, where we'd left off last night. Except I couldn't remember where we'd left off (begun, or done). Besides which, there was little hope of my resurrecting my boner that early in the day, me in the condition I was in. Quite frankly, there had been more and more times when I hadn't been able to get a hard-on at all. At least that hadn't been the case last night, to hear the kid tell it. Or had he insinuated any such thing? How much of a stiff prick would I have needed, belly-down, getting drilled by this teenybopper?

"I really do have to go," he said, performing another of his feats of prestidigitation to produce a second beer. "I just had to be sure you weren't going to pull a 'daddy' on me and drown in your own vomit."

"Jesus Christ, kid!" I complain of the picture he conjured for me.

"You, after all, the best fuck I've had since dear dad kicked the bucket," he said.

Kid did know how to stroke a guy's ego.

"Want to put it to me one more time before you go?" I volunteer.

He checked his wristwatch (Mickey Mouse?), as if actually considering my offer. I was so excited by the sudden prospect that he might stick around, my cock actually started to stiffen.

"Can't," he said. "Although, no doubt I'm tempted."

A likely crock of bullshit, if ever I'd heard one, except he continued to be just full of surprises.

"See," he said.

He veed his fingers along the inside thigh of his Bermudas to highlight an obvious solid ridge of his hard-as-a-rock pecker.

I hoped he was about to propose turning up on my doorstep a little later in the day. Give me a few more pick-me-up drinks -- already my fuzzy brain was beginning to clear -- and I might have been able to rustle up a respectable boner for him to figure out what to do with.

"I'm late already if I want to get ready in time."

Time for what, for Christ's sake! I couldn't think of anything more important than me and this little studly number getting together for a remembered -- this time by the both of us -- rematch.

"I'm off to play cabin boy on a friend-of-a-friend's yacht."

Oh, Jesus, fucking lousy luck, but I didn't believe it!

"However, call me in a couple of months," he said. "I left my name and number by your phone."

Out the door so fast, I somehow missed him going. Once gone, hardly ever seeming to have been there.

I'm convinced I've hallucinated it all. It wouldn't have been the first time.

I'm up, headed for the phone. I stub my big toe on the corner of the coffee table.

"Jesus, oh, Jesus, oh, Jesus!" I accompany with hip-hop on one leg. My kangaroo routine made me dizzy and want to puke. The phone table teetered as I took hold for support. The phone receiver spilled off its rest. My reflexive gag action kept me from hurling to splash everything in sight. I was sweaty as a zombie's clammy hand.

The dislodged phone receiver complained in plaintive wail, soon replaced by the computer-voice operator who instructed that I please hang up and try again.

I hung up all right, with a force that sent the phone into ding-dong chimes and hair-line cracked its supposedly durable surface.

"Jack Dory" said the neatly printed letters on the pad by the phone. Followed by a local phone number.

Except the kid hadn't look anything like a "Jack". He'd looked like a Joey. He'd looked like a Billy. He'd looked like a Jeffy.

Jack? What in the hell kind of name was Jack? Jack was a butch lumberman. Jack was the muscled mechanic down at the garage. Jack guzzled beer, sat around in his dirty shorts and constantly watched grab-ass sports on television.

So, when had I been so fucking drunk that I'd let a Jack into my condo, the guy so pleased by my performance that he'd jotted down his name and number before leaving?

I hadn't even bothered to thank the considerate little shit for having stuck around long enough to be sure I was okay -- not drowned in my own vomit like his incestuous father had done. Never even said thank-you for considerately donning a rubber when -- and suddenly I have the shakes as regards the what-could-have-beens -- I was too damned drunk to give a damn.

I headed for the door and picked up my robe en route. I entered the hallway and jogged to the top of the stairs. I hoped to catch Jack for a thank-you before he was out the front door. What I caught, instead, was my right bare foot in the carpet.

At the completion of my roll-a-ball tumble down a flight of stairs, scrunched into an obviously unnatural heap, a piercing pain in my right leg, a flashbulb went off in my brain, and I upchucked all that was left of the night-before debauchery, including the two beers I'd chug-a-lugged that morning. Then, Jack having thought he'd left me safe and sound, I passed out and almost did drown, a la incestuous daddy, in my own rancid puke.

"Jeez," said Jack, the next time he was in my apartment to hear the tale of my broken bones, my torn muscles, my cold-turkey time in the hospital where my every bellow for a drink had brought me nothing but physical restraints.

Jack was brown as a berry from having had his fun in the sun on that friend-of-a-friend's yacht, while I had been literally sweating out booze with enough accompanying pain, over and above my bad case of DTs, to convince me all the attending straight doctors and nurses had been in a conspiracy to punish me for being gay. No matter that my doctor was so much a queen that he sent everyone in his path into spontaneous curtsies.

"So, you're really off the bottle?" Jack said and sounded genuinely pleased.

"So, you're really of legal age?" I said and hoped against hope that he wasn't going to come clean, at this late date, about how much he'd had to pay for his phony ID.

I'd invested too much of my time on fantasies of a rematch with this sexy young kid to be turned aside now by any of his unwanted yes-I-am-underage revelations.

"I'm really legal," he said. "This..." and he pressed into high relief the ridge his cock made in the pants leg of his faded jeans. "... is teenage-hard, legal dick. You offering up your asshole?"

"For starters."

"Okay," he said. Stood. Unfastened his pants. Left his fly slightly ajar over a completely hairless vee of peaches-and-cream crotch, while he pulled his tight T-shirt up and over his pretty mouth, his snub nose, his blue eyes, his short-cut blond hair.

Legal he may have been, but his was still a very young-boy body. No muscle definition to speak off. Mainly smooth and roundcontours, baby-fat not yet completely discarded. Pink nipples. An asterisk belly button.

Frankly, I was relieved, when he dropped his pants, over his cock and ass, neither encumbered by underwear, to reveal a small blond bush of pubic hair veed at his crotch. Crotch hair definitely meant puberty, right?! Not that it necessarily meant legal, barely or otherwise, but I successfully told myself that anyone conscientious enough to have stuck around baby-sitting an unconscious drunk wouldn't lie about his age. If he still came off looking too young to me, I accounted it to my never having, before then, been all that turned on by youth, per se. Quite aside from Jack, my sexual preferences still pretty much centered more on men my old age, or only slightly younger.

Not that most men my age, or slightly younger, could boast cocks any bigger than the one Jack had sprouted from his lower belly. It looked big enough, in its streamline, prepuce-removed dimensions, to do permanent damage to any asshole, mine included. If it had already safely probed my anal depths, once, I'd been pretty much out of touch at the time. Presently sober, I saw what I saw, and I wondered if drunkenness was a prerequisite for safely taking his cock up my butt.

He knelt for his dropped pants, and from a front pocket he produced ... "Look, I even brought rubbers."

"And, my belated thanks for having brought them the last time," I said. I'd begun blood tests, so far reassuring, to assure myself I hadn't, during some other unremembered fucks of my asshole, allowed an unrubbered dick to pollute my vulnerable rectum.

"Want to put this rubber on my dick for me?" he said and sat on the edge of the bed.

I went over, unpackaged the lubricated rubber and rolled it down his dick. After which, he laid back on the bed, belly up, and watched me undress.

"I'll bet you've always been one helluva good looker, haven't you?" he said. No need for me to figure he'd provided false compliments, because he'd picked me up the first time, to hear him tell it, for some reason, hadn't he?

"Actually, I was an ugly child," I said and wondered if the same could be said for him. I doubted it, seeing as he looked so child-like, at whatever legal age he was. His the delicate looks that played well into old age. Mine the kind that wouldn't stand the test of time nearly as well, not that I couldn't hold my own at the time and place.

So, I provided him a slow strip, complete with muscled, black-haired chest; muscled, black-haired belly; muscled, black-haired cockroots. Firm, furry ass. Good bear-fuzzed legs. I provided him a nice smile that dimpled my right cheek, provided him a glimpse of teeth with nary a cavity or filling, and put a twinkle in my hazel eyes.

"How about you sitting down on this?" he said and levered his hand to hook its thumb beneath the back of his dick to push his erection to vertical.

I straddled him on the bed, feeling very much like an eagle hovering over a field mouse, at least as far as our comparative body types were concerned. His boyish delicacy came off decidedly vulnerable. My muscled, hairy bulk seemed almost predatory.

"I'm not a China doll," he said, as if he'd known what I was thinking.

On my knees, I reached back for my asscheeks, took hold of them and tugged them outward from their mutually shared asscrack. Jack directed his cockhead on target, his pulpy cockhead playfully running the hair of my anal valley before finally homing in on my sphincter.

"Yours the best asshole ever," he said, reminding me that he, of the two of us, well remembered having had his cock inside me before.

Made confident that he'd told me the truth when he'd said he'd fucked me, and pretty sure my ass could accept the return trip of his cock up my ass, helped along by the lubricated rubber, I began to sit.

"I'm fucking such a sexy ... sexy ... stud's ass," he said as I managed a butt-swallowing of at least half of his dick before I paused to give my rectum a chance to adjust to what it had swallowed.

I put my hands to his shoulders, and he seemed to become all the smaller and more vulnerable.

His skin was so soft, I could see faint tracings of blue veins. His stomach, despite continuing evidence of baby fat, concaved to provide prominent hipbones to form the saddle into which my ass had all intentions of sinking.

"Play carrousel horse on my dick," Jack said. Not exactly the vocabulary of a choirboy, but it didn't keep him from looking like one.

The ease with which I finally engulfed the total hunk of his stiff penis assured me that we both retraced familiar terrain. I've had smaller dicks that felt more uncomfortable than his did jabbed to his balls up my behind.

When I completed my sit, his cock thrust directly upward and into my gut, my thick cock laid like a redwood log on his belly, my cockhead rested almost over his navel.

He stroked my prick, as if it were a friendly snake and gently fondled its veneering foreskin in such a way that he cowled and uncowled my pulpy cockhead.

Momentarily, his attention was distracted by the puddling of my balls. He cupped each of my testicles, fondled the whole lot, as if he were a curious schoolboy fascinated by something hairy and alive found in his toy box.

"Big, big, hairy nuts," he said appreciatively. "Big, big cock. Big, big, hairy man."

He lifted my penis and began to beat it. Not in any frantic, schoolboy sort of way, either, but in slow and easy, long and sensuous, up-and-down, stroking. My nuts shifted on their own, my scrotum pulling in more tightly, my black ball-hair riding like buoys on a shifting ocean of contracting skin.

I feathered my fingers from the base of his neck to his nipples. Such small rosebuds: his titties. Rosebuds with entrancingly swollen centers, hard as tacks. When I pinched them, he provided a deep, very childish mewl and rocked his head slightly from side to side.

Still mauling his kiddy paps, I commenced, full-scale, my carrousel ride on his dick. Slow and easy, at first, as if the merry-go-round's motor was still working up steam. My bounces were pretty much timed to the continuing languid strokes of his fist along the length of my pecker. I progressed into a faster tempo, from there, and required his masturbatory strokes to catch up.

I slid my hands beneath his arms, my thumbs coming upward over his sides, my thumbs sliding until their pads claimed his nipples and rolled his hard titty centers, even as I increased the bounce of my ass over his sticking cock.

After the first few lucky bumps of his dick against my prostate, my dick leaked preseminal wet in sympathy, and I adjusted my various bounces so that I put my prostate under constant attack and caused a continuous gushing of pre-cum from the pouted mouth of my pecker.

That Jack seemed in no hurry to orgasm told me, more than anything, that he wasn't the innocent his packaging portrayed. When I was his age -- rather, when I was the age he looked -- I could cream with no more stimulus than the way my pants rubbed my dick whenever I walked a few steps across any room.

Jack had the control of a professional hustler, not that I'd been to bed with one -- not that I could remember, anyway. He knew just exactly what he wanted out of our fuck, and pretty well seemed to know how to get it, even to giving me instructions as to when he wanted me to bounce faster or slow down.

"Easy ... easy," he said. "That's right. Oh, yes. Now, you can go a little faster. No, not quite that fast, but ... oh, yes ... oh, yes ... yes ... just like that."

I took to following his lead, exactly because it was important I make him enjoy. Even the prospect of doing less a good job of it, while stone sober, than I'd managed while dead drunk, was a notion I found more than a little disconcerting. As if it would insinuate my need for liquor to break down my inhibitions sufficiently to get really into this gay male-male sex thing. As if, without the crutch of drunkenness, I was really a lousy fuck.

"Oh, you do fuck my dick well," said Jack. He did wonders for a guy's ego, especially for this guy who hadn't fucked or been fucked sober in as long as I could remember. So long ago had it been, in fact, that the memory loss was probably natural and not because of any brain cells killed off or pickled by the booze.

All the while I bounced my ass, Jack kept up a matching lift and drop of the loose cockskin around the harder inner core of my penis. Which he eventually supplemented by massaging my hairy balls with his free hand.

Before long, I actually had it figured I was going to pop my rocks before he did.

"Won't be long now," the cocky little mind-reader said. I thought he referred to my orgasm which had pretty much reaching a boil somewhere within those gonads he manhandled so expertly within the fully compact scrotum I had sprouted at the base of my cock, between my legs.

I would have slowed down, better attempted to staunch the flood of ecstasy already threatening to drown me, but he chose that exact moment to goad me into even greater speed.

"Ride me faster, stud-fucker!" he bellowed. "Jesus fuck ... faster ... faster ... faster."

He left off beating my meat and fondling my balls to slap my thighs, not once but twice, like he played kiddy on a rocking horse and demanded giddy-up.

The sudden freedom of my cock and testicles may well have provided me the much sought ability to keep my own explosion under wraps for those few extra seconds. Because, by the time Jack finished whopping my flanks and reclaimed my cock and my balls, his cock and his balls were hard-and-fast pumping his hot spunk up my asshole.

A mere micro-second after his cum let loose, my cum followed suit. It came flooding out in pearly streamers expelled with such force that the first of it splattered Jack's mouth and disappeared with a quick lick of the kid's tongue. The next landed in a webbing along his neck. At which time, a torque of Jack's fist around my cum-spewing pecker, sent several of my spewing comets sideways onto the sheets of the bed. In finale, my sperm oozed like slow-running magma from a caldera and covered Jack's gripping fist as if his fingers were fallen lumber swallowed by a volcanic eruption.

In total, that first simultaneous coming for that evening, followed by all the fucking and sucking that came after, wherein I got a sampling of the wonders up Jack's tight teenage ass, was good sex. Not can't-be-beat sex. Not tremendous sex. Not fantastic sex. But good sex. Which was more than enough.

Because I remembered it all when we were over and done, didn't I? Obviously, I still remember it to this day. And, in the end, when you reach the age I've now reached, memories are pretty much all there are.

VARIATIONS ON A TALE OF TWO CITIES

TV Programming Guide:
Starring David Cleveland, ABC plans an announced warning this performance may not be suitable for all family members.

Teen Scream Magazine:
What teenage heartthrob, with shy persona, still remembered for his ad campaign for Pallin Popcorn, now starring in his own TV sitcom, and soon -- if rumor has it correctly -- to emerge as the brightest light in a soon-to-be-released big-screen blockbuster, is spending more and more of his time in Cincinnati these days?

Teen Entrepreneur Magazine:
"I've seen 'em come, and I've seen 'em go," says Al Cincinnati. "What I offer here has never depended on what others do or charge. And never will."

So much for his competition! Al, associated with satisfying the needs of some of the world's most famous men, certainly isn't wanting for clientele.

Al's expertise in his business has kept him in great demand by big-name personalities, most recently teenage superstar David Cleveland.

In an era of assembly-line service, Al, just 18, has a yearly five-figure income based on some of the most personalized attention in town.

"Some people think selling any 'service' is a dirty business," he says, "but somebody has to do it."

In the George Tallaney decorated bedroom of Al's Manhattan Central Park South apartment, clients can relax in the opulent luxuriousness of a large king-sized bed.

Al's one unyielding rule: "My customer is always right no matter what. A buyer has every right to be demanding -- he's paying my bills. My ego shouldn't get in the way of a customer's wants and/or desires."

Consumer Informant Magazine:
It's always gratifying to be able to give credit where credit is due. And credit is due at least one of the 15 models tested for this report. The quality of the Cincinnati model was just about the best we've seen. It was the brightest, had the best looks, gave the most attention to detail, and had the most compact chassis. At $125 an inch, adding up to $1000 a ride, it's by far the best buy around.

After Dusk Magazine:
Good music, good costumes, and good performances added up to an entertaining evening with teenage heartthrob David Cleveland in Cincinnati last night.

Costumed by Piccolo, Regina Krowtiz, Bill Blass, and Jockey International, the on-the-rise young man paraded in high-fashion elegance while exuding his charming boyish attractiveness.

For some, the subject matter might have been difficult to handle, but Cleveland managed with his usual mixture of charm and innocence, curiosity and sincerity. It was an evening of tastefully rendered adult entertainment directed with skillfully choreographed aplomb.

The show offered an innovative and perceptive evaluation of homosexual relationships as well as an interesting insight into the gay subculture. It was the apotheosis of two natural, sensual, beautiful young men searching for a workable relationship.

Fashion's Last Word Magazine:
Teenage heartthrob David Cleveland is a triumph of understatement in his beige silk tussah sweater with shawl collar. (By Regina Krowitz, 7 West 22nd Street, New York, MY I0010, about $61). Shirt by Piccolo for Gates Shirts, about $28. Wool flannel pants by Bill Blass for PBM, about $50. Brown shoes: Gentlemen's Footgear, about $110.

David's International Denim T-shirt/brief ensemble by Jockey International, about $8. Socks by electric Sox, about $3.

Al Cincinnati wears a combination of the real and surreal. He teams up his orange cotton sweatshirt by S. Mantis, about $12, and his orange-grey-and-yellow plaid shirt by 5 Brothers, about $15, with green pants by Ronald Kolodzie, about $70. All available at Camouflage, NYC. Leather boots by Wolverine World Wide, about $55.

Al's sumo supporter with full tailored pouch from International Male, about $3.

Uttica Narcissus sheets by J.P. Stevens. Lubricated rubbers by Safety-First. Stereo equipment by Panasonic.

Bedroom design by George Tallaney.

In-Depth Sports Reporter:

Cleveland again rolled over Cincinnati in a ball game in Cincinnati last night. Cleveland was really hot and stayed on top of Cincinnati throughout most of the evening. Cleveland made several successful passes, and came through with only one near fumble early in the first part of the evening.

Cleveland managed to hold Cincinnati down well into the evening with some excellent ball handling.

Cleveland's final climactic touchdown, late in the game, was, as with all the others before it, attained via a successful squeezing through Cincinnati's tight defensive ring to penetrate the end zone.

There were no spectators on hand, but Cleveland obviously didn't need any large cheering section.

Cleveland and Cincinnati will meet again on Saturday, again in Cincinnati.

Prowl magazine:

"You look like a Christmas tree," David Cleveland said. He knew it wasn't what he'd wanted to say, the minute it came out of his mouth. Better at making conversation these days, he realized in quick retrospect that something like, "Looking good!" would have been more to the point. If Al Cincinnati's clothes were colorful that didn't mean Al didn't look damned sexy in them. David, though, didn't follow up with his amended version, even though it probably wasn't too late for its delivery. David simply wasn't good with words. Never had been.

William Maltese

Certainly not growing up on the family farm in Kansas, where the only conversation skills he and his illiterate parents figured he'd ever really need were the few words to get the pigs to the trough, or the cows to the barn. Not now, even though Mrs. Taylor, his personal tutor, tried untiringly to do her very best.

In fact, David's conversation skills were so totally lacking that he could wonder how he'd coherently managed those three now-famous words, required by him when he'd been literally plucked out of that Kansas cornfield, entirely against his will, by the director of the production film crew doing that damned popcorn commercial. He certainly didn't know how he now managed, again and again, to come up with all those required words the writer's of his sitcom expected him to say every week, week after week after week. He only knew that the mental exertion of doing so was getting the best of him.

Actually, the whole ordeal (because ordeal was how David still saw it, no matter the obvious material advantages provided his folks and himself by his new-found fame), had recently become so fucking much that David as much as told his agent to take modeling, and acting, and the whole ball of wax, and shove it. David was convinced he'd be far happier, as he professed, back where nothing more was expected of him than that he did his best to keep the farm from going under.

His agent, Tom Reynolds, who hadn't gotten to be successful by sitting around with his head up his ass, having spotted David immediately as someone "with potential", had, finally, as if pulling teeth, extracted from David what Tom figured the prime reason David was presently balking at the very lucrative net that held him. It simply boiled down to David not getting laid. Something Tom might have taken longer to discover, on his own, without David's reluctant input, because Tom was as well aware as anyone (more so, in that he counted the money increasingly filling the coffers), that there were literally hordes of available teenybopper little girls, who flocked to David, like mice flocked to cheese, who would have literally died and gone to heaven if their teenage idol would have put his schlong to them. That anyone, like David, so American-ideal farm-boy clean-cut, was gay, was something, without David's input, Tom would likely have taken too long to discover on his own, even in a business which probably had more gays, per capita, than just about any other on the planet. Before David's confession, Tom had figured he'd had the knack for spotting any gay right off.

Tom, in the business of making money, not judging other people's morals, surprised David by being surprisingly accepting of the young man's revelations. No way did Tom let a cash cow like David slip back to some Kansas farm, just because the kid liked cock instead of pussy. Certainly not when there were probably as many gays, in the movie business, who would have been as damned happy to be on the receiving end of David's cock, as there were teenybopper teenage girls scrambling for the same privilege.

That David felt too ill-at-ease around everyone, beyond the narrow parameters of his family's Kansas farm, however, to enjoy the prospects of bedding any fellow gay in the business, his inferiority complex about the largest Tom had ever come across, even with Tom's many years in the acting business which was known for people overcompensating for low self-esteem, was a complication which Tom, with his usual aplomb, took in stride.

Tom's eventual solution was Al Cincinnati, who now stepped back to let David into the condo, and who said: "Might as well come on in and see what latest present can be found for you atop this particular Christmas tree."

It was the kind of cleverness that David wished he had the knack for coming up with, but which he doubled he ever would. That David wasn't sent into a panic in the presence of someone who obviously knew more about just about everything than David did, although they were obviously pretty much one and the same age, was only because David knew, from his past sessions with Al, that the guy was being paid good money to make David feel at ease and not feel the fool. From the beginning, when David had been his most nervous, Al had managed to make him feel in good and safe hands.

"Would you be interested to hear there's a sumo jocksock in basic black hidden underneath all of this Christmas color?" Al asked and made a beeline for the wet bar, knowing David probably wanted a cold beer.

"I don't want a beer," David said.

"So, what do you have in mind?" Al asked, and not just because Tom Reynolds had instructed that Al's job, above and beyond good sex, was to try and bring David out of his shell. Al genuinely enjoyed his time spent with David. David's natural charm and shy self-consciousness were rarities in a city where charm and shy self-consciousness were usually nothing more than another exercise in acting. And, of course, as far as Al was concerned, his pleasure with David wasn't hurt by David epitomizing the true-blue American farm-boy stereotype, complete with tousled blond hair, sky-blue eyes, cleft rugged chin, square jawline. In a business with more than its share of good-looking participants, David was still a standout. "Want me to stand on my head while you fuck me?"

"Naw," David replied and blushed.

Al was always impressed by anyone who could still blush, especially when the resulting rosy highlights made a perfect peaches-and-cream complexion seemingly even more perfect.

"You're not very demanding, you know?" Al said. David's sexual tastes were still pretty standard fare, in the all-around scheme of things, to the point where Al often wished David would risk a bit more experimentation. "I thought all farm boys were jaded by fucking horses and getting head from little calves."

"Jesus, Al!" David protested.

David had never fucked a horse. He'd never let calf suckle his dick. All he'd ever done was fuck around with Terry Chandler. Sex with Terry had always the best-ever sex until sex with Al put all David's previous sexual adventures to shame..

"Why don't we take a look at your black sumo jocksock for starters," David suggested, pleased that he'd managed to say just what he'd wanted to say, just the way he'd wanted to say it.

Al peeled off his green pants and his brown-suede boots. He slipped off his orange sweat shirt and tousled his thick black hair in the process. He unbuttoned his orange-grey-and-yellow plaid shirt, unconcerned that David was making no immediate move to undress. It always took David, naturally shy, even after all of his exposure to Hollywood, a little time to get started.

Actually, it wasn't so much David's natural shyness that kept him rooted to the spot, although that, as much as he tried otherwise to deny it, was part of it. Mainly, though, it was just because he took so much pleasure in seeing Al strip down.

In a city full of handsome men, David still found Al's handsomeness something unique and special. What's more, Al's handsomeness became only more so as each piece of his clothing was removed to make more and more naked his one-hundred and seventy-five pounds of studly hard-muscled young teen, with cock-bulged sock of black material that emphasized rather than camouflaged his eight-inch cock and accompanying bull-like balls.

David knew Al's cock was eight inches, because David's cock matched it inch for inch. When the two pricks aligned, belly to belly, they were mirror-images of each other: two rockets on the same launch pad, both cleanly cut and streamline. The fact that David's cock held up so well by comparison to one with such a big-dollar price tag attached to it did marvels for David's ego. Had Al stripped to twelve inches or more of stiff meat, on their first encounter, David wasn't sure he would have handled it, knowing full well that he already had an inferiority complex, even before bringing the size of his dick into the picture. What David didn't know, of course, was that Tom Reynolds had taken just that possibility into account when he'd gone searching for just the right person to fit David's (and thereby Tom's) specific needs of the moment.

"Why don't you fuck me with your clothes on?" Al suggested.

David wanted to fuck Al. Clothes off, clothes on, any way there was: that's how he wanted to fuck him. Any time, anywhere: that's when and where he wanted to fuck him. Trouble was, he wanted to fuck Al so badly that the mere thought of doing so could still get David hot to the point of creaming. Without any self-manipulation of his cock, without Al even coming near it, David, turned voyeur, could feel his stiff prick giving those little jerks, his balls elevating, despite their heavy loads of cum, his insides telling him that if he didn't try to get his excitement under control, he was going to end up with the crotch of his underpants webbed with pearly cream.

Telling himself that he should, by now, have come far enough in his relationship with Al to get a grip, David kicked off his shoes and his socks. He dropped his grey-flannel pants.

"I still find it hard to believe that the person millions of Americans invite into their living rooms, one night every week, steps into my condo, without benefit of TV," Al said. He dropped his sumo jocksock around his firm hips and ass, freeing his erection and sending his impressively stiff boner into an upright position before his rippled belly. The base of his dick and his accompanying ball-bulged scrotum were a sight that almost overrode David's hard-achieved self-control. Suddenly, David thought for sure his cock was going to go into spontaneous eruption. Miraculously, though, and David didn't have a clue how he managed it, his orgasm aborted, at the very last second, although it still threatened to sneak up, unawares, if David, for any reason dropped, any part of his ongoing defenses against it.

David's sweater and shirt came off and left him naked except for tailored underwear of brushed blue cotton. The crotch of his underpants were bulged with David's cock and balls.

"Why don't I come right over there and suck your cum out of your cock through the crotch of yours shorts?" Al suggested, pleased his words caused a visible pulsing of David's hard cock beneath the stretched cotton of David's underpants.

"I don't want anything between your hot mouth and my cock," David wanted to say. Instead of saying it, though, he dropped his shorts and added them to the pile collected at his feet. He crossed his arms downward, across his chest and belly, took hold of his T-shirt shirttail and pulled the snagged material up and over his head.

All part of his business, Al compared David's body to those which had come before. Granted, Al had seen better bodies, in his time, but not many. He'd certainly seen a helluva lot more bodies in far worse shape.

With a bit more fumbling than he would have preferred, David first accepted the prophylactic, then freed it from its packaging and rolled it down and over his cock, hoping, all the while, that his on-the-rise-again excitement wouldn't see him filling his rubber before he got it on.

Al dropped to his hands and knees, invitingly aiming his naked ass in David's direction. Their very first session, he'd correctly assumed that a kid from a farm, who'd watched animals fucking their brains out, would more readily recognize the on-all-fours fuck position, over any of the others, even over missionary position so preferred by... well ... by whom else but by missionaries?

David had a delicious eyeful of Al's brown pucker that awaited filling by David's tumescent erection. The anal move was a magnet that actually seemed to pull David's cock down slightly and aim right for it as David took the few steps necessary to close the distance between them.

David dropped to his knees behind Al's asshole. He put his prickhead to the pucker and pushed. Al's sphincter rolled open, like the lens of a camera, and gummed along David's entering dick. The taut oval of the asshole slipped securely into the deep groove formed just beneath the impressive flare of David's cockcorona

Al dropped forward and lowered to his forearms, simultaneously delivering a backward shove of his ass. His butt greedily swallowed David's hard cock all of the way to David's balls. Al's hard asscheeks smacked loud and hard against David's washboarded belly.

"Oh, yes! Oh ... oh!" David responded.

Al revolved his hips to stir David's cock, angling just right so that some of those hard inches collided with Al's nub-like prostate. There was a resulting ooze of preseminal goo that exited Al's cockmouth and formed a translucent string that proceeded from his cockmouth to the rug, before breaking free.

With little more forewarning than David's ongoing knowledge that he was hotter than hell, that there was the continuing pressure Al's gumming rectum exerted along the length of his dick, that there was a fiery friction that seared his cockshaft with each and every movement of cock up butt, or butt around cock, David shuddered as his nuts erupted their floodgates and began filling to capacity the rubber socked so securely up Al's asshole.

Al expertly fluttered the muscles of his anal lining and milked David's dick so that it continued exploding all the more.

David's cock pulsed rhythmic jerks of pleasure. Automatically his hands clamped Al's hips and held on for dear life. Every part of his being seemed siphoned down to his balls for seeming expulsion, along with his cream, up Al's greedily sucking asshole.

"Shit!" said David. It wasn't any sort of complaint as to the quality of the pleasure he'd derived from his explosion. Christ, how could he complain of something so fucking good? What he could and did complain of was: "I'm still the quick-as-ever on-the-trigger hay-chewing kid from down on the farm."

"A quick cum, first go-round, merely tells me your interested, remember?" Al said, for not the first time. "It's not like you're some old fart who's through for the evening first time his nuts let go, is it?"

What it was was that David so much enjoyed the feel of his cock, so fully ensconced and cum-webbed within the snugness of Al's butt, that he never wanted to take the break required to pull out, wipe down, and re-rubber for another try. Nevertheless...

"There now," Al said, David's newly rubbered cock retracing its previous journey up Al's dog-positioned asshole. "Both of us none the less horny because of the pause. In fact, I can't speak for you, but I'm all the hotter knowing just how long and how hard you're going to be riding me before your next gooey wads squirt up my sexy behind."

David's belly molded Al's ass, like yin to yang. His chest curved over Al's back. His hands scooped beneath Al's belly. His left hand palmed Al's balls. His right hand wrapped as much of Al's hard cock as it could.

"Hmmmm," Al said appreciatively, He made it an even louder, "HMMMM", when David delivered a complete fuck stroke that pulled swollen cock out to its head, out of Al's asshole, and then pushed the cock all of the way back in, to David's balls. At one and the same time, David's fist stroked the entire length of Al's cock, and his other hand rolled Al's balls into collision.

David wished that, just once, Al would be as fast on the trigger as David initially always was. David would have liked to think that Al was as turned on by David, as David was turned on by Al, that the young prostitute could no more control his pleasure than David could. But, if David couldn't have that wish come true, he'd take what he could get. And what he got wasn't anything to complain about: his cock fucked yet again up a tight asshole, his hands full of sexily stiff meat and cum-bulged hustler-balls.

David stopped all movement of his cock up Al's butt, in order to concentrate a few moments on just his languid pump of Al's hard meat and his caressing manipulation of Al's hair-fuzzed scrotum.

"You do know how to give a guy a good ride," Al said, his hips providing the fucking motion that jammed his prick through David's fist at the same time asshole partially unsheathed David's thick dick. Al torqued his ass around David's cock and luxuriated in the twisting of his own hard prick within David's masturbating grip. David, who still wasn't much one for talking, didn't concentrated on words to explain his renewed soaring pleasure, nor on words to detail just how much he wanted to provide Al, as well as himself, with pleasures all the more. He concentrated on the doing. If he could master the memorizing of written words to be said before the camera, when that was such a goddamned fucking chore, he was confident he could far more easily master whatever the intricate techniques of fucking that would one day get even this professional hustler truly squirming from the genuine, bona-fide, pleasure conjured by hearty spearing from David's farm-boy cock.

What David couldn't know, of course, was that he met that very objective, each and every time -- beginning with the very first fuck. Even though, Al was a paid professional, fucked so many times, by so many people, that he'd perfected certain tricks of the trade that often allowed him to feign pleasure and excitement far more intense than the reality. Granted, there was no way Al, or any man, faked orgasm. In that respect, a female whore had it over a male prostitute every damned time. A tart could moan and groan, say she was coming up a storm, and no one would be the wiser. But if a guy moaned and groaned, said he was coming up a storm, but didn't produce creamy residue, well, he was found out, quick enough, wasn't he? Al, though, was lucky in that he always had plenty of cum ready and willing, no hard work required, to come exploding whenever David came a-calling.

"You've about fucked me to creaming, stud," Al said. "Just keep on fucking me, a little bit longer, with that luscious ... luscious ... luscious cock of yours ... up my tight ... tight ... butt ... and ... oh, yes, that's the way ... that is, is, is the way."

Al unabashedly blew his wad. Frankly, as always speared on David's cock, he was surprised he was so quick on the trigger, considering just how jaded Al should have been to this sort of thing. On the other hand, it was always a pleasure to know that he wasn't so completely jaded that orgasm had become no more exciting than blowing his nose. It being an extra bonus that he was being paid for it. Just going to prove: "Yes, Mary, there is a Santa Claus!".

Al's wads came from the mouth of his dick. His first juicy slugs splattered his overhanging chest. His following comets, only a little less forceful, collapsed into webbing along the ridges of his overhanging stomach. His final gushes, too heavy to be propelled all that far, either drooled to coagulating puddles on the rug or cocooned David's still-pumping fingers.

David, extremely pleased with himself, would have been more pleased if Al's first climax of the evening wasn't suddenly responsible for David's second. "Ugh!" David grunted helplessly. There was nothing he could do but go with the flow. No way did he swim upstream against it. Not the way his balls, miraculously full in spite of their previous spermal expulsions, pumped newly manufactured spunk so hard and so fast that it was hard to believe this wasn't David's very first go-round.

David rested a sweaty cheek against Al's equally sweaty back, shut his eyes, growled his pleasure, and drained what remained of his load.

So well had Al performed the job cut out for him that David was made strangely embarrassed and distraught. Because, the idea of returning to the farm for sex with the likes of Terry Chandler, even more of a no-nothing than David, was far less inviting than before Al had come into David's world. Because Al was merely doing his job, David not the only customer who paid for Al's services. Because David continued to feel, for every other reason, than sex, that he'd be far better off and far happier out of the Hollywood rat-race and back in the less complicated existence he'd had on the family farm in Kansas.

FOOD CHAIN

Raol Mowla was forty-seven, well-dressed, and spoke excellent English in a charmingly lilting way. He had been referred to Mark Matinson by UN Forces Colonel Talbot Cisco whom Mark had met at one of Charles Gilbert's parties.

"You have a penchant for poverty-stricken areas of the world?" General Cisco had asked the handsome eighteen year old, having learned Mark had vacationed in Egypt, Bangladesh, Haiti, India .... "Then go to Grawnli."

"You have come to the right place, at the right time," Raol affirmed to Mark, as both sipped an imported whiskey. "In Grawnli, anything can presently be had for a very reasonable price."

The next morning, they went looking.

"All Grawnli is your department store," Raol assured and drove Mark through city streets that seemed to have a beggar on every corner. He told Mark that when he saw something of interest to just say so. "Nine times out of ten, it can be had," Raol assured him.

On the grounds surrounding Cranduk Palace, Mark made his first selection: a kid who was painting a small watercolor of the Palace tree. Mark was a painter -- or, at least, had once aspired to be.

He tied the boy to a bed in a small rented room and fucked him until the kid screamed for mercy. For which Mark paid 642 Grawnli pahteen, the equivalent of two American dollars.

The young boatman on the Morg River caught Mark's interest because of the bulge the kid's cock managed within loose pants rolled above knotty knees. If most Grawnli men were rumored to have small cocks, the young boatman's eight-inch prick was a pleasant exception.

Mark beat the boatman's ass with an oar from the young man's own boat, then fucked him to climax. For which he paid 321 Grawnli pahteen, the equivalent of one American dollar.

Interested in archaeology (Mark had met Charles Gilbert while sketching the Baths of Caracalla in Rome), Mark had Raol take him to

Pow-far-ju. They spent the first day exploring the grounds of the almost-deserted Borgum Temple. On day two, Mark decided they should make the pre-dawn climb to the famed religious Grotto atop Gordum mountain, there to watch the sunrise.

Once at the Grotto, Mark liked the exotic good looks of one of the Grotto's attending novice monks.

Even Raol seemed a bit taken back by Mark's request, then arranged, after pre-payment to the young monk of 963 Grawnli pahteen, or the equivalent of three American dollars, for Mark to meet the teenage attendant that night in one of the large burial mounds dotting the valley floor.

The young attendant's body was shaved clean, including his head and his crotch. The latter emphasized his average-sized prick that would have been less impressive with an accompanying bush of pubic hair. Erect, his penis resembled a phallic mushroom whose cap was perfectly halved by a pit that leaked succulent, translucent juices.

Mark turned the attendant to one of the large granite grave guardians, raised the young monk's arms to wrap the thick neck of the stone statue. Mark tied the attendant's wrists in place and fucked him from behind while the young man's cock banged old stone and stained the rock with copious preseminal juices. All the while Mark fucked, he looked over the attendant's bare shoulder into the leering, torch-lit face of the granite totem the young man was tied to, thinking all the while that there had been a similar stone-faced monster in Mexico while he'd fucked a young peasant in the ruins outside of Veracruz.

Back in the States, Mark settled into the plush leather seat beside Charles Gilbert, while Charles' chauffeur put Mark's bags in the trunk.

They drove a few miles before Charles, with a wide grin, bent for the briefcase on the floor at his feet.

"I have a little something to show you," Charles said and unsnapped brass catches.

His briefcase open, Charles removed a small painting.

"Jesus, Charles, a Selchov!" Mark exclaimed. Frustrated in his desire to become a painter, Mark had compromised by coveting the works of those more successful in their resolve than he'd been. "Where in the hell did you get it?"

"A friend was in a bind and needed some cash," Charles confessed. In the basement of Charles' house, Charles watched Mark disrobe.

Charles liked what he saw. Maybe Mark, at eighteen, was a tad too beefy for some, but Charles liked a bit of meat on any trick's bones. Charles actually got turned off by recognizable ribcage, definitive hipbones, an obvious run of spine from back of neck to asscrack, each vertebrae present and accounted for.

On the other hand, too much muscle tone, as far as Charles was concerned, was as much a definite turn-off as too little. He had actually felt disappointment the first time Mark had stripped down to reveal a surprising amount of apparent body definition. Not chiselled work, like a body hewn from stone. Rather, a subtle molding of flesh that clearly defined rectangular pectorals and abdominals but without blatantly doing so. In the end, Charles had decided he could live with that after all.

"I see you got a bit of sun," Charles said. If he'd once had a decided preference for pale, almost pasty skin, he'd found Mark, once again, the exception to the rule, with skin that remained peach-toned, even with exposure to the sun. Sunshine merely enhanced the peach, rather than turned it distastefully, in Charles' opinion, bronze or dark brown. There was a nice contrast between Mark's sun-exposed peach to his unexposed lighter-tone peach where the young man's tan-lines emphasized his paler crotch and asscheeks.

Although Mark wasn't particularly well-hung -- Charles estimated seven inches, max -- Charles wasn't a size-queen. As long as a trick had a cock large enough so that there was no mistaking it for pussy, Charles didn't give a goddamn about anything else. He had very little use for any trick's cock, anyway, except as decorative appendage. Whether such a cock stayed soft throughout a session, or, like Mark's cock, sometimes managed a respectable erection, was really of no consequence to Charles.

What was of interest to Charles was teenage ass. He considered himself a connoisseur of teenage ass. And if Mark liked to pretend knowing something about painting and art, there was no doubting his young ass was the kind that turned Charles on.

Mark's ass was big without being too big. One buttock mirrored the other, right down to the dimple in each. Not a hair to be seen, where the two asscheeks met at their mutually shared crack. Even when the asscrack was pried open, the hair was few and far between. Like the rest of Mark's body, which was surprisingly hairless, except for the few strands around the young man's nipples and a few more around his navel, and a more hearty bushing around the young man's cock and balls.

Charles required that Mark affix the first of the two available hanging-from-chains manacles. It was symbolic indication that Mark entered into each session of his own free will. Some men liked to come across as rapists, but Charles preferred the role of someone bestowed with the right to do what he did by the willing consent of the teenager to whom he did it. How much more powerful he felt when his slave couldn't moan afterwards that he'd been raped against his will. Anyone could rape ass, but being given teenage ass on a silver platter, well, that was something else again; the very thought of which pumped more blood into Charles' already pretty thoroughly blood-glutted pecker.

Charles affixed the second manacle, this to Mark's other wrist. Mark finally pretty much sealed and presented for fucking.

Charles bagged Mark's head with a full hood, no eye slits. Charles didn't think it was the teenager's business seeing just how much exquisite pleasure Charles actually took in what he was doing.

Charles secured the hood around Mark's neck with a loosely pulled drawstring. Charles moved around Mark's hooded and hung body in order to better access the asshole which was what this was all about.

"I wish your ass wasn't so goddamned fat," Charles said. He didn't wish any such thing, but why tell Mark the truth? Rather, Mark should be made to think himself damned lucky that Charles even bothered with the imperfections Mark brought to the black room.

Charles gave Mark's ass a whack with the opened palm of a hand. The collision of flesh against flesh was loud. The impact immediately warmed the full span of Charles' palm and fingers, as well as set into motion tremors that vibrated all of the way to Charles' shoulder.

"Every time I whack your ass, I hit baby blubber," Charles pretended to complain. He gave Mark's teenage ass another slap. Charles' hand went even warmer. Mark's buttcheeks evidenced two red hand-prints on peachy skin.

Charles shed his clothes. He was in damned good condition, for his age, if he did say so himself. Not that he was one of those lucky guys so turned on by themselves that all he needed for sexual fulfillment was himself and a mirror.

To Charles' way of thinking, his main imperfection had always been his being way too muscular. Not that he'd lifted weights, because he hadn't. It was merely something to do with his genes. All the Gilbert men, even some of the women, had hereditary muscles. If Charles' had lost some of their edge, over the years, they still turned a few heads at the beach. If it was a nude beach, Charles' big cock turned a few heads, too.

Charles could never figure the big deal some people made of cock size, in general, of his cock size in particular. He truly believed his cock, smaller by two inches, hell, even three inches, would give him the very same pleasure it could deliver now. Sometimes, he genuinely found his big prick an inconvenience, like when trying to disguise it within a pair of well-tailored slacks. In straight company, there wasn't all that much advantage to flaunting his wares, and Charles spent a good deal of his time -- socially and professionally -- in the company of straights.

Too much time in the presence of straights, Charles decided. Still, his business didn't run itself. His family had certain civic responsibilities that he couldn't shuffle off onto others. So ...

Best not bemoan what little time he had for his particular kind of enjoyment. Best just enjoy, if and when he could take advantage.

His cock was a weight extended in front of him, its foreskin peeled back to reveal and turtleneck his purple cock corona.

To abort his admitted impulse for a quick fuck, he countered his mounting pleasure by, one by one, pulling out, by their roots, the three obviously white pubic hairs amid the otherwise black bushing at his crotch. Sooner or later, he'd have to leave off such frequent weeding, or he'd pluck his groin as clean as the crotch of a newborn babe.

He held off hand-slapping Mark's ass again only because a better job could be done with a belt.

He had several belts from which to choose, all neatly displayed in a cupboard against a nearby wall. He had whips, too: bull whips, cat 'o-nine-tails, riding crops, even a spatula-like rubber paddle once used during unofficial interrogations by the South African police. He'd tried them all but had decided, after years of experimentation, that ass-whipping with a belt was still pretty much his favorite way to go. There was just something about the way a belt colored a teenager's asscheeks in attractive swaths of variegated red, without damaging the skin as easily as a whip or riding crop.

He chose a wide police belt, black leather. He folded it over on itself and didn't waste time.

"Jesus!" Mark bellowed quick on the heels of the black police leather against his already hand-slapped behind.

"You and I know you're baby-fat ass needs warming up to make it of any real interest to me," Charles said. "You don't want me to come this far and lose interest, do you? Well, do you?"

"No," Mark said, his voice muffled by his hood.

Hardly needing Mark's permission, by this stage of the game, Charles decided another whack of the belt to the butt was warranted.

Mark grunted immediate response.

"That your way of saying thank-you?" Charles asked.

"Thank-you," Mark said.

Oh, but Mark knew how to play the game. Another reason Charles found him so enjoyable.

On the other hand, even as Charles delivered another whack to Mark's ass, Mark providing another sensuous response, Charles knew that Mark, this time, wasn't nearly as much the turn-on Mark had been the very first time, the second time, even the third. No fault of Mark. Maybe a flaw in Charles' character that required him not to stay with any one young stud for long. As it was, Mark had lasted longer than most.

Charles gave Mark's butt another smack, as if extra could make Mark extra attractive. It didn't work, but it had been worth the try.

Charles dropped the belt. It curled on the basement floor like a cock gone soft from lack of interest. Thank God, Charles' cock wasn't quite so jaded.

Charles rubbered his dick with lubricated prophylactic, obtained from a cupboard drawer. The target for which Charles would aim was clearly defined for him by the attractive vee made by Mark's uplifted arms and shoulders. The young man's spine, like the shaft of an arrow, pointed all of the way to the crack of Mark's ass.

Charles hooked his thumbs to Mark's asscheeks and pried the teenage asscheeks open along their mutually shared crack. What he unveiled was Mark's waiting pucker.

At its hardest, Charles's cock was a lever that needed to be pried down from before the man's belly. Now, however, it was merely a bridge between his belly and the opening of Mark's butt.

"Not long now," Charles said. The lubricated head of his dick touched pucker.

Charles pushed Mark slightly forward, the young man swinging on his chains. Charles stepped in closer, just as Mark began a backward swing. The momentum of Mark's backward swing carried the young man's pucker up and over the cockhead of Charles' aimed cock.

"You're too big," Mark protested.

"Naw," Charles denied and fed another two inches of his erection up Mark's rectum.

Charles probed even more of his dick up Mark's funky anal pit. Charles let go his handhold of Mark's ass and let the young man's asscheeks fall in along their crack. Where the asscheeks couldn't meet, because of Charles' hard cock thrust between them, they molded snugly around the shaft of Charles' sticking penis.

Charles' hands on Mark's hips, the curve of his fingers felt the flesh-padded ridges of Mark's hipbones, and Charles bucked his pelvis forward, pulled Mark's ass back, and fed Mark's young asshole all the man-cock Charles had to offer.

"Ugh!" Mark provided sensuous sound effect.

"Nothing like a tight, hand- and belt-whipped teenage ass for good fucking," Charles said. His stomach firmly mated Mark's ass. His chest hugged Mark's back. His mouth whispered close to Mark's hooded right ear.

Charles' hands slid Mark's sides.

Charles' hands found and cupped Mark's pecs. Mark's taut nipples punched Charles' palms.

Charles tented his fingers. His fingertips claimed Mark's nipples and squeezed them ... hard ... harder ... hardest.

"Jeeez!" Mark rewarded Charles' efforts.

"I'm fucking baby-fat ass," Charles said. He hands came up and over Mark's shoulders and locked there. His chest was really tight against Mark's back.

If he lifted his feet, he could hang from Mark's body, maybe even dislocate the young man's shoulders. He knew someone who liked doing just that to tricks. Charles' tastes, though, were simpler. All he ever asked from any kid was to take a few slaps on the ass and a good fuck up the butt.

"You going to give me a good fuck, aren't you, kid?" Charles asked.

"Yes," Mark said. He sounded as breathless as he was.

"Sure you are," Charles agreed. It would be a good fuck, too. But it would, also, be Charles' last fuck of this asshole, no matter how many more times Mark might be prepared to offer it up. It was simply time for Charles to find an even more perfect teenage butt. Time for Charles to find an even more perfect teenager to manacle and hang from chains in Charles' basement black room.

Charles eased back. The fit of his cock up Mark's butt, lubricated or not, was so snug that Mark's ass followed right along. Charles needed his hands back on Mark's hips to hold Mark's body static, in order to break the vacuum and allow Charles' cock maneuverability within Mark's asshole. When Charles cock came partially unstuck, it did so with an audibly sucking "Slurp!"

Looking down, Charles watched his cock coming out. He watched it going back. He watched his pubic bush sandwich between his belly and Mark's ass.

"Mmmmm," Charles hummed appreciatively. It did feel good. It did feel real good.

Charles got the rhythm he wanted. It was a coordinated combination of his hips, swinging back and forth, and Mark's body, swinging forth and back. Whenever Charles bucked forward, as Mark's ass came back, there was a dull thud as Mark's teenage ass and Charles' man-belly smacked.

"Like that, don't you?" Charles asked. Not that he really cared. Charles liked it, and that was all that really counted.

It got better, too.

Charles' pleasure intensified with each slide of his prick up Mark's butt, with each slide of Mark's butt over Charles' fuckIng erection.

Charles liked the way Mark's chains rattled. Something about that clink of chains, like sexy wind chimes, combined with Mark's increasing moans, got Charles nicely hot and bothered.

"Ready for a butt full of cream?" Charles asked. More importantly, Charles was ready to provide that butt full of cream. By the feel of his weighty balls, he carried far more cream than a mere butt-full. He might end up drowning the both of them with his creamy overflow.

He moved into higher gear. It wouldn't be long now. Orgasm had suddenly become the most important thing.

"Come on, baby-fat ass," Charles said. "Coax the cum right ... out

... of ... my ... Jesus ... cum-filled ... man-balls ... man-balls ... man-balls!"

Charles buried his cock to his nuts and left it there. He dropped his head back on his arched neck and let go a howl. He revolved his hips in ecstasy and creamed ... creamed ... creamed ... until he was sure each and every one of his guts had turned to liquid, flooded into his gonads, and exploded out through his stiff dick into teenage butt.

He feared for the viability of the rubber. Surely, no condom was designed for so much flooding cum. Was it, even then, ballooned to bursting?

In the end, far less cum was produced than Charles imagined: maybe only a teaspoon of the stuff. All of it easily contained by the rubber. All of it successfully pulled from Mark's asshole and contained within the protective rubber, the latter quickly tied off at its open end and deposited in a convenient wastepaper basket.

After which, Charles Gilbert paid Mark Matinson one Selchov painting, or the equivalent of three-thousand American dollars.

ROBINSON HOLE, WYOMING

I can't tell by looking, because the kid looks far younger, but Bobby is eighteen. Eighteen years, six months, two weeks, four days, three hours, two minutes ... forty-five ... forty-six ... seconds.

Although he looks young, he hasn't a trace of baby-fat. Good thing, because nothing turns me off more than even a hint of baby-fat plumpness. I like my men (albeit young), lean and compact and well-muscled; so as I know they're men and not some kind of male-female hybrid that hasn't yet decided whether or not it's going to sprout tits. Lucky for me, most of the guys that I see in my line of business are athletic types already having pretty well honed their physiques.

Bobby, I know, without being told, has been doing a helluva lot more than caving before he got around to visiting me in Robinson Hole, Wyoming. He has the physical makeup of a varsity swimmer or runner who has obviously supplemented with a bit of weight training on the side. This kid has hard pecs and ripped, albeit slightly concaved, abdominals. You can see his every muscle grouping hard-etched and well-defined. His biceps and triceps show all evidence of having pumped more hard cock than his own, since he's reached puberty. Nice legs, too, that go well with the rest of his body. Surprising how many guys overlook leg development and concentrate only on the upper body, ending up looking top heavy and ready to fall over.

And you want to see the epitome of young male ass, take a look at Bobby's. Not a giant ass. Not a small ass. A just-right ass. Two compact, hard as nails, globes, aligned along a common crack, each inviting a hand (preferably mine) to come along and take a firm hold, maybe push the buttocks wide, along their shared crease, and check out the kid's I-know-it-will-be sexy pucker.

I haven't missed what he has to offer in the cock department, either. Little chance of missing his eight inches soft that I imagine are ten inches hard. Although I have seen/felt cocks at eight that stay that way, whether soft or hard, I imagine his as only getting bigger.

Not to confuse me with a size-queen, because those guys and I are in a completely different ballpark. I check out a whole package, and if good points override bad, then things are a go. Sometimes, believe it or not, a cock can come off too big for a pleasingly perfect physique. Not that I'd reject a guy for ever having a fourteen-inch dick. It's back to how I perceive the total, and as to whether or not certain flaws (a cock too big, or too small, an ass too flabby, a belly unripped), are sufficiently overshadowed by corresponding points of goodness.

Bobby, though, pretty much perfect, no matter where I look, as he swims the Green Grotto's lake; no matter where I looked, as he'd stripped down for his present plunge; no matter where I may decide to look whenever he hauls his naked body out of the warm-spring pool.

"You coming in?" he asks and runs his hands up and over his head to squeeze water out of his black hair. Little beads of moisture catch in his thick lashes and cling to the tanned baby-bottom-smooth skin of his Adonis-handsome face.

Have I mentioned his eyes, black as obsidian, with all the sparkly reflectiveness of that natural-glass stone?

How about his slightly upturned nose? His two dimples, both in one cheek? His sexy chin cleft?

"Think I'll pass this time around," I answer his invite. Although I do have every intention of joining him, it's not going to be in the water. "I just might have a cold in the making, or some kind of allergy acting up."

Actually, I've a boner in my pants that, if the kid saw it face-on, would likely put the fear of God into him. He'd certainly get the clue that what I have in mind for him is more than a mutually shared paddling around some underground pool.

"Be back in a sec," I tell him, "Got to drain the snake."

No way any piss gets up and out the stiffy I'm toting in my pants. Actually, my dick is so hard, I have to bend slightly as I walk to better accommodate it within the usually ample space provided inside my trousers.

The steely hardness of my cock requires me to unbuckle, unfasten, and drop my pants around it, once I'm behind a convenient rock. No way do I force-feed the monster out through the small space that would have been afforded by a merely opened pants fly.

By the way, I'm not dropping my pants because I figure to take a dump, since my cock is too hard for me to drain my bladder. What I do

I do purely in preparation for what will come, and for what I can only hope will come as a result of what comes.

From my shirt pocket, I pull out my special designed cock-sock. Actually, cock-socks is more apropos, in that there are two: a sheer silk one on the inside, with a corresponding bulky white sweat sock over the top. The sock openings have been combined, one to the other, but not sewed closed, round a cockring. All designed so that both socks, more like one sock with silken lining, drop down over my hard dick like a cozy over a teapot. Once down, both my balls are likewise fed through the opening and through the cockring. Total result: my cockringed cock and balls securely enclosed within a comfortable and well-padded genitalia container. All of which gets crammed into my pants, which I hoist back up around them.

I adjust the whole caboodle into an upward alignment, double-socked cockhead to my belly button, so its bulkiness is less evident than it would be had my hard dick jutted downward along my left thigh.

I have mixed feelings about my inability to join special guys like Bobby in the Green Grotto's pool. Since me stripped down and bare naked would certainly be a prime opportunity to give them a peek at just what they're about to be offered.

Let's face it, I can hold my own with just about the studliest of guys, what with blond hair and blue eyes, and a body well-conditioned by almost daily traipsing in and out of Robinson Hole, not to mention a regimen of mountain hiking, biking, and weight-lifting. If I wish my nose didn't look as if it had once been broken in a fight (I was born with it that way), and if I wish my lips were a little thicker (my upper lip way too thin, in my estimation), the total picture still comes off damned aesthetically pleasing, if I do say so myself.

No way, though, as I've told myself over and over, does presenting all of my goodness to guys like Bobby, at the Green Grotto, come across anything but scary when I accompany it with my giant dick looking hell-bent on finding asshole or mouth into which to do considerable damage. Unless, of course, the guy splashing around in the pool, is gay and gets turned on by stiff monster-dick inches. Unfortunately, "Are you gay?", is not one of the questions we're allowed to ask, or place on the release form everyone signs, before someone heads with me down into the cave complex.

It being a fact, though, that we are able, indeed are required by law, to ask a caver's age and have him provide verification. Which is why I so well know Bobby's young but legal age at the present time.

Given a couple of days, I figure I can ferret out any gay guy from any straight, no matter how deeply ensconced the gay might still be in his closet, but it's not nearly as easy when there's only the few hours of only a day trip.

"Jeez, that was neat," Bobby says, coming out of the water, just as I rejoin him.

His studly body sloughs water, from head to toe, some of it draining off the end of his circumcised eight-inch cock as if the kid were pissing.

I toss him a towel and watch him dry off, all the while pretending I'm not paying all that much attention. No one can say I'm not a good actor.

"Must be great owning a place like this," he says, having clumped the towel to drag it from his asscrack, upward beneath his cock and balls, leaving his pecker and testicles swinging seductively between his legs by the time he gets around to wiping his washboarded belly.

"Admittedly, it does have its advantages," I admit, and I'm not referring to my ability to access the pool in the Green Grotto whenever I feel like it.

Robinson Hole having been in my family ever since great-great granddaddy discovered the cave complex while trying to evade an Indian scalping party. I say "trying to evade", because the Indians knew of the place before great-great granddaddy did, and they knew he had to come out eventually the way he'd gone in. Had they gone about flushing him out quietly, his rescue party wouldn't have heard the gunfire that brought them to the scene. Great-great granddad not having survived but one day after he was pulled, wounded and bleeding, to freedom.

Bobby doesn't seem in any hurry to get dressed, but I don't interpret that as any major signal that he knows I'm ogling and he's consciously out to give me a long and leisurely look. Most guys simply like being stark naked in a wilderness setting. Even I have to admit there's something liberating about allowing my cock and balls to flap freely in the breeze.

And there is a breeze. A couple of bolt holes, only big enough for pack rats, break free a couple miles back, causing an intake of outside air that eventually warms up when crossing the heated water of the Green Grotto pool. That breeze, even now, gently dries the black wiry hair that rides Bobby's impressive teenage scrotum.

"This is genuinely marvellous!" he says and sits on a nearby rock. His balls spill over the stone and provide a pillow for his elephant-trunk cock; whether he knows it or not, for my sheer enjoyment and viewing pleasure. "So many places have rules and regulations about how you shouldn't get in the water."

"That's because a lot of the cave systems in the US have ended up in government hands, or under government control," I say. "Not that they haven't tried getting their hot little bureaucratic hands on this place, too."

Uncle Sam and his state of Wyoming counterparts can try all they like to get Robinson Hole from we Robinsons, but this is one Robinson not about to give in without a fight. Not only does the privately owned cave complex provide me with more than a substantial living, but I'd miss its ability to pimp for me, even more than I'd miss the money.

"So, toasty warm," says Bobby. The warmth yet another reason guys don't mind keeping their clothes off a little while longer.

The whole area is situated over a hot spot in the Earth, as nearby Yellowstone Park can very well attest. Nonetheless, there are very few accessible underground hot springs, like those in Green Grotto, especially that yearly maintain a constant temperature for safe and comfortable swimming.

"Beats coming into a clammy damp old hole, doesn't it?" And don't I make that statement all rife with double entendre?

"Well, time to dress, I guess," he says, apparently innocently oblivious to any of my intended sexual reference. He slaps his thighs, just above his shapely knees.

He's reached the point where he feels staying naked any longer will likely come off as something more than merely a young guy simply enjoying a bit of natural nudity. Not that I would give a damn if he stayed stripped bare for a few additional hours, even came right on out and started playing with his thick prick, and maybe even ...

"I'd better get suited up before I catch a cold," he says and proceeds to do just that; dress, I mean; not catch a cold.

It's the way out of the Green Grotto that I really love. Granted, it's the same way as one comes in, actually only the one entrance/exit, but heading out is always my very favorite time. All because of the way the entrance/exit narrows at one spot to a tight-tight at-mid-thigh crawl space. On the way in, I'm subjected to the grand picture of wriggling studly butt, as the person ahead of me heads on through, in that I always send my guest through first. On the way back out, however ...

"Better let me go first," I say. "For some reason, it's always a little more tricky headed this way. Kind of like one of those exotic flesh-eating plants with hair-like appendages that provide easy access to bugs but try to keep them permanently on the inside."

"Yipes!" he says, sounding genuinely concerned.

Another reason I so enjoy the young ones, like Bobby, aside from the fact that they're just more attractive when they're that young, is how most of them haven't been spelunking all that long, realize they don't know it all, and are willing to take the word of someone they figure an on-site authority.

As if designed by God, just for the likes of me (Mother Nature, with her cunt, not likely to have been so obliging), the exit hole is just the right height so that a bend at my waist gets most, but not all of, my upper body into the hole for my supposed wiggle to the other side. God knows, it would be easy enough to enlarge the hole and make it far more convenient. More than one Robinson, in the past, even proposed such excavation, the Green Grotto being such a popular draw. In the end, though, it was always decided that something like the Green Grotto is always more appreciated when it takes a bit of time and effort to get to it. That line of reasoning working perfectly to the benefit of this particular present-day very-queer Robinson.

So, I lean forward into the space and present Bobby with what I hope is something equivalent to the marvellously wonderful male ass he'd presented to me on the way in from the other side. I lean in even farther, and the sock-cushioned bulge of my stiff dick fucks snugly between my belly and the solid stone of the rocky squeeze. Just a little more wiggling, and ...

"Jesus, I think I'm stuck!"

"What?"

"I fucking-Jesus think I'm stuck."

Considering I'm lodged within a doughnut hole of solid stone, the acoustics aren't all that bad, as I've long ago discovered. Although I'm' speaking pretty much into the empty space in front of me, my ass aimed in the completely opposite direction, my voice, up front, and Bobby's voice, behind, don't have all that much trouble maneuvering the available cracks and crevices.

"Stuck?"

There's always an initial moment of genuine panic, for my companion, at times like these, considering I presently clog the only feasible exit from the Green Grotto.

"Not to worry," I reassure. "This happened once before."

A decided understatement, but it's not as if I go through this routine for each and every guy who pays his entrance and guide fees for a glimpse and a swim in the Green Grotto. In fact, mine, more often than not, is a long wait between perspective candidates for this bit of show and tell, because I'm pretty damned selective.

"I forgot to factor in my boner," I say.

"What about your honor?"

Remember, I said the acoustics were good, not perfect.

"My boner. B...o...n...e...r."

"Boner?" he says, with I-must-have-it-wrong disbelief.

"I like men," I say. "Can't help it. You all naked and all just got me too horny. Usually, I'm not so hard that I can't maneuver. Just give me a few minutes, no movement, and chances are good I'll soften up enough to squeeze right on through."

He grabs the back of my pants and gives a hearty tug that might well have dislodged me if I hadn't been prepared for it. The first guy who tried that maneuver, and caught me unaware, greeted me with his face all red from indignation and not from his expended effort to haul me free. "Get yourself help," was what that prick told me. "Trust in Jesus!"

To counter Bobby's attempts, I'd merely levered in both arms to keep me tightly where I am.

"Pulling me in half isn't likely to get the top part of me unstuck," I tell him.

"Sorry," he says.

"It's just a matter of time," I say. "You ever seen a boner that lasts forever?"

"Some of mine," he says with a nervous laugh.

"Just give me a few minutes," I reassure.

"You say this happened once before?"

"Actually, my boner occurred on several occasions. Genuinely takes a mean stiffy, though, to provide the extra bulk to cause this kind of predicament. You shouldn't be so damned sexy." Clever me to blame all of this on him.

"How long before you went soft the last time?"

"About fifteen minutes, but those were extenuating circumstances. Probably, you should count on being here a bit longer than that."

"What kind of extenuating circumstances?"

"Turned out the guy on your end was gay. Took advantage and fucked me up the ass. I got so excited, I blew my wad in no time. Ever know a cock to stay hard after it spits its goo?"

"Only mine."

Talk about raging teenage hormones.

"Aren't queer, by any chance, are you?" I venture.

"I've a girl friend, thank-you very much."

"Any chance, then, that your bi?"

"Where in the hell would I get the dope to get high in this place?"

Once again, blame those good but not perfect acoustics.

"Bi, not high," I provide clarification.

"Buy what?"

"Bisexual."

"Nice try, but no."

"Never wanted to give it a try?"

"When I've a girl friend with a cunt? No way!"

"A cunt may be a cunt may be a cunt, but it sure ain't male asshole, buddy, I can tell you that much."

"Anyone ever tell you that you are one sick doggie?"

"Not as many guys as you may think. For whatever the reason, a whole lot of guys of your generation are usually quite liberal and understanding about this sort of thing."

No need to mention the few genuinely uptight young studs who genuinely freaked out even before this stage of the game. Luckily, for me, my ass in their face never presented them with much of a target upon which to vent their frustrations, and they calmed down before I came unstuck enough to allow them their freedom.

"I thought you said this only happened once before," he says. Don't anyone call him stupid. "So, what's all this shit about a whole lot of my generation being liberal and understanding?"

"So, maybe, there were two or three other times I failed to mention."

"You're so full of bullshit, you're sure it's not that overload that's got you stuck in there?"

"If you could see the size of this boner you've given me, you'd have your answer."

"How about if I have an alternative?"

"Alternative?"

"Like I pull down your pants, not to fuck your ass, but to give it a few hearty whacks with the flat of my hand."

"You ever hear of pain as an aphrodisiac?"

"At this point, I don't give a damn about your sore back."

"Nothing to do with a sore back, buddy," I say loudly. "Aphro...disiac! Sexual stimulant. Major turn-on. You ever hear of b&d?"

"I thought you just peed a few minutes ago."

"Look, kid. Picture this girl friend of yours in black panties and black bra, black silk stockings, black garter belt, black spike heels, whacking your bare ass with a riding crop. You think that's going to give you a softy?"

"I'm not wearing black panties or black bra, or black silk stockings, black garter belt, or black spike heels."

"You're wearing flannel shirt, camouflage pants, hiking boots. For me, that's even more sexy. Granted, not as sexy as you wearing nothing at all, but ...."

"I figure I'll just hit you extra hard. Your cock getting the message, good and fast, that we're not playing sexual games here."

Even I suspect there might just be a degree of butt whacking that would overstep the boundaries of pleasure, but I hate to think this clever fuck is going to weasel out of this one.

"My old man used to go that route, when I was merely a snot-nosed kid," I lie. "He used to really lay on a razor strap. You know what that is, kid, reminding me, as you do, of someone who wouldn't know a straight razor if it jumped up and cut you on the ass?"

"I know what a razor strap is."

"All it did was give me a boner when other kids my age didn't even know that the thing they had between their legs was good for anything other than pissing."

"Let's give it at try, anyway. What do you say?"

"Look, kid, you a sadist? That it? You get turned on by swatting vulnerable guy's buttocks?"

"I'm just a guy suddenly anxious to get out of here, who sees paddling your ass as probably quicker than waiting for you to go soft on your own, or my risking screwing you soft without a rubber."

"Who says you'd be doing any screwing without a rubber? You think I'd risk your naked cock up my behind?"

"No matter, I suppose, that I never thought to bring one, no notion whatsoever of rubberizing a stalagmite on which to sit down on?"

"I've rubbers in my back pocket."

"Why, I wonder, doesn't that surprise me?"

"Just rubberize that dick of yours, fuck us both to rip-roaring climax, and we'll be out of here in no time."

"Thanks for the offer, but I think I'll pass."

After which, there's a good ten minutes of silence.

"Your dick any softer?" he asks finally.

"Can I help it that I can't seem to get out of my mind the thought of you spanking my naked ass."

"Jesus!" he says.

Another five minutes of silence.

"Someone is going to come looking for us, right?" he says. "Eventually, I mean."

"Sure," I say. "My cousin stops by every evening after he gets off work. He'll come checking to see if anything is wrong. Except, no way he takes hold and pulls me on through from his end."

"I can't fucking believe this!" he says. "Trapped by a giant cock."

"Be encouraged with tales of how I'm bound to go soft in old age."

"Come on, asshole," he says and takes hold my of my back pockets for another couple giant tugs. "You can't really be stuffed in there as completely as you say!"

Isn't he surprised, though, when I very well make it appear as if that very well is the case?

"Fuck!" he says, giving up. I'm glad he's stopped, because my arms are skinned raw from my efforts to keep me positioned right where I am.

"You haven't even wondered what it's like having your cock fucked up another guy's butt?" I ask. "Hell, I know straight guys who wonder all the time but who never get the opportunity to find out. Here you are with my ass served up for you on a silver platter. Not only can you find out, once and for all, if male ass isn't for you, but you can do us both the favor of finding out in a way that gets us out of here in time for supper."

"I'm not about to fuck your ass."

"How about playing doctor, then? Your finger might do the trick."

"You saying I should put my finger up your asshole?"

"It's not like doctors don't do it every day. Straight doctors, I might very well add. Straight doctors who don't consider themselves queer afterwards, either. For that matter, didn't Freud say that every man experiences a bit of same-sex experimentation in his life time?"

"He was talking about slap-ass locker-room shit and, maybe, a couple of circle jerks," he says. "I'm way passed those kiddy things now."

"You must have enjoyed them at one time, though," I say. "The good times you've had slapping ass in the locker-room what makes you so hot, now, to drop my pants and start with a hearty laying on of hands?"

"Considering your present vulnerable position," he says, "you might consider not getting me any more ticked off at you than I already am."

I begin to wonder if a bit of ass-warming, under his large and skillful hands, would be all that bad, after all. It isn't as if I can't come unglued quickly enough if he genuinely gets carried away.

"Okay, you want to pound on my ass for my confessing I find you boner-making sexy, go ahead. Maybe it'll work. Not exactly the way I would prefer it, but you're obviously anxious to be on your way, and I seem unable to accommodate you, any other way, at least for the moment.

"I can't believe you still have a boner."

"Feel free to try and cop a feel, via any route at your disposal."

"This is so fucking unbelievable!"

Another moment of silence, and he's back tugging my trousers.

"I think you're going to have to cut them off," I say.

"Your balls? Think I can get to them from here?"

"My pants. Whether you want my ass bare for whacking or for fucking."

"Who says I need your ass bare?" he says and delivers a couple of loud whacks with the flat of one hand.

"Jesus!" we both say in unison.

"That stings!" he says, and I have to agree.

None of which stops him from doing the exact same thing all over again.

"Now, that you've worked up a boner yourself, you sadistic shit," I say, "maybe you'll have second thoughts as to the good use to which you can put it."

"I think I'll use all this extra time for another swim."

"Wrong thing to say, stud," I say. "My mind just flashed yet another boner-producing vision of sexy and naked you in the pool. Making my cock -- well, not even I believe it possible -- even harder."

"What a crock of shit!"

"Crock rhymes with cock. Nothing better than cock for packing shit."

"Get your mind off sex, why don't you?"

"It's not as if I'm not trying."

"Try multiplication tables, or something."

"That works for you, does it, when you're socking it to pussy?"

"Some times it does, yeah."

"One times one is one. One times two is two. One times three is.... Doesn't seem to be working, buddy."

"Such a fucking queer!"

"Speaking of fucking queer."

"Oh, for Christ's sake, do shut up!"

He gives my ass another hearty whack which does nothing whatsoever to soften my dick, everything to stiffen it firmer.

A mere few seconds later, he's changed from whacking my butt to pinching it. I'm likely to end up, from this one, with a pretty well bruised ass.

However, it's a sudden waft of cooler-than-usual air on my ass that tells me he's merely pinched up enough material from the seat of my pants to cut through it with his knife.

"Better make sure the hole is a big one if you expect enough room for your big cock to slide on through," I say. "Even if your cock doesn't get any bigger hard than it is when eight-inch flaccid."

"Don't get your hopes up, stud," he says. "We're talking just my finger here, and I've yet to decide if even it's going to make the trip."

"Be daring," I tell him. "Be adventurous. Risk a bit of sexual adventure away from your usually pussy-dominated existence."

"So, do I drape my finger with a lubricated rubber, or what?"

"Ever hear of spit?"

"Maybe we just better wait."

"Up to you. Can't figure out a way to make you do otherwise, or I would have used it by now to prod you to prodding."

"How could you want my finger up your ass, let alone my dick up there?"

"Easy, kid. Easy."

He may not be convinced, even as regards his venturing a finger-fuck inside me, but I can tell he's down for a closer look at the breach he's cut into the seat of my pants.

"I'm not made out of glass, kid," I say. "You need to survey the terrain, don't be afraid to do a bit of manhandling."

"Why do I feel the distinct impression you're enjoying this?"

"Could it be because I am enjoying this?"

"And, I had you figured for a really nice guy."

"I am a really nice guy. You can find out just how really nice by losing all your straight he-man inhibitions and dipping your teenage weenie deep between my buns."

What he does is squeeze open my buttocks in search of my pucker.

"Hope your preferences runs toward blond-haired asscrack," I say.

"I'm supposed to find your asshole among all that fur?"

"Use the Braille method, kid, and I'll tell you when. Yeah ... stud ... a little bit more to the right and .... See, it wasn't all that damned hard, was it? Fingertip feels slightly damp, too."

He squirrels his saliva-slicked finger up my butt with such genuine expertise that he's either studied pre-med somewhere, or he's practiced a bit on his own asshole. Like magnet to iron, his finger finds my prostate in nothing flat and screws hard against it.

"Maybe ... just maybe ...." I say and abort with a low grunt.

"Your dick going soft, is it?"

"Maybe this the wrong way to go, kid," I say, "because that does feel mighty damned good."

"Jesus H. Christ!" he says and withdraws his finger so quickly that I swear I hear, even through the insulating stone, the sound of cow's foot pulled from the mud.

"So, why'd you stop?" I ask. "Afraid of how all that discovered tightness will play your hard dick to the kind of orgasm you've yet to find up that barn-big slit that's your girl friend's cunt?"

"I can't believe I just had my finger up your butt!" he says.

"Take it from someone who can believe -- it was, indeed, up there."

"Smells like shit," he says disgustedly.

"Granted, probably not as aromatic as what perfumes your butt, but what were you expecting? From another standpoint, what are you sniffing it for, anyway?"

"I didn't have to sniff it," he says. "The stink fills the Grotto."

"Okay," I give him that much. "Which leaves us where exactly?"

"It leaves us no farther than my finger having been up your asshole, so don't even begin to think otherwise."

"So, you're scared, kid. I understand that. It's probably hard to resist the temptation to fuck my butt now that you've experienced just how snug the fit of it is likely to be bunned around your hot-dog."

"What scares me is that I'm going to be stuck in here forever, with you out to talk my cock up your butt."

"Going to take more than talk to get it there, kid."

"You can damned well say that again."

"Going to take more than talk to get it there, kid," I repeat.

"Funny!" He makes it sound anything but.

"Will you tell me one thing, kid?"

"Like what?"

"No kidding me, now, kid. Okay?"

"You my Father-Confessor, offering deathbed absolution, or what?"

"Your dick even the least bit hard?"

"My dick ... hard? Let's focus on your hard dick, which is the cause of this farce."

"It's just that I do know how tight my asshole is. I do know that kids your age still haven't lost their yen for experimentation and exploration. Hell, it's that very quality that has you here, in this cave complex, isn't it? What a temptation it must be for you now to explore an even deeper, tighter hole than the Green Grotto. Forbidden territory, even, that must seem all the more enticing because of all the taboo, no-no, and don't-touch signs nailed up at the very door."

"I'm not seeing any signs hung on your ass, except the one that says 'Welcome!'"

"So, come on, kid. I'll bet you another swim in the Green Grotto that you'll enjoy."

"I'm not queer," he says. Sooner or later, that's usually what all the I'm-straights say.

"But not so straight that one fuck of one male asshole will turn you forever queer, surely? Amazing!"

"Fuck you and your asshole."

"Okay, I'm game if you finally are."

A long pause.

"You aren't really stuck in there at all, are you?" he says.

"I sure as hell feel stuck," I say. "Can't deny, though, that I'd much appreciate being firmly stuck on your stiff dick as well."

"My finger-fuck didn't make your cock go soft, that's quite apparent. I'm to believe, though, that my sexy dick is going to do the trick?"

"Your finger might yet do the trick, eventually, if you leave it up my asshole long enough. However, I guarantee your cock up my butt, for just a few minutes, will perform the miracle. You ever met a guy, before me, who can cream with just the run of hard cock up his asshole?"

"I haven't gone around asking."

"I'm telling you without your asking. Promising it'll happen, in fact, if it's your cock up my asshole."

"Bullshit!"

"No, kid, I can tell. I can spot those magic cocks, like yours, from a mile away."

"You can cream with just cock up your butt?"

"Not just any cock."

"You can cream with just my cock up your butt?"

"You do know just how sexy the package: you and your cock?"

"Nothing to do with how you'd probably be fucking your cock between your belly and the rock, at one and the same time?"

"Not a thing. Besides, just how much movement do you think I can manage, socked in here as I am?"

"If I were queer, I'd probably say yes in a minute."

"But you're not gay?"

"I'm not gay."

"So, it's going to take a bit more time for you to say yes?"

"I'm not likely to say yes, am I?"

"Does 'not likely' constitute a definite, honest-to-goodness, one-hundred-percent 'No!'?"

"I'll bet you're one of those loud-mouthed queers who would have it broadcast all over the place before I even pulled my cock out."

"Even assuming that's true, how many mutual friends do we have? Not that many, I'd say. You having the added advantage of a girl friend ready to swear on a stack of Bibles that you put cock to her pussy, on a regular basis, and, therefore, don't need some guy's asshole for getting off."

Goddamn, I'm good at this!

"I don't believe, for a minute, you really have rubbers in your back ..."

"See!" I know he's found them.

"You saw this coming."

"Wanted to see you coming. Would like to feel you coming. What's the big deal anyway? A kid your age always has plenty of hard cock and gallons of cum to spare."

"I'll bet you could pop right out of there if you wanted."

"You wouldn't say that if you knew just how tightly my hard boner has me wedged into this stone doughnut hole."

Is studly, oh-so-straight Bobby going to take the bait? I don't know. Is there any take-a-risk teenager, anywhere, who can turn down the temptation to just see what the big deal is about cock up another guy's butt? Answer: Yes, there are, indeed, a few just such uptight young dudes, usually, I suspect, deep closet cases who are so afraid of their own possible homosexuality that they're afraid to risk even the slightest chance of full conversion by and to it.

"Damn, my dick is hard!" he says but doesn't sound nearly as pleased as I am to hear it.

"There, now, that wasn't so hard to admit, was it?"

"Just how many cocks you had up there before mine?"

Does he realize he's just insinuated his cock is about to make the trip?

"Not so many that you won't think you're fucking virgin asshole."

"I can't believe I'm even thinking of doing this, especially since I don't believe for a moment you're really stuck in that hole and need me to fuck you out of it."

"How boring life would be without a few uncertainties."

I've sure as hell got that right, all right.

"My fucking some guy's ass!" he says. "My girl friend would have a heart attack. My father would turn over in his grave. My mother would shit bricks and build a house around me. My priest would be sure I was destined for hell."

"Your priest is probably just as hot for your dick as I am."

"Right!" he says but doesn't sound convinced. "Trouble is, he's a damned ugly sonofabitch."

"And if he were young and good-looking?"

"I never once thought of fucking male ass, priest's or otherwise, until you came along and so conveniently presented yours."

"Never?"

"Never -- seriously -- considered it."

"Then, you are -- seriously -- considering fucking my ass, now?"

"You know how hard my cock is right now? So hard that if you'd pop on through that hole, right here and now, I'd probably get stuck trying to follow you on through."

"That is hard, buddy," I say. "I'm flattered. I'm disappointed that I can't get turned around to see it. I figure, though, I can make do with the feel of it up my butt. Want to take the few seconds to get your rubberized penis thrust from its pulpy cockhead to your big balls? You do have that cock of yours rubberized by now, don't you?"

Pause.

"Come on, Bobby. What's the big deal to merely saying, 'Yes'?"

"Yes."

"See there." I swallow, because my throat is dry and my cock is wet from all the leaking it's been doing into its silk-sock lined cocoon. "We've covered every lead-in, all that's required now is that you put your prick on target and send it all the way home."

Pause.

"Bobby?"

"I haven't gone anywhere."

"Time for you to go forward into my asshole."

"Oh, hell!"

He fumbles with the knife-slice in the ass of my pants. I feel his cock poke every which way along the crease of my asscrack.

"Easy kid," I say. "I'm not going anywhere. My asshole can be found simply enough, if you just take your time. Remember where your finger has been and put your cock right to that place. Down just a bit. Just a bit farther. Just a ... see ... ah, yes ... there."

"Jesus, fuck," he says, making it sound just as hard as it probably is for a heretofore perfectly straight young man to realize he has embarked upon a journey that he's never really intended to take -- at least not without a helluva lot more forethought.

"You can do it, one of two ways," I say. "Push in slow and easy, enjoying each and every sensuous inch as it slips inside of me. Or, if you're genuinely paranoid you'll change your mind, halfway through, you can just go ahead and feed my ass all you've got in one mighty heave."

"And split your asshole from your backbone to your balls?" Straight guys, with big cocks, have long been brainwashed by women who moan and groan that cocks are simply toooooooo big, need to go soooooo slow, lest they damage sensitive pussy. Bobby sees a small asspucker, like mine, finger-fucks its tightness, and he's suddenly convinced he's hung way too large for me to survive him.

"I'll take a chance, whichever way you want to go," I say. I wonder if he's one of those guys I'm going to have to remind that any asshole, if he'll just use a bit of logic, can be assumed to have shat turds as big as submarines, so that it would have to be an exceptionally big cock to ... "Ohhhhhhhhh!"

At least two good inches of his hard cock take me by surprise. He hears my response and just as quickly pulls completely free.

"Jesus," he says. "I knew it, I knew it."

"A guy can't give a groan in pleasure, Bobby?" I say, frustrated as hell in his having fed me a piece of his dick only to have so quickly withdrawn it. "You want I should try my best to make this a silent screw?"

"I didn't hurt you?" he sounds amazed.

"You'll know when and if you truly hurt me, kid. You telling me your girl friend doesn't moan and groan with pleasure every time you stick her with your dick?"

"She's not all that into fucking."

"That's because all women resent not having a choice," I say. Oh, they have the choice of saying fuck me or don't fuck me, but if it's a fuck me, they're always on the receiving end. Unless, of course, they go the dildo route. We guys, on the other hand, can give or take. Having that option, I can truthfully tell you that I genuinely enjoy receiving a thorough fucking of my asshole."

I want his goddamned cock so badly that I'm tempted to come unstuck from the stone hole, bowl the sexy bastard over in surprise, and sit down over his stiff dick before he has a chance to realize what's hit him. I'm kept from it only by the encouragement I receive from his cockhead returned to my asscrack for hopefully another go at my pucker.

Having learned from his past attempts how to position his cockhead to the entrance of my rectum, he manages placement, this time, far more easily. Less shy about it, too. Probably figuring a fuck of male ass is his to be blamed for, whether he's put in a mere two inches of his cock (quickly withdrawn), or goes all of the way, with accompanying strokes to orgasm, he gives me his all.

"Yes!" I say and grunt, wanting there to be no mistaking that he's provided me cock inches with which I can deal. "Yes ... yes ... fucking ... yes."

"Oh, sweet God!" he says.

I've known grown men to cry real tears their first shove of hard cock up another man's asshole. Maybe it's because they know they've stepped over some invisible line, and there's no turning back. More likely, it's from the pure pleasure, better than any yet known, that they feel flooding them with an intensity sure to prove addictive.

"Grind your dick home, buddy," I say, his cock so far up my ass that its pressure against my prostate genuinely has my cock thrust to additional hardness.

"Fuck, oh, fuck, oh fuck," he chants.

The disadvantage for me, of course, is that I'm like the proverbial ostrich, his head in the sand, being fucked up the butt without being able to enjoy the picture it presents. Although, my mind's-eye view is just great, by way of conjuring the way Bobby's belly flattens my ass ... his balls still hanging low but elevating quickly ... his hands flattened against the stone just above the crawl space ... his legs wide-spaced, his feet firmly planted. His cheek, too, against the cold stone. His mouth providing a slight drool of saliva to match the drool of preseminal juice which his dick simultaneously provides the interior of his rubber up my butt.

Even I'm surprised by just how good his cock feels inside me. I'm convinced that Bobby's inadvertent incorporation of ass-beating, in prelude to the eventual passage of his cock up my anus, has somehow made my pleasure more intense than any I can remember. Then again, maybe my good time is just because this kid, out of all the visitors to Robinson Hole, is the most handsome, the most studly, the most perfect. Whatever, I'm determined to figure out how to persuade all who come after Bobby that they should serve me up a few butt-smacks before their thorough cock-fucking of my ass.

Give the kid credit, he knows enough about the mechanics of screwing to know male asshole may not look like cunt, may not be cunt, but needs treating pretty much like cunt. Mere cock up asshole not nearly enough. A bit of vigorous movement required, Bobby quickly into the first slide-out to his cockhead, quickly followed by another slide-in.

"Got it right, stud," I say. "Drilling required. Skewering necessitated. Pistoning wanted ... relished ... enjoyed."

Bobby the best kind of butt-fucker. In that, he could have been straight as a stick, since Day One, but once he's decided to try the male-male thing, he goes about it whole hog. No holding back. So quick to get the hang of things that he might well have been fucking his buddies' assholes since he'd been old enough to come.

Marvellous -- the rhythm his fucking cock achieves in its in-and-out butt pumps. No in-stroke or out-stroke the same as the one before it, varied each time, however slightly. His probing pecker always seeming to know right where my prostate is, battering it, each and every time, as thoroughly as any boxer's glove pommeling punching bag.

Oh, his lucky, lucky girl friend, to have such a natural humping her bones on a regular basis. Silly, silly-assed girl friend for ever pretending she doesn't enjoy this kid's cock inside her. No way do I believe, not for a second, that this broad of his, whomever she is, wherever she is, doesn't enjoy all of this as much as I do. Her problem, and it is a problem, being that she carries around all of the whole female baggage thing about how it's the male of the species who's the more hedonistically sexual.

"Ohhhhh," I say, his belly pounding my ass, his cock in its continuously speedy slide from its balls to its cockhead, then back again.

No one fucks as exuberantly as a young kid fucking his first male ass. If an older man, with more experience, fucks with more finesse, finesse is sometimes overrated. Especially when, for me, a good deal of my turn-on occurs during leads-in, when it sometimes hangs in the balance as to whether or not I'm going to get what I want, no matter how hard I work for it.

Except, the lead-in that's got Bobby's sexy teenage truncheon fucking my butt, combined with just how stunning a looker the kid is, and how good he is at doing what he's doing, does make his fucking of my asshole genuinely better than those that have come before him. There's just something about the way I'd been so keyed for my asshole to get his dick, then to get it, then to lose it, now to have it tightly packing my shit, that really has me flying.

"Fuck my ass ... ass. Fuck ... my ... ass ... ass!" I say, as if he may yet change his mind and pull out before climax.

"Fuck it, fuck it, fuck it!" he chants, and his sped-up fuck strokes reassures me that his cock isn't going anywhere, except in and out, in and out, until this studly young kid fucks himself into cum-blasting eruption.

Final announcement of his blast-off occurs when he punches his cock up my rectum to his balls, in one butt-whacking thrust that pins, then locks, his love muscle deeply inside of me.

"I'm coming!" he says and, without farther fanfare, proceeds to do just that.

The nippled tip of his rubber goes water-balloon big up my butt, and the pressure of its expansion against my prostate, as his cock spits even more of his steamy teenybopper load, has me high enough to leave the Earth's atmosphere.

His deluge is as profuse, as hot, and as forceful as I expect from such a virile, young, attractive stud, whose cum-producing possibilities are at the max. His pulsing erection floods enough spunk to fill my asshole to peak capacity.

When he's finally over and done, he pulls his cock out slowly. Whereupon, I play snake and begin the slow wiggle that takes my fuck-exhausted body on through the crawl space to the other side. I spill out onto the floor, where the tunnel again widens, and I just lie there, back to the ground, a good view of the stalactite-phallic ceiling. I breathe hard.

Bobby follows me on through, stands over me, his exploded cock back behind the closed zipper of his pants.

"You really get off with just my cock up your ass, or was all of that nothing but a crock of shit?" he asks.

I unfasten my fly, I fish through the breach and bring out my still sock-sheathed prick.

"Looks like you've got your packet bundled up for Alaska," he says.

"It's mighty tight inside that rock slot," I say, "and I get pretty excited. All this cushioning merely protection for my dick. As for whether or not

I came while you fucked me ..."

I unhook the cockring from beneath my balls and thread my softening dick back on through. My penis emerges soaked and sloppy with my slimy discharge.

"What's all this evidence tell you, Sherlock?" I say and turn the cock-sock partially inside-out so he can see the spiderwebbing of cum my cock leaves behind it.

"Every gay able to manage that kind of come?" he asks.

"I don't know about every gay," I say. "I do know, though, that it's hard to know what you can, or can't do, with a hard cock rammed up your ass, if you're never adventuresome enough to let yourself be fucked by one."

"How about if I come back?" he says. "You and I both into the Green Grotto when you don't have a cold coming on, or an asthma attack in the offing, or whatever other excuse you may have for not striping down to join me for a swim? You cavorting in and out of the water ... maybe all I'll need to get my dick all hard and ready for a protective cock-sock. Me through the crawl space ahead of you ... maybe to get stuck. Me possibly the one needing a bit of an assist -- from you, no maybe about it."

"How about this Tuesday?" I say. "I can put a closed sign on the access drive, and we can spend the whole day down here, doing all sorts of exploration."

"And I'll maybe hang an 'Open for Business' sign on my ass," he ventures speculatively.

"Sounds great to me," I readily assure him.

He shakes his head. I'm disappointed, because I figure he's changed his mind, when I see him as someone with such exciting stud-fucking possibilities. As it turns out, though, his head apparently shakes in amazement, more than in denial.

"I can't believe I'm actually coming back for seconds," he says.

"Didn't our advertising promise you wonders beyond belief in the fabulous Robinson Hole, Wyoming?" I say and vise my cockroots, beneath my balls, milking upward through my scrotum and along my cock to ooze one final bit of tardy cum into an enticing, inviting, icing for my looking-forward-to-his-return penile cake.

COUNTERFEIT COWBOYS

Leather dark with horse sweat and man sweat.
Straw yellow with cow piss and cow shit.
Hay ripe within the heated barn.
Fear.
The smells.

Horses nervous in their stalls.
Cows lowing in their pastures.
Spurs wind-chiming on scuffed boots.
Breathing erratic with ...
Fear.
The sounds.

Spit stale and tepid.
Blood heavily salted.
Snot sniffed through an unblown nose.
Fear.
The tastes.

The smells, the sounds, the tastes, all come to eighteen-year-old Brad Waynewright III through a blackness that magnifies them. A blackness that, likewise, magnifies his ...
Fear.
And, the blackness remains until his blindfold is ripped away.
Seeing gives substance to his fear, letting it form a tangible knot in his guts that ropes his young but large balls and squeezes them to aching. Seeing gives substance to things previously sensed: leather, straw, hay, spurs, boots and ...
The man: Roger. The cowboy who isn't cow -- or boy. Standing, looking down, a permanent smirk on a face that would be right at home in a Marlboro cigarette ad. Handsome. Jesus, handsome! With blue-

black hair beneath the black (Stetson?) cowboy hat.

Roger. With black eyes beneath black brows. With dimple in right cheek, even when he doesn't smile. He isn't smiling now.

Square jawline

Cleft chin. How does he shave inside that deep crevice?

His body poured into tight-fitting clothes that accentuate a superb physique. From riding fences? Bulldogging cattle? Pitching hay?

Rectangular pectorals. Round nipples, taut and pressing hard against the pale blue chamois of his work shirt.

Stomach washboarded, although unseen.

His belt, thick, hand-tooled black leather, fastens with a buckle showing a gold stallion rearing against a silver backdrop. "Colt Firearms": the raised inscription. On the back, an engraved signature, "Sam Colt, " and the warning, "BEWARE OF COUNTERFEITS."

Not designer jeans. He won't be caught dead in Calvin Kleins. His are Levi's, an identifying cloth tab sewn on one back pocket to prove it. The crotch buttons over a cock that would be equally at home on a stud with four legs instead of two.

"I used to fuck horses," he says. It's easy to believe him. How many four-legged stallions has he pleasured, spewing hot, steamy spunk up clutching animal orifices? No thoroughbred colts issuing from those unions! In ancient Greece, he would have fathered centaurs. "Now, I fuck young men."

Boots. Tony Lamas? Justin? Larry Mahan? Black like the hat, like the belt, like the curly hair visible at the vee formed by the open collar of his shirt.

Spurs. Gold ones. Wicked with star-burst rowels.

Brad knows he's going to get fucked by this cowboy and is afraid, never having been fucked before ... while tied ... after being beaten. Never by a cock as big as this cock.

He shudders, intuitively knowing the still-concealed erection in Roger's pants is as big as it looks. Not counterfeit. Nine inches of the real thing. Thick and meaty. Heavily veined. A "leaker" that has sopped cupping elastic jocksock with preseminal discharge.

"No," Brad says, wanting, yet not wanting. His voice sounds strange to his ears. The gag, now gone, has left his lips and tongue numbed to the point where they can't form words correctly. It's like he's been to the dentist, his mouth shot full of Novocain.

"I ride for a living," Roger says. "I'm a pro. You won't get ridden by better."

In emphasis, his right hand drops to his crotch, his large fingers and thumb parenthesizing his cock to more powerful advantage. He bounces rhythmically on the balls of his booted feet.

Brad's mind rushes to fill the gaps that'll give how and why to his being here.

He'd been hitchhiking across country: New York, Pennsylvania, Ohio, Indiana, Illinois, Iowa, South Dakota, Montana. He'd been heading for Washington. He has friends there.

"You must be out of your mind, hitchhiking in this day and age!" Who would have told him that? His mother? His brother? The queer who gave him a lift and a blow-job outside Newton, Iowa?

He'd grown short of cash just west of Billings, or maybe Great Falls. Anyway, somewhere on the Yellowstone River, since he had always wanted to see Yellowstone Park. He'd figured, yes?, that if he made a little extra, hiring out as a ranch hand, he might detour through the Park before heading on to Washington.

What did he know about ranching? Nothing! He's a city boy, born and bred in asphalt jungles. Two ranchers told him they couldn't take the time to train a transient greenhorn. Too busy at that time of the year?

Roger hired him, though, even after getting Brad to admit he'd never worked a ranch before.

"You look as if you've got a body capable of standing up beneath a little manual labor." That was something Roger would say.

Brad should have been suspicious, warned off by the ease with which Roger had taken him on when everybody else had been so reluctant. But, Roger had needed the money. And, the job had made him feel good. He had always been physically oriented. In the city, it was weight-lifting at a local gym and jogging. In Montana, it was chopping wood, riding horses, digging holes for fence posts, repairing the roof of he barn. This very barn in which he is now tied, helplessly waiting to be fucked.

His body shows the results of his past and present workouts. It is in good condition. It is "tight".

"I'll bet your teenage asshole is one tight motherfucker!" Roger says, his fingers starting to unbutton his trouser crotch, his eyes taking in the interesting groupings of muscles caused by the way Brad is tied.

Yeah, Roger is thinking, this stud does look good. Looks real good!

Brad's hair blond. Thick, cut short at the sides but long enough on top to bang in an attractive leftward sweeping over his forehead. Not really much hair on either his chest or belly, but a curling vee of it at his crotch. More on his balls, growing down beneath his powerful legs and up into the crease of his highly muscled young ass.

Roger likes his men young and blond. Young offers vigor and virility. Blond offers an exotic contrast to Roger's own naturally dark complexion.

Roger likes his young men studly. There is nothing more erotic than muscle straining against muscle. Not like sex with a woman, where he is made lethargic by softness. Since his first man, he has never fucked another woman, considers the time wasted that he took to fuck any cunt he'd ever deigned screw.

He is looking forward to fucking Brad. Not just because of Brad's youth, blond hair, and exquisitely chiselled physique, either. There is Brad's masculine, attractive face. There is Brad's pair of enormous balls. There is Brad's large and impressive teenage cock, even if that cock is presently soft. Roger is confident he will soon have that cock hard. He knows intuitively, whether Brad does or not, that his supposed victim is going to take to this scene like a cow to winter fodder.

"Get on your knees, stud," Roger instructs. His right hand is lost within the open crotch of his pants. His fingers are prying at his cock, simultaneously peeling away a soaked jocksock to secure it beneath his hairy balls. His cock comes out, followed by his scrotum, the former jutting straight up, the latter waterfalling over the lower vee of his fly.

"And if I don't?" Brad asks.

Roger only smiles. It's a smile devoid of humor, reminding Brad that his earlier beating might well be repeated.

Brad comes to his knees, his ankles tied, his hands secured behind his back.

"Now, crawl over here, you sonofabitch, and wet down this cock of mine!" Roger commands. His right hand is stroking his cock, milking for clear, pre-sex juices that bead momentarily in the cupping cockmouth before overflowing.

The prick is more than a handful, Roger's large fingers barely able to wrap it. It has been circumcised, the resulting scar well healed to nonexistence. The cock looks as if it has always been the streamlined missile it now is.

Roger fingers his balls, tugging on scrotal flesh that, black with hair, is contracting around his two large nuts.

"Come on over here, stud," Roger says. "I don't plan to make that request a third time."

Brad crawls, his flaccid cock swinging back and forth like the trunk on a bull elephant. It strikes first his left thigh, then his right, and then repeats again for as long as he is on the move. The battering makes the cock elongate, pushing pink meaty tip almost beyond the protective darker cowl of his foreskin.

His arms hurt at his shoulders, his wrists and ankles chafing on the ropes that bind them. His knees, though, move across a convenient cushioning of straw and hay.

Roger reaches out both hands, his fingers cupping the back of Brad's head, simultaneously pulling forward. In an accompanying forward swing of his hips, he brings his upjutting hard cock to Brad's face.

"Kiss horse cock, cocksucker!" he commands.

Brad kisses the warm, hard erection, disturbingly excited by the feel of it as he wets it with his tongue. Such pleasure seems somehow perverse. He, after all, isn't here willingly. Is he?

Roger had called him into the barn and had then jumped him from behind. The two had wrestled, it taking long moments for Brad to realize the scuffle was for real and not tomfoolery. What had convinced him could be a split lower lip that flooded his mouth with blood.

"My horse cock wants a blow-job, slave," Roger says, giving another grind of his cock into Brad's face. "And, you're going to play toothless calf to this studly farm boy's hard prick."

He pulls back his hips, using his left hand to lower his cock into fucking position. Meaty cockhead glosses Brad's lips with sticky liquid that tastes vaguely of salt, reminding of blood.

"Open ... open," Roger says, his right hand pulling Brad's face forward as he watches his cock disappear faster ... faster ... into the warmth Brad's open mouth has offered it. "Oh, Jesus, yes, yes. Yes. Jesus, yes!"

Brad can't breathe. What with the cock in his throat, there seems room for little else, certainly not for air. He tries to pull his face free, but Roger won't let him.

"I haven't choked a slave to death, yet," Roger assures, a sudden bucking of his hips making Brad's throat raw with an additional insertion.

Brad gasps, his mouth pried so far open that his jaws ache. His lips are pressed so tightly against his teeth that they are bitten, releasing more salty flavors to dissolve in wet-warm spit. He thinks he's going to black out. He commences a reflexive gag.

Ride your face over my cowboy cock!" Roger grunts, accompanying with a hearty series of partial thrusts and withdrawals. On the final withdrawal, he pulls his cock completely free of Brad's gasping, fucked face.

His massively thick cock, soaked with spit, slaps back, its head splattering juice on a golden horse reared against a silver backdrop of belt buckle.

"I hope to God you're a better fuck," Roger says. He raises his right foot, putting his boot to Brad's chest, toppling Brad backwards.

"Jeeeeezus!" Brad squeals. He has landed on wrists which are crossed and tied behind him.

"You'll be more comfortable on your belly," Roger tells him, the toe of one boot insisting that Brad perform the necessary roll.

Rowels on gold spurs produce faint jingling.

"Nice ass," Roger says. His hands go to his belt buckle, unfastening the metal hook that, jutting just to the right of Sam Colt's signature, has dug neatly into one belt hole. The buckle comes free. The belt exits denim waist loops with an audible sigh.

There is a loud crack of leather connecting with Brad's sweaty ass.

"Ohhhhh!" Brad groans in surprised pain.

Beneath Brad's belly, his cock swells larger, his cockhead completely free of a foreskin that's become a turtlenook beneath his coronal flaring. Another lashing of the belt makes his cock go harder, simultaneously letting his asscheeks flush the beginnings of a crisscross design.

"I always whip my studs to show them who's boss," Roger says.

Brad's ass jerks in response to the continued whipping, blushing a deeper pink that soon converts to scarlet. His cock is a stiffness laid out beneath his belly, fucked deeply into the fragrant hay, leaking clear and viscid fluid that can't yet be called cum.

Roger drops the belt to the floor, stepping to straddle Brad's prone body. He squats, his ass resting on the bends at the back of the teenager's knees. His fingers take hold of Brad's asscheeks, his palms feeling the heat generated by the whipped buns. He pushes open the cheeks along their mutually shared crack. He sees blond hair running the length of the anal valley. He sees a light brown pucker haloed by that hair.

He drops his face to the crease, smelling the heady aromas of teenage stud in heat, dissolving those aromas in spit, converting them to exotic tastes on exploring taste buds. His forehead, nose, and chin nuzzle even deeper. His tongue licks, rolls, and then darts inside Brad's asshole to sample whatever flavors have been kept from him by the kid's guarding sphincteral ring.

"Noooooo!" Brad moans, helplessly brought to the point of enjoying this fuck by tongue, wondering when he's destined to enjoy a fuck by the bigger (and better?) cock.

Roger feasts, despite Brad's verbal protests, eating until deliciousness has been reduced to the blandness of untainted spit. He pulls away a face smeared with saliva and perspiration.

"Ready for a real ride?" he asks, rubberizing his dick and sliding the result along Brad's asscrack like a wiener parenthesized by cupping hot-dog bun. His belly falls over Brad's bound wrists. His chest is snug against Brad's back, going more snug as his hips lift. His cock isn't prepared to lower naturally into a convenient fucking position, it too stiff in its alignment parallel to his belly. So, he uses his right hand to pry it down, his left hand widening the kid's asscrack and pinpointing the pucker for the blunt head of Roger's cock.

"Don't fuck me!" Brad says. But, in truth, he wants to be fucked. Hasn't he always fantasized being fucked by a cowboy? Isn't that what this is all about?

Roger's cockhead is at the opening, poked into the spit his hungry mouth has already leaked there.

Brad gives a startled grunt as Roger's hard cock begins to enter his body. He's being pinned to the floor, and there's no way he can prevent it. He's being dominated, ridden by a cowboy whose jeans are chafing Brad's vulnerable nakedness.

Roger wastes little time in driving his cock home, leaving Brad breathless with pleasure and pain. He grinds his hard belly against Brad's asscheeks, stirring his cock inside the teenager's ravaged asshole.

He moves reflexively, expertly, his hips yanking his cock outward, only to stick cock in again. On each ensuing in-stroke, the black hair on his crotch and balls mingles with the blond hair running Brad's asscrack.

Brad grunts. If he has something coherent to say, he can't manage it. He's too caught up in the fuck, too lost in the exquisite pleasure of his pain. He's only able to grunt, groan, utter breathless, indecipherable sighs.

Roger continues, his body growing sweaty, his chest sticking to Brad's back, his belly sticking to Brad's butt. His cock sticking to Brad's asshole.

Brad's cock fucks the straw beneath his belly. The hay is drenched with his leaked juices. His scrotum is losing its flaccidness, converting to a prune-like consistency. Both of his cum-swollen balls will soon be hoisted to the base of his throbbing erection.

He gasps for breath, a dull aching in the pit of his belly spreading to his chest and throat.

Roger continues pounding his thick inches into Brad's tight asshole, knowing he can't fuck it forever, but wishing he could, nevertheless.

"Screw me, screw me, screw me!" Brad chants, punctuating with loud groans each time his tender prostate is battered mercilessly by Roger's entering man-cock.

There's a definite change taking place inside Brad's body. Pain, once there, is now gone, his butt adjusted to the fat cock fucking it. His body is relaxed, surrendering to the complete luxuriousness of the screw.

"Ride me, cowboy!" he bellows, feeling another surge of pleasure send him bucking into uncontrolled ecstasy.

"Hell, yes, I'll ride you," Roger promises, his whisper guttural in Brad's ear, his cock not missing a stroke while he holds on for dear life. "I'll ride you until my horse cock creams up your studly young butt."

"Yes!" Brad begs, continuing to be battered beneath Roger's riding fuck. "Fill me! Jesus, fill me with cum, cum, your thick and creamy cum!"

And Roger, as if on cue, obliges, his guts blasting. He grunts pleasure, biting Brad's shoulder as he does so.

Brad feels the eruption of the cowboy riding him. He hears loud squeals and quickly joins in the chorus as he experiences his own gut-shattering explosion.

And when it's over and done, Roger's cock makes a lewd noise as it's released from the vacuum formed by Brad's thoroughly fucked asshole. Free of its rubber, Roger's cock trails a snot-like string of cum which Roger pinches free with his thumb and forefinger.

For Roger, this fuck has been an exceptionally good one. They aren't always this way, this being an exception rather than the rule.

He stuffs his cock back into his pants, not too difficult now that his prick is going soft in the aftermath of explosion. He squats slightly in order to unfasten his jocksock from beneath his balls and roll it back to its original cupping of his genitals. That completed, he buttons up, wiping his sticky hands on his denim trousers.

He kneels beside Brad and unties him.

When Brad rolls to his back, massaging chafed wrists, Roger is already disappeared into a surrounding darkness which has become noticeably silent.

Brad crawls the short distance to his discarded clothes and dresses. In Levi's. In Pendleton shirt, open at the collar. In Tony Lamas boots. In Stetson hat.

He finds the exit, pausing before opening the door, reluctant to shatter what's left of the expensive illusion. Finally, though, he opens the door and steps into the hallway beyond.

There are two flights of rickety stairs separating him from the street below.

Outside, the city is just achieving that dull grey glow so often gotten before another colorless dawn.

A fog horn sounds forlornly from somewhere on the East River.

He has parked in a narrow alley between two dilapidated warehouses. His car's expensive upholstery exudes a small of leather.

Nothing helps now, though. Not the smell of leather, nor his Pendleton shirt, nor his Levi's, nor his Tony Lamas boots. The fantasy gone, the reality is another Monday morning. He has to be at his summer job, at the family-run business, in a little over three hours.

He sighs, knowing his summer job is necessary, because his trust fund doesn't kick in until he's twenty-one. Without his job, how could

William Maltese

he rustle the spare change needed to get his ass ridden every weekend by cowboys? Cowboys like Roger, and all the illusion that comes with him, don't' come cheaply in the big city.

Maybe next time, Brad will pretend he's a hardened criminal, finally ridden to the ground by a sexy marshal so frustrated by the skillful chase Brad has given him that the silver-starred cowboy will decide to rape his prisoner's ass before hauling it off to to the slammer.

CALIFORNIA CREAMIN'

In the beginning days of surfing here in the States, when surfing was an official rebellion against a society that was supposedly out to stymie individuality, surfers had some pretty raunchy reputations. I've had some granddaddies of the surf tell me that Joe Q. Public looked upon them as something in the same category as the Hell's Angels or Jack the Ripper. In other words, when the surf was up, proper beach communities locked up their kids for fear they'd be raped by some scruffy and unshaven guy playing Neptune with his single-pronged trident (unident?).

I missed out on those dim beginnings of surfing as a life-style. I came along later, after middle-class America had taken surfing to heart, and it was suddenly an acceptable thing like football, baseball, or any of the other jock sports. As a matter of fact, if you lived by the ocean like I did, then you were usually expected to go out on the waves and excel or be left behind by your peer group. Schools everywhere were rife with their little cliques, and find me one of those schools anywhere near a good surfing area where the surfers didn't claim a pretty high spot in the pecking order.

So, by the time I appeared on the scene with my custom-made Hobie Alter surfboard, through some act of God (or more likely because of all those Beach-Blanket-Whatever movies), everyone and his grandfather looked upon all of us surfers as good, clean, all-American, jock-type kids who probably went through our teens more concerned with boards than broads. Or, if we did notice girls (no one would ever insinuate there were gay surfers anymore than there were gay football players), we always did so in the same chaste way as TV-rerun Frankie Avalon always chased chaste Annette Funicello.

Well, it's time someone let the cat out of the bag. No matter what quality of bullshit has been fed the public, I do know that "hanging ten" is as much the length of the cock hanging between my legs as it is a surfing position. I know all about cock and about where to put it for a good time. And, when the surf isn't up, I also know how to ride other things besides the waves.

I'm not the exception to any rules, either. As a matter of fact, I'm just your typical blond, blue-eyed all-American, butch-next-door surfer. Picture yourself a stereotypical stud-surfer teen, and I'll bet you two-to-one you've got me pretty much down to a tee.

I stand five-feet-eleven. I weigh one-sixty stripped naked and soaking wet. I've well-defined pectorals and a nicely ridged belly. I've a ten-inch, circumcised, rocket-shaped cock, and a large pair of blond-haired nuts. My cock and balls are difficult to hide within brief-cut swim wear, or within a wet suit, but hardly noticeable when I wear the standard surfer boxer-type swimsuit. My ass is firm and tight, inside and out. The only hair on my body is on my head, beneath my arms, around my cock, around each of my dime-size nipples, my brows, my eyelashes, and a line of hair that runs up (or down?) the crease of my ass.

What all of this boils down to is that surfers, myself included, may look like you've always imagined, but they aren't those all-I-need-is-a-good-wave celibates you may possibly have been led to believe. Nor are they exclusively heterosexual, any more than all the big jocks in football and soccer are all that straight. There are gays out there riding the waves just like there are gays playing grab-ass (and grab-other-things), in many of those butch NFL locker rooms. I know. I surf. And, I'm gay. And, I've fucked and been fucked by enough surfers to know that I'm not alone. Let's face it, when you load your boards in the Range Rover and take off for some isolated beach for the weekend, worried parents aren't likely to condescend to your taking along any Carol or Mary-Joe. But, if you share a tent with Carl of Marty-Joe, then what parents gives a fuck?

You think surfers haven't been into gay and straight sex since those once dim beginnings? You think no surfer would ever think of plugging another surfer's butt or mouth?

Sure, there's still that communing with nature that you're always hearing about. Sure, there's still that big thrill of being out there on a wave and knowing nothing but the wind and the water and the slide down the glassy surface. But, surfing has lost some of its original mystical aura, because it's usually no longer a case of just you and the wave and nature. Now, there are those twenty other surfers out there trying to maneuver on that same wave as you are. Somehow, surfing and surfers have been the losers in the adoption of surfing and surfers by the masses. Not that there still aren't loners who live expressly for each new wave. Not that there aren't guys who insist "getting it off" on a wave is a helluva lot better than fucking some guy or some chick. Sure as hell, those aficionados of the sport are still there. It's just that, over the years, they've gone from the majority to the minority.

What you mainly have out there, these days, are guys like me. Not that I'm shooting down my own skill on the board. Because, I'm good. You want to see someone do a good nose-dive, a spinner, a head-dip, a backward-turn, I can show them to you without having to make any excuses for my skill. But most of the guys I know are no longer apt to head out into the water at daybreak and stay there until their skin puckers up like adolescent cock after its first masturbation. There's more to a surfer's life these days than just wind, water, and his surfboard. We may no longer have neighbourhoods locking up their kids, but that's only because the surfers of today are those kids who used to be locked up. The majority of us are no longer loners whose lives (sex included), revolve around making it with one more great wave. We want an occasional good ride, sure. But, when the ride is over, we want something in addition. As I've already mentioned, heading off with a buddy or buddies to a good surfing beach does indeed offer opportunities for a little fooling around among healthy young men.

Take that week Pete Windgate and I went up the coast about a hundred miles to one of the few remaining beaches on either US coast that can still be deserted on occasion, maybe, because it's a day hike to reach. It's known for having point surf; and, its long walling waves are ideal for some pretty long rides.

We arrived in the afternoon, found two other groups, two surfers to each, already there. We spent a couple of hours, jockeying for position on some good sets, and doing a few of the hot-dog maneuvers which are now the "in" thing with my peer group. After which, Pete and I lit up the third of three bonfires and concerned ourselves with roasting on a stick the kind of hot-dog that comes in a package from the corner grocer. Only then did Pete and I retire to the seclusion of our two-man tent in search of each other's stud-wiener.

Pete's cock isn't as long as mine. We once measured his in at a little over seven inches. But, it is admittedly thicker. Even when it's soft, it looks more like a beer can than a penis. It's uncut; but in erection, its foreskin is completely peeled back to reveal one fucking big cockhead complete with deeply sliced meatus. I've had that cock up my butt more than once, and goddamn if it isn't one beautiful buttful! His nuts are big ones, too. They fit the picture I always get when I read about bull-like balls in all those fuck books. His scrotum is covered with a furring of brown hair.

The vee of pubic hair at his crotch is also brown. Which says, better than anything, that he's not the natural blond he otherwise appears. During the time I've known him, he's been various shades of blond, some from bottles, some from peroxide, some from the combination of lemon juice and sunshine which he's taken to using because he likes the streaking effect it gives his full head of hair. He just squirts a bit of lemon juice into the palm of one hand, rubs his hands together, and combs his fingers through his hair. That, with regular doses of sunshine, produces a really attractive effect that so epitomizes the surfer "look" that Pete was on the cover of "Surfers International" just a couple of months ago.

Like me, Pete is pretty hairless, otherwise he might have difficulty keeping chest hair, arm hair, and leg hair the same attractive shades of blond. What additional body hair he does have is of a fine, downy quality that easily bleaches out in just the sunshine, without any need of any other help-alongs.

He has a really nice body. It's the kind of natural physique that provides adequate muscle definition without appearing pumped up in some gym. Slender, rather than bulky Square pectorals across a shallow pectoral cleavage. Dime-size copper nipples. Indented navel that punctuates abdominals that are obviously firm but not so much so as to appear strikingly washboard. Nicely firm legs, too, with surprisingly good calves, considering the latter can often come off too thin on guys, like Pete, who don't at least spend some time working out on the side. Sexy feet, too, if you can believe Talbort Jones who has somewhat of a foot fetish and knows these things. All I can tell is that Pete's toes don't overlap, he doesn't seem to have any noticeable calluses or bunions, and his toenails are always neatly clipped and clean.

Pete and I have had a lot of sex, in the time we've known each other, but we're not lovers. Fuck-buddies would probably be a better way of putting it. We enjoy doing a lot of things together, mainly surfing and sex, but we're not tied to each other by any kind of monogamous strings or jealousies. I guess we're both pretty easy going, in that way, even having gotten down and dirty together in more than one three-way or orgy, without ever begrudging the fun the other was having. It was kind of hard for me when he took up kind of regular with Suzy Peniars, a surfer-groupie girl no less, but that was short-lived, as I knew it would be. Pete likes to think of himself as bi, but I know differently, and no two-week fling of his with some surfer chick is going to prove to me otherwise, not the way this boy likes my dick, mouth, and asshole, as well as most other dicks, mouths, and assholes that come his way.

"I do like your cock," he whispered in that tent, after our afternoon of riding the waves at that isolated beach up the northern California coast. That he hadn't said it any louder than was necessary for me to hear was because of the two other tents, and four other surfers, parked along the beach, several yards away. I'd only seen one of the guys in the other two groups before. Met him while riding the waves in Hawaii. He lives somewhere down around Santa Barbara, and I guessed he was straight. Which meant, his friends were likely straight, too. Best to assume anyone you don't know is straight, until you find out for sure. Straight surfers, as liberal as they pretty much like to think they are, can still get a little upset if their night's sleep is disturbed by two guys fucking and sucking up a storm. Granted, we'd pitched our two-man tent as far away as possible from the others, without coming off downright unsociable, but the acoustics at that beach can be finky at times. Sometimes you can hardly hear what's being said to the guy sitting next to you, while you can hear the jokes told by someone around a campfire a mile down the beach. So, while both Pete and I could be pretty confident that what we said and did was said and done pretty much in privacy, the breaking waves putting up quite a fuss, as well as the low moan from the in-blowing wind that blasted the bluffs that separated the beach from the mainland, better safe than sorry.

Our other precaution, besides speaking in whispers, was our having doused the Coleman lantern before we hit the sack. I'd once spent a very amusing evening watching the sexual shadow-show provided by two studs against the canvas of their tent when they'd forgotten, or not bothered, to turn off their light before getting down and dirty.

All absence of artificial light didn't mean that we were rummaging around in the dark, like two blind guys who had to resort to sex via the braille-method. It's genuinely surprising how much light can be found on a beach, even near midnight, what with the moon and stars in the dark night sky, and the luminescence that, more often than not, glosses the white water like white material gone all shiny under blacklight.

Actually, once my eyes had grown accustomed to the natural lighting available, I could see damned well.

My hand lifted Pete's stiff cock so that I looked down its entire length, from its fat head to its thick roots, all of the way beyond his nesting of brown pubic hair at the base of his dick, to where his flaccid scrotum pooled on the blanket between his open legs. When I drew my fist upward along the shaft of his dick, I could easily spot the way his thick foreskin could be stretched to pretty much duplicate the snout it provided Pete's cock when his cock wasn't in full erection. When I stroked my fist back down the length of his pecker, I pulled loose outer skin completely free of his cockcrown, once again, and not only fully revealed the deep slit of his cockmouth but made his prickslice gape even wider.

I was astride Pete's supine nakedness, my head to his crotch, his crotch to my head. He fisted my dick as thoroughly as I fisted his, and he pulled my stiff prick down from where it projected parallel to my overhanging belly. He had my cockhead so close to his mouth that I could feel his breath each and every time he whispered. His other hand not only clamped my ass but slid his fingers into the crack of my butt where his fuckfingers was within ready striking distance of my snugly shut pucker.

I had to be very careful that Pete didn't prematurely launch one of his favorite double attacks on my body, namely gulping my dick while simultaneously cramming his fuckfinger fast and furious up my tight asshole. It was something he liked to do, because he'd learned from practice that it could really get guys, in general, and me, in particular, really hot and horny. I still remember the first time he came at me, both barrels, my ending up creaming my wad while he merely chuckled at his success. Which was okay, in that I'd gotten my nuts off, but I prefer reciprocity, and it's sometimes hard for me to get immediately back into the game when I've just come down from a massive spermal explosion.

Not that Pete seems to care. In fact, I once accused him of being more turned on by turning on other guys than being turned on by other guys' attempts to turn him on. Something, by the way, which he didn't deny, then or since. Nonetheless, we've reached a mutual understanding that I have every intention, each and every time we screw around, to make him come just as often as he persuades me to pop my loads. By now, I know enough about Pete's sexual likes and dislikes to pretty much give as much pleasure as I get. He tries something funny, and I have a few aces up my own sleeve. Although, he still tries, on occasion, to get the better of me in one of his who'll-cream-his-load-first little games.

That night, in that tent, though, on that northern California beach, Pete was on his best behavior. When he licked the head of my dick and sucked his lips to the tip of my prick, like a kid savoring a lollipop, he went no farther than that until I, likewise, latched my hungry mouth to the bulbous head of his stiff dick and began wrapping and unwrapping my tongue around his cockshaft.

His dick tasted like shushi. Supplemental flavors were purely those of young, virile, surfer-stud.

"Mmmmmmmmmmm," his low voice vibrated around my cockhead, then waited for my "Mmmmmmmmmmmmmm," to do the same for his sucked-up dickhead.

I worked both my hands beneath his ass, and he obliged by lifting his hips in a way that gave my fingers freer access and, at the same time, poked another inch of his cock into my face. I curled my fingers along the in-curves of his butt, and my fingertips slid into his asscrease until they touched bottom.

I kept my mouth over his extra inch of dick when Pete's ass lowered back to the blanket and anchored my hands. So, Pete had carte blanche to suck up at least another inch of my dick. He vacuumed up not only that additional inch, but all the rest of my dick as well. My balls, still held within their comparatively flaccid sac, sagged his nose, one nut to each side. He snorted hot air that stirred the blond bush that furred my scrotum. His chin nestled firmly against my lower belly.

My lips remained taut and slid the shaft of his dick, my mouth forced wide by the entrance of his beer-can cock all of the way to his thick cockroots. My face was down into his crotch almost as far as it would go, my chin buried within his brown pubic hair, my nose pinioning his fairly compact scrotum. My face burrowed even more securely and forced one of his balls to either side of my nose, like boulders to either side of a wedge. My nose was thrust almost as far as his asscrack, and his butt smelled of seaweed and salt water.

When his face slid off my dick to the halfway point and paused, I knew what he was up to. That my nuts, still hung my scrotum and weighed the bag just about halfway along the length of my downjutted cockshaft, made them vulnerable, and Pete, as usual, was prepared to take every advantage. To counteract the pleasure he'd soon provide by opening wide for first one of my nuts, then the other, squeezing both to pleasurable pain against the shaft of my swallowed cock, I squirred both of my hands more completely beneath his ass until his resulting grunt announced one of my fuckfingers had successfully located his pucker.

His mouth exerted the suction out to siphon one of my large nuts between the small space offered between his pursed lips and my cockshaft, and my finger crooked and shoved up his butt.

"Aaaghhrrrr!" he growled around my dick, at the same time he successfully claimed my one nut. Hung from my lower body by one hand, like a monkey hung from the thick limb of a jungle tree, he maneuvered my remaining free testicle so it soon joined its companion, as well as my cockshaft, inside his mouth.

"Aggggggghhhh!" I said, his sucking of my second ball having caused a good deal of additional discomfort that was thankfully balanced by attending pleasure.

Assaulted by the combination of pleasure and pain, I wasn't so occupied with those two forces battling for predominance inside of me that I forgot to punch my fuckfinger even deeper up Pete's dry asshole and crook it there in farther search of his prostate.

"Ughhh ... ughhhh ... ughhhhh!" he said, when I found his prostate and massaged his nut-shell gland with sufficient expertise to provide him his own dosage of pleasure-pain combination.

Both his hands again anchored securely to my ass, he used his handholds as leverage to hoist his face up the total length of my dick, taking along for the ride my two large nuts compressed between his cheeks and my solid cockshaft. His nose, unimpeded by my sucked-up scrotum, poked deep into the crack of my ass, and I imagined his nostrils snarfing my pucker.

I lifted my face, my lips taut so they pulled with them the loose outer layer of foreskin that coated his thick dick. I rode up his dick so far that my mouth actually surrendered his cockhead, while it retained his prepuce which was now pinched off over the end of his corona. I torqued my finger deeper yet up his asshole, and crooked it more substantially to maintain contact with his prostate.

"Ahhhhhhhh," he said. His head fell back down my dick and pulled my scrotum as far as my compacting scrotal skin would stretch. Then, he attempted to stretch it even farther, his snug lips tugging on my balls which wanted escape, between his lips and my cockshaft, but weren't allowed it.

"Ooooooooeeeeeiiiii," it was my turn to verbalize the exquisite counterplay of pleasure and pain he kept actively warring for the high ground inside me.

My face lowered and pushed his foreskin back over his dick and down along the stiff shaft of his penis, making his prepuce form its thick turtlenecking around the very roots of his pecker. From there, I progressed into a more eager chewing on his dick, combined with an up-and-down rhythm of my head over his cock that had his dick fucking my face like sixty.

I had the advantage, in that it was easier to bounce my face down and up the length of his straining erection than it was for him to muscle his face up and down my downjutting dick. What's more, my finger could fuck his butt pretty well, even when his ass ground against my hands and did its best to flatten them to the blanket beneath him. Where for him to fuck his finger up my ass, and maintain his sucking cadence over my dick, would have required that he perform the equivalent of one-arm chin-ups.

As it turned out, he successfully calculated that he didn't need his finger up my butt, as long as he continued to contain both of my balls inside his mouth, along with my cockshaft. Whatever activities my finger performed up his anus, his mouth countered by massaging, mashing, tonguing, and washing my balls, each and every time his head moved down or rose up along the stiff inches of my erection.

My washing his prick with spit was aided by gravity which claimed every ooze of my saliva between my lips and his cock and drooled the length of his fat meat to form translucent beads among his brown pubic hair. On the other hand, his efforts at spit-lubricating my dick were less easily achieved, in that his saliva, acted upon by the same gravity, and more easily caught within the residual vacuum from his sucking face, each time his mouth ran down my cock to my cockhead, hardly ever gained a nesting within the blond netting that ringed the thick base of my sucked penis.

Every so often, I felt his mouth and throat contract heartily against my stiff inches, and accompanying balls, in order for him to swallow his excess saliva. Each and every time, the compression of his cheeks and throat against my dick, and the accompanying smash of my testicles against the shaft of my dick, rocketed me to a higher state of sexual ecstasy.

We had both fucked around with each other enough times so that we knew just what the other liked, by way of getting really hot and bothered. We'd eliminated all the excess and wasted motions, which made for far quicker ejaculations than when we'd been two people needing to explore what worked and what didn't work for the other.

My signal to him that his chewing of my dick was about to feed him a mouthful of my erupting cum was the frantic in-and-out fuck motion of my finger up his butt, still keeping my fuckfinger crooked so that it rammed his prostate on each inward and outward phase of every slide.

What he did, to clue me, likewise, that I wasn't alone in the degree of pleasure I had swirling through me, was to vary the way his head came upward into my overhanging crotch and then retreated from it Rather than a straight rise and fall, he varied the angle of his head, so that my cock slammed in and retreated against his left check, then slammed in and retreated directly into his throat, then slammed in and retreated against his right cheek, then slammed in and retreated directly into his throat, then

Our sucking had taken on all the aspects of a foot race where friendly rivals ran neck and neck, each knowing that their breaking the tape would result in a photo finish, but each wanting the altruistic satisfaction of knowing the other had gotten there first, if just by a few fractions of a second.

By then, our guttural grunts and groans were probably loud enough for anyone to hear within miles, kinky beach acoustics, or not. However, likewise, by that time, neither of us much cared. We were barreling down on the finish line, and there was no stopping either of us.

Final indication for Pete that he had me on the very brink was when my scrotum contracted to such an extent that it was no longer possible for Pete to hold onto either of my nuts and still provide the length of my dick with the sufficiently vibrant up-and-down bounce of his face that he wanted. In order to maintain the fuck of his mouth and throat over my erection, he had to surrender my nuts whose containing bag immediately compacted all the more, my testicles suddenly hoisted almost to disappearance within the base of my belly.

Each poke of my nose into Pete's scrotum saw me snort into a brown-haired sac that was less pillow than hard canvas over hard boulders. If his balls never climbed as far into his lower belly as mine did into mine, their containing scrotum nonetheless underwent sufficient change, near each and every sexual finale, to let me know, no question, that his testicles were as poised to let go their load as my disappeared gonads could ever be.

My overhanging hips began a definite fucking rhythm to coincide with each fall and rise of Pete's face. His hips bounced on the blanket in a cadence that matched my up and down sucks of his erection.

He was hung from the very tip of my prick when I lost our race, by winning it, and spewed my spermal cream. My cum kept on shooting as Pete's face rose up over the entire length of my erupting cock, one final time, and leeched to the base of my belly like a child securely sucked to his mother's pap.

"Grrrahhnngghhh!" I said, and it was that very growl that was the last impetus Pete needed to erupt his own hearty load.

No one ever said Pete was stingy with his cum. When his jism came, hot and fast, sticky and viscous, it ballooned my cheeks almost to forced spilling before I successfully, finally, managed to swallow it all away.

"Mmmmmmmmm," he hummed over my cock which, gone hypersensitive in the midst of eruption, throbbed within his still containing mouth and throat.

I burrowed far and deep into Pete's crotch and concentrated on successfully swallowing each and every bit of his exploded cum which, like seawater, was salty on my tongue but, unlike sea water, wasn't so salty that it gagged or burned my sinuses.

We continued to feed and be fed, almost as if our cum was one massive flooding of the stuff that merely circled from my cock to him, from his cock to me, from my cock to him, over and over again.

The intensity of it all, combined with the energy spent, earlier in the day, hiking into the beach, and spent later that day, riding the waves, left us limp as rag dolls as we finally came apart and spread out, naked and sweaty, satiated and exhausted, next to each other on the blanket within our two-man tent.

"Jesus!" Pete said.

I don't remember saying anything in response, merely surrendering, contentedly and willingly, to a sleep that was fast and furiously upon me.

When we woke up, miracle of miracles, we were alone on the beach. The two other groups, who'd been there when we'd arrived the afternoon before, had apparently pulled out some time during the night or, more likely, earlier that morning.

The waves weren't anything to brag about; but, they had potential for getting better. Pete and I decided to go out. We took the tandem board into the water A tandem surfboard, by the way, bigger than a normal one. This one was over twelve feet long and twenty-five inches wide, but it was still quite buoyant in that it was designed to hold two people instead of one. While traditional tandem is a boy-girl thing, Pete and I use the tandem board mainly for other things on those rare occasions when we find ourselves somewhere without two-million other surfers in the water with us. Those instances of privacy on the waves, I might add, are getting to be as rare as hen's teeth.

We paddled out to the calm beyond the break line and maneuvered our board so it aimed toward shore. We took one more look at the beach to make sure it was still empty, and I unbuttoned the small front pocket of my trunks to retrieve the contraceptive packet I had there. With the packet secured between my teeth, Pete and I stripped off our swim trunks. Anticipating what we both had planned, our cocks were already harder than hell.

Since I wore the tether that connected my ankle to the surfboard, in order to more quickly retrieve the board should we, for whatever the reason, be momentarily toppled from it, I slipped the leash off my foot and threaded the legs of our two pair of swimming trunks onto the cord before reattaching the line to my ankle. No way did we want to loose our trunks, en route to shore, only to discover someone had taken up residence on the beach to watch us exit the water stark naked.

Pete went belly-down on the board, the top of his head facing shore. I faced forward, too, and knelt on the board between Pete's legs. The board shifted, this way and that, with our combined weight, but Pete and I had a good enough sense of balance, having done what we did so many times before, that neither of us was really in any danger of being tipped into the water. Additional balance was achieved by Pete's hands and arms, drooped and moving like stabilizers, on either side of the board.

I ripped the condom packet open with the help of my teeth, and I unrolled the lubricated latex down the length of my stiff dick.

I fell forward, my chest over Pete's buttocks, my legs outstretched on the board, between the backs of his open thighs. My cock fucked the empty space immediately behind his ass. I reached my arms up along Pete's torso and looped my hands underneath his arms and curled my fingers up and back over his shoulders to face me. I used my handholds to scoot my body farther up Pete's body, until my belly rested against his ass. The head of my cock, parallel my belly and the board, touched the crack shared by Pete's sexy assbuns.

I humped my crotch up, just slightly, and gave Pete room to reach on back with one of hand, find my cock, and guide my cockhead to target.

"Okay, stud," Pete said when he'd achieved his purpose, my cockhead aligned for perfect entrance up his butt.

I lowered my crotch and simultaneously used my handholds on his shoulders to drag my body farther upward along his back. As I pushed my hard cock into the slot offered by Pete's asshole, he sent his hand back into the water and raised his butt to make sure my cockhead gained an even more ready entrance. All of which was no mean feat, considering that if we didn't do it right the first time, maintaining our balance all the while, we could have ended up sexually frustrated and dumped in the drink.

With a little more coordinated maneuvering, I ended up spread out along Pete's body: my chest on his back, my belly on his butt, my cock rammed to my blond balls up his brown-hair fringed shithole.

"What do you think?" I said. I knew it felt right, but I wanted to confirm.

"I think your cock is up my butt, and my cock is smashed between my belly and this hard board," Pete said. Then, apparently lest I think he complained, he added, "Feels good, stud. Feels damned good."

That was the position in which we proceeded to fuck, slow and easy, making sure that we renewed our acquaintance with the board and reaffirmed all that was necessary to stay balanced aboard it. A smaller board would have had us sinking beneath the water on its far more precarious perch, but the tandem board allowed only an occasional slopping of ocean over its edges to pool along our bodies before almost immediately draining away.

"Oh, nothing like fucking a surfboard while you hump my ass," Pete said. It was his way of letting me know that his cock was provided pleasure from its snug fit between his muscled belly and the board, in supplement to the pleasure of my cock working Pete's studly surfer ass.

However much pleasure Pete felt, I was the one more likely to get the most out of this particular ride. While orgasm, purely from my cock up his butt, and his cock fucked between his belly and our board, had, on the very rarest occasions, provided enough pleasure to rupture Pete's nuts, as well as my own, that was the exception rather than the rule. Usually, reciprocity required that we repeat the procedure, a bit later on, with my ass upturned for fucking on the board. We could only hope the beach remained deserted until we'd both benefited from the temporary seclusion it offered.

The idea was for me to fuck and keep on fucking Pete's ass to a point where I was almost into orgasm, but not so far along that I'd lost all ability to exert conscious control. It was a finely tuned performance that sometimes didn't work, even after so many times of our having run through it together. The need for us to play our parts to perfection, each and every time, had increased, over the years, as it had become less and less likely that we'd find locations that allotted us the privacy and/or the time needed to fuck the way we were then fucking. Therefore, despite the pleasures within me, birthed by my each and every thrust and withdrawal of my hard cock within Pete's tight asshole, I fought to maintain control of the fuck and not let the fuck take complete control of me.

There wasn't much within the format that allowed for innovative fucking, above and beyond the where of doing what we did. What was required, and what I delivered, was a series of slow pumps of my cock, in and out, in and out, of Pete's rectum. Not that there was anything wrong with that time-proven method of building ecstasy to the point of blast-off. It worked very well, thank-you very much. Pete's asshole was plenty tight, so that I really didn't need to perform any kind of fancy cockwork to slowly but surely prime myself to the point where my nuts grouped at the base of my dick in preparation for feeding cream deep up Pete's sexy surfer ass.

I slid my dick to my cum-bulged balls, once more, only this time left it there.

"Next big wave, buddy," I said, and dropped my arms and hands into the water with his.

We paddled us and our board to catch the very next swell, not caring whether what we hopped was destined to break small, medium, or large against the shore. Our present schedule for my orgasm didn't allow us to be as picky as we would have been had we been out there purely to sample the existing surf.

Although the wave we caught wasn't a genuinely large one, it proved far larger than the ones produced by the ocean before we'd swam beyond the break line.

When the nose of our board tipped over the leading edge of the finally formed wave and angled a slide down and across the concaved face of water on the other side, Pete and I aboard, and locked cock to ass, ass to cock, it was quite a thrill, let me tell you, in no way diminished by our having fucked on far larger waves in our time.

Our paddling kept the board in position, and we stayed belly down, no attempts made at any sexual gymnastics that might have seen us, somehow, miraculously standing up, still sexually locked.

Like riding a roller coaster, the bottom suddenly dropped out from under us and that sensation, along with Pete's ass suddenly clamped tightly around my cock, as Pete filled with his own degree of wave-riding excitement, pretty well gave me the final push over the edge into full-fledged orgasm.

"I'm fucking coming!" I screamed, my voice lost in the roar of the water, in the splash of the spray, in the singing of the wind, as we completed our long slide down the face of that perfectly curled wave that headed for the shore.

My spermal foam pumped its gallons up Pete's butt, as all around us the ocean foamed its orgasmic climax destined for completion upon the sandy shore.

I guess what all of that says is merely that everyone should know that gay sex is alive and well within one international sport, even if it's becoming harder and harder to get the privacy needed for literally "getting it off" on one of those waves. For those of you who interested, even when the waves get so crowded with people, there'll still be plenty of action among us surfers on shore.

So, the next time you hear some kid screaming "Surf's up!", rest assured that somewhere, at that very minute, some surfer's cock is up, too. And, that cock is most likely going at it, hard and fast, up another sexy surfer's tight young asshole.

Come on down and join us.

In the interim, gotta go. Surf's up. And so is my ten-inch dick.

USERS

Half-naked boys splashed like dark-skinned dolphins in the crystal water of the Camino del Rio swimming pool. Blond, blue-eyed John Molay, at eighteen years of age and probably only a few years older at best, tried to decipher their mirthful squeals of communication but couldn't. Although the swimmers looked like mere kids, John would still liked to have known if they were of legal age, a couple looking really prime. If only he were better at learning their language, he'd be set. Problem was, he'd never been all that much good at anything scholastically, which was what let him to realize at a very early age that if he wanted to enjoy the good things in life he was going to have to go about it some other way than through capitalizing upon any kind of superb academic background.

"Great beginnings for a fine tan!" John's lover, Brian Caspen, complimented, arriving poolside while John continued his lazy attempts to put some meaning to the ongoing chatter of excited Spanish.

"Why not get your swimsuit and join me for some splashings with the locals?" John suggested. Brian, after all, spoke great Spanish, and if John were particularly clever in the way he worked it, he'd have the age of each kid in the pool in no time.

There being no reason Brian couldn't put on his swim trunks. He'd finally received a clean bill of health. Exercise and physical therapy having given him a well-muscled physique that rivaled the one he'd had when he'd somehow misgauged a simple warm-up vault at a university-level regional gymnastics meet and had done serious, erroneously diagnosed as permanent, damage to his spine. However, there were, as John well knew and continued to advantage, Brian's accompanying mental injuries, from so many years of recovery time, which hadn't healed quite as well, and possibly never would.

"I thought you were out soaking up some local color," John diplomatically changed the subject.

Brian had all of the dark good-looks that John found so much a turn-on in younger packaging. Not that Brian, being as old as he was, at twenty-five, was so old that John couldn't sexually get it on with the guy, and manage to pretend a really good time, as John had very well proved, and would continue to prove, as long as Brian continued to be generous with the inherited money in his bank account.

"Another of my ideas that sounded good only when I was drunk," Brian confessed. He could still feel quite lost without John nearby.

"Okay, then let's go somewhere together," John suggested.

"Go where?" Brian wanted to know. Despite knowing what was best for him, he would have preferred a nice quiet place, maybe drinks, just the two of them.

"I've seen enough of this first-class hotel for the moment," John said, "and since it's just about lunch time, I happened to spot this little place ..."

The teenager had spent the last couple of days spotting just such little places which usually came complete with fly-specked menus. He was forever insisting that Brian order them goat, or deep-fried ham hocks, or turkey tacos. All of which Brian would never have ordered on his own, especially not in his excellent but stilted tutor-learned Spanish that left him ill at ease and feeling inadequate around people who came by the language naturally.

John's latest gourmet discovery was Montaga's Bean and Tortilla House.

When they went in, every head of every in-situ customer turned in the pair's direction. Heads often turned, most usually in amazement at so much attractive maleness in such studly combination.

A waitress came from behind a greasy counter. She went first to John. They always went first to John, as if they sensed intuitively that, despite his younger age, he should be the one in charge. Brian was admittedly envious of how at ease John always was around people. Brian's younger brother had certainly felt the undeniable attraction afforded by this charming teen, only Timmy's masochistic pleasure having allowing him to play martyr and give John up when John began, more and more often, to "hang out" with Timmy's older and recovering brother. Timmy had since moved on to Harold Wyler, but there was no denying that certain bittersweet longing he got in his eyes whenever he found himself in the same room with the young man into whose hands he'd so generously and unselfishly surrendered his older brother. Of course, what Brian had sensed of John's rampant and promiscuous sexuality, from the start, had likely saved dear Timmy from a helluva lot of heartache and sexual frustration in the long run. Brian had learned to control John's tendency toward sexual excess by putting John into situations where the young man's inability to speak the local language didn't give the teenager quite as much leeway to advantage every sexual possibility that would otherwise have presented itself.

John smiled at the Mexican waitress. He had an attractive smile, very wide, very sincere, very warm. His teeth were white and even.

"No hablo espanol," he said, taxing his couple days of accumulated vocabulary.

So, it was Brian who ordered them beers, hating the exposure but knowing just how desperately he needed John's silent and sometimes-not-so silent prodding to get out and function in society like a normal human being.

Knowing, down deep, that just being out in the world again, and doing everyday things, like an everyday person, was good for him, Brian could be -- and was -- passively indulgent when the forever-horny John commenced obvious ogling of the young Mexican at the adjoining table. About John's age, maybe a tad younger, the Mexican kid had dark hair, dark eyes, cleft chin.

These occasions, when Brian was prepared to lengthen John's golden chains, were designed to keep the kid happy until Brian was through with him.

Brian knew John's sexual preferences, and this Mexican kid matched every one of them, so it could be expected John would soon start up some kind of conversation, it making no difference whatsoever that John didn't speak the language, because John figured that was what he had Brian there for -- although he didn't know Brian knew just how John had it figured. For not the first time, John would use Brian as middle-man, insisting later that it was good practice for Brian -- which it was -- who needed to start feeling more at ease around people -- which he did.

Brian moved things along by excusing himself to find the toilet, seeming more innocent than he was, and returned to find more beers.

"The extras are from Pablo," John commented, nodding toward the young Mexican. "Go over and thank him, will you? I'm sure he'd appreciate a little more than the feeble 'Gracias!' I was able to come up with. Why not even invite him on over?"

Brian did as John suggested, hardly surprised when Pablo accepted the invite to join them.

Brian and Pablo talked. Occasionally, Brian stopped to translate the gist of the mundane conversation for John's benefit. John mainly just sipped his beer and looked for his moment to leap without Brian noticing the leaping.

Finally, Pablo took the lead and excused himself to go to the bano.

As soon as Pablo was gone, John pushed back his own chair and came to his feet.

"Yours-truly has suddenly got to piss, too," John said with a wide smile. "Don't go away, will you?" He punctuated with what Brian was supposed to interpret as a naturally suppressed yawn which, if it fooled anyone, didn't fool Brian.

John headed for the door marked caballeros. He had no difficulty finding it, because the way was marked with wet footprints from all those who had gone before.

A toilet, absent of any seat cover, was rooted in a pool of what (at least from the smell), must have been about one-hundred percent one-hundred-year-old piss. A sink held a rust-encrusted faucet, a leaking stream of urine-colored water flowing over a cracked ceramic surface but failing to clean it. No mirror. Walls streaked with grime and Mexican graffiti.

Although Pablo was going through the motions, his cock was in no condition for pissing. It was rock-hard, jutting from unseen hairy balls. Its powerful, heart-shaped head rested against the silver buckle that held Pablo's belt shut.

Pablo's penis, dark like its owner and looking as if it would have been right at home attached so someone far older, was a thick truncheon. Its foreskin was rolled to a turtleneck that encircled the flared base of the prick's rubbery crown. Its shaft was lined with large veins.

Pablo smiled in greeting.

"You look as red and as unappetizing as a fire ant," Pablo said, knowing by now that John wouldn't have a clue. He'd wanted to follow Brian into the can, when the more attractive older stud had left the table, but John had, from the beginning, proved the one more interested in Pablo's obvious charms, and Pablo had to advantage such opportunities when they presented themselves. Luckily, he could get hard for just about anything, this sunburned, otherwise pale, American boy included.

John mumbled a quick "Si!", which he intuitively suspected would be more than adequate response. His more universally interpreted response, though, was the large-denomination American bill, part of the extremely large travel allowance Brian allowed him, which he pulled out of his front pants' pocket, folded exaggeratedly into a small square, and extended in Pablo's direction.

At least Pablo hadn't had to go into all the bullshit sign language to let the American know he wasn't about to do anything free of charge; he'd give the kid credit for that much smarts, anyway. Actually, Pablo wouldn't even have been there, on a bet, if it wasn't for the money. He far preferred his cock buried to his balls up Maria's tightly gripping pussy. However, there was his mother, his little brother, and his little sister's well-beings to think of. Tortillas and beans were expensive in the Mexican capital, and a guy had to do what a guy had to do, even if it was tricking with a rich little American kid to whom Pablo wouldn't have given the time of day under less dire need-the-money circumstances.

Only after Pablo took the money and pocketed it did John unzip his own pants. By which time, Pablo's balls had been fished out. Pablo hooked his Mexican dick with the thumbs of both hands. When John stepped in even closer, Pablo extended nine fingers to gather in and hug John's white cock, belly-to-belly, with the stiff meatiness raised before Pablo's teenage belly.

"Si!" John said.

He spit into the palm of his right hand and dropped his hand, and its pooling of saliva, to the uplifted pricks, forming a cupola over their sexily dual mushroom-like cap.

Pablo was the shorter, but his cock was sufficiently longer so that it seemed to be perfectly equal to John's cock when viewed from the top, looking down. If Pablo's cock was also bulkier than its companion, that was primarily because of the extra girth supplied by his uncut foreskin. By comparison, John's cock was circumcised and streamlined: a thoroughly modern missile holding its own when measured against what, before the recurring popularity of skipped circumcision in the States, would have come across as a decidedly archaic Third-World model.

John's left hand went deep between them, cupping his balls and those of the Mexican youth. The silkier blond hair on John's sizable scrotum mingled with the wirier black strands that made Pablo's contracting sac like a puff of steel wool. John squeezed and, if Pablo didn't groan because of John's cracking of the kid's nuts, the Mexican's eyes did get larger and water just a tad.

With a small buck of his hips, John fucked his cock upward through Pablo's fists, the belly of his cock rubbing sensuously against the pillowing of Pablo's hard, prepuce-cushioned erection. The resulting ride caused a pleasant friction. With both of his hands, Pablo expertly began masturbating both cocks while John continued to massage their balls.

John wondered if the Mexican wanted to kiss? Some studs did, some didn't. Even John had his days, his moments, when his primary interest was sex below the belt, no time for the business of battling tongues and exchanging saliva. Though, he wouldn't have minded kissing the Mexican. Pablo had kissable lips, firm and slightly pouted. They fit perfectly in a face that, like the youth's body, was still handsome and not yet gone to the later-years' chunkiness John noticed prevalent among so many of the Mexicans north of the border. Maybe the more trying economic circumstances in the Mexican capital kept its inhabitants, unlike their US cousins, less prone to fat.

With his free hand, his other hand still busy with its skillful rolling of hairy scrotums and fat nuts, John hooked the back of Pablo's head and tried to pull the kid's handsome face closer.

Pablo, though, was having none of that. The last thing he wanted, already having to endure this American kid's pasty cock up snugly against Pablo's more enticingly brown Mexican dick, was being forced to have this kid's red-as-a-lobster face force-feed his probably long-as-Quetzalcoatl slippery pink tongue down Pablo's throat. Rather, hoping to get this whole distasteful procedure over as quickly as possible, Pablo feigned swelling ardor by increasing the rhythmic cadence of his stroking fingers over their hard cocks.

John wasn't so caught up in the moment that he'd lost sight of the time. How long, after all, was this taking, compared to how long it took for a couple of guys each to manage a simple piss? Brian had seen enough of the can in question to know there was no way John would linger for a crap, not with a sanitized toilet awaiting any of their dumps back at the tourist-oriented Camino del Rio.

John wished he had more time to work with, because he found this Mexican kid a real charmer. He had no doubts, whatsoever, that with a bit of additional persuasion he could seduce Pablo into sucking face -- maybe into even sucking John's dick. On the other hand, it was lack of time that added to the turn-on. The danger that John's lover might come to look for them, or the possibility that a stranger might materialize to use the can, contributed to all the ecstasy John was feeling, to all that excitement spiralling through his guts in preparation for that one final and concentrated explosion of his cream from the pouted lips of his stiff prick.

John's handful of scrotums had become less fluid and more leathery, and Pablo's handfuls of cocks had become too large a circumference to be completely contained. The young Mexican's grip was forced wider and wider as each successive stroke of his hands over their mated dicks swelled both pricks toward a hope-for dual explosion.

"I'm going to come," John said.

Pablo had heard the English words before and said the Mexican equivalent of "Thank the Lord for fast-shooting American twits!"

John didn't understand what Pablo said, nor did he care. His money paid and accepted, it was only John's soon-to-be-depleted balls that primarily concerned the teenage blond now.

John's hand, the one still in Pablo's glossy black hair, rerouted to cap what quickly became a dual-pronged gusher.

Pablo had had to work damned hard to get his own dick off, considering how distasteful he actually found this teenager and this teenager's pale dick. Pablo wouldn't have bothered with orgasm at all, except he knew from past experience that Americans liked the illusion that they were giving as much pleasure as they were getting. He didn't want to get into any argument with this little shit about how John should get some kind of refund since Pablo had kept his cum in his nuts and not shared any.

John contained as much as possible of the soupy shots of sperm that erupted simultaneously from all four balls. Not to have done so might well have resulted in incriminating stains on shirts and/or pants. John didn't want to have to make any unnecessary explanations to Brian.

A final upward stroking of Pablo's fingers milked the cocks for the last oozes of stale sperm remaining within both penile tubes. John added that additional mess to his present handful and, since there was no toilet paper on the lone dispenser, he transferred his claimed part of Pablo and his mess to tissues he'd conveniently stuffed into his pockets before leaving the hotel. He wiped his fingers and his cock clean. Pablo used an absorbent, albeit slightly used, hanky, to perform his own mop-up.

Finished, the two young men paused embarrassedly. They might well have been two straights having raced to the same urinal, each offering, despite equally building bladder-pressure, to let the other piss first.

John checked his watch, and Pablo high-tailed it out of the restroom, anxious to be completely free of the thank-God-it's-over scene. John stayed behind and counted slowly to ten. When he exited, he wasn't really surprised to find Pablo not sitting at the table.

"Pablo?" John asked, pulling out his chair and sitting down. Brian looked nervous, but then he always looked nervous in public places.

"He had a previous appointment and was late," Brian explained. "At least that's what he said, if I got it right. He was speaking pretty fast."

"I think he might have been trying to tell me as much in the can," John alibied. "He was chattering up a storm, but I certainly couldn't understand any of it. However, between his trying to tell me something, and the wretched state of the restroom, I didn't think I'd ever get my plumbing working for that needed piss."

Brian didn't need genius IQ to know what had been going on in that restroom between John and Pablo. Pablo had emerged flushed and sex-sweaty, and John's lighter skin had gone absolutely beet-red beneath his attractive but thin veneering of brown tan and pale-pink sunburn. It more than just a bit insulting for Brian to have John thinking the kid was so thoroughly clever as to have, once again, pulled the wool over Brian's eyes.

Well, Brian, at least for the moment, was willing to let things proceed as-is, in the face of the benefits he genuinely believed he still derived from his and John's relationship.

"Yeah, I know just the can't-piss-feeling conjured by that particular toilet," Brian agreed. "What took me so long in there, when I went first, was my uncertainty as to whether I was supposed to whiz in the toilet bowl, in the sink, or just go on the floor like everyone else seems to have done?"

John didn't have a clue that Brian knew the truth. The way John had it figured, his lover's mind would have been completely blown had Brian even suspected John of doing dirties with the young Mexican in that horrendously dirty can.

"Shall we go back to the hotel?" John suggested. "Find a quiet spot and have a cold glass of something? Then have a long draft of hot and heated sex?" John was always pleased by the speed with which his dick could be expected to resurrect, even for the less pleasurable responsiblity of work.

"Yeah, sure," Brian said. No denying he was relieved to be exiting what seemed like center-stage. Obviously, he still needed a few more venturings out into the big wide world to feel genuinely at ease, when left alone, within it. Maybe a trip, with John, to somewhere even more far-flung, like to Spain or to one of the Spanish-speaking South American countries, was called for. It was certainly something to think about before, somewhere, up the road, he dumped this two-timing little hustler-shit by the wayside.

FOOTBALL

I know when: Three years ago, this March sixteenth ... two-forty-five in the afternoon ... more likely two-fifty-five, because I ran a little late that day, and it always takes time to get settled in for a session.

I know whom: Kenneth Jalonson ... above the age of consent, if barely ... football player, varsity, at Palladium School ... handsome kid ... looked straight off the farm ... blond hair ... blue eyes ... high cheekbones ... sexy mouth ... milky complexion... real nice body in a sport where jocks tend to blubber over muscle ... muscles neither bulky nor ugly ... somewhat small-appearing for football, until, I guess, on the playing field, he hit you like a ton of bricks.

I know how: the sole of his foot tight against my groin.

Here, let me show you. Sit there, across from me. Take off your right shoe and your right sock. Don't worry, I've seen countless feet probably in a helluva lot worse condition than yours. Unless you're talking a bad case of athlete's foot, or flesh-eating crude. I didn't think so. So, let's do this. A picture worth a thousand words.

Kenneth, call him Kenny (he said), sat across from me, just like you sit now, only at the clinic. I had him put his foot up here, toes up, between my legs. I took hold of his foot, and I scooted up tight against its sole, like this, so his right knee was forced to bend slightly. I told him to push, like I tell you to push.

You can push harder than that. Don't worry about my nuts. There's a technique to all of this. I'm a physical therapist who's damned good at what he does.

Kenny's was to be an exercise program, involving stretching, to work a bothersome recurring kink out of his right thigh. Right about here, by way of illustrating on your leg. I won't bore you with the medical terminology, or with the Latin names of the muscle, actually the two muscles, involved.

Stretching: the key. That's what I told Kenny. That's what I tell you, because you'd do well to do a bit of stretching yourself, if you want your legs to last you into old age. Push a little harder, so you'll straighten your leg. Except, you can't straighten your leg, can you? That's because most everyone's muscles, even in the best of times, have a tendency to shorten. Yours no exceptions.

Admittedly, some guys have muscles that seem to have memories. Those muscles get adequately stretched out, and they retain the memory of how good it is, and they do their best to remain flexible, sometimes managing all the way into middle age. Few guys, though, certainly not you, are lucky enough to have memory-retentive muscles. In fact, most of us have muscles that can't remember shit from Shine-O-La. We neglect them, and they neglect us. That's the story of your leg muscles. That's what Kenny's thigh muscles did, but his only did it now and again, usually when he was on the playing field trying to win a football game.

What I don't get is why I got a hard-on, Kenny's foot tucked into my crotch, when I'd never gotten one with any of the other young jock-feet I'd had tucked in one and the same place. Kenny some kind of ... what's the damned word? Yeah, catalyst. But was he a major catalyst, or was he just the last in a long line of little catalysts that finally hit critical mass and swelled my dick to that erection?

At the time, I was scared shitless that Kenny would be offended by my erection. The kid was with a legitimate and well-respected physical therapist, and suddenly, out of the blue, I can't even keep my dick soft in my pants. It was a bit disconcerting, you can bet your sweet ass.

Speaking of your sweet ass, you might think about doing a few butt exercises. Most people don't realize there's help for sagging ass, especially if they catch it early. Yours not yet into all that much of a butt-sag, but ...

So, where was I? You sure you want to hear this? Teddy says your expertise is fetishes. Maybe you can tell me if this kind of thing is usually so spontaneous. Before that first time, with Kenny, I never dreamed I could get turned on by someone's foot. Especially after all the feet I'd seen during the course of any one workdays, up until then.

At first, I figured it was Kenny, in total, not his foot, who was the cause. I thanked God when he didn't make a big issue of my arousal. He pretended to ignore it, although it was a bit too big to ignore, take my word for it. Or, maybe, you don't have to take my word, since my dick seems to be doing it's going-stiffy routine, right here and now, just for you.

I can argue that boners are often conjured by therapy sessions, more likely on patients than on their therapists, but I started wearing a plastic jock-cup whenever Kenny came in for therapy.

My cock still got hard but, as long as I wore my plastic cup, Kenny no longer could tell and/or be embarrassed by the obvious swelling of my dick. Out of sight, out of mind, was how I had it figured.

At first, my hard dick stuck around only for as long as it took Kenny to get out the door. After awhile, though, it mysteriously assumed a longer life. Suddenly, I had to wear the plastic codpiece to sessions with whomever the next patient scheduled after Kenny. It didn't seem to matter, either, if that next patient was man or woman, young or old, cute or ugly, gay or straight, or whether he/she had feet rife with the most odious types of corns, calluses, and bunions.

I started jerking off, immediately after each session with Kenny, just to be rid of my bothersome boner which, otherwise, became damned distracting.

I told the girl in charge of scheduling, "Ink me in a break right after every one of the Jalonson kid's appointments, will you?" As we were allowed two breaks in the morning, as well as two in the afternoon, no one found my request unusual.

I'd whack off in the can. Initially, all it took was a few seconds of some steady, hard beating, and my dick spit cum. After which, I could count on my dick staying soft for the rest of the day.

That go-soft-after-a-whacking, though, didn't hold true if I shut my eyes and fantasized Kenny, his foot tucked against my groin, while I whipped my dick to climax. If I added fantasies of Kenny to the mix, I'd have to cream at least twice before my cock lost its starch. So, I tried not to fantasize Kenny and his foot all that often.

Not that I ended up with too much choice, in the matter, since fantasies of Kenny and his foot started accompanying me home. I'd wake up in the night, with a raging boner, and realize I'd dreamt of hugging Kenny's foot against my stiff dick. I'd be in the middle of supper, and my dick would get stiff before I realized I'd been concentrating not on my food but on thoughts of Kenny and his foot.

All of those thoughts of Kenny and his foot, and my raging hards-on because of them, continued even after the kid finished his prescribed series of sessions at the clinic. Some people have to keep coming back, pretty much the rest of their lives, but other's, once we've given them the basic exercises to do at home, don't need constant supervision. All Kenny needed was to be sure he regularly made the concerted effort to keep his thigh muscles flexible, especially before and after a game.

It was only after it became painfully clear that I wasn't going to be free of my fantasies of Kenny and his foot, or feet, no matter how much I wanted that to happen, that I began methodically beating my resulting boners into submission and trying my best to live with them. Made uneasy by how those orgasms always seemed a tad more intense than climaxes via more regular jacks-off, I, nonetheless, decided that pure fantasy was entirely harmless and infinitely different than if I actually had Kenny and his feet present with me at the time.

I took to propping a shoe between my legs, toe-up, sole as a belly-rest for my hard dick, whenever I flogged my hog. One of my old slippers worked particularly well and got splattered with my spunk more than once.

Just when I figured the Kenny "thing" was no more nor less than just a nice little addition to my fantasy life, Carlo Morandillini showed up at the clinic.

At first, I didn't see Carlo as a problem. I had his foot stripped down and tucked into my unpadded crotch for two sessions without experiencing even a hint of an erection.

Not that Carlo wasn't a good-looker. I even preferred his Mediterranean handsomeness to Kenny's Scandinavian peaches-and-cream.

Carlo had black hair. Carlo's eyes were just as black as his hair, and they came with dark-dark eyebrows and lush eyelashes.

He had a classical Paul Newman nose. He had full lips. He had two dimples, not counting the one in his chin.

He had a dark fan of body hair across his rectangular pectorals, funneled through his pectoral cleavage, and marched down his muscled belly to the denser pubic hair bushed at his crotch.

Even the first time he provided me a good look up the left leg of his boxer shorts, as far as his impressively uncircumcised dick and his black-haired balls, Carlo didn't see me "losing it" like I had with Kenny.

Carlo played varsity football for Genesse, a rival of Kenny's Palladium. A fact that never once had me make any connection between Kenny and Carlo. I'd never had more than basic exposure to team sports, throughout my schooling, in that I'd focused more on sports that emphasized the individual. I assumed members of rival football teams only met on the playing field, didn't chum around afterwards.

"I'm a little disappointed," Carlo said, during session three. Up until then, he'd been talkative and friendly, but not overly so.

"It just seems progress is snail's-pace," I said, having misread him completely. "In no time, you'll be amazed that the discomfort is completely gone. What's more, it'll stay gone as long as you continue the regimen of stretching you'll learn here."

"It's nothing to do with my leg," he said. I had firm hold of his leg, gently massaging his muscled thigh, while he exerted push of his foot against the niche provided between my legs.

I was so innocent that I was willing to let what he'd said pass, without comment, merely continuing on with my own therapist-babble, "Push a little harder, Carlo. Not so much that it genuinely hurts, because the notion of pain for gain is a bunch of crap. Pain merely means muscles are being asked to do more than they've been adequately pre-programmed to do."

"Kenny Jalonson said the first time you had his foot against your dick, you got a boner the likes of which almost split the crotch of your pants."

I was so taken back that I did the very unprofessional thing of clamping Carlo's thigh muscles too tightly and making him grimace in pain.

"Sorry," I said.

"You should be sorry," Carlo said, his comment having nothing to do with the discomfort I'd just caused him. "Sorry, because you deprived Kenny of a good deal of pleasure by, thereafter, capping your dick with some kind of tin cup, each and every time."

"Yes, well," was about all I could come up with, not about to volunteer that the cup in question was actually, as Carlo probably already very well knew, of hard plastic. "Such things as spontaneous erections often happen in therapy, therapy being the hands-on healing process that it is. It's just very important that such things be taken in context and not misinterpreted."

"How come my foot doesn't give you a stiffy?" Carlo asked and actually wiggled his toes and burrowed the sole of his foot deeper into my groin. "And, don't tell me you've a tin cup covering your dick, at the moment, because I can tell that it isn't so."

"This conversation, Carlo, is inappropriate," I said and looked around, as if there were someone else in the room to hear us.

"I'm of legal age," Carlo said, calm as you please. "You're of legal age. I'm gay. You're ...?"

"Jesus!" I said when he didn't finish his sentence but left a question mark hanging on its end, as if he were talking conversation that warranted my frank response.

"You're Jesus?" he said and flashed me a very wide smile that deeply sank each of his matching dimples and showed his very white teeth to every advantage.　　　　"Funny!" I said. Just how unfunny I found it was evident in how I completely left off massaging Carlo's thigh.

"So, are you gay?" he came right on out and asked.

If my mouth could have gone any further agape, it would have.

"If you're not, I'll save myself the bother of any further come-ons. Unless, of course, you're bi. Unless, of course, you're as straight as a stick but always wondered what the much talked-about male-male sex shit is all about, me happy to oblige with your education."

"We're here for one purpose only," I said and got back into the routine that had my fingers trying their professional best to unknot the muscles still well-knotted in his thigh.

"It's because I so like the way your magic fingers work my leg muscles that I have these wild fantasies of turning those same fingers loose on that other muscle of mine that tends, at times, like now, to get so horribly hard and knotted."

"Look, Carlo," I tried to be reasonable. I tried to ignore the reaction all this had on my dick. I scooted back on my bench so Carlo wouldn't misinterpret the sudden swelling of my cock between my legs. "This is my work place."

"Who says a guy can't have sex where he works?" Carlo said. "Certainly not that swelling boner of yours."

"I could be fired for what a co-worker might insinuate goes on here."

"I've heard it's unprofessional for a doctor to seduce his patient. But, for a patient to try and seduce his physical therapist?"

"No way does either of us seduce, or get seduced, without

compromising ethics."

"I really do like your long, lean look," Carlo said. "As does Kenny, by the way. Kenny far enough along to admit he's gay but not so far along that he's done 'it' yet, if you know what I mean. Although, I truly do believe he wanted to do it with you, if you'd have given him a bit more evidence, besides your hard prick, that you were interested in taking him on."

I convinced myself that the swelling of my dick was less genuine sexual turn-on than harmless response to my meeting one of the new breed of homosexuals, so young, so confident, and so early out of the closet.

"You should have been a little less uptight with Kenny, by the way," Carlo said, "and you could well have been the first one to sample his virgin body. Because, he really does like you. Everything about you, as a matter of fact, from your short blond hair, to your Liz-Taylor violet eyes, to your pert little nose, to your kissable lips, to your compactly thin-but-not-skinny physique, to those runner's legs of yours that seem to extend all of the way to your neck. Your truly monster-size boner another obvious draw."

He gave me another unbelievably seductive smile.

"Aren't you going to tell me that compliments aren't going to get me anything?" he said.

"Compliments aren't going to get you anything," I said.

His laugh was genuinely something you wanted to hear. Low and bubbly with mirth. Something seldom heard on clinic premises where most people suffered physical discomfort and were afraid they'd be subjected to even more before they were let go.

None of this to insinuate Carlo wasn't at the clinic without a real muscle problem. That it was the same problem that Kenny had was purely coincidental. Not so hard to believe when you remember every athlete probably suffers from it, somewhere along the line. Some jocks grit their teeth and bear it. Some jocks intuitively sense the cure is in more stretching and correctly self-prescribe their own cure. Some jocks have the resources to seek professional help.

"I wonder what my chances of seeing that now-hard cock of yours outside your pants," Carlo said. "I kept hoping you'd strip to your underpants, just once, and give me a peek. I even went out of my way to be sure my cock and balls were well-displayed, whenever you had me strip to my briefs. It doesn't seem you're swayed by subtlety, though, so ..."

I didn't unzip and yank out my hardening dick, but I did shift my cock manually to ease the pain from it having stiffened into an inconvenient bend.

"Come on," Carlo said. "Pull out your dick and let's have a look."

"This hardly the place or time, " I said.

"You want me to keep the ball rolling, that it?" he said and hooked his thumbs front-center his brief's waistband. His fingers angled downward in parenthesis and in emphasis of his erect penis.

"Don't!" I said and knew what he was going to do even before he did it.

His thumbs pulled out the elastic, and he tugged the waistband, and the attached underpants crotch, down the total length of his stiff dick, finally letting the elastic snap into place beneath his testicles. The only balls Carlo had kept "rolling" were his, up and over the elastic spillway he'd so skillfully provided for them.

His long cock was made fat by a copious foreskin that coated its steely inner cockcore as sufficiently as any Arctic parka. So thoroughly was his cockhead cowled by his prepuce, even with his cock erect, the flare of his cockcorona, and most of its knobby shape, were discernable only as a familiar piece of furniture is recognized when draped by a dustcover. His balls were large and shifted within his hairy scrotum like weasels furiously fucking in a burlap bag.

"Someone can come in at any time," I said and visibly sweated. "Someone to tell me to take a call on line one. The receptionist to say there's someone to see me. Something to do with a change in a scheduled therapy session."

"How many times I been here now?" Carlo said. "Twice before this one, right? Kenny here how many times? No one interrupting any of those sessions with word of any incoming phone call, or need for you to see someone, or some change in scheduled therapy. Even Kenny said you and he could have fucked and sucked up a storm, any old time, you had so much privacy. Nothing I've seen to prove differently."

"Just because someone hasn't walked in before, doesn't mean it's not going to happen any minute. There's even a law that states anything that can go wrong will go wrong."

"Yeah, The Peter Principle," he said. "And, speaking of peter ...."

"Actually, The Peter Principle, though it may seem to fit, considering the size of the peter you've on display, and the one I've in my pants, has more to do with job performance and where it inappropriately puts someone on the corporate ladder."

"Whatever," he said. "I'll concede this may not be the best place to have our dicks out, my foot pressed against yours, me flogging my boner to eruption."

He made no effort to re-pants his swollen pecker. He stroked his stiff meat with one hand, and his other hand cupped and fondled his nuts.

"Which means," he said and grinned from ear to ear," that the sooner you agree for us to take up, where we leave off here, in a totally safe place, the better off we're both likely to be. How about we schedule something for my place?"

"Your place?" I didn't find that a viable alternative, and he immediately guessed why.

"Mom and Dad out of town this weekend," he assured me.

"And if they come back unexpectedly?" I couldn't help but count upon the very worst scenario.

"I've a whole wing of a very big house to my very own, so there'll be plenty of time and opportunity to slip you out the back way."

"I don't think so," I said. I was made more and more uneasy, not only by the danger of his sitting there, his hard cock and balls flagrantly on display, when no way would anyone interpret his dick, hard and naked, as part of any professionally acceptable therapy program, but because there was something I found tremendously sexy about the triad of his hard cock, my hard cock, and the sole of his foot. The latter was still aligned with, although no longer touching, the length of my stiff dick.

"Then, I guess we're talking your place," he said and gave his cock another caress, gave his balls another languid fondle. "You fancy Saturday or Sunday? I realize you might have to work me in and around other plans you may have previously had for this weekend."

"I really don't think our meeting at my place, your place, any place, ever again, is a good idea," I said.

"It's not like I'm giving you a choice, beyond the where and when, though, is it?" he said. "My hard cock and studly balls stay naked and on display, here and now, until you've inked me in for either your place or mine."

"That's sexual blackmail."

He laughed. You had to see all his white teeth, and the way his dimples caved so fucking attractively into his cheeks, to believe just how sexy he looked when amused. It was a sexiness that had nothing whatsoever to do with the complementary sexiness of his feet, his stiff dick, and his studly balls.

"At least I'm not hearing you scream sexual harassment," he said and eyed me mischievously over the thrust of his hard cock and the hang of his nuts. "While it may be difficult to tell if a woman means no when she says it, it's pretty obvious, by the evidence in your pants, that you saying no means the complete opposite."

I told him to come to my place Saturday night. What else could I do, except call his bluff and end up, as a result, with him still there, in that room at the clinic, his hard cock long enough and hard enough to provide him a chin-rest, when my next patient came in?

After I finally got him to put his cock and balls back in his shorts, got him through his scheduled routine of stretching exercises, got him dressed and out the door, I asked Jerry Winesap to take my next patient while I took care of a bellyache. In the can, I whipped off my stiff dick three times in quick succession. Even then, my seemingly spent pecker, finally stuffed back into my pants, was nowhere nearly as soft as it could be.

Come Saturday, I figured to spend the day, until Carlo's arrival, doing nothing but regularly beating my dick and wiping up its spilled cream. If I could prove to him that the whole idea of sex with him didn't give me even the hint of an erection, my boner at the clinic purely an anomaly, I could send the sexy, precocious, and studly bastard on his way, our relationship back on a purely professional therapist-patient basis.

First thing Saturday, I wrapped my conveniently hard pecker with my fist and beat it like sixty. I didn't get it to a climax, though. I stopped even before any sign of preseminal goo. Something warned me that beating my meat once, even a hundred times that day, merely cut off my nose to spite my face.

After all, Carlo and I were legally adults. If he still lived with his parents, still went to school, that had nothing to do with his every right to propose sex with me, and my every right to say, yes. If I remained vaguely concerned about the ethical aspects, it wasn't as if I'd taken unfair advantage of a patient's vulnerability. Two therapy sessions were hardly enough for me to seduce anyone who'd not come through my door hot to trot, even if I'd been hell-bent on seduction. Hell, I was the one seduced! Obviously, Carlo had a helluva lot more experience in seduction than I did, more than I'd probably ever have.

I carted around a genuinely rampant stiffy for the whole day. It was a genuine test of will not to grab hold, at least once, and whack it to creaming. By the time Carlo arrived, silly-ass grin on his handsome face, I thought for sure, when and if I dropped my pants for him, it would be to display the hardest cock and the most vibrant pair of blue balls since the dawn of man.

"At least your dick's happy to see me," he said.

No missing my hard-on, even with it in my pants. The crotch of my trousers had all day been so strained and chafed by my hard cock, anxious to be free and whipped into submission, that the material came across as having been worn paper thin.

"Just so you know that me and my cock feel the same way ..." Carlo unzipped, grabbed each side of his open fly and widened the existing gap, to provide me a glimpse of one thick section of his hugely erect dick. His cock was so thoroughly stiffened, I knew his cockhead had to be thrust beyond the low-water ride of his trousers on his hips. In confirmation, I saw the bump his cockhead made in the belly of his T-shirt.

I was beyond fighting against what was about to happen. I'd gone over all the pros and cons. What it came down to, in the end, were two healthy, horny, males, one just of legal consent, the other not all that many years older, controlled by basic wants, needs, desires, and pure sexual instinct.

Carlo's pants were unbuckled and it's waistband unfastened before Carlo had gotten as far as my living room. His shoes were left on the rug beneath the archway that connected entranceway to living room. His pants dropped halfway to the chairs I'd placed, facing one another, on the far side of the room. His T-shirt peeled off just before he sat down, his socks peeled off shortly thereafter.

I'd seen him in one state of undress or another at the clinic, but completely stripped bare, he was a genuine piece of masterful craftsmanship. A compact physique of diamond-cut muscle definition that had bulk without being bulky. Seemingly perfect body symmetry, meaning even I, who knew muscles and muscle groups, would have been hard-pressed to tell him where to focus his weight-lifting efforts when next in the gym.

"How's your thigh?" I said, my mouth dry. He was naked, and I was still fully clothed. I even wore my underpants, because my cock, hard and drooling throughout the course of the day, had required more than one change of briefs.

"I've only one muscle that need concern you," he said and fisted his dick in emphasis. "Damned pecker has been hard since morning. I thought I was going to break it off at its base every damned time I had to piss."

I didn't sit down. Maybe I waited for my dick to shrivel as proof-positive that I didn't find Carlo and his feet as attractive as I definitely did find them. Since Carlo and his feet had entered my life, my thoughts of Kenny and his feet had dimmed like pale moon to supernova.

"The only muscle I need be concerned with," he said, "besides my cock, is your cock. So, what say you quit playing reluctant virgin and pull out that dick of yours so I can see it before you prop it up against my foot?"

I undressed, feeling very much the virgin. I'd never been with anyone who seemed so much in fucking control. No matter that Carlo looked just as young as he was, there was no doubt in my mind, then and now, that he'd seduced before. Probably not specifically seduced a guy hot and bothered by Carlo's feet, but seduced enough men, in general, in enough sexual situations, to handle his seduction of me with far more aplomb than I could ever have mustered had our roles been reversed.

I wasn't really virgin at the time, by the way. Some guys, despite all their bragging to the contrary, need years and years to get laid, but I ...

What? Well, that's nice of you to say, but I've never thought of myself as genuinely handsome. Certainly not handsome like Carlo was handsome, or like Kenny was handsome. Fair-to-middling good-looking, I guess, so that I had my first sex, not counting masturbation, when I was twelve. With another guy the same age. Which had me feeling so guilty I next tried sex with a girl, actually a woman. She showed me a damned good time, too. At least enough of a good time so that I fucked two more women before I decided, once and for all, that I genuinely had a thing for men. Not for men's feet, you understand, at least not back then. The feet thing didn't start until Kenny, didn't escalate until Carlo, and wasn't full-blown until Teddy arrived on the scene.

Teddy said you're interested merely in hearing first-times, so I'll let Teddy fill you in on Teddy, me, and Teddy's sexy feet, if and when you're interested. I'll get on with the telling you about Carlo, me, and Carlo's sexy feet. Kenny's feet actually having been the first to turn me on, as I've said, but I didn't get to advantage that attraction until six months after Carlo officially stopped being a patient at the clinic, although he'd kept up regular visits to my place. One day, Carlo just showed up on my doorstep, Kenny in tow, and said, "Virgin boy, here, decided you're to be his first gay experience, after all." But that's an entirely different story.

So, where was I? Carlo naked in the chair, right? I, finally naked, as well, and sitting across from him.

"Nice cock," Carlo said. "Really nice dick. You were so damned shy in showing it that I had it figured as probably one of those pricks with ugly moles, or with a bend or a twist, or with veins like whole river systems. Granted, I couldn't detect any of that, my sole pressed against your pecker at the clinic, but a guy can't tell if a cock has a birthmark just by feeling it with the bottom of his foot, now can he?"

He put his foot between my legs, back of his heel against the chair cushion, his toes pointed toward the ceiling. It was as if his foot were a powerful magnet, my stiff dick an ingot of solid iron. My ass slid across the cushion of my chair as fast and as easily as any new-fangled magnetic train ever elevated and slid its rail.

I can't tell you the intensity of the jolt that shot through me at contact. Remember, we're talking a first here, as far as my naked cock against anyone's naked foot. With Kenny, and with Carlo, at the clinic, I'd always had my pants and underpants in between. With Kenny, there had, except for the first time, even been the additional barrier of protective plastic athletic cup.

The feeling with Carlo, his foot against my dick, was just ... Actually, I can't find the words. Maybe you could if it happened to you, but I'm still at a loss. It was something I'd never experienced before. A super warmth that took hold, at the exact moment of contact, and sunburst inside of me. Not orgasmic. Not that at all. No cum. Even the bit of stickiness at my cockmouth was leftover drool from my whole day of waiting for that moment. What the feeling was ... was just ... well, indescribable. Wonderful. Marvellous. Enough to tell me, right then and there, that there was definitely, and don't ask me why, because, as I've told you, I still haven't a clue, something going on between Carlo, Carlo's foot, Carlo's cock, my cock, and me.

"Hey, now, that does feel damned sexy!" Carlo said and scooted down a bit in his chair, his leg slightly bent, his foot nudged all the more securely against my naked groin.

My hands wrapped his instep. My thumbs and palms curled the sides of his foot. I mashed my cockbelly securely against the sole of his foot.

Surreptitiously, I checked his foot for any signs of blisters or athlete's foot; after all, he was an athlete. Had I spotted any breaks in the skin, I would have put on a rubber. I've never heard of anyone getting AIDS from balling a foot, but my motto, from the outset, has always been better safe than sorry.

Would you be surprised that I've checked out your feet, even as we've talked, and found them in pretty good condition? You're obviously someone who takes care of his tootsies, and I'm not saying that just because they've so recently been prettied up with a pedicure. Tell me, did you get your pedicure specifically because of your scheduled visit with me this afternoon?

Ah, I've embarrassed you, and I'm sorry. It's just that most people, Carlo included, if they know their feet are going to be on display, go to the bother of getting a pedicure. I pay particular attention, because careless toenail clippers can cause small cuts that probably shouldn't end up cum-covered. So, hold on just a minute, and I'll slip on a rubber over my dick, just like I did with Carlo, that first time, just in case you've a nick somewhere around a toenail, or a nail pulled away from its quick, that I can't see just by looking.

See, that didn't take long, did it?

The problem with most people is that they inaccurately assume that one pedicure, at the same time they're in to get a manicure, puts their feet in A-one shape. It doesn't.

You know the main feet abusers?

Yes, you might well think athletes, wouldn't you? A lot of people do, as a matter of fact. It's not, though. Athletes have the benefit of coaches who have learned from past experience that bad feet make for bad players who make for bad ball games that make for coaches losing their jobs.

The main offenders, aside from professional dancers who don't have feet as much a hooves, so mangled are their tootsies by the time they're finished with them, are average woman who constantly cram size-six feet into a size-five shoes. Then, come amateur hikers who decide to break in a new pair of boots on their first attempt at Mt. Everest.

Carlo's feet were in damned good shape, by the way. He'd actually washed them and powdered them, as well as had them pedicured, for presentation.

Carlo had a callus on the ball of each foot. A lot of athletes do. Each callus was quarter-size and rough to the touch. I liked to press one of them to the belly of my dick where the belly of my cockhead flares from the belly of my cock. That part of my cock is as sensitive as hell. Yours, too? I got off once, all the way to climax, just by putting a fingertip to that spot on my cock and exerting an intense circular pressure. Kind of like a woman playing her G-spot to orgasm.

Your feet, now, don't have calluses on their balls, but you already know that. The soles of your foot would have an entirely different feel to them, when pressed against the belly of my dick. Which doesn't mean the feel of them would be any the less sexy than the sexiness of Carlo's feet, merely different.

Maybe someday ... Say, would you really mind if ...? Just let me unzip my pants, quickly, and ... Yes, that is better. How about your cock? It can't be any more comfortable in your confining pants than mine was in mine.

There, see how right I was? That has to be far more comfortable for you, your cock and your balls out in the open.

Now, where was I before I got distracted by your foot, your cock, your balls?

Speaking of your cock, whomever the doctor who circumcised it did a helluva fine job. Hardly any scar tissue, is there? Not even one bit of webbing. Nice shape, over all, too. Something mighty impressive about the way it so decidedly fattens in its middle, like a snake having swallowed a hippo, tapering as it does at each end. Looks too damned hefty to stand so tall. Can you even get your hand around the fat part? I thought not. Your balls obviously more than a handful, too.

Nicely haired scrotum, by the way. More hair than I'm used to seeing on a blond.

How about your chest and belly? I mean, as far as hair goes. Could you pull up your shirt just a little ...

Yes, damned lot of hair for a blond. Sexy actually.

No doubt, is there, that I find your feet incredibly sexy? Likewise, having found Kenny's feet sexy, and Kenny, a blond, had very little body hair.

Kenny had green eyes, did I mention that? Sometimes I think your eyes are green. Sometime I think they're blue. What color are they? Blue-green! Why didn't I think of that?

You should shave that little mustache of yours, though. I'll bet you think it makes you look older. Actually, it does. However, one day you'll be older, and you'll wonder what in the hell ever possessed you to add ten years to your appearance when you didn't have to.

I've been side-tracked, again, haven't I? Okay: haven't we? I'll gladly shift half the blame to you, thanks for the offer.

So, this is pretty much exactly like I had my hard cock mated to the belly of Carlo's foot, except we were both naked. My hands here. Now, bend your toes just slightly so that your big toe and the one right next to it ... That's right. Those two toes cupping the head of my dick like tines of a ring cupping a gemstone.

Carlo a little less shy than you. Yes, I do think you're shy. You don't? I know you've got your foot propped against my cock, your cock and balls out of your pants, but look how long it's taken to get us this far. Not that I'm complaining. What's to complain? Carlo was sexy, because he was aggressive, when I wasn't used to aggressive kids. You're sexy, because you're shy. Sometimes, I like to take the initiative, like when asked if I could pull out my cock and balls, then asked if you'd like to pull out yours. Variety the spice of life.

Carlo a talker. You a listener. I'll give you Carlo's phone number so you can call him and ask him about his and my first time. He'll be delighted to give you his perspective. You'll come away with at least one ear talked off, maybe both.

I'd no sooner mated my cockbelly to Carlo's foot than he said: "Go ahead, fuck it."

So, I fucked it. No hole to screw, so I made a compact passageway out of his foot and my fingers.

"Better than any foot massage," Carlo said. "I thought it would tickle." By that time, I knew my turn-on had a good deal more to do with Carlo's foot, pressed against my dick, than I'd originally thought possible. The usual combination of Astragalus, Calcaneum, Metatarsus, Phalanges, Entocuneiform, Cuboid, Navicular, Ectocuneiform, and Mesocuneiform had been lifted out of any purely medical textbook context for me and made sexy as hell. Made his foot as much a sex organ as his cock was.

The same way I find your foot sexier than your big sexy cock. I prefer rubbing the belly of my dick against your foot to rubbing it against your cockbelly, any time.

When I do this, my cock shoved up so that its head pushes even farther above the horizon of your toes -- see my inches saying hello? -- I get a genuine rush.

You can tell, can't you, your heel against my nuts, that my scrotum is contracting around my balls: a sure sign that I'm getting more and more sexually aroused?

In the end, Carlo would have enjoyed my cock mated to his cock, more than my cock mated to the sole of his foot, but he gave no indication of that at the time. He'd had plenty of cock mated to his cock, but that was the very first time anyone had ever pressed hard prick up nice and cozy to the bottom of his foot. One of the disadvantages of his being so aggressive and as sexually driven as he was, going out and getting each and every sexual experience he wanted, was his risk of running through the whole gamut of available experiences all too quickly.

Since that first time I humped my dick up beyond Carlo's toes, then pulled them back into seeming hiding, like this, then up again, peekaboo!, he moved on to some pretty kinky stuff. I don't really envy him his need to always keep looking.

"Hope you don't mind if I jack-off while I watch you busy with my foot," Carlo said, that first time. "No way does hot and horny me just sit here, as sexy you foot-balls me."

By the way, if you want to whip your dick, like Carlo did, feel free. If your leg muscles were a little more flexible, we could bend your leg back so the heel of your foot hunkers against your ass, my dick still fucked to the bottom of your foot, and I'd be able to stretch the distance to put my mouth to your cock. Carlo couldn't manage that the first time, either, though, because of his thigh problem. We got to it, later down the line, and the novelty kept him coming back for a couple more private sessions. Now, he's too into handcuffs, dungeons, and chains to be coaxed back by what I have to offer.

Lucky for me, the way I have it figured, is how all I need is a handsome stud, a nice cock (not even necessarily a big one, although yours is admittedly big), and a sexy foot. I need all three, though. Just one, or two, of the three, and the magic isn't there. Which means, Granny Higgins, at the clinic for a sprained ankle, still doesn't have to worry about my humping her foot. You, on the other hand, had you come by the clinic, would have been a likely candidate for just what we're up to here and now.

Your hand looks sexy stroking that big poker-dick of yours. Carlo's hand looked sexy, too, stroking his boner, while I rubbed my cock against the sole of his foot -- just like this.

I used to think riding a foot, like my dick rides your foot, like it rode Carlo's on more than one occasion, had be like a cowboy in a western saddle on a horse -- you know? like the cowboy's crotch gets up close and personal with his saddle horn, he even holding to the saddle horn over rough terrain. Except, I went horseback riding not that long ago, western saddle and all, and it was nothing like this. All that horseback shit did was give me a sore ass. The saddle horn was hard as steer horn. No give to it at all, where there's plenty of sensuous give to the sole of your foot.

Mmmmmmm, this does feel good. Felt good with Carlo, too. Almost always feels good. Really, such a turn-on, especially when I've the additional eyeful of a stud like you whipping his naked dick.

"Finger-fuck your asshole," Carlo said, as if he'd had countless experiences with guy's fucking his foot, and he knew just how he wanted it to go. He told me later that he had laid awake nights, between the therapy session at the clinic, and the sexual session with me at my home that Saturday, just imagining how to choreograph our playtime.

I wasn't at all sure I wanted to free a hand to stick one of its finger up my butt. Two hands kept my dick nice and snug against his foot, like they keet my cock hard against your foot, and I didn't want to risk something so right for whatever the possibilities offered by a poke of my finger up my asshole. Especially since I could provide myself with just that kind of poke any day of any week.

"Come on," Carlo encouraged. "Just give it a try."

By way of further encouragement, he slobbered one of his fuck-fingers with spit and fucked his hand beneath his ass to jam his finger up his butt.

How about you? You want to give your asshole the pleasure of your finger, like Carlo did? It would be easier, of course, if you were stark naked, like Carlo and I were stark naked, but I'll bet, if you try, you can burrow your hand through the open fly of your pants, down beneath your balls, and ... Better soak your fuck-finger down with spit first. That's it. Then, lift your ass, just so. A little more, and ... How's it feel?

I could tell Carlo got a charge out of his finger up his butt, because his eyes got wider as he worked his finger deeper and deeper up his asshole. It looked as if he had such a good time, I decided to give my finger up my asshole a try.

While doing so meant that I could no longer completely encircle his foot and my cock with both my hands, I could keep my cock in place with the curve of one thumb. Like this. Then, licking the middle finger of my free hand, like this, and getting it soaked with saliva, like this, and lifting my ass, like this, and working my hand beneath my balls, beneath my ass, like this (only a bit easier because I was stark naked at the time), and sitting down on my finger, like this ...

Oh, but that does feel good! Carlo having intuitively known what was right for him and for me. He was good at that sort of thing. As our private sessions continued, he was always improvising little variations. When Kenny made it a threesome, there was even more for Carlo's fertile mind to work with.

That first time, though, the overall uniqueness, for Carlo and for me, didn't require we venture too far from the basics. Although, I did have a little something of my own that I threw into the works, which ended up really nice for me, and was an additional charge for Carlo who hadn't had even his imaginative mind playing it out quite the way I did.

You know what I did, while rubbing my dick up and back, up and back, along the sole of his foot, like I'm rubbing my cock against the sole of your foot now? While sitting my butt down farther and farther over my fuck-finger? Crooking that finger, up my butt, so that ... oh, there it is! there it is! ... I made contact with my nubby prostate and coaxed the very first run of my preseminal juice into my rubber?

Here, I'll show you exactly what I did. Well, maybe not quite yet, because I want to milk a bit more out of just my cock's fucking your foot, and my finger fucking my ass, and your fist wrapping your dick, and your finger plugging your asshole.

"Ohhhhhh, this is quite the trip!" Carlo said. Yeah, I agreed, just like you agree now. Quite the trip, it certainly very well was and certainly very well is.

Who could have imagined, certainly not I, that there was so much ecstasy conjured from simply adding someone's foot to the sex act? Or, maybe, I should say, adding someone's foot or feet to the sex act, because two feet in the mix can often prove just as good if not better than one foot. Although, that first time, with Carlo, only his one foot came into play. So, we'll make your one foot do for this occasion. Of course, if you and I had known, from the beginning that you and I would get into this in more than just verbal terms, we might have started off stark naked and tried to duplicate more exactly, from start to finish, my first sex with Carlo.

Oh, do that again, please! That thing you just did with your toes. Working out a small cramp, were you? Cramp-free, now, are you? Nevertheless, it felt good, the way a couple of your toes tapped my cockhead, just as my dick was sliding ... That's it. Oh, yes ... oh, yes.

You've taken to this like a duck takes to water, haven't you? Maybe, this isn't your first time doing this kind of thing. Teddy says you interviewed how many guys, like me, for this paper you're doing?

That many, huh? To think, for so long, I figured I was the only guy in the whole universe who had this thing for feet. Carlo and Kenny didn't really count, because, in the end, they were in it just for the sex, the foot thing just a bit of kinkiness that additionally turned them on, like the introduction of bondage and discipline now turns Carlo on. Less adventuresome Kenny has settled in with a lover and is content with sex of a more conventional nature, no supplementation, foot or otherwise, needed any longer.

I the only one of the three who definitely requires a foot, or feet, for good sex. Oh, I can get off in more conventional ways, but it's never the same and certainly never nearly as intense. Nothing like the ...

Ohhhhh, that does feel so very, very good! Not duplicated with my cockbelly jammed against even the biggest and best cock any stud might offer up on a silver platter.

But, I want you to tell me how many times you've done this before, because you're getting way too much of a charge out of it, and are a bit too well and too quickly into the game, to be as virgin as I first thought.

You think I'll be ticked off if you tell me you've done pretty much this same thing with everyone you've interviewed? That your shyness is really just an act? That you know what you want and, like Carlo, go out and get it, even if you're a bit more subtle in your methods than Carlo ever was?

Hell, I don't give a shit if you've had your foot hooked up with ten-thousand dickbellies that've webbed your toes with creamy eruptions. It's my pleasure to find your foot sexy as hell, no matter how many times it has been around the proverbial block.

So few times? Once I started thinking about it, I would have guessed more, but I know how it goes. A guy can have had countless of feet propped between his legs, nothing happening, until one day, one foot and one guy comes along that changes everything and sets into motion a whole new life-style. Likewise, a guy can have had countless of people, like me, tell him stories of first times with a foot, or with feet, in the sexual mix, until one day, one story, and one guy telling it, and one particular cock fucked up against the sole of one particular foot, makes everything different. We've all a different catalyst to set that special ball rolling, only a few of us lucky enough to have found it.

So, let me show you the little extra something I did with Carlo, for Carlo. The little something I came up with on my own. You might not have come across this yet, either, considering you're really not all that far into your journey for these good times.

I've not met too many guys who can do this, because not too many guys have muscles that retain the flexibility of youth. Muscles have a tendency to tighten up so far and so fast, usually beyond the point of a genuine return to original flexibility, that some guys even forget they've once, way back when, been capable of doing what I'm going to do.

My muscles kept flexible, because I learned at a very early age the advantages for keeping them that way. What advantages, you ask? Well, let me show you.

See how, keeping hold of your foot and of my cock, like this -- no need even to pull my finger out of my butt -- I bend on over your foot and on over my cock, like this, kind of scrunched down in my seat, like this, and put my face on a beeline for your foot and for my hard cock pressed against the sole of your foot?

Yeah, you've guessed it. I can suck my own cock, when I've a mind to do so. I don't know how many guys have told me that they'd have it made if only they could self-service their own pricks. Not that I haven't had some really good times, my cock sucked up my mouth to my balls, but never good times to the extent I've had when I've sucked someone's toes right along with a good part of my stiff pecker.

Now, this might tickle. Even guys who insist they aren't susceptible to ticklishness, Carlo comes to mind, tell me the sensation of my simultaneously sucking their toes and my dick makes them tend to giggle. Not because it's so very funny, but because the pleasure is so unique, so almost like, but not quite like, being tickled.

Mmmmmmmmmmm ... good.

That does feel quite nice, doesn't it? I thought maybe you'd like it. Carlo certainly did. For months afterwards, Carlo tried to regain the lost muscle flexibility that would let him at his own cock. Unfortunately, he never quite got it back, even pulled a muscle trying, and I'm not talking all the pulling he and I performed on the muscle usually hard between his studly young legs.

I'm going back down on your foot and my dick now. I'll probably stay there, sucking away on your tootsies and on my peckerhead until I cream. I'll let you know when I'm about to blast, by giving you another long and loud, "MMMMMMMMMM." Probably not too far up the road, by the way, because I'm almost ready to cream, here and now, having found all of this, with you, so fucking sexy. My sounding off will be your cue, if you're anywhere close to climax, to start whipping your meat like sixty if you want to join me in spurting hot and heavy cum.

First, though, something you might be able to answer for me.

If I'm a foot fetishist, are you a foot-fetishist fetishist?

OPEN FLY-FISHING SEASON

I loved my grandfather for his having taken over raising me from a very early age (grandma dead of a stroke, both grandparents dead on my mother's side, my parents dead in the eruption of Mt. St. Helens).

I loved my grandfather's collection of feathers, because it never ceased to conjure visions of exotic birds and exotic places far removed from Washington State's Olympic Peninsula. Of my favorites feathers were those from the birds of paradise: the exquisite emerald feather from a shoulder tuft; the very long tail feather, little or no vanes, which looked and glistened like pliant steel wire; the velvety red erectile fan plume, with purplish sides tipped with green and white highlights.

Granddad had pen pals and long-standing business acquaintances, worldwide, who sent him packets of ibis feathers from Egypt; parrot feathers from Australia; turco feathers from Africa; fulmar feathers from the Arctic; toucan and seriema feathers from South America. His collection included feathers from birds, like the Japanese hooded crane, the Haitian white-necked crow, both since put the endangered species list.

It was while tickling my newly dropped testicles with the delicate wing plume from an adult male ostrich, my other hand experimentally stroking the amazingly discovered erectile state of my suddenly pubescent cock, that I experienced my very first self-masturbatory climax.

All of the myriad feathers, in his collection, except for the extraordinarily rare or irreplaceable, were fodder for granddad's real passion, which was tying artificial flies for fisherman, himself included.

Of equal fascination, albeit on a more macabre, possibly even gross, level, was granddad's real flies, done in by carbon tetrachloride and stuck to corkboard. These ranged from the notorious tetse, to the edible Ephydra, to the more common house and horse fly, all used as models for granddad's artificial flies. Except, he was always quick to point out that some of his best and unqualified successes looked nothing whatsoever like anything produced real-life by Mother Nature. The trick was, if possible, to come up with something a fish merely discerned as irresistibly tasty.

That I eventually came to take up tying artificial flies for a living was a happy coincidence of granddad's enthusiasm for, and success in, the business; my early association of feathers with sex á la my first, and many subsequent masturbations); and my, perhaps, sacrilegious desire to improve upon God's work by presenting a fish with something fake he could deem more delicious than anything real. And, last, but not least, there was the undeniable fact that, once my young body had experienced its hormonal explosion into puberty, I found a good many of my grandfather's customers sexually attractive. Not usually those who were merely collected granddad's flies as pieces of art, but those actual sportsmen who got out from behind their desks and kept themselves physically fit while fishing.

Terry Salvor a case in point. Junior, not Senior, although I suspect the latter may have been a prime stud in his day. Terry, was twenty-two. He had ebony hair, a bit too long to please Salvor Senior who always found reason to complain about how it shouldn't even hang the very little it did over Terry's shirt collar. Terry had black eyes, lush lashes, and eyebrows that, while they didn't meet over his nose, looked as if they might yet do so if left unattended. He had a square face and the trace of a dimple in his right cheek. He had full lips and white teeth. His cheeks and chin had this sexy blue-black overcast that came from his dark beard that, though always kept completely shaved, seemed capable of sprouting full-grown overnight. His perpetual tan made his five-o'clock-shadow look far less blatant that had it existed on, say, my thoroughly blond complexion.

What I could ever see of his body indicated that it was in damned fine shape. Once three buttons of his flannel shirt had been unfastened, and I'd caught a glimpse of a deeply corrated pectoral cleavage; it and its accompanying vee of chest surprisingly smooth and bare -- taking into account the profusion of hair on his head and, if given the chance, the hair likely to have sprouted on his face.

His legs were made strong by lots of vigorous hiking into the backcountry. His ass was solid as a rock, the mere sight of it having given me the stirrings toward more than one hards-on before I was old enough to make any possible connection between his asshole and the shiftings of my dick, or, for that matter, between my asshole and his penis.

As for his cock ... well ... it always mysteriously enticed by seeming so perpetually hard. My cock, by comparison, always so soft and malleable, before my hormones kicked in, saw me, at first, quite disbelieving I actually saw Terry's cock swollen to such definition within his pants that anyone could tell he had a circumcised penis. Even when my cock got hard and seemed to stay that way, forever and a day, Terry's cock-bulged basket continued to impress me. So much so that it became, as much as that ostrich feather, a part of my earliest sexual fantasies.

Once my testosterone kicked in, it didn't take me long to figure out what it was guys did together, when the heat was turned up. After all, I was a child of the Internet, wasn't I? Once I started surfing The Net, checking here, clicking there, lying about my age on-line, I became knowledgeable, in no time, as to what one guy could do to and with another guy's hard cock and/or tight asshole, or have done to his own.

Knowing and doing, however, were two different things. Which didn't prevent me from including Terry in my ever-wilder sexual fantasies. As often as I made-pretend fucking his asshole, sucking his cock, and giving him similar access to my hard virgin cock, and my tight virgin asshole, I didn't believe for a minute the daydream would ever become reality.

"How's it going?" Terry said, over to my work station, after having purchased another of my granddad's original flies.

"Pretty good," I said and shifted my position to make room for my cock to go as hard as it usually did when Terry was close and personal.

He picked up two of my finished flies for a look-see. "Think these will get me any trout?"

"My grandson is going to be one helluva fly-tier, one of these days," my granddad said from across the room. "However, for the time being, I wouldn't count on anything he ties putting dinner on your table."

Granddad wasn't being facetious or sarcastic, or putting me down, only being truthful. I sometimes had trouble concentrating. As a result, hard as I tried to follow his instructions, my flies never quite came out looking right -- to me, to granddad, or to the fish. Not, as granddad said, that he didn't hold out hope for me. In fact, once he realized I didn't exactly have genius IQ, and couldn't get excited about school, in general, or college, in specific, he pretty much set us both on the course that would eventually see me taking over his fly-tying business from him.

"What say your grandson and I take these two flies of his out for a try?" Terry suggested to granddad. "We catch even one fish, and I'll buy the both of them."

"You wouldn't just be expecting the kid to lead you to a good fishing hole?" granddad ventured.

Granddad owned King Creek, the only private trout stream in the area. He was an ecologist before ecology became such an "in" thing. He was a tree-hugger from Day One who had bought up extensive Olympic peninsula old-growth timber and had such good rapport with the elders of the Quinault Indian tribe that they excluded granddad's land, under special dispensation, when they successfully sued to reclaim property illegally seized from them by the public, by the state, and by the Federal government.

A good many of granddad's regular customers bought his flies every year just for the privilege of fishing King Creek.

"Get your waders, kid," granddad said. "You can probably give Mr. Salvor Junior, some fly-fishing pointers while you're at it."

I was excited and uneasy. Excited because I was suddenly about to experience, in reality, what I had only, theretofore, experienced in fantasy: namely, some time alone with Terry. Uneasy because I had a boner that wouldn't quit, and Terry or granddad noticing it might ... what? Hell, a kid my young age was just as apt to have a boner twenty-four hours a day as not, right?

Access to King Creek was only a short walk. I had all intentions of taking Terry to a spot I figured had a fish ignorant enough to bite at least one of my flies, but Terry manhandled my shoulder, albeit softly enough for my runaway imagination to fancy it a caress, to steer me in another direction.

"Let's try near Deep Hole," he said. "If we don't luck out with the fish, at least we can take a refreshing swim."

Right! As I were going to strip down to my shorts, what with the boner I presently had inside them.

"Actually, I often come here just to have private access to Deep Hole," he said. He headed off in its direction and left me to follow. "You know how difficult it is, these days, to find an unpolluted creek for skinny-dipping?"

Wasn't skinny-dipping swimming completely naked ... in the buff ... naked as a jay ... not even a skimpy piece of underwear to do its piss-poor job of concealing the family jewels? Granted, the idea of seeing Terry naked was more than a little stimulating: more bulged ... most bulged ... went the already stiff dick I carried around in my pants.

Whether or not Terry had a penchant for unpolluted swimming holes, he was a damned serious and skillful fly-cast fisherman. A proponent of the old-time wet-fly method, he whipped the stream with each cast of a fly, and shifted the fly from place to place, as opposed to the dry-cast method which dropped the fly atop the water, dry and natural, and left it there for a fish to come along.

His butt was a marvel to behold as it moved, however slightly, as he performed each of his many intricate casting maneuvers. All his casts, I knew from personal experience, only possible after years of long and hard practice.

After no caught fish had resulted from his series of initial casts, he -- to his likely surprise, and certainly to mine -- hooked a rainbow trout that was a real beauty. I knew he usually returned his catches to the water, it being easy to do, in that cast fishing usually, as had been the case that time, only caught the fish's upper lip and did very little physical damage

"I think we'll save this one to show your granddad," he said and placed the trophy into his creel.

"Now ..." he said, obviously finished with fishing for the moment. He sat on one of the larger rocks on the bank, and I came out of the water to stand near him. "How about we discuss my chances of getting access to your third fly?"

I asked if he meant granddad's sand-salmon dabber which I had stuck in the baseball hat I wore.

"Naw," he clarified. "Think farther south."

As many times as I'd fantasized him propositioning me, I didn't have a clue until he reached out and actually brushed the back of his hand across the ridge my hard cock made in its leftward plunge down my left thigh. My response was a pogo-stick hop backward that almost landed me back in the water.

He laughed. He had a nice laugh. Deep-throated. Bubbly between sexy lips.

"You never guessed I was gay?" he said.

I shook my head. Hoping wasn't knowing.

"All those times I literally drooled at the sight of those boners you suddenly started sporting in your pants?"

I shook my head again.

I was at a complete loss as to what to do or say. "Too good to be true" was what I was thinking. I figured my brain had short-circuited: he saying one thing, completely harmless; I hearing something entirely different and sexually oriented.

"Tell me you're not a virgin," he said.

"I'm not a virgin," I lied. For some reason, innocent that I was, I'd falsely equated virginity with the last thing any experienced cock's-man would want in a young man.

"Well Not-A-Virgin," he said, "I know rubbers are de rigueur these days, but don't you think our full-body condoms a bit overdone?"

For a moment, I didn't get it. Then, I realize he referred to our waders that actually came mid-chest.

"And, since I was thinking of eating your young dick, we don't really need rubbers at all. Assuming your cock is legal. You are, if I've calculated correctly, eighteen, yes?"

Jesus, he wanted to eat my dick! Jesus, I wanted him to eat it! My worry, then and there, was that I'd come in my pants before I could even get my dick out.

"I'm a virgin," I changed my story.

Actually, he didn't look in the least surprised.

"In which case, I'll pay..." he mentioned a price which I found exorbitant, at the time, and consider impressive, even now.

I thought he kidded, in that I equated experience with high-dollar value, the same way my granddad's flies went for higher prices than mine did -- and would, for years to come.

"Okay, then," he said and, without waiting for my comment, upped his offer.

I blushed: something I could still do in those days. I felt the pinkness make itself known, even through my tan which, although decidedly less intense than his, was still respectable.

"Charming," he said. "Absolutely charming. Especially since I haven't been able to blush since before my cock was virgin."

"I want to see you naked," I said. Novice, I might have been, my whole body blushed red as a baby's spanked ass, but I knew I wanted Terry naked as a jay if and when he sucked off my dick.

"Well ... I suppose I've not yet gone so far to seed that I can risk the comparisons we're both bound to make between your teenage perfection and my older, far more used physique."

He stood, unleashed the shoulder straps of his waders and let them drop. Waders are of waterproof material so stiff that his didn't drop all that far, actually pretty much standing on their own. He sat down to tug them off, and I, anxious as hell, now that the ball was rolling, gave him a helping hand.

I clumsily unbuttoned his shirt, widening the vee of his visibly bare flesh at its open collar. His deeply serrated pectoral cleavage came into full view, then his washboarded belly as far as his navel. His belly button was raised in its exact center: like a miniature doorbell. It was the very first and last navel I ever saw that remained without any surrounding hair, without the assist of a razor. In fact, his shirt completely undone to the waistband of his pants, I saw no real evidence that he had any pubic hair at all.

He shrugged his shirt off over his powerful shoulders and revealed an even greater expanse of hairless, muscle-rippled flesh. It was all toasted golden brown and had this velvety texture. I touched it, without asking, running my fingertips from the indentation at the base of his throat, through the chasm dividing his rectangular pecs, all of he way to his navel which I pressed gently.

"Ding-dong!" he said with a wide smile that made him all the more handsome.

He unbuckled his belt but stood there, waiting for me to unfasten the top button of his pants and release the zipper tab that sealed his crotch.

Since he wore no underpants, his black pubic hair appeared as soon as the teeth of his fly zipper sighed slightly open. As if to make up for its stinginess elsewhere, this hair grew in wiry profusion, puffing out, more and more, like a black man's Afro, with each additional slide of the tab.

When the zipper was opened to its bottom, a thick slice of his monster cock was visible where it inserted downward into the left leg of his pants. That section of revealed dick was wide across its back, darker brown than the rest of his body, and lightly filigreed with blue veins.

William Maltese

His pants were more prepared to oblige with a fall around his feet, than had been his recalcitrant waders, but were kept from it by the way his muscled body, including the impressive curvature of his supporting ass, had been so thoroughly poured into them.

He took my hands and guided them along his waistline, my fingers beneath the waistband. A downward movement of my hands slid his pants over his firm hips and solid ass, freeing his downward-aimed cock as far as his still-concealed cockhead.

He dropped his pants the extra inch to free his dick completely.

His prick leapt to standing-tall position with a forceful upswing that would have knocked silly anyone, or anything, in its way. It presented its impressive belly for my viewing pleasure, where before I'd only had a view of its back. As equally wide as its back, its stomach was slightly round, and I could see exactly where the large inner tube had been God-inserted, within all that steely vein-striated erect flesh, in order to propel his piss and/or cum all of the way from his large-reservoir balls to his pouty prick mouth which punctuated the head of his circumcised erection.

His balls were even better revealed when he squeged his pants as far as his knees. Magnificent balls they were, too. The left hung in his scrotum slightly lower than the right, but each moved of its own accord and made the wiry black hair on its containing bag shift like floating birds on a shifting sea.

Large uplifted cock and drooped bull-like balls, now fully free, made his sprout of black pubic hair, veed at his lower belly, less explosively dense than had been the original impression. His total genitalia-package represented pure perfection: one large nut in perfect complement to the other, both in complement to his large dick, all in complement to his bush of curl-billowed pubic hair.

He bent to force the remainder of his tight-fitting pants down to his ankles. It gave me a good look, along the back of his neck, along the sexy curvature of his spine, to where the small of his back disappeared into the funky crack of his perfect ass.

"Okay," he said, unfastening his boots while he was down there, and stepping out of them and out of his pants at one and the same time. His cock, as he stood, was so close I could not only reach out and touch it, but I did just that.

He didn't jerk away, like I had when his hand had brushed the indisputable evidence of my stiff dick. Actually, he used my fisting of his pecker as a kind of counterbalance as he raised one foot, then on the other, and peeled off his sweat socks to make himself completely naked. All the while, my hand felt the sensuously sexy shift of his hard inner cockcore within the velvety sleeve that had remained even after the so obviously skillful clipping of his original foreskin.

"My cock feel pretty much like yours, does it?" he asked.

God, there was all the difference in the he world! Mine was still kiddy-dick, no matter it's size; his was undeniably studly man-erection.

"Just as hard as yours, is it?" he added. "Just as powerful? Just as stiff? Would be nice if I could see for myself."

He was stark naked, but I was still completely covered for fishing the creek, including my waders up to mid-chest, and my everyday clothes beneath those. All of which made his sculptured nudeness all the more sexually stimulating.

I actually trembled when he stepped in closer and dropped my wader straps for me, one off each shoulder. The complete drop of the waterproof material was hindered, aside from the material's stiffness, by the fact that my hand still clung greedily to Terry's dick.

"Unless we're both masters of double-jointedness, you're going to have to turn loose of my dick for the couple of seconds necessary for us to get you undressed," he said and flashed yet another of his dazzling smiles. He was so close I could smell peppermint on his breath.

Reluctantly, I unfastened my hold on his dick, my palm still warmed by its recent handful.

Terry was genuinely expert in getting me undressed. He physically placed my hands on his shoulders, while he knelt to aid my shedding of my waders. He stayed down to unfasten my boots, remove them and my socks. On his way back up, he unfastened, one by one, the buttons of my shirt.

I was a little uneasy as to how my body would come off by comparison to his. While I didn't consider myself too skinny, or too fat ... while my physique admittedly had far more muscle definition than other naked kids I'd seen my age ... mine was definitely a teenager's body, compared to his which was obviously all man. Odd how a mere few years of age difference, between the two of us, provided his body with a physical maturity that mine was mainly lacking.

"Perfect," he judged and ran his open hands through the breached material of my shirt, over my taut nipples, up and over my shoulders, carrying shirt material over and off.

Whether he really meant his compliment, or had intuitively sensed my concern and had moved swiftly to abate it, I hadn't a clue. I did know that I'd come way beyond the point of no return with this handsome young man who wasn't all that much older than I was. Granted, I was a virgin, from the word go, but I had no doubts or qualms that I would emerge, on the other side of whatever, no longer a virgin and possessed of a helluva lot more beneficial carnal knowledge than before.

My shirt off and on the ground, he wasted very little effort on releasing my belt buckle and unbuttoning the waistband button of my pants. His quick and easy opening of my zipper provided an immediate influx of cool air that evaporated, even through the cotton of my undershorts, the sweatiness my crotch had gleaned from tight encasement within skivvies, trousers, and waders.

He let my briefs remain, while my trousers fell. The snugness that remained within the hug of just my underpants, however, was no longer sufficient anchorage for my so-hard dick. My whole boner, except its belly-locked base, shifted leftward and upward, providing a moving ridge that wedged its leading tip almost against my left hipbone, but didn't quite thrust upward beneath the more tightly held line of elastic waistband.

"Oh, yes," Terry said and surprised by squatting and providing the first suck ever of my dick, doing so through the concealing fabric of my shorts.

The damp heat of his breath, filtered by white cotton, was like a jolt of electricity delivered directly to my cockhead. I needed balance to stand, and my hands automatically clamped his shoulders.

His spit was moist and warm as it soaked the material capping my cockhead. His saliva mingled with the deluge of preseminal ooze my cockmouth provided from the other side. All of the combined moisture, flavored by such close contact with my stiff dick, was siphoned by Terry, like liquid through straw. All that was left behind was a circle of dampness slightly darker than the surrounding areas of undrenched white cotton.

My orgasm was completely unexpected. Oh, I knew full well the intensity of pleasure his ministrations were causing, but it had been some time since I'd first played my dick to climax in mere seconds, and I'd frankly forgotten just how quickly the novelty of new sex can cause fireworks.

"Oh, Jesus, no!" I protested. Even as I was beset by the wondrously cataclysmic shudders that took hold to shake me senseless, I though: "Please, please, not to be over and done so quickly. Not when I've waited my whole life for this particular man's head burrowed over the teenage hardness extended from my crotch." Even as the first slugs of my pulsing seminal discharge were blasted into what cramped available space there was, Terry unveiled my entire exploding erection. With the skill of a troubleshooter who coped with recalcitrant gusher misfirings everyday of his life, he skillfully opened his mouth to immediately cap my cock, locked it, and conveniently reroute its each and every rhythmic blast that followed.

My cheeks, as well as his, concaved. It were as if the tremendous suction he exerted pulled so heartily on my cum, and on my guts, that it extended all of the way through me to collapse my cheeks from the inside-out. I sucked my gums, my spit, my teeth. I sucked, I swallowed; I swallowed, I sucked.

He sucked and swallowed. He swallowed and sucked ... cum from my dork ... essence from my very being.

He had become a physical part of me, an extension of my penis, as if another more perfect Adam had sprung full-grown from the head my dick.

My fingers helplessly combed his black hair and entwined those inky strands like snakes entwined silky grass.

A reflexive buck of my hips popped the remainder of my dick into his face, my blond pubic hair mustaching his upper lip, my balls providing him with a beard.

"Oh, sweet ... sweet ... Jesus-sweet," were the words I managed to find at that moment.

I was thrust to the tip-top heights of Valhalla, and I didn't want to come down so tried to stay there. Not the least because I feared Terry would be critical of my obviously premature blast-off. For the price he'd agreed to pay to service me, I figured he'd expected something a bit more long-lasting.

No sexual high lasts forever, however. Thank God, lest we'd all overdose on such pleasure! My first climax, under the tutelage of another man, was no exception, although it was longer than any I'd achieved up until then and have seldom matched since.

Rather than complain about how fast I'd been on the trigger, Terry was obviously more cognizant of the recuperative powers of any teenager's dick than, even I, a teenager, was prepared to recognize. While I prepared to offer him his money back, or at least a partial reimbursement, he munched my exploded dick into full and complete resurrection. The degree of his success, so fast upon me, quickly refocused my total attention on his hotly gobbling mouth, on my stiff cock, and on the recognizable waves of pleasure again at play within me.

Looking down along my chest and belly, I saw my cock inches move in and out of Terry's mouth in the small space provided between his head and my stomach. The shaft of my cock was glossy with his spit, the slick of my cum already washed away by his cream-dissolving saliva.

His mouth had complete control of my cock; actually, it had never surrendered complete control of it. His hands slid my ass, lifted the bit of my skivvies' waistband that clung so tenaciously to the upper curve of my buttocks; the front of my shorts having already been lowered to provide a shelf over which my cum-refilling balls cascaded like a blond-fur coat over the arm of some chair.

He tugged my shorts down my thighs to my ankles, not missing an upward or downward glide of his face over my erection. He didn't miss a beat, either, when I stepped free of my shorts to become as completely naked as he was.

His hands returned to my ass and his fingers slid inward along my asscrack, one fuck-finger beating the other to touchdown on the puckered entrance to my rectum. His loser hand completely vacated my ass and dropped all of the way to the hard-on sprouted upward between Terry's muscled thighs. I sensed, rather than had an uninterrupted view, how his fist smoothly began stroking the complete length of his steely pecker. Reinforcing my mind's-eye vision, of his hand-fisted dork, was how his shoulder muscles and arm muscles moved and sensuously shifted with his each and every whip of his clenched fingers along the shaft of his penis.

For me, the moment could only have been more perfect had I had a better view of the activity going on at his lap ... if I could have touched and stroked his cock, fondled his balls ... even as he stroked and re-stroked his dick and simultaneously sucked off my penis.

When he stopped the bounce of his head, his pursed lips once again locked to a halt around the very base of my dick, he swallowed, and the corridor of his throat closed inward for an more snug sleeving of my erection.

His hand, with its fuck-finger still petting my pucker, slid away, down my ass and inward between my legs to push my balls toward his face. At which time, he claimed both of my nuts within the very same suction that contain my hard dick. The decidedly painful squeeze of each of my testicles between his pursed lips, to join my dick inside his face, plus the resulting collision of my gonads together and against the shaft of my erection, caused me to provide him with a thoroughly helpless groan.

I couldn't believe he'd eaten as much of me as he had. Granted, my cock was no gargantuan monstrosity, but it and my balls, in total package, seemed too substantial a mouthful to have been so successfully gobbled -- gagless at that. That he still managed to find the room to shift my testicles with his tongue was just amazing.

I wanted Terry's secrets at sucking cock, munching balls. I wanted to learn the how of burying my face in the guy's crotch and pleasurably surprising him, like he'd so pleasantly surprised me. Except, it was hard for me to concentrate on mastering the secrets of his technique when the pleasure flooding me remained such a distinct distraction. Rather like a novice who tried to master the finesse of proper fly-casting, distracted each and every time, no matter how good or how bad his efforts, by catching fish hell-bent on pleasing him.

Terry's mouth pulled up along my dick and tugged my balls with it, my scrotum, pretty much compact by then, still managing to stretch with them. When my nuts popped out, both at once, their warm wetness immediately converted to icy coolness within the outside air. They didn't droop very far but kept tightly hugged, by their contracted scrotum, to the base of my dick, like burls sprouted from the trunk of a tree.

His fuck-finger was back on my pucker. His fingertip had been wetted down in its short absence, possibly by some of the residual spit that had ridden my balls out of his mouth. The slipperiness of his fingertip allowed him to do more than just stay poised at the door of my ass, this time, actually poking on through.

Oh, Christ, was it hard to concentrate on anything, except the pure wonderment of the exciting things he did to and for me.

Within every man who has reached the age of sexuality, myself included, I've discovered the capability for reflexive action, beyond conscious control, that allows for an instinctive going with the flow. My hips, seemingly all on their own, commenced the swinging momentum that coincided with Terry's continuing ministrations to suck my cock in and then spit it out to its head. In and out ... in and out ... in and out: an amazingly graceful cadence that stacked pleasure upon pleasure upon pleasure inside me.

I clamped my fingers to Terry's ears, first merely allowing my hands to ride along, then more anxiously trying to determine the momentum of his head-bounce over my face-fucking dick.

"Oh, yes ... so ... so good ... yes," was about all there was to my limited vocabulary at the moment. Even it came out pretty well garbled because of my accompanying grunts and groans as the teetering stockpile of pleasures inside of me threatened a collapse and thoroughly rumble my guts in consequence.

There were wet sounds from my cock entering and exiting Terry's eagerly sucking face. There were additional wet sounds from where Terry flogged his hog, his stiff dick gone sloppy with leaked juices that were precursors of the creamier stuff yet to follow.

My naked asscheeks dimpled during each forward thrust of my hips, my lower belly banging Terry's face with a force that bruised his lips.

"Oh, stud, stud, Jesus, stud!" I complimented.

I was flying high. God, how high! Certainly higher than I'd ever flown before. Somewhere close to Neptune; maybe even close to Pluto. Way, way up there. About to be consumed by some intergalactic cataclysm that would match the universal Big Bang in size and scope.

My cock sucked his face, harder and faster. I hung to his ears for dear life, fearful he might pull free and deprive me of the orgasmic release that had suddenly become of such paramount importance to me.

No denying I ... HAD ... to have climax. I might well have killed anyone, or anything, attempting to keep me from it. I was that keyed ... that primed ... that on the verge of complete digestion by the marvels of male-male sex turned lose inside of me which remained beyond any of my wildest imaginings and expectations.

"Gotta come, gotta come, gotta come," I said in guttural mantra. There no mistaking my uncontrolled compulsion to feed my roiling cum to Terry's expertly feeding face.

As I pumped into my final moments of face-fucking, prior to ejaculation, he commenced a slight rolling of his head that gave new variation to each and every up and/or down slide of his mouth over my erection.

His fuck-finger delved all the deeper up my butt, crooked against my prostate and sent a surge of electricity from my butt ... to my balls ... to my spine ... to my brain ... to ....

Blast-off! Creaming! Coming! Orgasmic release!.

I locked my belly hard and fast to Terry's face.

Erupting!. Blowing! Spewing cream!

"Aaaghhrrrruugh!"

Shooting his face chock full of my hot and heavy load!

I was awash in sheer wonder, totally amazed as to my high-keyed state ... as to how Terry didn't choke on the gushings I force-fed him.

He swallowed ... swallowed ... swallowed again.

He drank all of me, every last drop of me, unabashedly sucking for even more of me.

I trembled all over, my legs weak-in-the-knees.

I held tightly to his ears, as if I were a driver clinging tenaciously to the steering wheel of a race car and fighting to regain control.

When I finished ... rather, when I thought I'd finished ... thought I was over, done ... had blown the last and whole of my wad ... Terry dragged his fuck-finger out of my asshole, along the crack of my ass, to my balls. His milking caused one last oozing of tardy cum from the neck of my now orgasm-sensitized penis. He was as eager to feast upon those leftovers as upon the full meal which had come before.

"Ugh ... ugh!" I grunted as his head, with my permission, finally, slowly, came free of my dick.

He stood and allowed me full view of his cum-soaked fingers which still gripped his big pecker which he'd successfully whipped into an eruption that had coincided with mine.

"About that swim," he said with a wide smile. "I know the old wives' tale about not going into the water after eating, but ..."

"We swam. We sucked; this time my time, albeit amateurishly, to make my attempt at giving head.

Terry's hard cock not the only boner I ended up sucking in those very woods, in that very spot, on the edge of that very creek, over the next few years, all in the excuse of getting in a bit of fly-fishing.

In the beginning, certain customers, like Terry, bought my tied artificial flies which, in reality, bought them sex with the teenage fly-tier. Although by the time granddad died, I'd become just the expert at tying flies he'd always predicted; serious collectors so hot to have my work that I had constant back-orders. Even guys, like Terry, who no longer wanted sex with me, by then, because I'd grown too old and too jaded for their particular tastes, were still cognizant enough of fly-fishing to buy my artificial flies as the ones to catch the really big fish.

That said, I still have an ongoing list of regulars, who come primarily for sex with me in the woods; most having come along later in my life, preferring the more mature fuck I can now provide, over anything I every managed during my naive teenybopper years. My having finally achieved that Terry-like physique I always wanted.

Not that lovers of chicken don't still regularly visit, as they did in my early days of sexual exploration. These days, though, they come to buy Dillon's flies and fish Dillon's pants fly.

Dillon the nephew of a collector and regular sex partner of mine who inherited the kid, Dillon sixteen, from parents who caught him with the neighbor's dick stuck down his throat. The understanding parents having figured Dillon in need of the positive gay role model his uncle offered.

Dillon is no more good in school than I ever was, but he's genuinely skillful with his hands, as anyone can attest -- including me -- who has ever let him jack them off. He quickly saw how learning to tie artificial flies, when presented with the idea by his uncle and by me, when he turned eighteen, was an excellent opportunity for him to learn a well-paying profession and supplement with a well-paying pastime.

Since then, so many guys wait to take him on, he and I are sometimes tempted to beat them off with a baseball bat.

Not that baseball is the kid's favorite sport. Fly-fishing comes first and foremost. His pants fly being fished comes in a close second.

Someday, I predict, Dillon will be better at both than even I am. But, that's not going to happen until he gets in a little more practice as to the all-important nuances needed to be a genuine success in both sports.

UNIFORM SEX

Once again, I slot each and every inch of my sizable cock into the snug tightness of Laker Corrigan's sexy asshole. My pleasure having built considerably during the course of our fuck, I stay put and hope the pause will check the ecstasy enough to allow me to extend our screw a bit longer.

Laker has no difficulty with my game-plan.

"Do love your stiff dick firmly anchored to your big balls up my behind," he says. His legs, their ankles locked over the backs of my thighs high enough to contact the muscled swell of my butt, tighten so I'm more firmly locked in place.

My pubic hair, around the base of my fucked-to-its-roots cock, and Laker's pubic hair, running the crease of his ass, are so much one-and-the-same curly black that it's hard to tell which belongs to whom.

Laker's impressive cock is stiff between the press of our bellies. His chest is hard against my chest. His breath, when his nicely muscled arms loop my neck and take hold to pull my face down to his, is sweetly peppermint.

"Oh, so fucking marvellous!" he says.

I can't deny sex with Laker is good. My question is, why is it never better?

He's everything I think I find physically attractive in a man. His hair, inky black, lush, and banging his forehead, is cut short on the sides and in back. His eyes are as green as the China Sea, his eyebrows sexily arched, his eyelashes sexily lush. His cheekbones are high. His nose is perfect in that it's not perfect, having once been broken on Aspen ski slopes. His mouth is full-lipped and sensuous. His jawline is so sharply defined that even when he exaggeratedly tucks in his chin, as military men do while standing at attention for inspection, there's not a trace of a double chin.

His body is to die for, the result of good genes (I've seen pictures of his studly old man on the sports pages of our local paper), and his three-times-a-week workouts at the gym (we first met at a high-Nautilus machine and discussed the pros and cons of steroids which we both decided, since we were into muscle definition, as opposed to muscle bulk, weren't for us).

His physique has just the right etching and solidness of muscle to look as terrific in tight jeans and in tight T-shirt as it does in suit, shirt, and tie. You look at Laker, when he has his clothes on, and you never say, there's a teenager who obviously works out. You say, there's a young man in damned good shape.

He's got it all, as I've been told I've got it all. Together, we're enough book-end attractive to have had more than one voyeur approach one or both of us with proposals that we sexually perform for a fee.

Even now, on the bed, reflected by the big mirror that extends the whole bank of Laker's closet doors, I can't deny we present quite an erotic picture. Something about our suntanned skin, except for our skimpy bikini lines, forms one very attractive variation of the fabled two-backed beast.

So why isn't the sex more than good? Why isn't the sex stupendous? What's missing from all the seemingly perfect ingredients that make the end result less than perfect?

Not that I can complain too much. There are guys who go whole lifetimes not feeling even a fraction of the pleasure Laker and I milk from our bodies. My orgasms with Laker are always rip-roaring, and it's not likely this next orgasm is going to be the exception. Still ...

"Hmmmm," he says, and his anus gives my hard cock a squeeze that massages like the belly of a snake feasting on its own tail.

I kiss him, full and deep on his lips, and play my tongue against his tongue. Our relationship has progressed to where we freely exchange spit, convinced by all the doctors, and because we both take such pleasure in it, that there's little danger of AIDS being passed, one way or another, that way.

If Laker knew me less well, less confident that I wear a rubber each and every time I have sex with anyone else, he'd probably have the more to fear about getting AIDS from me, than vice versa, because I'm admittedly more promiscuous. Laker feels he's found all he wants, by way of a guy and sex, by having me in bed with him. He's even suggested, more than once, that we room together. I've resisted, although my resolve is weakening. My hopes of discovering that certain someone, who has the magic to unlock all the sexual potential I still feel untapped inside my teenage body, seems less and less likely as I continue to sample, and be disappointed by, the stud-pool out there.

Of all the guys I've sucked and fucked, been sucked by and been fucked by, Laker comes in right at the top of the-best list, every damned time. If only I could be sure he sits at the very tip-top, no one out there likely available to provide me with better sex, I'd feel a helluva lot better providing Laker the monogamous relationship he so desperately desires, now that we're both out on our own.

I resume fucking and begin the slow and easy slide of my stiffy out of Laker's rectum. I continue the withdrawal until only the rubberized head of my dick is popped through his anal doorway, his tight sphincter gummed around my foreskin where my cockcorona flares from my cockshaft.

"Ah, yes," he says. "Yes ... yes ... yes."

His hands run the length of my back, all of the way to the swell of my muscled butt. Each hand anchors to an asscheek for the ride down that pokes my cock back up Laker's butt. Once my cock is fully inside him, Laker's hands keep where they are for a brief fraction of a second, then clamp to hoist, at least seemingly, my butt toward the ceiling and slip my dick, one more time, out to its bulbous tip.

He rolls his hips beneath me, and my cock stirs in his butt like a swizzle stick stirs a gin and tonic. Hard and hot as any ingot of steel popped from the fiery furnace, his stiff dick masturbates between our muscled bellies.

Next time my cock takes the deep dive up his butt, I assume more of a push-up position. I like the view of his handsome face, slightly flushed even through the deepness of his tan, several strands of his inky hair wet and sweat-plastered to his forehead. His green eyes dilate farther, and he turns his head to one side and moans response to pleasures that linger from the way my hard cock so recently prodded his prostate before sliding right on by.

There's a sexy pool of perspiration in that little notch at the base of his neck. There's a glossy sheen of dampness down his pectoral cleavage and along the sides of each washboard ridge of his muscle-etched belly.

Another thrust of my dick up his behind, a farther lift of my torso, my back actually bowed, I can look deep between our chests and our bellies and see his cock. Naked as the day it popped from the womb, but considerably larger, his big and circumcised erection has its head pillowed by the slight and sexy protrusion of his navel. The halo of black hair that encircles his belly button now provides a dark halo for the head of his dick.

Nice cock. Beautiful cock. Cock perfectly designed for fucking my mouth or my asshole. I've never found a cock that fits better, does a better job of fucking. I genuinely wish I could quit holding out hope of a cock, out there somewhere, that can do better.

His dick is flat across its belly and back but curved along each flank. Not a dowel of a dick but more a two-by-four dick with beveled edges. It's circumcised coronal flare is free of all webbing, all of the way around. His erection an impressive piece of meat even when it's not anything but passively on display.

I can't see his balls, but they're just as impressive and are perfect complements to his dick. Some guys have big dicks and surprisingly small nuts. Some guys have big nuts and surprisingly small dicks. Laker's nuts and dick combine for a perfect package, even when, at orgasm, his scrotum loses much of its sag and assumes an exotic fruit-bearing appearance in its hang from the base of his dick.

His hands, off my ass, take advantage of the breach between our chests and bellies and fan their palms over my pectorals. His palms securely cap my nipples and rotate tighter to chafe them. It's more pleasure added to the precarious stockpile already inside me. It's pleasure that takes my fuck strokes from slow and easy to harder and faster.

"That's the way, stud," Laker says.

His fingers tent my tack-like titty-nubs, his thumb tips and fingertips pinching hard and steady.

"Right on," I say.

To which, he keeps right on pinching, and I keep right on fucking, and my scrotum keeps right on contracting, and my orgasm keeps right on building in my guts.

I go even higher into push-up to signal Laker that I'm not likely to control the situation for very much longer. I've about reached the point where my conscious brain checks out and leaves control to more primitive impulses.

One hand pinching one of my nipples, Laker's other hand searches for his dick, finds it, fists it, pumps it in pretty much the same steadily increasing cadence that my stiff cock assumes up Laker's butt.

"You've got me hot. You've got me hotter. You've got me hottest," I say. No lie!

"Feels sooooo good," he says and, then, provides more color commentary: "My hand whipping my dick. Your cock screwing my ass. Your balls elevating along my asscrack. My nuts swelling ... Jesus, swelling!... with hot and heavy cream."

The mirror shows us as two gold statues about to go liquid, our sculptured surfaces already seemingly beaded with our precious metal.

I shut my eyes to concentrate on the wet sounds. The slap, slap, slap of my belly against his butt. My lubricated cock fucking his ass within a vacuum almost farty each and every time I push, almost each and every time I pull.

I think of providing another pause to the fuck, in order to keep orgasm again in temporary abeyance. Thinking, though, is as far as it gets. I'm too far gone for pauses now. My fuse is lit. I'm into countdown, no chance of any demolition's expert coming to my rescue.

"Fuck me, fuck me," Laker says and punctuates with puffy little grunts.

I actually think I can feel the rubbery hardness of his prostate scratching its groove into the back of my erection each and every time my dick goes in his asshole and each and every time my dick pulls out to my cockhead.

"Jesus, stud!" I say. I want to say more. I want to tell him that I'm standing on the brink of orgasm and am already leaned too far over the abyss to be saved from the fall. I want to tell him to beat his thick steak however hard and fast necessary to trigger the release of his cum from his spunk-ballooned nuts. I never manage anything more, though, than the "Jesus, stud!" My constricting throat closes off all other words, allowing only the most primitive and guttural sounds to slip free.

"I'm going to come!" Laker says, and I think he's realized my temporary muteness and speaks for me.

As it turns out, though, Laker speaks entirely for himself. Even as my seeming gallons of pearly spunk begin their mad rush from the compromised reservoirs of my testicles, up the channel provided within the stiffness of my dick, destined for final ejaculation from the mouth of my cock, Laker's dick lets go.

Streamers of Laker's cream fly free. Great stringy ropes of the stuff speckle my chest and belly and drool like stalactites from my hard-muscled flesh. Those are followed by juicy parabolas of pearly translucence that are more easily captured by gravity to splatter, hot and heavy, like great puddles of volcanic magma, across the muscled plains of his chest and belly.

All the while, his asshole does marvellous things. Fluttering things, squeezing things, massaging things, fondling things, petting things, eating things ... attempts to swallow my dick. So intense is the vacuum suddenly at work up Laker's ass that I'm fearful, as always, that it's going to tug my rubber completely off my cum-spewing prick and flood his asshole with my creamy mess.

"Sweet, sweet Jesus!" I say, although it doesn't come out sounding anything like that. Such primitive howling must have been made by prehistoric creatures having discovered the wonders of procreation for the very first time.

I slot my cock up his butt one final time and leave it there, completely succumbing to the wave after wave of pleasure that sweep outward from my ass-pressured cock and throughout the rest of my body, from my head to my toes.

My fingers clutch bed-sheet. My still-releasing balls, like those bulbous rubber syringes used to clean ear channels, seem to have a human hand wrapped around them to squeeze, then squeeze gain, to release more and more cream from my nuts, through my cock lodged deeply up Laker's spasming butt.

When it's over and done, a long time coming for both of us, I collapse on top of him. I rest my cheek against his neck and hear his heartbeat, rapid but not as rapid as it was just moments before.

My full weight on him, I lift my hips to pull out my cock.

"Goddamn!" I say.

"Was that good, or what?" he says and runs his fingers through my hair as I turn my face deeper into his neck and kiss his sweat.

I tell myself sex can't possibly get any better. Something, despite all my conscious efforts to subvert it, tells me I'm wrong.

"Stay the night," he says.

"Wish I could," I say.

I never stay the night. It's become such a foregone conclusion that, though Laker continues to ask, he no longer requires that I come up with some logical or less-than-believable excuse.

Not that it's ever wham, bam, thank-you, man. It's another two hours before I'm actually up, showered, dressed, and out the door. There's more petting on the bed, before the shower. There's more sex in the shower, before I dressed. There's a final kiss and simultaneous mutual grope before I'm out the door.

I tell myself that I cut through the small park because it's the shortest way home, which it is. I tell myself that, sated from my sex with Laker, I'm not in the least interested in the sexual sounds in the bushes around me, nor in the gay men who make those sounds.

Nonetheless, I stop to watch a black kid's ass getting banged, his face, chest, and his belly jammed tightly against the trunk of a tree by some muscled and tattooed white guy who fucks him hard and fast. When the white guy rams cock home the final time and yells, "I cum!", loud enough to scare the birds, although none take wing, I can't help wonder if this has been the best-ever sex for him. Will all his other fucks, after this fuck that nailed this black kid to the tree with white beer-can fat prick whose head is tattooed with a skull and crossbones, be one varying degree or another of deteriorated intensity?

I move on, momentarily distracted by sexual activity, off to one side. I veer slightly, for a better look, at first thoroughly discouraged by what I see. In that, I'm not that fond of skinny people. I've yet to fuck or be fucked by a redhead that I thought worth the time or the effort.

So, what's different about this skinny redhead, and what he's doing, to bring me up short?

I try to get my cock out of my pants before my dick gets stiff and makes its removal more difficult. By the time I unzip, reach through the breach and through the fly of my briefs, my prick is about as hard as I've ever seen it. No way do I get it to make the twists and turns necessary to thread its way successfully through the piss-hole openings of my underpants and pants. So, I drop my trousers, then drop my shorts, and get full access to my standing-tall erection that way.

Pretty nice cock I have, too, boner or soft, or so I've been told. Compared to some pricks I've seen, complete with veins that look like the whole Amazon river system, or with strange little bends that can set the top half of a dick at a forty-five degree angle to its bottom half, or circumcision-scar webbing that makes a cock seem more butchered than clipped, my cock is pretty uniform in size and shape. Although, at eight-and-a-half inches, it's admittedly a fairly large size and shape.

Rocket-like best describes my pecker, especially when it's erect. It's a bit larger at its base than at its tip, but not much. My black-haired balls droop from my cockroots like cocoa pods droop from their tree. My cockshaft is round, golden in color, and doesn't show even one blue vein. My cockhead is a perfect thimble-like cap on the end of my dick. My cockmouth isn't one of those cleaver-slice indentations but merely an ice-pick hole.

I fist as much of my erection as I can and begin pumping away.

I'm hotter than a pistol, hotter than I ever remember being, and I wonder if Rudy, the skinny reason, can really,somehow, be the mysterious reason why.

I know the skinny redhead's name, because that's what Todd Rainwald, getting his ass fucked hard and fast by Rudy's cock, calls him. "Fuck me, Rudy! Jesus, yes, fuck me, fuck me. Ram your big cock through my butt, through my belly, and sock it into the base of my throat."

It's not Todd who causes my exceptional hard-on, because I've seen Todd before, have had sex with Todd before, and Todd has never turned me on the way I'm turned on now, my hand whipping my dick so damned hard my fingers are a blur.

It's not the voyeuristic element, Rudy and Todd fucking up a storm, there in the park, Todd's pants dropped around his ankles, Rudy's cock thrust through the open fly of his camouflage trousers, Todd slung over the back of a park bench, me peering at both of them from behind a bush. I've been in this park plenty of times, seen plenty of sex, whether singles, doubles, ménage a trois, foursomes, fivesomes, downright orgies of sucking and fucking. I've been made horny by all of those, but nowhere nearly as horny as this horny.

It's not just the tremendous stiffness of my cock that tells me Rudy is somehow special. It's that little extra something in my gut, down deep in the pit of my belly. My nuts, rolling this way and that, in my quickly contracting scrotum, ooze a unique pleasure that's been hidden up until now. Even my own caress of my penis provides enjoyment previously lain dormant during countless previous masturbatory leads-in to orgasm.

Standing there, my pants and underpants pooled at my feet, watching Rudy's rubberized cock pump Todd's funky asshole, I try to make rhyme or reason as to what's so special about Rudy to get me in the state I'm so obviously and so quickly in.

Rudy's not have-to-bag-his-head ugly, but I've certainly come across more handsome young men in my time. Even Todd is better-looking.

Rudy's best feature is his red hair, and I've never been overly fond of red hair. It's white-walled along its back and sides, enough still on top to let anyone know that, if left to grow, it would come in thick and lush.

The red hair of his eyebrows and eyelashes is a less distinct red. It's almost blond and gives his face a kind of washed-out quality. His grey eyes are too wide-spaced, his nose too small, his mouth too thin.

He doesn't even have much of a physique. His camouflage trousers, from which his cock sticks, as well as his camouflage T-shirt, are both so baggy it's hard to tell if Rudy even has a chest or an ass.

As far as his cock, admittedly impressive in the way it fucks Todd's ass, like sixty, it's been flattered when Todd called it "big". Fair-to-middling is more like it, although it's difficult to tell any cock's real size when the prick is always being kept at least partially thrust inside an asshole.

Nonetheless, there's something about all of Rudy's not-so-grand appearance, there in that park, fucking Todd's willing asshole, that has had me hooked from the get-go.

"Fuck me, Rudy! Fuck me!" Todd encourages.

"Yeah, buddy, I'll fuck old Todd's asshole until I have you screaming like a banshee," Rudy says.

"Yeah," I echo, in mere whisper.

While the two wouldn't likely do what they do, where they do it, if shy about having an audience, I don't want to say anything, or doing anything, too noisy, that'll interrupt their screw-in-progress.

"Mighty tight ass, Todd, boy! Mighty fine," Rudy says. Which convinces me Todd isn't the only one who can flatter. Because if Rudy's cock isn't all that big, Todd's asshole isn't all that tight. Having been there, I know. My cock not having been positioned all that snugly, at the time, it unlikely that Rudy's smaller tool fares any better, now, than mine did.

Their fuck progresses to sloppy sounds.

There's the smack, whack, smack, whack sounds of Rudy's crotch slamming Todd's asscheeks, although those sounds are muted by Rudy not having dropped his camouflage pants for fucking.

Other sounds turn out to be my sounds. The swoosh of my swift fingers over my stiff dick, my guttural little pants from somewhere deep inside me as my pleasure builds in a way I can't recall ever so exquisite in all the other times, and there have been plenty, my dick has been coaxed into squirting its sizable loads of cum.

"Like that, Todd?" Rudy says. He bends into an even more pronounced hunch over Todd's rear end. His cock keeps its constant in-and-out prodding of Todd's asshole. "Tell me how much you like it."

"Really like it," Todd says.

Todd can't like his ass fucked nearly as much as I like it fucked. For the life of me, I still can't figure what there is about Rudy, or what there is about the way he fucks Todd, or what there is about my watching all of it, that has me in such sexual arousal.

I'm amazed by how my dick becomes suddenly slippery in my couching palm, because I figure I've somehow cum without knowing. My amazement increases when I realize my cock leaks preseminal slime, my dick not having been a leaker since the days I first discovered sex, those first moments of sexual discovery so far back, by total count of my sexual encounters since, that I've come to believe my dick had never been a leaker at all.

To prove the leakage isn't my imagination, my pumping fingers milk an additional overflow from the barrel of my dick and spread it over my cockshaft, like sugar syrup over phallic cake.

The slime momentarily decreases the friction between my dry fingers and my dry cock, but it provides a new kind of pleasure to compensate.

"Wow, I'm hot and getting hotter," I say to myself, as if only the saying confirms the reality.

Every so often, I see slight indication that Rudy may have some kind of ass inside the baggy seat of his camouflage trousers. More often than not, though, the rear end of his pants looks like empty sail that constantly catches then loses the wind. As appreciative of nice butt as the next guy, I find it curious as to how a seemingly ass-less Rudy keeps me so enthralled.

"Oh, stud!" Todd says. "Have I a load of cream to baste this park bench."

"Wait until you feel my cum ballooning the rubber up your ass," Rudy says.

All of which worries me that they're going to pop their rocks before I do. The last thing I want is to be standing there, unexploded cock in hand, helplessly beating my pud, after they've recovered enough, from focusing on each other, to catch sight of me and realize what I'm up to. Not that I'm adverse to doing what I'm doing in front of an audience. Even now, there may be several pairs of eyes, out there in the dark, focused on me, just as I watch Rudy and Todd's impending eruptions of pearly cum. I just don't want to give Rudy any indication of how hot and horny he makes me, because it'll give him the advantage. I don't want him too cocky (mentally, in that he can never be physically too cocky), should I decide to take this farther.

"Oh, yes, stud, yes!" Todd says, and it might as well be me, because I feel the click inside me that says I've pumped my meat beyond the point of no return. Even if I turned completely loose of my dick, then and there, it's likely my erection would independently proceed to orgasm.

Not that I have any intentions of setting my dick free. I grip it all the harder and pump it all the faster.

I grab a hearty handful of my nuts, in the bargain, able to handle both testicles only because of how securely they're contained within my leathery scrotum. I give a squeeze. Not too hard but hard enough to inject a bit of pain into the mix as a supplement, not a detriment, to my skyrocketing passion.

"Take it, take it, take it!" Rudy chants and hunches all the more over Todd's receptive body.

"Sweet Jesus!" I say, although it's more a hiss.

My balls erupt. We're not talking Mt. St. Helens but Krakatoa, my spewing cum so far and wide that I suspect some globules of the sluff set down somewhere east of Java.

I think my legs are going to give out beneath me: weak-in-the-knees suddenly something more than just a hackneyed expression.

As there's nothing to hang onto, the nearest bush flimsy enough to be pulled to the ground with me, should I fall, I take a firmer hold of my cock, as if something so powerfully big and steely stiff can keep me firmly anchored where I stand.

While I'm coming, I keep right on pumping ... pumping ... pumping. This time, it's not preseminal juice webbing my fingers but real, bona-fide, thick and gooey, wet and warm sexual spunk.

My ass, just the right size to let anyone know it's tight and muscular, no matter what trousers I wear, dimples as my sphincter purses.

Still more loopy parabolas of my sperm hurl from the pulsing mouth of my dick, pearly streamers fired from my massive phallic cannon.

"Ooooeeeiii," I say, because my cock is hypersensitive from ejaculation, but I can't make my fist stop beating ... beating ... beating ....

The ground is cratered from the soupy pearls of my hard-hitting sperm, some of the resulting lakes so big I half expect life to begin within them and crawl from out their primeval ooze.

My dick is soaked with my spent slime, my fingers as netted with the stuff as a fly cocooned by a spider for serving up later.

With a few quick flicks of my hand, I send flying a lot of my soupy spermal glove. I use a handkerchief to clean up most of the remainder, counting upon the absorbent crotch of my cotton underwear to absorb whatever I miss.

By the time I have my shorts and pants up and fastened, Rudy has his cock stuffed in his pants, and Todd has hoisted his dropped underpants and pants, fastening the fly of the latter.

Normally, this is when I do a quick fade-out. Except this isn't like anything I've ever experienced, and I just stand there.

Rudy and Todd exchange words. I'm still too awed by the mystery of my feelings to get anything, at least initially, than the gist of what they're saying, Rudy extremely upset

"You said ..." is what Rudy says.

"Sorry," is what Todd says and turns and walks away. Thank God, he heads off at an angle to where I stand, or he could have plowed right into me.

"You fucking, lying shit!" Rudy calls after.

I just stand there, the nearby bush no more genuine concealment than it's ever been.

I know the moment Rudy realizes I'm there. I feel his realization, even before he turns towards me.

"You know that shit-for-brains?" he asks me. Considering where we are, what just occurred, what occurs in the park nightly, how many eyes always watch it, I'm not surprised he's not all that surprised to see me.

"I've seen Todd around, yeah," I say.

Rudy walks on over and, I swear to God, my cock, so recently depleted of what I assume must be a good week's supply of cum, begins stiffening again within the still-damp crotch of my undies.

I find him no more attractive close-up than at a distance, although I must think him somehow attractive, lest why the little dance to elongation my cock is doing in my trousers?

"I like your looks far more than I liked Todd's," he says.

He smells of spent sex. The musky aroma clings to his camouflage T-shirt; to his bloused-at-the-cuff camouflage pants; to his black and shiny military boots; to his dog tags, two of them, each with rubbered silencer and dangling from his scrawny neck. Or, maybe, it's my rutting smells emanating from each and every pore of my body. Or, maybe, it's my blasted cum, going stale on the landscape, on the handkerchief stuffed in my pocket, on the crotch of my underpants in which my cock continues to expand.

"What exactly are you looking for, tonight?" he says. "Keeping in mind that jerk-boy Todd has undeniably depleted my wiener." He cups his crotch with his right hand, camouflage material crumpling like a hot-air balloon. "But I'm sure I can come up with something to show you a good time, if ..."

"If?"

"I'm kind of at loose ends tonight," he says. "Todd boy having promised me a place to crash, only to renege on the deal once he'd taken advantage of my stud services. You have someplace to stay?"

"Sure," I say. Do I actually want to take this guy home for a whole night? "Maybe we can figure something out."

"Well, as I've said, Todd got the best of my old pecker, at least for the moment. That doesn't mean the old dick won't be up and rearing to go before the night is done. Whomever takes it home can count upon it being extremely grateful before sunrise. In the meantime, I've an experienced mouth and throat that can show that lively pecker in your pants a good time it isn't likely soon to forget. Or, since I like your looks, I'd willingly drop my pants and let my asshole do some skillful cock-swallowing of your pecker. Provided, on the latter count, that you've a rubber, my having wasted my last one on Todd's ungrateful ass."

"I've a rubber," I say and produce it from the several in my pocket. Luckily, sex with Laker never leaves me without extras.

"Well, then," he says. "What's your pleasure, stud? Because, I'm yours to command, now and later, just for a bed for the evening. My trusting you to be more a man of your word than Todd boy who I should have beaten the shit out of for being such a shit. Not that I'm complaining, mind you, now that you're in my life. Todd not nearly the hunk you are."

I'm doubtful Rudy could beat the shit out of Todd, or out of anybody. He wears a military uniform, but he doesn't look military. He looks a kid, and a not very old or attractive one, who has raided his soldier daddy's closet. Of course, even the frailest woman can be trained in martial arts and be given the advantage should any Mr. Universe come at her with ill intentions, but Rudy doesn't come off as Bruce Lee, Claude van Damme, Jackie Chan, or even Chuck Norris.

"You want to let me stick my dick to you, dog-style, here in the park, promising a bit more action at my place later," I say, "then I've a bed you can use for the evening. Providing you've no qualms about sharing that bed with me."

I've got to find just what about this guy gets me hornier than I've ever been. Granted, my dick has always been quick on the recovery, but I'm amazed at how, after sex with Laker, after more sex with my hand, my boner is more than willing, more than ready, more than able to take on Rudy's doubtlessly less-tight-than-promised asshole.

"You've just found yourself a genuine genie, stud, to grant your each and every wish," he says.

He unfastens the rectangular brass buckle, all shiny, that latches his webbed military belt. He unbuttons and unzips his camouflage pants. He drops his military pants and his military-issue boxer shorts.

"Private Rudy, ready for short-arm's inspection, sir!" he says and manages a half-ass semblance of stand-at-attention.

No doubt, even to me, that he looks downright ridiculous, his batam-rooster legs, prominent hipbones, concave belly, and flat ass, exposed to me and to the night. Not to mention his small dick, for which "short-arm" is right on the money. Actually his cock, made even smaller by having so recently blasted up Todd's butt, has a rose-hip quality as it nestles, almost obscured by the deep thicket of red pubic bush that grows his crotch like out-of-control fireweed grows a corner of some neglected garden.

So, why is my dick made all the harder by a vision so less-than studly that I could never have contemplated it a turn-on, even in my wildest dreams?

"I guess this is what's of more interest to handsome-stud you," he says and turns his flat ass more in my direction.

What does he know about his butt, which has the gaunt cheeks of a man gone without food for forty days and forty nights in the deep desert, that allows him to know I find his skinny ass sexy? Despite my, as yet undefined, fascination with his rear, even with the way its flesh unattractively stretches its boniness, I can't conceive Rudy, all that often, coming across as anyone, front or back, up or down, that anyone would ever find all that sexy.

"So, what say you give me a peek at that dick of yours," he says, "so I'll know just what I've let my asshole in for, this evening? Here to tell you, your dick looked damned impressive, doing its erection-bit in your pants, buddy. Here to tell you, it looks damned impressive even now. Bet you don't find too many guys, like me, willing to risk splitting their bungholes, from their balls to their backbones, by taking on your monster dick, do you? Luckily, my butt isn't shy. Not that you're going to find it any less snug than if it were virgin."

He has to be kidding! Then, again, maybe not, in that how many cocks, big or small, besides mine, could maintain an erection long enough to go exploring, and thereby stretching, what he has to offer?

What remains so surprising, about the here and now, among the other surprising things, is how there's no way I get my stiffy conveniently out of my pants without unfastening my trousers and dropping pants and undershorts, at least as far as to the base of my balls.

"Oooooeeeiiii!" he says when I put my cock on full display. "Big I thought it was. Big it truly is. So big and so beautiful that merely looking at it makes my cock to do a bit of swelling on its own."

He turns to show me how the head of his little rose-hip pecker, complete with red-lipped mouth, extends a bit farther out, although the majority of its cockshaft remains puffy and telescoped.

"A sure sign," he says, "that my dick is going to be more than ready for whatever you may have in mind for it later. In the meantime ..."

He turns and bends at the waist. His hands slide the backs of his legs to his calves and take hold, his flat ass once again aimed directly at me.

I walk on up, keeping my unfastened pants in place just beneath my ass and balls. When I stand right behind Rudy, I totally drop my pants and underpants.

Nothing about his ass, as I consciously note, should be as attractive to me as it is. It's skinny to downright bony. Its sickly pale white seems to glow in the moonlight, like white cloth glows under a black-light. When I put my hands to his gaunt asscheeks, I open his asscrack to reveal a sweaty, narrow valley; perspiration-soaked red hair, a clump here, a clump there, like rain-flattened bushes that cling tenuously to each side.

His asspucker isn't round, more lozenge-shaped, that illusion intensified by its medicinal pink color evident even in the poor lighting. The slightly bulged pucker comes complete with encircling ring of wet red hair, the red-hair-to-pink-skin contrast so noticeable as to invite some fashion coordinator to shake his/her head in dismay at anyone with so little taste as to have combined the two.

Except, there remains something else, albeit inexplicable, that draws my cock and me to Rudy and to Rudy's pathetic anal landscape, like a rocket programmed for one particular target area.

I remove the rubber from its packet, and I roll the latex down, over my cockhead and over my cockshaft, making damned sure the condom is fully anchored at the base of my dick.

It doesn't take much effort, just one of my hands, to keep Rudy's asscrack open along its crease, my other hand's thumb hooking my dick and pulling my cockshaft from vertical to horizontal between my belly and his ass.

"Don't worry about hurting me," Rudy says, his voice coming up to me from where his head hangs just about touching his knees. "My asshole isn't made of fragile glass."

I touch the nippled tip of my dick to his lozenge-pink pucker and follow with my cockhead mashing against his anal gate.

It's a back swing of Rudy's hips, though, that rolls open his sphincter and causes it to swallow a good half of my cock.

"Just like virgin ass, didn't I tell you!" Rudy says.

Just like virgin ass, if virgin ass is barn made roomy by all its animals having been let loose ... if virgin ass is so roomy that it takes me a few seconds to realize I haven't missed it completely and fucked the air between his legs.

"Oh, Jesus, that cock of yours does fill me up," he says and gives another backward thrust of his butt to claim all of my cock that's remaining.

If his ass is so loose, and it is ... if his butt is so ugly, and it is ... if Rudy, in total, is someone I still can't imagine, in my worst nightmare, as being anywhere near my real taste in a man, as far removed from Laker as our sun is removed from Betelgeuse, and he is ... what is there bout Rudy, about his ass, about his asshole, that gets me so damned excited and keeps me there?

"Good, yes?" Rudy asks.

"Good, yes," I say. Not a lie, but I'd really like to know why it isn't.

"Only to get better," Rudy promises and revolves his butt and stirs my dick within the seemingly far and wide expanses of his asshole.

I hold his hipbones. My thumbs overlap his asscheeks and press his buns inward, along their shared crack, hoping to puddle any loose assflesh against the sides of my dick and provide a bit more friction. Except Rudy's butt doesn't have any excess flesh. It has merely enough flesh so his ass can be called an ass only by the wildest stretch of the imagination.

"Fuck me! Fuck me!" he says.

He reaches back and up between his legs and grabs my nuts, the feel of his fingers on my scrotum sending a shock wave of pleasure into my wiener that's socked to my balls up his butt.

"Jesus, what big nuts," he says and tugs them for a meeting with his own.

My body goes into automatic fuck, although I can't imagine there ever being enough snugness to his asshole for my dick to get coaxed to ejaculation. During my next few strokes, he massages my balls and his, in close contact, rolling the four nuts on continual collision courses that spill pleasure-pain into the pit of my belly.

When he frees my nuts, I figure he's tired of working them over. Until it hits me that he's let go because he can no longer maintain balls-to-balls contact, my scrotum already compact to a point more basketball than shopping bag. No way does the leathery, getting more leathery by the minute, skin around my nuts any longer make the stretch required by his one-time handhold.

"Yes, yes, yes." It's not more of Rudy's horse-race encouragement; it's me.

My hips go into higher fucking gear. My belly whacks the bones of Rudy's ass so hard and so fast that I bruise my abdominals.

"Ride me!" Rudy commands. "Ride me ... all the way ... to creamy ... creamy ... blast-off."

He asks for miracles. Even if I somehow screw his butt to some semblance of orgasm, on my part, my nuts certainly haven't had enough time to replenish cum so thoroughly depleted by my sex with Laker, and by my sex with my hand, the later which I performed while Rudy fucked Todd's much-more-desirable-and-tighter asshole.

Nonetheless, no cum available, I feel the budding of something on its way. A something felt, in the past, as sure sign I'm headed for orgasm. A something, this time, decidedly unique. I'm not certain whether the uniqueness is good or bad, only that it is.

"Oh, but I can tell you've fucked butt before," Rudy says, and his ass commences another series of bumps and grinds, rocks and rolls, that persuade my dick, more and more, that fucking what it fucks isn't fucking-bad at all. The friction of his asshole against my cock is no greater, but something besides friction primes my cock for climax.

I've a fast and furious fuck in motion, my swinging hips maintaining fuck strokes that pop my dick all the way out to my bulbous cockhead, all of the way back in to my stalwart nuts, each and every time.

"Got me humping," I say. Superfluous, in that there's no doubt what I'm up to. No doubt I'm really beginning to enjoy it.

"Ohhhhhh," Rudy says. "I do so love it when that cockhead of yours butts my prostate and slides on by."

The accompanying roll of his hips is the movement that best assures a repeat performance. His resulting moan confirms when, once again, my dick finds his rubbery little anal gland, though I can't consciously detect the where and when of our cock to-prostate meeting.

"My prick is hard enough now for me to pump, would you believe?" Rudy says and proceeds to provide himself a hand-job. "Sorry, buddy, but you have me so hot and horny that there's no way I don't pound my pud in accompaniment."

"I've a good view down the present curvature of his back. His camouflage T-shirt slides, because of his bent-over position, and because of gravity, and because of the growing intensity of our fuck, to reveal half of his back and all of his belly, although I can't see the latter or the jerking of his dick that goes on underneath it. I can see his right arm, bent at its elbow, moving, this way and that, as his hand, having captured his swollen dick, proceeds with its phallic beating.

I even think I hear his dog tags jingle in their hang from his neck, until I remember his tags are nearly as rubberized as my cock which is headed for climax up Rudy's marvellous, getting more marvellous by the second, asshole.

"I'm about to..." I say.

About to what? Blow? I'm still not sure I've the cum to spare.

"... orgasm," I finish my thought. Orgasm possibly not requiring an actual release of cream, in that someone told me guys with vasectomies still gets off without seeding furrows.

"Make it last, buddy," Rudy says. "Make it last ... just ... a little bit ... longer. So I can ... oh, Jesus, it would be so great if only I could ... oh, let me cream ... right along with you."

At the beginning of this screw, I would have bet money I'd have no trouble making it last all damned night, it seeming, as registered by other than my subconscious, to be so downright unappetizing. Now, there wasn't a chance in hell I was going to hold out much longer.

"Better hurry," I tell him.

He takes me at my word and whacks his dick all the harder. He pumps his meat. He gyrates his ass. His dog tags swing left and right on their chain, and I catch glimpses of them.

"Hurry, hurry!" I emphasize.

It's my own orgasm that heeds my commands for swiftness, suddenly upon me, like a flash flood, all-consuming.

"Jesus, fuck!" I say, all mouth-agape amazement as I slot my dick, hard and fast, up his rectum to my balls, one final time. My basketball scrotum flattens against the gumming mouth of his pink and pursed pucker.

I hold his hips tighter. I worry my hips forward, my head thrown back, my back arched like a longbow being drawn. I try to feed more of my pecker up his ass but I've no more pecker to give him.

"Oooohhhh!" I howl at the moon.

For the first time, I feel the corridor of his asshole hugging my dick, clamping down and taking hold.

Only vaguely do I hear his, "I'm coming!" After which, all I hear is the tremendous roar inside me. A cataclysm turned loose, of such strength and magnitude that new cum, a deluge of it, has been manufactured by my balls, just for the occasion.

My cock rockets spermal bullets, hard and fast into Rudy's ass. The rest of me rockets into a heretofore unexplored, undiscovered, and totally unknown domain.

Afterwards I take Rudy to my place, after a short detour at the bus terminal to pick up his bag. It's a scruffy and battered duffel, stenciled name and serial number obliterated by black ink, probably from a felt pen, which leads me to suspect it, like Rudy's military-issue boots and camouflage outfit, has been picked up at some Army-Navy surplus store.

He asks if he can shower. I give him a brief tour of the bathroom, off the bedroom, showing him where there are extra towels if he needs them. I leave him to his washing up.

I strip down and collapse face-up on the bed. Impatiently, I wait for him to finish his shower.

Hard to believe, but my dick is hard. Between the park and my place, my quick-recovering pecker has regained all the stiffness lost after blast-off up Rudy's asshole. I know just where and when resurrection occurred. Rudy was pulling his duffel out of the bus-terminal locker, and he brushed against me. A mere touch of his camouflage cotton against my blue denims, and it might as well have been fast-setting cement injected into my pecker. I had a full and raging boner before we left the building.

"Aren't you a marvel," I say to my hard cock and hook its back with thumb and forefinger. I push my erection to vertical. It feels as if it might snap off at its base.

I look at it, amazed. It's as if I've never seen it before, as if its hardness is a new metamorphosis of my limp dick that I've only just discovered. Actually, that's exactly the case, in that never, in my whole life, has my weenie come to life so often and so quickly as it has this evening; not even when I was newly discovering those miracles of which my hey-my-dick-is-swollen erection was capable. Since Rudy remains the only new ingredient to the mix, I continue in my belief that he's somehow responsible.

"How is it that that skinny, tiny-pricked, no-ass scarecrow does this to me?" I ask my pecker, as if my cockneck will sprout vocal cords and an Adam's apple and my cockmouth will move verbally to articulate the correct answer.

I give a series of pinches to my pulpy cockhead that makes my cockmouth at least go through the motions of mutely mouthing words.

"Rudy's secret powers of arousal is this cock's to know, yours to find out," I throw my voice, like a ventriloquist to his phallic dummy.

I hand-wrap as much of my erection as I can and give a few masturbatory strokes. Rudy has only been in the bathroom a few minutes, his shower water hardly turned on, and already I'm anxious for him to finish, for him to head back through the door, for him to do with me whatever magic he's able to do.

I contemplate showering with him. I even go so far as to prepared my dick for just that by unrolling a rubber down its entire length. Except, my dick is so heavy with engorged blood, it seems too weighty to make the trip from bed to shower without disconnecting from its anchorage at my belly and thudding to the floor.

In the end, bolstered by an inner something that tells me, loud and clear, that Rudy needs a thorough and uninterrupted washing, probably not having had one in a helluva long time, I leave him to it. My consolation is my languid stroking of my dick, shutting my eyes and fantasizing what's to happen when Rudy emerges from the bathroom, squeaky clean, smelling of soap and water, maybe even with a hint of herbal essence, from shampoo, lingering in the strands of his damp red hair. His dick standing hard and tall because, in my fantasy, I make Rudy just as hot and horny as he makes me.

Except, I'm jolted by the sudden realization that my fantasy makes Rudy something he definitely is not. Namely, an attractive young man. Behind my closed lids, Rudy's eyes become less pale and less wide-spaced, his nose less pencil-thin and his mouth less skinny-lipped. His body loses its skin-and-bone and puts on a bit of meat and muscle. His chest gets pectoral definition, instead of boyish flatness. His belly gets ridged abdominals. He gets an ass. He gets a tan. He even gets a bigger dick.

My eyes open, and my dick is still wondrously thick and stiff in my caressing hand.

If Rudy is such the turn-on for me that he is, why am I performing mental plastic surgery on him and putting him through a pseudo regimen of diet and exercise? Shouldn't I be content? Actually, I would be if I only knew just what he has that does to me what it does. Is it his red hair, when red hair has always before been a turn-off? Is it his cadaveric body, when I've always had a preference for far more muscle? Is it his small dick, since I've always known I'm not a size queen? Is it his no-ass, although I've always gone after guys who had enough sexy butt to fill out the seat of their trousers?

Or, am I on the wrong track completely? Can it be that it's not just one thing about him that does the trick but the sum of his parts? Are all of his obvious negatives brought together into something powerfully volatile, like common household cleaning agents combined by terrorists to make powerfully volatile explosives?

Am I even wrong to question the why? Should I just be content that whatever it is, it's there in my bathroom, an alien creature, newly popped in from another dimension, prepared to show me sexual vistas and landscapes never known to another mortal man?

"If only you looked less man-from-space," I say to Rudy who's still in the other room, still surrounded by falling water, and deaf to my words. "If only you ..."

The shower water turns off.

My dick pulses anticipation against the palm of my hand.

I want Rudy stark naked, small cock, no-ass, skin and bones, and all, out of the bathroom and on the bed with me. I want to fuck and suck him to within an inch of his life. I want him to do the same to me. I want our bodies and the bed so awash with our exploded cum that the results clog shower and wash-machine drains for days, weeks, months, even years to come.

Just imagining is so good, it's hard to contain the bounce of my hand over my dick and the bounce of my naked ass on the bed. I have to remember that as great as fantasizing sex with Rudy is, as is beating off my dick in accompaniment, the reality is destined to be so much better than any blasting off in my hand could ever be.

The knob of the bathroom door turns. The door begins to open. I'm so hot and horny in anticipation of what's about to happen that I almost rupture my nuts, then and there. It takes a concentrated effort, and a violent pain-producing squeeze of my gonads, to keep my pleasure in check.

Suddenly, there he is, my miracle worker personified, stark naked, dewy moist from his shower, his little prick stiff and leading the way.

His balls two little marbles in their red-furred little purse.

So, why does my dick immediately loose its hardness? I'm not talking a slow fade to oblivion, either. I'm talking major deflation. One minute hard, stiff and ready to pop its load from here to China, the next a spineless slug erect only because I've got it firmly contained within the wrap of my fingers, like Jello locked inside a steel mold. It's shrinking sheds its condom, like a snake sheds unwanted skin.

"God, that shower felt good," Rudy says and comes over to me on the bed.

He spots my newly limp dick right off. No disguising it as other than the poor example of stiff dick that it is.

"I thought that impressive meat of yours would be up and rearing to go," Rudy says. No way he can tell my prick was up and rearing to go until the moment he came through the bathroom's open door.

To say I'm confused is the understatement of this year and next. It's like I've been hit by a two-ton truck that's come barreling down the freeway, doing fifty miles an hour over the posted speed limit. I'm stunned, I'm speechless.

"No harm done, though, "Rudy says. "My pecker is hard enough to get us through whatever fun and games your cock'll need to get it back into full operation."

Where I would have believed his divination as Gospel, a few brief moments before, now I'm full of doubt, as if the magician has lost his power. Damn-it, lost it, how? Lost it, why?

"What say I fuck your studly ass?" Rudy suggests. "It was your cock fucking my butt, if you remember, that got the starch back into my pecker, there in the park."

The magic possibly gone for good, I have visions of the evening stretching into eternity.

"Sure," I say and get him one of the condoms sequestered in the dresser by the bed. "You fuck my ass. You fuck my dick into full erection."

I want to tell him, "You fuck the miracle back into our relationship, buddy, or you tell me what in the hell mysteries you controlled, but minutes ago, that have now seemingly deserted you."

I roll to my belly. No way I let him fuck me face-on until I figure how I can bring back whatever it is, now gone, that makes his skin and bones, his washed-out facial features, his red hair, his tiny dick, his no-ass hind end, something far more than the mere sum of his thoroughly unattractive parts.

If I look at him, before I bury my face into the sheet, it's only to reassure that his dick is sufficiently rubbered to explore my butt. It's only because I want to be damned sure his dick isn't too small to wear the latex in the manner the manufacturer intended and in the manner safe-sex requires.

"Goddamn, I thank my lucky stars you turned up in the park," Rudy says. "I don't know when I've come across anyone who turns me on quite the way you do."

The feeling was mutual, buddy. Notice the past tense?! Hopefully, he will resurrect the wonder by merely slipping his prick inside me.

In the end -- rather, in my hind end -- I find the insertion of his pecker vaguely pleasant, especially when I shut my eyes and pretend it's Laker's cock inside me. Actually, the Laker fantasy doesn't work all that well, because Laker's dick was never so less-filling. Surely, there has to have been someone, anyone, whom I'd once let fuck my asshole with a cock quite as small as the one Rudy uses. In the end, I pretend I've a little finger rammed up my butt, because that's the comparison that best fits.

"How's that monster dick of yours?" Rudy asks, doing what I assume is his best at dick-stretching my asshole.

"Just needs a bit more rest," I say and wish I'd had the foresight to whip my dick to climax when I'd had it stiff and ready to go, not all that long ago.

"How about I give it a bit more incentive to balloon?" Rudy says and pushes his hands between the bed and my belly. "I've been told, by people who know such things, that I've magic fingers."

Hell, at this point, I'm willing to try anything. I lift my hips to give him more room for manhandling my dick and nuts. His body weighs so little that my butt lifts him far more easily than any bronco ever lifted a chowed-down cowboy.

"Easy on the ball-crushing," I say, because I'm not enjoying nearly enough pleasure to counteract the ache his fingers cause by fondling my tender testicles.

"Mmmmmmm, good!" he says against the back of my neck. At least one of us is having a good time. "What a perfect ass. What a perfect body. What a perfect cock." He gives a squeeze of the latter. "What perfect, horse-size nuts." He mistakes my moan of discomfort, caused by yet another of his forceful squeezes of my gonads, for pleasure on the rise, because he says, "See, didn't I tell you I'd get your cock primed in no time?"

I can't believe he believes my dick any more primed than when he first took hold of it. If anything, my prick is even softer.

"Tell me how you like my dick up your asshole," Rudy says.

"I like your dick up my asshole," I say. Not a total lie, in that it's not causing the discomfort his fingers on my balls continue to do.

"Want me to go harder and faster?" he asks. "I can go harder and faster."

"Go harder and faster," I say. I'm beyond believing that harder and faster is the answer. However, I feel guilty enough to want to do my best for him by counteracting my sudden desire to make Rudy pay for providing less than I imagined I'd get from him. "I'd like the feel of your cock speedily streamlining my asshole."

"Yes ... yes," he confirms and immediately progresses into higher gear.

His chin is bony against my back. As are his ribs. Whenever he varies the angle of his fuck, so that one of his hipbones collides with my butt, I end up with another bruise on an asscheek.

"Oh, stud, I do so like my dick stuck to my balls up your asshole," Rudy says.

I'm glad he's glad, at least content that his swelling pleasure has momentarily distracted him from mauling my nuts.

"Oh, stud ... oh, stud," he chants. "How fucking fast this tight butt of yours gets me ready to cream. How ... fucking ... fucking ... fast."

Rudy got off in Todd's ass in the park. Rudy got off in his own hand, while I fucked his ass in the park. Rudy is about to get off inside my ass. I should be so lucky! My only consolation is that Laker had pretty much sexually exhausted me before I even met Rudy. Possibly, all I now suffer is the recovery period needed by any normal stud who has already fucked himself silly, during the course of any one evening. Some guys are only able to pop their rocks once, and that's all she wrote until another sundown. I've done a helluva lot better than those guys, and here I am still bitching.

Except, my cock had been hard, on this very bed, not that long ago, Rudy in the shower. Or, do I imagine it firm, its mad rush towards orgasm curtailed only by the intervention of my fingers vicing my nuts?

"Jesus ... but I do believe ... I'm going ... to come," Rudy says, more than a little breathless.

A little jiggle of my butt is probably in order. Rudy, poor jerk, might as well fuck a corpse for all the animation I'm providing. Not that he seems all that hindered by my non-participation. Why shouldn't I believe him when he says he's about to come? His pumps of his tiny dick up my behind are genuinely piston-like as he pokes and pulls, pokes and pulls and pokes.

"Oh, stud ... oh, stud ... oh, sweet, Jesus ... handsome ... handsome stud," he says.

It's hard to be down on somebody so free with compliments. If he knew what the problem was, even knew there was some kind of problem, he'd probably be the first to try and fix it. It's hardly his fault that my psyche has somehow taken a nose-dive and ended up completely out of whack.

I provide a half-ass uplift and partial revolution of my butt. I follow through by clamping down on his primed dick with all the effort my ass lining can muster around so small a prick.

"Ah ... ah ... ah," he voices in final countdown.

"Feed me your pearly cum!" I tell him.

"Aaggghrrrahhhh!" he says and pops his cream into my butt.

"Oooooahhhh!" I say. Not because my cock is resurrected, because it isn't. Not because I've basted the sheet and my fingers with cream, because I haven't. I groan, and follow up with another groan, because Rudy, in his spasming ecstasy, frantically grips my nuts, not once but twice, and floods my belly with fast-following twin aches of genuine discomfort.

I don't immediately chuck Rudy out on his no-ass, even though he continues to fail in living up to my original expectations. I keep him around for four days in my attempts to figure out what in the hell went wrong. I had felt something when first seeing him fuck Todd in the park, when first fucking Rudy in the park, when first fantasizing how good fucking would be for us once he'd finished his shower.

For awhile, I convince myself his original scruffiness, washed off by soap and water, was what had pushed all my right buttons. Some guys get turned on by dirty shorts and/or by funky body odor. Despite how hard I try to convince myself I'm one of those guys, I can't make it happen. I'm turned off by my own skid tracks, even by my own body odor when it's particularly ripe. That I should so dislike some things so personal about me, but get turned on by them in someone else, doesn't make sense.

I'm relieved that, beginning the day after my major disappointment, I at least -- somehow -- begin managing hards-on with Rudy. I even manage to keep them, if I don't dwell too closely on Rudy's peculiar physicality. I manage more than a couple of so-so orgasms with him. It's just that the promise for us, once seemingly in the cards, obviously isn't going to happen. It's been a mistake, a misinterpretation, a fluke, an anomaly. It's been an-almost something that'll never materialize. Keeping Rudy around, in hopes of hooking the illusive dream, is no longer something I find acceptable.

Rudy a slob and a thief.

Rudy-the-slob readily evident after his very first of his many showers. The kid can't seem to get enough of my soap and hot water, much of the latter ending up splattered on the walls, the ceilings, and on the floors. The kid can't seem to get enough of my towels, either. It's not uncommon for me to find four of them at a time on the bathroom floor, each sopped, shower water oceaned in the floor-space in between.

I come home early one evening to tell him it's time he moves on. I should have called first. He's not there, but there's no indication, unfortunately, that he's gone for good. To the contrary, there's his by now all-too-familiar trail of discarded clothes, obviously the result of more indecision as to what to wear for his latest afternoon foray into the park, or into one of the surrounding city's gay bars or baths.

I pick up his blue T-shirt, his green T-shirt, his polo shirt with ridiculous alligator logo, his tennis shoe, his non-designer tie he uses as a belt but never as neck-wear

I stop at the coffee table, lift the lid of the small, wood, Balinese box that contains my cache of petty cash, and I correctly guess, even before counting, that it's again short.

Rudy-the-thief (and the slob) has to go.

Laker's feelings are hurt that I've let some mooch move in off the streets when I won't even stay at Laker's overnight. Just my luck, Laker had called when I was out and Rudy was in. I'm not sure what Rudy said. I'm not sure I want to know. Although I suppose I'll have to ask

Laker if I ever want to defrost the chilly treatment he now gives me.

I pick up more of Rudy's clothes and know full well, from past experience, that the trail he's left will dead-end at his duffel bag. I spot it, flipped open on its side, by the side of our unmade bed, as I enter the bedroom.

I pick up his camouflage T-shirt and his camouflage pants. They're what Rudy wore that first night in the park. I haven't seen him in them since, although I can tell, by a quick sniff, that both have been recently washed.

His camouflage T-shirt, his camouflage pants, his military-issue boxer shorts and boots and belt, his duffel bag, his dog tags: an isolated costume. Nothing else I've seen Rudy wear even hints of military service. There are, in his limited wardrobe, at least two cowboy shirts, a pair of jeans, three pairs of shorts. One pair of shorts is so short that you can spot even Rudy's short dick if you look just a short ways up its short left leg, whenever the short sonofabitch wears them.

I discard everything in hand, except for the camouflage T-shirt and camouflage pants. I ball those and give them another sniff, coming up with nothing but the scent of the clothes-freshener strips I use in the dryer.

I like something about them, even if its just lingering memories they conjure of their and their owner's potential somehow lost. I check to see if they're made of something besides regular cotton. They're not.

I rub them against my cheek and simultaneously adjust the lie of my cock in the crotch of my trousers. I'm similarly inclined to adjust my dick only seconds later and realize my pecker gives me so much trouble because it's stiffening in my pants.

"I'll be damned," I say, pleased and relieved that spontaneous erections haven't become solely things of my past. Recently, I haven't seen the onset of any of my boners without an extensive and concentrated effort to coax them into being, more often than not including some form or another of incessant fondling. "Yes ... yes ... yes."

I carry camouflage T-shirt and camouflage pants to the mirror attached to the back of my bedroom door.

I take a good look at myself in the reflective surface.

"Looking good!" I say and concentrate on my crotch where my dick is so stiff it's not really adequately concealed by the crotch of my pants.

"Looking damned good."

I drop Rudy's military garb, and I begin to undress. I've always taken great satisfaction in my body. Just how much satisfaction has somehow been overlooked, these last few days, with Rudy as a houseguest. It's time I get back in the groove. No need to wait, either, until after I give Rudy his scheduled little push out my door.

I put shoe trees in my shoes and put the results in the closet. I crumple my dirty underwear, my shirt, and my pants, for deposit in the bathroom hamper, except I don't make to the bathroom.

Narcissistically, I stay in the bedroom and enjoy the weight of my dick, sprouted from my lower belly, as well as the way my weighty dick plays back from the mirror. It's almost as if I've never seen my dick stiff before. I try to remember if what I feel now is anything like what I felt the very first time I discovered my cock in erection.

I toss my soiled clothes as far as the bed and concentrate fully on myself in the mirror. I look carefully, critically, as if my having missed a couple of evenings at the gym may already have me converted from stud-muffin to fat-young-man with love handles.

I check specifically for excess fat, along my face, beneath my chin, down my neck, across my chest, down my belly. All I detect is velvety-textured and tanned flesh molded sensuously over an admittedly still-impressive framework of well-etched muscle.

I palm my scrotum and let it overflow my fingers while my hand, albeit barely, contains both nuts.

I bend forward slowly to test my flexibility. I wait for telltale muscle tinges to tell me I've gone way too long without my regular regimen of stretching exercises.   I slide my hands down my legs, behind my calves, and I bend my torso even farther forward.

Every indication tells me I'm still limber enough to lick my dick, if I choose to do so.

What a discovery, that first time I realized I could actually suck my own cock. It had taken viewing some double-joined kid, performing self-fellatio in a fuck movie to convince me I should give it a try. Not that I met with instant success. It took me a good year of private yoga lessons, and only then because I asked for special attention from my instructor whom I'd correctly figured would know the secrets of eating one's own dick, if anyone knew. It helped that he'd, also, been covetous of my young ass. The stretching program he tailored specifically for me more often than not had my legs thrown over my head, my dick getting nearer and nearer my mouth as his dick shoved deeper and deeper up my asshole.

Before my bedroom mirror, I lick my dick but get distracted by Rudy's camouflage gear still pretty much heaped at my feet.

I squat for the camouflage T-shirt and the camouflage pants. I stand and squeeze the material into a large ball that I press tightly up beneath my balls and against the base of my erection.

Maybe it's the pressure of the camouflage cloth against the spot that connects my balls to my ass ... Maybe, it's my re-discovery that I can get a spontaneous hard-on ... Maybe, it's my preparedness to discard my hopeless search for perfect sex, at least with Rudy ... Whatever, my cockmouth leaks a bead of preseminal goo which I immediately lap, made excited by the slightly saline taste and oily consistency that brings back a flood of childhood memories directly linked to my initial sexual awakening.

I tuck the camouflage T-shirt under an arm. I shake out the pants and hold their waistband to my waist. They're obviously a bit high-water, in the legs, but they otherwise look as if they'll fit. After all, Rudy inside them looks like a pismire swimming the Pacific.

However, do I, so recently undressed, want to put them on? Isn't there a known degree of pleasure to be had in doing myself while I'm stripped completely naked? Don't I spend so much time in the gym just so I'll look studly whenever naked as a jay?

I crumple the camouflage pants and the camouflage T-shirt with all intentions of giving them a toss. Instead, I give them another sniff, another rub against my cheek. I dust-rag them down my neck, my chest, my belly. I balance them atop the head of my dick and force feed them down and around my erection.

My dick leaks new juice. I'll have to wash Rudy's little costume, or he'll ask how it got dotted with goo. I can't remember whether my these-days-oh-so-rare preseminal juice will stain like oil, or if it will dry solid to flake like dandruff.

I give a few hearty pumps of snug material up, down, and around my cock. I use both hands to squeeze the material in on itself and in on my cock, in order to make an even more compact package for fucking.

"Feels damned good, yes?" I ask my reflection and see only camouflage material bunched and moving at my crotch. I answer my own question: "Yes, feels damned good. Skinny, no-ass Rudy finally providing me something that's got me finally genuinely excited again."

I hold tightly to the clamped ball of camouflage material, a hand firmly placed to each side of it, as I would hold someone's head while fucking my hard dick into sticky mouth and throat. Although, I'm better able to move this cloth head, because it's detached from any constraining body. I've got a pretty good swing to my hips, too, so the combined fucking rhythm allows my cock to sock a space that's tailor-made for it. All the while, my fingers, clamping tightly inward on their handhold, allow the space to maintain its snug integrity.

The corridor that my cock fucks is quickly slimed by more leakage from my dick. Granted, some of the wet is absorbed by the cloth, but some of it oozes slickness that coats the hole, like mucus coats a mouth and throat.

"Eat me, soldier boy," I say and slam the camouflage head down my dick at the same time my hips come forward. "Swallow this gay guy's hard dick all of the way from my pulpy cockhead to my bulky cockroots."

I shift my position, no longer coming at the mirror face-on but turned sideways to it. It gives me better viewing pleasure of what's going on. I can see my cockshaft when it pulls out to its bulbous tip, the clumped camouflage material suddenly perched atop my erection like the mushroom cloud of an atom blast gone off in the Nevada desert.

I've the makings of a sizable bomb inside me, too. No doubt about the genuine thrilling my fucking of pseudo soldier-boy head sends through me, from my head to my toes, although staying mainly concentrated in the pit of my belly, very damned near my scrotum-containing balls.

Each forward thrust of my dick, accompanied by the forceful pull of cloth down and around my prick, causes my asscheeks to dimple, and causes my pectorals to squeeze almost to contact across the narrowed gully of my pectoral cleavage. The muscles of my arms, too, are put into attractively high relief.

"Ever had such a delicious dick as this one?" I ask my phantom military cocksucker. "Ever had a dick quite this big shoved quite so far into your not always so amicable military mouth and throat?"

My dick slides out to its head, naked and slick with its own preseminal slime. Its veneering of oily natural lubricant makes it golden and glossy in the artificial lighting of the room.

I'm genuinely delighted, doing what I'm doing, discovering the potential offered by Rudy's camouflage T-shirt and camouflage trousers that hasn't been advantaged since Rudy's scarecrow, no-ass, body was couched within the excess material. Although I can't yet tell, this might be even better than with Rudy present to compromise my pleasure by his being so damned opposite my ideal of physical perfection.

This way, I have the benefit of military pants and military T-shirt and the ability to fantasy anyone I damned well please decked out in them. Laker comes to mind. Laker's studly body would fill out the camouflage material like Rudy's never did and probably never will.

"Sexy, sexy soldier-boy Laker," I say and imagine Laker on his knees, recruited by Special Forces, warned against sucking male dick but unable to resist the temptation of my erection. Laker with an ass to fill out the seat of these camouflage pants in a way Rudy's ass never could to do them justice. "All the military telling you how eating cock is a no-no, and you're still unable to resist the deliciousness you find while sucking mine."

Yeah, I do like what I've got going. It's made even better by my having had such poor sex, by comparison, with Rudy, over the last few days.

Bunched camouflage material gives better head than Rudy ever gives. Hell, it gives better head than most guys I know. It gives better sex than my own hand, because I genuinely get turned on by the fantasy of fucking soldier's face.

I try to remember if and when I've ever incorporated a military man in my sexual fantasies, before; whether I've ever, in real life, had sex with a genuine soldier. As often as I've had sex, with so many men as I've had in and out of my bedroom, on and off my stiff dick, in and out of my asshole, there must have been one soldier in the lineup. Except, I don't remember him, certainly not as someone who openly wore his uniform. Most soldiers are so paranoid about the consequences of loving male dick, other than their own, they're not likely to be on the prowl in-uniform.

I can't have gone all my life without having spotted some gay, somewhere, whether in a bar, in the park, in the baths, even on the street, advantaging the butch come-on of the ever-popular military look. Rudy certainly couldn't have been the first. Nonetheless, I can only remember Rudy in camouflage, fucking Todd's ass, Todd leaned over that park bench. Except, already my mind's-eye replaces that Rudy-in-the-park memory with the better-looking Laker. Rudy never having quite the degree of sensuousness I demand from the memory in question.

"It's you, isn't it, Laker?" I say, and my cock gives the camouflage clump, now imagined it not as Laker's face but as Laker's ass, a couple rabbity socks and withdrawals. "It's been you all the time, you sexy bastard. Masquerading as no-ass, small-dick, Rudy-the-scarecrow. When you and I could have been making some really sweet sexual music together."

Ah, yes, Rudy out of the picture, and all the pleasure-potential still intact. Perfect!

I'm building to a rip-roaring orgasm. If only I can maintain its swell to conclusion and not see it aborted like that time, me on the bed, waiting for Rudy to materialize from his shower.

"Where you been hiding your uniform, Laker?" I ask, shove my dick deep into camouflage butt, and take the time and effort really to squirrel my dick inside. "Thinking to bring these duds out on a very special occasion to surprise me? Well, I am surprised. And, you can bet your studly ass that you're not going to soon file these items of clothing back into some dusty drawer."

If I listen really carefully, I hear echos of the sloppy noises I make when fucking Laker's ass.

I've got this hump of pseudo ass into really high gear. The camouflage bundle is pretty much a blur as I coincide its up and down, rise and fall, with the in and out, back and forth, fuck of my big and priming dick into and out of the very pre-cum slicked heart of the variegated green-black-brown material.

"Oh, soldier-boy, this is truly good for me," I say. "Is it as good for you? Tell me it's as good for you."

God as my witness, I hear Laker, down on his hands and knees, doggie-position, fucked royally by me from behind, my cock accessing his asshole through a small split in the crack of his camouflage pants: "Damn right, you fuck me real good," he says. "You fuck my soldier-boy camouflaged ass better than anyone ever fucked it before, better than anyone but you is ever likely to fuck it again."

"Damned right!" I agree and really jab my dick far and deep into soldier-boy's rectum. I leave my dick inserted to my balls.

My testicles are hugged tightly by the leathery ball my scrotum has become, as if the hairy sexual sac has been vacuum-packed around my gonads.

I twist the bundle of material around my dick, like a dog worries a bone. I clamp my handholds down hard and tight, compressing the slick-slimed corridor into which my dick remains fully submerged.

Which is all she wrote!

"Yes!" is pretty much all I can say in response to the wonder, as speechless as any witness to the first atomic explosion must have been.

I'm not talking paltry, puny, tiny-weenie eruption of my guts here. I'm talking genuine big time. I'm talking an explosion suddenly going off inside my belly that rivals the biggest orgasm of my life, to-date, including the one had in the park with my cock buried to its balls up Rudy's naked no-ass.

"Ugh ... ughhhhh ... ughhh ...ohhhhh ... ahhhhhh ... eeeiiiiii," is pretty much all I can come up with in follow-up.

For a few painfully pleasurable seconds, I think, like some guy who has had his tubes tied, that there's going to be no cum freed for ejaculation. All the right pumping mechanisms seem in effect, my asspucker pursing and un-pursing, my dick throbbing and pulsing, but I don't feel any cum, until ...

"Oh, sweet Jesus ... fucking, holy shit!" I bellow so loudly that all my neighbors surely hears me, despite all the sound-proofing in between.

Although having seemed AWOL for a few brief fractions of a second, which seemed endless stretches of days, my cum, when it comes, out my balls, up my cock, and out my cockmouth, into what little space exists for it within the fucked camouflaged material, is a flood of Biblical proportions.

"Sheeeeeeet!" I squeal, and the vacuum formed behind by all my jettisoning spunk is so intense I actually believe I'm being turned inside-out.

My luxurious torment isn't short-lived, either. It goes on and on ... and on ... and on. It takes control of me. It grabs me thoroughly and inserts me totally into the very heart of the maelstrom.

I pump so much cum into the bundle of camouflage material that excess backs up, along the full length of my dick, along the hole my dick pokes, and drools pearly globules into the curly black pubic hair that nests my crotch and balls.

I'm panting like a man genuinely out of shape who has, nevertheless, through some miracle, managed not only to complete the Boston Marathon but win it. For long, agonizing seconds, I lose all capacity to siphon enough oxygen to breathe. I'm light-headed. I'm on the verge of collapse when ...

"Ohhhhhhh!" I manage a long and heady intake of air as intoxicating as any shot of whisky had by an alcoholic two-years on the wagon.

My eyes focus on my reflection in the mirror. I expect a man obviously the worst for wear. I see a stud in his prime who has never looked better.

My whole body has an attractive blush, evident even through the deepness of my tan. My veneer of sweat makes my skin velvety and sensuous. My muscles are as deeply etched as I've seen them, without giving me even the slightest illusion of unnecessary bulk. My hair bangs attractively over my forehead, my eyes still sexily dilated. I lick my lips red-ripe as any strawberry on its vine.

Slowly, I pull the cum-soaked material up and off my miraculously still-hard dick.

I lift the cum-oozing bundle slightly above eye-level, as if it's a conch, and I'm a South-Sea islander prepared to blow it. Pressure to its sides purses its mouth, poked into existence by my recently exited penis, and it drools my spent cum, like a resident mollusk oozing escape.

I taste the creamy evidence of my explosion and savor its saltiness. I French kiss the hole for even more of my spermal discharge.

My smell permeates the material. Not Rudy's smell. Not the blander smell of soap and water. Not the vaguely sweet smell of freshener strip transferred during the spin of the dryer. I sniff my heady essence and am turned on by it, convinced it's laced with powerfully aphrodisiacal pheromones.

As if to make up for its more recent recalcitrant past, my dick doesn't soften in the least. My excitement doesn't dip to zero, like it always does after sex with Rudy, but remains on a fairly high plateau that might, with proper coaxing, be elevated into another orgasm.

I shake out the bundle of camouflage material and watch the results of my sexual intercourse become more widely dispersed, like pigment on die-dyed material.

Several slash marks of spent cum, as if designating military rank, are dark against the variegated coloring of the camouflage. Three such cum stains are on the T-shirt, one on the pants, all of which give clues as to how the material was originally rolled around my dick and, there, saturated with my cum and pre-cum. In addition, there are individually gelatinous lozenges of my stale jism that resemble slugs, wet trails from which resemble pathways slugs may have conceivably taken. Besides, there are several pearly seeds of spunk, like tapioca, centering wet circles that evidence absorption of whatever moisture those original dollops had to offer. Finally, there is thread-like cum gone gossamer against two segments of the foliage-patterned material.

I slip the camouflage T-shirt on over my head. The cum-soaked parts of the cotton material are cool against the warmth of my sweaty flesh.

I step into the legs of the camouflage trousers and pull the pants up, my hard cock and balls parenthesized by the open fly. I close only the top button of the pants and allow my cock to maintain its impressive thrust through the cunt-like opening. My balls cascade the opening's lower lip.

I tuck in T-shirt, and I check the results in the mirror. I rotate my lower body slightly to better see how my ass -- Rudy should be so lucky! -- completely fills the seat of the trousers.

"'Tench-hut!" I say militarily loud and come to demanded attention. My cock, a miniature soldier, already stands tall and shows no immediate signs of At Ease.

I like what I see. The illusion of a military me is a far better fantasy than any Rudy ever presented. Laker will look just as respectably serviceman as I do, and I can't wait to recruit him.

The camouflage pants, as I'd originally assumed, are too high-water at their cuffs to be a perfect fit, but they'll do until I get a more tailored replacement. It's easy to imagine the too-short pants legs merely bloused for wear with boots.

Are Rudy's boots in his duffel? Is that where I'll, also, find his military-issue boxer shorts and dog tags? I'm tempted to go digging, in order to flesh out the picture I present of military studliness, but I've not reached the low that would have me willingly violate Rudy's privacy. Although, he's had no qualms about stealing money from my petty cash.

I give myself a salute, hold it, right hand fairly flat, thumb tucked under, the tips of my forefinger and fuckfinger positioned to my forehead, just above my right eyebrow.

"Private Stud, reporting for sexual duty, sir!" I say. "Private Stud, requesting sexual instructions, as regards his hard stud-cock, and your hard-stud cock, sir!"

My stiff dick is too much a temptation to be left to fend for itself. The little soldier needs a helping hand (or mouth) from his Private-Stud buddy who's a genuine connoisseur of cock, in general, of my cock, in particular.

"Yes, sir!" I say to my reflection. "I'll suck it, sir! All of the way to my stud-balls, sir! To stud-eruption, sir!"

I open my mouth. I bend from my waist and hold to the backs of my thighs. I give head to the head of my pecker. The taste of me, my cockhead smeared with residue pre-cum and cum, is aphrodisiacally delicious as it dissolves in my spit and is swallowed away.

I suck my head farther over my dick. My handholds pull from where they're anchored to the backs of my legs. I watch my cockbelly enter my mouth, just beneath my nose.

I don't recall my cock ever so tasty, not even the first time I licked it clean.

"Hmmmmm," I hum over my mouthful and continue to swallow on down. Sound vibrations do wonderful thinks to my dick, actually making my erection a tuning fork that vibrates sympathetically.

My balls hang from the base of my dick and shift with a life all their own. I pause in my swallowing, before my nose reaches my nuts. It's been awhile since my face has been this far down my erection, and I want to be sure, in my eagerness to get the job done, that my back doesn't get thrown out of whack. Although, my spine provides little, if any, protest, at bowing so tightly for the wonders of the moment.

My nose, quite close to my balls, but not yet smashed into them, smells sperm-drenched camouflage pants. It smells, me too. The heady air is rife with the palatable sweat and sex smells of this healthy male in rut.

My head commences a slow back shift that even better positions my dick inside my mouth and throat. When my mouth eats my down my cock again, it keeps right on going until I've no more cock upon which to dine.

Having gotten this far, I somehow manage to stuff one of my nuts into my mouth, in the bargain, but I'm too out of practice for extensive complementary ball-swallowing, this time around, so I let the spit-soaked nut slip free.

My nose pokes my hairy scrotum, the bag raising from its droop like a curtain rising on Act I. The funkiness emanating from my asshole would be even more pungent if not filtered through the bit of camouflage pants stretched between my asshole and my nose.

A bit of my hairy balls is about all the panorama I'm offered, my scrotum so close that I view it cross-eyed.

I remain acutely aware of the cotton camouflage material that covers most of my body. While, up until now, complete nakedness has usually accompanied any self-gobbling of my cock, there's no denying the pleasurable aspects of self-sex with military trappings.

My mouth slides up my cockshaft to my cockhead, then descends. As if I'd eaten my dick just yesterday, I'm as acquainted with it as a duck is acquainted with water landed upon again, after days of migratory flight.

"Hmmmmm," I again hum around my dick, again enjoying the vibrations that penetrate my dick and resonate as far as my balls.

There are definite advantages to self-head. Just as there are definite advantages to beating one's own meat. No one is more likely to know what a cock likes best than the guy who owns the cock in question. It's always possible to provide instructions to some second person, verbal or otherwise, to the effect that, "Center a bit more attention down my cockshaft, a little more to your right. A little farther. Lick there. Not with the full belly of your tongue, but only with its tip. Still too much tongue, buddy, but you're getting there ..." But it's far less time consuming just to do yourself.

The disadvantages, and there aren't all that many that I've been able to find, include a tendency toward quick orgasm, if only because a guy who blows his own cock is so familiar with its likes and dislikes. Therefore, anyone who gets much of his enjoyment from the build-up to orgasm has to be sure to program in a bit of fumbling around, or else orgasm will always seem to happen way too soon.

The precariousness of my position, standing while sucking my cock, risks loss of balance and the possibility of frustrating and even dangerous consequences. I could completely alleviate that precariousness of my stance by sitting in a chair, or by lying on the bed, but I've always found an extra sexual charge in doing what I'm doing with the inherent possibility of falling over in the heat of passion.

My head bounces in nice and easy rhythm. Up, down, up, down, up. I pause at the apex of an upswing long enough to tongue-wrap my cockhead and rub my taut upper lip over the supersensitive spot that exists where my cockhead flares its belly from the belly of my cockshaft.

Don't ask me how, because that answer pretty much remains a mystery, but some heretofore unknown responsive mechanism, somewhere inside of me, has obviously been triggered not so much by Rudy as by his clothes. Not just any clothes but those he wore when I saw him fuck Todd in the park. These very clothes, with the exception of boots, boxer shorts, and dog tags, that I wear now.

What's so unique about this camouflage T-shirt and camouflage trousers, compared to the many others I must have seen, may end up the greatest mystery of all. I'm just relieved I can send Rudy on his way and no longer feel gypped in not having had him come across like I'd expected.

So much more a turn-on, his camouflage T-shirt and camouflage pants, than the scarecrow, no-ass kid, in them, ever was!

I really suck myself in earnest, my cock deliciously tasty as any phallic lollipop. My tongue performs sensuous curlicues that wrap and unwrap varying segments of my entering and exiting meat.

Along the length of my tongue, to the very base of my throat, my leaking cockmouth feeds me preseminal wet that tastes distinctively mild, yet distinctively saline.

My nose snorts, on a downslide, and the hair on my scrotum shifts in the resulting breeze. While all of the way down, my chin and upper lip snugly press pubic hair, on my belly and on my balls, that temporarily provides a beard of black and curly hair. My pubes smells of my sweat and my spilled cum.

An ocean of my saliva joins my preseminal ooze and lubricates my face-fucked penis. Some juice copiously bubbles out, some is sucked out by the slides of my erection from my hungry mouth. The exited wet forms a lacy cockring around the base of my erection.

I expect orgasm far less intense than its predecessor, but I'm mistaken, except for how my mouth, down and anchored to the base of my dick, probably gets a bit less cum than was fed into the camouflage asshole.

"Ugh ... ughhhhh ... ughhhhugh!" I grunt loud and long around the base of my dick, my throat swallowing cum and trying to swallow my dick to the digestive juices of my belly.

My hands clasp the back of my legs more tightly. I hold on for dear life and depend upon my natural sense of balance to keep me from falling over and biting my cock off at its thick base.

When I next see Rudy, conveniently after having washed and dried myself, as well as his T-shirt and trousers, I break the news that it's time for him to leave. He argues against it, because he knows a good thing when he has it. Free room, free board, and free access to petty cash not all that easy to come by.

"I know we've had less than the best sex," he says, indicating a tendency for gross under-exaggeration, "but I'm willing to make the extra effort if you are."

I grease his exit by giving him enough cash for a couple of weeks in some downtown flophouse, and I ease him on out with more difficulty than my greased dick ever had getting through the tightest sphincter.

He's no sooner out the door than I'm off to the nearest Army-Navy surplus store, the address already retrieved from the Yellow Pages of my local telephone book.

I buy a camouflage T-shirt and camouflage pants that fit. I buy military-issue socks and boots. I buy black wax and cotton balls, after instructions from the store owner on how to use them, along with a bit of water or spit, to produce the face-reflecting shine any soldier is expected to provide for his footwear, unless, of course, in the field where the enemy might advantage the glare.

Getting dog tags isn't so easy. I finally persuade the store manager to part with his for a price that would likely tag every dog in EurAsia.

Everything in hand, I whack off a couple of times at my place to make sure the costume hasn't lost its magic. I'm wary of too-high expectations, after having so misjudged Rudy's potential, but my orgasms come through with rip-roaring intensity and leave me convinced I'm no longer far removed from the ultimate sexual high.

Next is to get Laker out of his little snit and on board. Which isn't as difficult as Laker could make it, were he really a bastard, which he isn't and never has been.

"I just can't see what you saw in that skinny little mutt," Laker says. Since I'd never introduced him to Rudy, and since Laker doesn't have superman abilities to see over phone lines, he must have bothered coming by for a clandestine peek at my recent houseguest.

Getting Laker to dress up for our reunion, though, is more of a chore than I expect.

"Jesus!" he says. "You know damned good and well how much I loathe this kind of game-playing nonsense."

I know no such thing. If he's ever mentioned it, it's something I'd not likely forget.

"This a bit of kinkiness you picked up from Mr. Skin and Bones?" The way he says it convinces me the last thing I should say is, yes.

"It's just a little variation I thought might be fun," I say. "No need to lay an egg because of it. You don't want to give it a try, just say no."

I worry he might take me up on the offer to pass. I'm more certain than ever that Laker and I, and camouflage pants and camouflage T-shirt, and military-issue boxer shorts, socks, boots, and dog tags, are all the magical ingredients necessary for really monumental sex.

"I just feel so fucking ridiculous, dragged for sex like for Halloween," he says. Which isn't exactly a definite no-I-won't-do-it.

"What about if I do the dressing up?" My having gotten off, like a house afire, with Rudy in dress-up, later blasting like blazes when just I was in costume, it doesn't seem as if it'll much matter whether Laker or I go military for this particular session of sucking and fucking.

"I've never needed gewgaws to get off on you, or with you," he says. His insinuation is that I now need supplements.

"Look, Laker," I say. "This military stuff isn't necessary, really. You don't want to give it a shot, fine. What I want, and only want, is to have sex with you, once again, one way or the other. The military gear is something I thought might make for something to tell our grandchildren."

He laughs and, for the first time, I suspect he's going to give me what I want. After which, he's going to be more than willing to play horny and studly soldier-boy, off to war, or back from war, whenever I want him to.

"When your granddaddy was just a young man, Tommy," Laker says to a pseudo grandchild, "he and Grandma, here, had a slight falling out that was made good by Granddad dressing up like he was going to war and fucking Grandma's tight asshole."

"Kids love that sort of reminiscence," I say.

"Hand over the pants and let me see if they fit," he says.

Ten minutes later, he's a young recruit about to go on maneuvers, and I've a cock in my pants that can poke holes in enemy lines.

"Jesus H. Christ!" he says to his reflection in the mirror. "How am I going to get a hard-on looking like this?"

"Maybe this will give you incentive," I say, and my fingers highlight the impressive length and breadth of my boner beneath the stretched cloth of my left trouser leg."

"All fine and good for you, but ..." he doesn't finish his sentence but merely shakes his head at himself and at me in the mirror.

"Best reel out that big gun of yours before it does get hard and refuses to come on out all that easily," I say. "Because it's going to be hard enough, soon enough, trust me."

My dick is certainly way too stiff for me to get out easily. I have to drop my pants and my underpants, my cock just too damned hard to be maneuvered successfully through the twists and turns that'll thread it through the small pisshole of my briefs and out the only slightly larger opened fly of my trousers.

Laker's dick is out and playing elephant trunk in front of his belly. He folds his arms across his camouflaged T-shirted chest. If his cock continues in its reluctance to get rock-hard, my cock continues to be made harder by Laker's soldier-boy off to war getup.

No way did Rudy ever hold a candle to the realism Laker brings to the picture. There's something about the compactness of Laker's body, fitted into those particular clothes, dog tags strung around his nook, that says, here's a soldier honed by military special training and more than capable of meeting any enemy and kicking ass.

If there's any fly in the ointment, and it's nothing I feel can't be made right to both Laker and my satisfaction, it's Laker eyeing me as if I'm the enemy and it's my ass that needs the kicking.

I've him pegged as merely a little shy. First-times at anything can seem strange, weird, even turn-off ridiculous. That doesn't mean they have to stay that way. Laker just needs time to maneuver himself out of this glitch in proceedings. I've something planned to help him do that.

I get down on my knees in front of soldier-boy Laker and immediately siphon up his total dick as if it were a thick length of spaghetti and I was a starving Italian.

"See," I say, coming up for air, relieved as hell that his dick has given just the swelling response I'd hoped for. "And, I'll bet you thought it wasn't going to happen."

Granted, his cock needs more swelling to get stiff enough be to be draped with rubber for a trip up my asshole, but no way has Laker gone impotent on me.

"That it has happened is only because I shut my eyes and pretended I don't really look like an Ugly American off to torch some village and gun down innocent women and children," he says.

"Goddamn it, Laker!" I criticize. "No wonder your cock is giving me such a hard time. Or, is it a not-so-hard time? This is pure fantasy, you asshole! You only need pretend you're the good guy, having just saved a village from being torched into oblivion, just saved countless women and children from being gunned down and/or raped by the real enemy. You're about to get your just reward for deeds well done."

"Right," he says. "I'm a good soldier when today's wars are never defined in definite black and white but in indecipherable murky greys."

"Look, Laker," I say and grab his impressive nuts with enough force and attending squeeze to make him exclaim ...

"Fucking, Christ, man! Be careful of the family jewels!"

For a regretful moment, I think my unkindly manhandling of his nuts will negate all progress made in getting Laker's cock hard. I'm encouraged, though, by his cock getting plumper, rather than going back to hanging its bulbous head.

"You genuinely want out of that military uniform, all you have to do is say so," I say. "That's all you had to do from the get-go. Did I ever say there was no way I go to bed with you if you don't get all soldier-boy for me? I think not!"

"Okay, I promise to be less an asshole," he says. "Maybe I'm trying to be difficult because you threw me over for some skinny sonofabitch off the street."

"I made a mistake with Rudy, all right," I say. "An exceptionally big mistake in bringing him home. Once I had him home, he was harder to get rid of than a bad case of head lice."

"What do you know about head lice, good case or bad?"

"I read about someone who had them. In Africa, I think."

"God, but literacy always turns me on to a man," he says. As if his joking comment is Gospel, his dick -- finally -- begins a genuinely hell-bent surge toward full erection.

"Why not give my dick a few more of those pump-strokes only your slurpy mouth knows how to deliver?" he says.

I'm happy to oblige. I'm delighted. I'm downright ecstatic. Suddenly, I've a mouthful of Laker's hard prick the way I remember it. It and my dick are on their way to good times I still have figured as likely being the best ever.

"Christ, but I have missed you, you sexy bastard," he says and clamps his hands to my head and holds me where I've deep-swallowed his pecker. "I've always thought no more perfect fit than your mouth and my hard cock, unless it was my hard cock and your asshole, or my asshole and your hard cock, or your hard cock and my mouth, or ...."

"Mmmmmmm," I say, because it's about all I can manage as long as he keeps my head firmly anchored where it is. I can and do release a flooding of spit along the total length of his submerged dick.

He eases the pressure his fingers exert on my scalp, and I take my cue to begin a return up his cockshaft, at least as far as the bulb of his cockhead.

Once I've only his cockhead sucked in my mouth, my lips gummed to rubber-band intensity within the groove formed by his coronal flaring, I turn my head slightly to catch sight of us in the mirror. My resulting surge of voyeuristic pleasure surprises with its intensity. My cock's responsive jerk brings my uplifted cock back with a force that smacks my cockhead against my belly and sunbursts my preseminal juice far and wide upon my abdominals. Automatically, my jaws clamp. My pursed lips garrotes Laker's cockshaft where it blossoms his dickhead.

"Don't pop the top off my lolly, you greedy sonofabitch!" Laker says with an accompanying and reflexive step backwards that puts his dick more on the horizontal. "The last thing I need is a decapitated pecker, and not just because I'd miss the additional inch it gives my erection."

I completely un-suck his dick just long enough to say, "Sorry 'bout that!"

"No harm done, I guess," he says, as if still not sure. "Anyway, my brief look-see tells me I still seem to have a cockhead where I once had one."

My face heads back into the headily masculine smells rife where his dick sprouts from the hair on his crotch. I bury my nose in his pubic hair and take a big sniff, at the same time my throat muscles commence their latest welcome-home squeeze of his erection.

His groin reeks virile soldier-boy-natural eau de cologne. My hands clamp the backs of his thighs, just above the backs of his knees.

"No one sucks my cock like you suck it, you bastard," he says and his fingers sensuously comb my hair. "No one."

I've no doubts, now, that I can successfully suck him, military uniform and all, to an orgasm he won't forget. Toward just that end, I provide several snug rides of my mouth up and down ... up and down ... up and down ... the length of his cock. However, I've no intentions of continuing to climax, this way, even when his little gasps and grunts confirm that I'm well into doing just that.

What I want, Laker decked out for war except for any other weapon besides his penile gun, is his uniformed body stuffing his soldier-boy cock hard and fast up my asshole to stellar climaxes for the both of us. If I suck him to climax, his passions might well cool sufficiently for him to have second thoughts, yet again, about continuing in-costume. To this point, I suspect my sucking has him so primed he'd now easily be persuaded to burn villages, gun down innocent women and children, or fuck my tight ass, just to see his nuts shooting tension-relieving cannon-shots of heavy cum.

My hungry, spit-drooling mouth takes its final upward journey, along the length of his prick and comes completely free of his erection.

His saliva-glossed dick assumes a quick, easy, impressive, and very professional stand-to-attention.

"I want your soldier-boy cock buried up my asshole, Laker," I say.

I go to all fours and angle my butt in such a way that, whenever he decides to probe it with his soldier-boy cock and starts humping me, like a victorious soldier raping one of the just-conquered enemy, I'll most easily access the voyeuristic pleasure had by seeing it all played back to me from the mirror that lines his bank of closet doors.

I'm really hot for his dick. It's as if my ass dies from some deadly poison, Laker's cock the only antidote. I show how much I want his cock by taking hold of my asscheeks and pulling them open along their mutually shared crack, baring for Laker's viewing pleasure the black hair that runs my asscrease and points the way, as surely as any road signs, to the location of my ailing asshole that awaits his phallic cure.

"Stick your soldier-boy dick up my butt," I say by way of additional

William Maltese

encouragement. "Up my belly to where, when I open my mouth to squeal my pleasure, anyone who looks can see your cockhead clogging my throat from the inside-out."

Obligingly, he dons a rubber and drops to his knees behind me, so well positioned that it's a simple maneuver for him to put his cock on the horizontal and align its head to my awaiting pucker.

"Yes," I say.

He slots the head of his cock through my sphincter which opens up, over, and around it.

"Jesus, yes," I say.

His hands hook my waist, his fingers curling downward and around to my hipbones.

"You really do want this soldier-boy cock of mine, don't you?" he says.

Before I can say, "Yes, please!", he feeds it to me in one gut-shuddering slide that thuds his camouflage-cloth-covered belly against my naked buttocks, the collision causing his balls to swing forward and up to whack my nuts that hang beneath my ass.

"Yes ...yes ... fucking, yes," I say. His cock is even better than I remember.

"I'll fuck you," he says, his cock already on its way back out of my butt, at least as far as his knobby cockhead. "I'll fuck you to within an inch of your studly life."

"Love the feel of your young soldier-boy cock," I say as his dick jabs back and pokes my prostate on the way in.

My dick, aligned along my belly, like a missile hung from the wing of a warplane, leaks a string of preseminal goo that remains unbroken all of the way from my cockmouth to the floor. The leading end of the goo forms a dime-size pool on the carpet. When the translucent string finally snaps, its lower half adds itself to the puddle, its upper half boomeranging, like a bungee cord on the recoil, to loop wet and sloppily over the head of my erection.

"Feels good," I say, Laker's cockshaft once again walloping my prostate and milking that gland for more goo to drool the mouth of my erection.

"This soldier-boy's cock better at fucking your studly butt than soldier-boy Skin-and-Bones' pecker ever was?" Laker asks and provides a roll of his hips to stir his cock full-length within my behind.

"No cock ever fucks my asshole the way your cock fucks it," I say and mean it. I've been oh-so-right in my assumption that, like a wizard with all the crucial potions, there's magic being made here and now.

I reach beneath my belly, beneath my cock, through my legs. I have every intention of grabbing Laker's balls and mine, or as much of their combined mass as I can master. I figure rolling them on a collision course will add a bit of pleasurable pain to the already heady mix. His scrotum and mine, however, have already contracted way too far to respond to even my insistent tugging to mate them. I must be content to manhandle Laker's testicles and hear him groan response, then vise my balls until I grunt.

Laker curls forward so his dog tags dangle my naked back. I feel the rubber silencers that wrap the hard metal tags, and I'm turned on by their touch.

I want this fuck of my butt to last, Laker's screwing dick to be savored and enjoyed.

Something in the core of my being tells me that if I'm patient, Laker's fucking alone will bring me to the brink of orgasm and tip me over the edge. If I had perfect control, I'd take full advantage of that potential offered by Laker in uniform and by Laker's cock fucking my butt. After all, never, even when before having been subjected to Laker's expertise as a cocksman, have I ever yet creamed with just the feel of his cock up my rectum. It's the very uniqueness of this fuck, the special turn-on from Laker in uniform, and from Laker humping my ass like sixty, that hints of new pleasures and experiences to be mine just for the waiting. However ...

Helplessly, I reach for my dick, fist it, and start pumping like crazy.

"Getting off on my soldier-boy dick, are you?" Laker asks, his prick working my insides with a skill I can't remember his ever having called into play before.

"Getting off ... getting off," I agree. "Goddamned ... fucking ... fucking off ... getting ... off ... on your ... soldier-boy ... big ... giant ... dick."

My hand milks my cock for preseminal goo, as well as usurps whatever natural lubricant already smeared to my dickhead prior to my hand having taken hold. My prick is a slick truncheon beaten not beating.

It's all reflected in the mirror: My whipping fingers a blur beneath my belly and blurring my lengthy cock as well ... Laker hunched all the more, like any male of any species about to fuck his sperm into any receptive partner's hole.

Laker's sweat wets a spot down the center of his camouflage T-shirt. The expanding stain begins at the notch of his neck, where are beaded small droplets of perspiration that match the sheen on his throat and face. The stain presently ends where the bas-relief, provided by the intricately etched muscles of his chest, indicates his pectoral cleavage ends and the ripples of his muscled midsection begin.

Laker isn't the only who sweats. I've a drooling forehead. I've trickles down the crack of my ass that additionally lubricate Laker's dick, like hot oil drooling hot and pumping piston, each and every time Laker's cock appears from the mouth of my asshole.

There's a decided sensuousness to the way the camouflage material of his pants parenthesizes his thrusting cock and contracting scrotum, while it simultaneously chafes my ass. I've been fucked by plenty of guy's who have left on their pants, by plenty who have dropped their pants, by Laker who prefers naked flesh to naked flesh. I don't recall anything quite the turn-on of camouflage cotton caressing my buttcheeks, on each of Laker's in-strokes.

How fast I climb the mountain and stand on the verge of tumbling into the abyss! It can't have been all that long since Laker dropped behind me and slotted just the head of his dick up my butt. Oh, but I'd like the sensations inside of me to last, to build farther, to pile ... one upon the other ... upon the other. However, I've been primed for orgasm enough times to know when I've very little time remaining in which to enjoy the precariousness of the ledge upon which I'm perched.

If I turn loose of my cock, or grab tightly of my nuts and squeeze, or even request of Laker a pause in his screwing, I might well extend the length of our fuck. But I can't turn loose of my cock. I can't make my fingers make even the short detour that'll clap them tightly to my balls. I can't find my voice, or the words, to tell Laker to ... please ... please ... slow ... down.

"Getting what you want, sexy bastard?" Laker asks. Rather than slow his fucking rhythm, somehow clued into how that's the best way to make it last, he speeds his cock's thrusts and withdrawals ... thrusts and withdrawals ... outs and ins ... outs and ins. My asshole becomes a rubber glove for his erection.

"Uggghhh ... unghhhhunggghhhh ... uuuggghhhhunghragh!" is all I can manage, tipped on the very edge of the sexual chasm with no handholds to save me from the plunge.

Sweat stings my eyes, but there's no way on God's earth I can wipe it away. My beating hand simply won't be pried from my explosion-primed cock. To use my other hand, or my other forearm, will most likely, in the face of Laker's suddenly robust fucking of my butt, tip me off balance.

Despite the stinging sweat, I'm too excited by Laker and my reflection in the mirror to shut my eyes to it. If the viewing, through my sweat-irritated eyes, somewhat deteriorates that reflection of my getting so thoroughly fucked by Laker's soldier-boy cock, what I can see is voyeuristically far better than nothing.

"I'm coming!" I somehow manage, although I'm too far gone to have a clue if it comes out decipherable. "Goddamn soldier-boy cock ... cum ... cock ... Jesus ... fucking ... ohhh ... ahhhh ... AAAGHHHRUNGH!"

It's so unbelievably intense, I honestly wonder if I'll survive it. Never has earth been rendered so thoroughly by earthquake than my body is spasmed, then and there, by thundering ecstasy that takes hold of every atom of my being and vibrates me into mind-numbing senselessness.

Great comets of my creamy cum jettison the mouth of my erection and fly so far afield that they beard my chin. I taste saltiness that can be cum, can be sweat, can be blood from a bitten lip.

My fist torques my exploding dick, captures erupting cream and converts it into more lubricating slime upon which my hand continues its ride around my pulsing boner.

I lose consciousness, or, more likely, shut my eyes. Tidal waves of pleasure pound and crash inside, around, and over me.

I pant even when the cataclysm is finally over and done.

"Jesus ... Jesus ... Jesus," I say and shudder helplessly as my cock-pumping fist still helplessly manhandles my cockmeat made hypersensitive by orgasm. Only reluctantly is my hand persuaded to stop.

"Genuinely liked that, didn't you, you sexy bastard?" Laker says.

Did Casanova like cunt? Do misers like gold? Does a man dying of thirst like water? Will tomorrow's sun rise in the east and set in the west?

"Liked it?" I say. "I fucking loved it!"

Which suddenly has me wonder ...

"Jesus, Laker, tell me you creamed right along with me."

Distinctly, I remember his cock, up my butt, shooting enough cum to make my anus expand with it. Distinctly, I remember Laker's animalistic grunts and growls as his butt-fucking dick exploded his hot and heavy cream in accompaniment to the explosions of mine. Or, do I remember? Was I too caught up in the wonders of my own eruptions to have paid all that much attention to Laker at the time? Could it be that I actually got my rocks off by my lonesome? That Laker ...

"Oh, I got off, all right," he says and has to hear my sigh of thank-God relief and satisfaction. As if to prove what he says, he tugs his cock from my asshole, slides his cum-filled rubber off his studly dick, ties off the open end of his condom, and holds the results up for me to see in the mirror. "Which doesn't mean I'm going to oblige you by again playing soldier-boy any time soon."

I'm genuinely confused.

"You really don't get it, do you?" he says.

Did the Pope get that the Earth revolves around the sun when that fact was first presented to him by Galileo?

"You did come, right?" I say, although he's already admitted as much and has the copious evidence of his eruption presently on display in his cum-drooped rubber.

"I once came in a baggy stuffed with raw liver," he says, "but haven't been persuaded to repeat the performance."

"Come on, Laker! You can't possibly equate what we've just had with your fucking a baggy of raw liver."

"Not what 'we've just had'," he says, "because it's obvious to me, as it would have been to anyone attending this masquerade, that 'you' were the one so obviously thrust to some higher plain from the get-go. My problem ... a problem only from your standpoint, not from mine, by the way ... is that you and I both enjoy uniform sex, but with a big difference. Your 'uniform' means the camouflage T-shirt, camouflage pants, military-issue boxing shorts, boots, and dog tags. My uniform merely sex with little or no variance from the more widely accepted norm."

"You're in a rut, you mean." I don't make it a question.

"Maybe it is unrealistic of me to want to be wanted for myself and not for the uniform I'm wearing."

"Come on, Laker. You can't doubt that I want you. For Christ's sake!"

"Then, why do I have this gut-feeling that your orgasm would have been just as intense if you'd fucked one of those plastic sex dolls dressed up like a soldier?"

"That's too damned silly to dignify with a reply."

"Maybe, but I'll tell you one thing that isn't two, and that's that it's going to be a cold day in hell before you see me duplicating what we did here today."

Which he's pretty much sticks to, although I have every confidence I'll eventually win him over to my way of thinking.

In the meantime, I roll over in bed beside Danny, the sex doll I bought at Stan's Sexual Emporium and XXX Video Arcade. I've Danny decked out in camouflage T-shirt, camouflage trousers, dog tags, boots, military-issue boxer shorts. Presently, Danny is on his belly, his camouflage trousers and military-issue boxer shorts pulled down beneath the lower curves of his admittedly sexy butt.

Danny isn't your low-budget, blow-up-through-a-valve-in-his-back sex doll. He's the latest ultra-deluxe model. His plastic is supposedly more flesh-like than any of his predecessors, although there's definitely still a lot more research and development needed for perfection. It is a nice touch, though, that he's water-filled, which gives him an almost realistic warmth when I fuck him.

"Like getting your soldier-boy ass fucked, don't you, Danny?" I say and roll on top of his back, quickly find his asshole and ease the full length of my erect cock inside it.

His ass is a completely separate containment cell for hotter water than fills the rest of him. So, although I've already fucked his butt once already, his anus is still nice and cozy, if a bit slippery with my spent cum.

One nice thing about Danny being that I don't have to use a rubber when I fuck him. Another advantage is that I don't have to make small talk, either before, during, or after our screws. I don't have any trouble being rid of him, either, once I'm finished with him for the evening.

Granted, soldier-boy Danny hasn't yet come up with the intensity of that fuck I had that one evening with soldier-boy Laker, but Danny is a loads better screw than Rudy ever was. Danny's performance, also, beats out most of the other tricks I've since brought home to do their soldier-boy routines for me.

"You're a pretty good, all-around, damned fine piece of ass, aren't you, soldier-boy Danny?" I say. "And, you'll do just fine until I can persuade Laker, selfish bastard that he is, just what he's making him and me miss out on."

I squirrel my dick full and deep up soldier-boy Danny's butt, my pubic hair pressing slight indents into the plastic, that doesn't really feel like real flesh, of his asscheeks. I fumble briefly for the switch which I eventually click to "on", as I settle in to enjoy the vibrator the clever manufacturer has provided to make soldier-boy Danny's ass all the more lively.

more sexy novels from

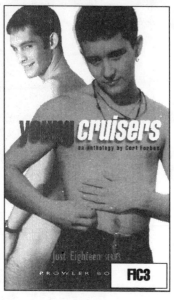

Corporal In Charge   FIC4   £5.99
Twenty short stories of hot and sleazy sex. Fritscher details each story down to the last drop of cum. From teenage wank sessions to college locker room fun to hard sex in the army, this book covers every fantasy.

Young Cruisers   FIC3   £5.99
The third novel to cum out of the Just Eighteen series is a tantalising selection of short stories on sleazy first time adventures. Black and Blue is a passionate story of how a young guy gets fucked for the first time by his fantasy man, a stud with a giant cock. Been There, Done That takes us into the world of hustlers where Ty unsatisfied with his tricks goes out and gets his fair share of hot spunky action.

PROWLER BOOKS

FIC2

FIC5

Slaves FIC2 £5.99

Slaves is the tale of Jack's sexual encounters which begin as he joins the mile high club. Cumming off the plane he falls headlong into one horny sexploit after another. Under cover as a journalist writing about the slave trade, Jack gets more than his fair share of native cock.

HARD by Jim Hardacre FIC5 £5.99

An all-new collection of 19 tales of shocking, SLEAZY, stories of dirty young men. Jim Hardacre has written for numerous publications including Hunk, Prowl, Spunky and EuroGuy. This is his first collection of red-hot short stories.

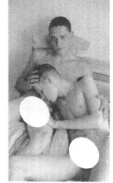

Young And In Love   JE7   £15.99

A beautifully shot voyeuristic & erotic film of young love.
Two young'n'cheeky English couples go on a hot'n'sleazy
holiday to Amsterdam. Let well endowed PJ and slim
Mark turn you on as their passionate clinches reach a
steamy climax. See Sean and big Brian's smooth, naked
bodies as they writhe in ecstasy. Good storyline & five
sexy boys who obviously enjoy one another as much as
you will. 75 MINS   BBFC CERT 18

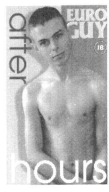

EV18

malexpress

EuroGuy After Hours EV18 £15.99

Here's your chance to find out what really goes on in a
shop after closing as five sexy boytoys let you in on their
horny exploits. Slim smooth Dave shows what you really
do with a penis pump. Discover cheeky Viper's intentions
as he gets caught by blond Matthew for stealing. Cute,
hung and ready for anything these guys are the best we
have seen in ages. 60 MINS BBFC CERT 18

Prowler Press publish Europe's hottest gay magazines; *Spunky, EuroGuy, Prowl & Real Men* as well travel books, erotic novels and video titles.
They also distribute gay toys, fetish, leather and rubber, sports & scenewear.

MaleXpress are Europe's leading gay mail-order company. Drop us a line, or call for your free se catalogue: 0800 45 45 66 (international +44 181 340 8644). Fax +44 181 347 7667.
Or write to MaleXpress, 3 Broadbent Close, London N6 5GG

In the US call **MaleXpress US** toll-free 1-888-EUROGAY.
Or write to 759 Bloomfield Avenue, Suite 342, West Caldwell, Jersey, NJ 07006 US.

Prowler web-site is where you can see the hottest new pictures from up-coming magazines and videos. PLUS you can order direct. Find us at **www.prowler.co.uk**

PROWLER SOHO is Europe's largest gay superstore situated in the heart of London's Soho. Design clothing, mags, erotica, videos, books, rubber and sex toys. Plus lots, lots more. 3-7 Brewer Street London W1. Behind 'The Village', opposite 'The Yard'.

 prowler

sweaty farm guys
first time wank
squaddie pick up
straight boy toilet sex
HOT CONFESSIONS
08961 106474
£1 PER MIN AT ALL